THE WHALE SONG TRANSLATION

THE WHALE SONG TRANSLATION

A Novel

HOWARD STEVEN PINES

pRp | Pacific Reefs Publishing

Published 2013
Printed in the United States of America
ISBN: 978-0-989479-70-7
Library of Congress Control Number: 2013912410

For information, address:
Pacific Reefs Publishing
PacificReefsPublishing@gmail.com

For Ying, Josh, and Jamie

Prologue

THE UNFATHOMABLE DANCE

"For the animal shall not be measured by man. In a world older and more complete than ours, they move finished and complete, gifted with extensions of the senses we have lost or never attained, living by voices we shall never hear. They are not brethren, they are not underlings; they are other nations, caught with ourselves in the net of life and time, fellow prisoners of the splendor and travail of the earth."

—Henry Beston, 1928, *The Outermost House*

FAR AWAY FROM human eyes and ears, in the depths of the North Pacific Ocean, a group of great-winged creatures cleaved curling trails through an underwater forest of sunbeams. Rotating clockwise in a heliocentric formation, their motions traced out sweeping elliptical contours, like the orbits of the planets. An incarnation of nature's great closed-loop cycles, these titanic beings soared and whirled in a Copernican adagio.

With graceful undulations of its fifteen-foot pectoral fins, their leader directed from the center, like an impassioned maestro waving twin batons. The whales performed in perfect synchrony to their choreographer's cadenced vocalizations, gliding effortlessly, propelled by the hypnotic beating of their wings, and responding to every nuance of melody.

Like a chain reaction of chemical eruptions, the titans spewed a steady stream of bubbles into each of their separate wakes. Their effervescent contrails sketched the outlines of their movements, as if they were a team of spiders weaving a web of foam. They pitched and yawed with such uncanny precision that the rate of their ascendency matched the speed of the rising bubbles. When the soloist's song finally ceased, they paused and gazed up at their colossal creation—a rendering of concentric rings, oriented perfectly parallel to the surface.

The pod trailed in the halo of their breath-sculpted tapestry as it climbed ever higher, shimmering in the shafts of morning light. Rising to the surface, the whales pierced the sky with a blast from their nostrils. It was time again to breathe.

Whale Watchers Anonymous

Maalaea Bay, Maui—an early January morning

"YES!" BOOMED GREG.

Dmitri turned his head to windward and gasped in unison with his fifty shipmates. The sun-drenched panorama of sea and sky had been fractured. A trio of leviathans had breached the ocean's skin, rocketing into the air, suspended in space before his eyes. The arc of each giant's body bridged two worlds. Dmitri gazed upon what seemed an illusion, a magician's trick. The forty-five-ton, forty-five-foot-long whales had transformed themselves into birds, each with the wingspan of a light corporate jet, soaring alongside the cruising tour boat.

Dmitri's world stood still. He viewed the striking features of the closest colossus in slow motion: the deeply grooved tire-tread pattern stamped upon its snow-white underbelly, the black and white mottled markings, like fingerprints, painted on the fifteen-foot tail fluke, and the colonies of barnacles clinging to the knobs, folds, and creases of the humpback's body. While he blinked, the fleeting vision melted back into the sea.

The titans' explosive, sub-orbital reentry back to their home world unleashed a frenzied chorus of screaming and cheering. "What a rush!" Greg hollered above the din of the crowd.

Dmitri spoke directly into his hearing-challenged friend's ear. "I know. It's incredible."

"Like Marine World," replied Greg, "only a hundred times better."

"It's more than that," said Dmitri, his heart still pounding. "Their brains are four times larger than ours, mostly gray matter, and their minds have evolved over thirty million years. Think of the possibilities."

With the crowd still abuzz, Dmitri thought about his mission with mounting anticipation. He'd scheduled this winter-break vacation to crack the codes of a mystery language. Three years before, his beloved mentor and former thesis advisor, Professor Theodosius McPinsky, had published his controversial challenge to the research community. Inspired by the professor's paradigm-busting proclamation, Dmitri had adopted the "McPinsky Challenge" as his own: "Decipher the languages of earth's other big-brained beings before they are crushed by the juggernaut of human exceptionalism."

As the double-decker catamaran ploughed across Maalaea Bay, crashing through aquamarine swells, the deck swayed beneath him. Dmitri gazed at the horizon. Silvery ribbons of morning light danced from crest to crest. Textured hues of blue suffused the air and water canvas. A perpetual crown of mists veiled the volcanic peaks of Lanai and Molokai. He heard the splashing of the prow and the flapping flags upon the mast. He breathed the seaweed-scented, salt-infused air. The sights, sounds, and smells of Maui cast a spell upon a man who'd spent most of his life in the suburban sprawl of Los Angeles.

Rounding Papawai Point and tacking northwesterly toward Lahaina, the view that gradually emerged seemed yet another surreal vision. The cane fields ascended the slopes of foothills and embraced the haunches of towering sentinels, the West Maui Mountains. Dmitri's eyes traced the sensuous curves of a verdant carpet.

"Dmitri, this is a blissed-out paradise!" Greg Bono, as well as the rest of David Dmitri's friends and associates, addressed his best friend by the preferred moniker of his surname. Greg reached out as if to touch the mountains. "Like a Gauguin landscape of Tahiti. Totally awesome."

They slapped their hands together, high-five style. Dmitri smiled at the sight of Greg's boyish grin and his golden, shoulder-length hair teasing the wind. They'd been colleagues for nearly a decade, associate professors of engineering and math, respectively, at Southern California Scientific University, more popularly known as SoCalSci. Dmitri had long admired his closest friend's tenacity. Greg Bono had trained many years to overcome the auditory dysfunction he'd acquired during a childhood illness. In the parlance of communications engineering, it was a signal-to-noise ratio problem. Compared to a person with nominal hearing, Greg had to labor to conduct conversations in noisy environments. When necessary, he compensated by reading lips.

Dmitri forcefully enunciated each word. "You know Maui is my favorite place on the planet. That's why I wanted to bring you here first before we cross swords about the whale song stuff."

"Yes, they are amazing creatures. But talking to them?" Greg arched an eyebrow.

"Oh, quit exaggerating. I'm an acoustics engineer. I'd analyze their songs for the elements of language. It'll make a great research paper, and my CPA tells me I can write off my trips to Maui."

Greg pursed his lips, a sign of grudging approval that Dmitri had come to relish. The thrum of the boat's engine ceased, allowing Dmitri to resume at a lower volume. "I've already contacted the director of the local whale foundation."

"You're swimming in dangerous waters." Greg furrowed his mathematician's brow into a familiar pattern, reminding Dmitri of the symbol for the square-root sign. "Don't forget. Your illustrious mentor was banished from our university for preaching about interspecies communication."

"I appreciate your concern and I promise to fly low."

"Aloha, and welcome aboard our PICES whale watch expedition boat." An amplified male voice, bearing a distinct New England accent, had spared Dmitri the sting of another of Greg's barbs. "I'm Tom, your PICES naturalist and tour guide. I think you'll agree. PICES is much easier to pronounce than Pacific Institute for Cetacean Educational Studies, especially after a couple of mai tais." His baritone voice exuded confidence.

As the crowd laughed, the guide brushed a hand across the red bandana wrapped gypsy-style around his head. Wherever Dmitri looked, he saw female gazes, like radar beams, admiring every conceivable angle of Tom's movie-star profile.

"You've just witnessed a surprise greeting from the commuters of Hawaii's Humpback Highway," said the naturalist. Dmitri's upper incisors tingled with a frosty chill as he strained to comprehend the man's noise-distorted message. "Consider yourselves extremely fortunate. I've never seen three humpbacks breach simultaneously and rarely this close when the engine's at full power. Now that we've stopped we should have even more action."

Greg's tortured expression, as if he'd bitten into a lemon, confirmed that the guide's electronic megaphone vibrated like the sound of scraping metal. Dmitri leaned closer to Greg and said, "An intermittent short circuit in the preamp. Totally nonlinear."

The guide slapped his palm against the side of the loudspeaker horn. "Testing, one, two, three." He nodded with satisfaction. "Sorry about the malfunction. Marine biologists are still speculating about the humpback's breaching behavior. There's no consensus explanation. Our staff divers have studied the breach from underwater. It takes only a few beats of their ginormous tail fin, no more than a couple of seconds, to generate the power to fly through the air with the greatest of ease."

"Mommy, look!" A freckled, red-haired girl near Dmitri pointed to twin geysers erupting from the sea. Like giant water pistols, they erased the precise V-shaped formation of a flock of jabbering cormorants.

"Don't be alarmed, folks," said the guide. "Humpbacks are air-breathing mammals who, remarkably, can hold their breath for up to forty-five minutes. They surface and exhale through their blowholes at speeds approaching three hundred miles per hour to generate the twenty-foot-high vapor plumes you just experienced. They're called 'blows.' After they replenish the air supply in their lungs, each the size of a Volkswagen bug, they can dive for another ten to fifteen minutes. Since the blows are visible at great distances, they're a surefire way to locate the pods."

Dmitri's thumbs played across the touch screen of his iPhone. He tapped Greg on the shoulder. "I just did a calculation about the breach." He pointed to the numbers on the display. "It's simple physics. The kinetic energy of the humpback exiting the water is the same as the potential energy of its body at the maximum height above the surface. Since I estimated its center of mass nearly twenty feet above the water, then its exit velocity is close to twenty-three miles per hour."

"Very cool," Greg replied with a sly smile. "Amazing what engineers can discover using basic algebra."

"So here's the punch line," Dmitri went on. "If the whale is about forty tons, then it only takes him a fraction of the time to accelerate to the same speed as a fully-loaded eighteen-wheeler."

"I'm impressed." A heavy-set, middle-aged woman stood next to him. "I couldn't help but overhear your conversation." Smiling, she removed her big-brimmed straw hat and waved it in the air. She would have smacked Dmitri in the face, but he ducked. "Excuse me," she singsonged at the guide, "but I believe the gentleman next to me has something interesting to share." She pointed directly at Dmitri, who slipped behind Greg.

"No need to be shy, sir," said the guide in a teasing tone.

With urging from a few bystanders, Dmitri submitted to his fate and repeated the story to his fellow passengers. The shared discovery was greeted by oohing and aahing. Greg turned the bill of a blue L.A. Dodgers baseball cap backward and launched into an exuberant fan's display of handclapping and shrill whistling. His enthusiasm was contagious. The crowd roared.

The guide grimaced and thrust his hands skyward. However, he couldn't resume until the celebration had passed. In a half-hearted tone, he said, "Very impressive, sir. Most folks on a Hawaiian holiday leave their calculators at home. This is the first time anyone on my tour ever put a Bill Nye spin on the physics of whales."

Already embarrassed by the scattered laughter, Dmitri turned to see the guide staring directly at him, eyes narrowed. "I'm sorry for the interruption."

"No problem." The guide brandished the megaphone with an authoritative flair. "I—" His words were swamped by a collective outcry. Like a giant periscope, a whale's head slowly emerged straight up out of the sea until its eyes were a foot above the water line. Then it rotated a full one-hundred-eighty degrees to scan the boat, like a submarine commander searching for friend or foe.

"The whales seem to enjoy studying us as much as we study them," said the guide. "This type of head display is known as a spy hop."

Another humpback surfaced, circling the vessel, getting closer and closer, until it finally snuggled up to the starboard side. When the whale began to rub its backside against the hull, a dissonant mix of shrieks and laughter abounded around the upper deck. Animated hands reached in vain to touch the gregarious giant. After a brief massage, it backed away, rolled languorously on its side, and extended its fifteen-foot pectoral fin toward the boat. It tilted its head with an eye open, appearing to look up at everyone on board.

"See," announced the guide. "This boat's no more than a scratching post for the mighty cetaceans."

The red-haired girl waved her arm and hopped in place. "What's a citation?"

The guide summoned up a grin. "That's a very good question, young lady." He gazed only at her, as if addressing a VIP. "Cetaceans are the dozens of species of large, air-breathing marine mammals, including whales, dolphins, and porpoises." Reengaging with his audience, he said, "In recent years, many humpback whales in this population have approached boats for friendly encounters. Such behavior has increased each year. It might be because of the relatively recent national and international bans on hunting humpbacks. These new generations of whales have never known whaling. They're curious and they initiate contact. They often stay for several hours, investigating."

The girl's eyes were huge as she listened.

Dmitri raised a hand. "It strikes me that their behavior indicates an extremely inquisitive mindset, not to mention the fact that cetaceans have, by far, the largest advanced brains in the solar system. Has anyone attempted to signal back to them during these encounters?"

The guide crossed his arms and clutched the megaphone like a shield. "There was one occasion when everyone on board started to dance the Macarena, which resulted in the whale splashing them."

He drawled the last few words.

The snickers swirled around Dmitri like the buzz of bees. He fumed, not accustomed to being the butt of a public joke, particularly when perpetrated by a cocky alpha male. Seeing Greg's concerned expression, he realized he'd better count to ten in an effort to calm himself.

"Seriously, folks," the guide continued. "The typical reaction is to wave back and shout greetings. Moving along now, the humpbacks have the most diverse repertoire of filter-feeding methods of all baleen whales. Their most inventive technique is known as bubble-net feeding. A group of up to a dozen whales blow bubbles while swimming in circles to create a ring. The ring of bubbles, sometimes a hundred feet in diameter, encircles the fish, which are confined in an ever-tighter area. The whales swim in smaller and smaller circles until suddenly they burst upward through the bubble net, their mouths wide open, swallowing hundreds of fish in one gulp. Some of the whales dive deeper to drive fish toward the surface while others herd fish into the net by vocalizing."

A gum-chewing, teen-aged girl raised her hand. In the span of a few seconds, a volley of expanding purple spheres emerged from the space between her lips.

Dmitri stage whispered into his companion's ear. "Humpbacks aren't the only intelligent species with the mastery to blow bubbles." Greg's trademark sign of approval, puckered lips and a thumbs-up sign, more than offset the nearby straw hat lady's "Shh!" of rebuke.

"My boyfriend gave me an iPod download of whale songs for my birthday," said the bubblegum girl. She popped a headphone bud from her ear and raised it above her head. "I'm listening to them right now. They're so cool."

"Thank you," said the guide. "As this young lady just reminded us, a humpback's haunting melodies can last for fifteen to twenty minutes. Some singers have been observed repeating the song cycle for a symphony lasting longer than twenty-four hours. Those of a particular region, like the North Atlantic, all sing the same song while the humpbacks of the North Pacific sing another. Each population's song changes slowly over a period of years, never returning to the same sequence of notes."

The guide waved up to the pilothouse. He was answered by an amplified broadcast of the song of the humpback. He closed his eyes and paused, his head scarf rippling in the breeze. With a lilting rhythm, he said, "Reminds me of a rhapsody, filling the air with grace." As if on cue, another cetacean missile blasted into the sky, igniting the crowd once again.

"Happens all the time," the guide intoned serenely, quieting the clamor. "Scientists are still unsure about the purpose of these songs. Only male humpbacks sing. Some have speculated that this indicates a high level of intelligence. It's still a great mystery. If you're interested, we have recordings produced by our own marine biologists for sale. Are there any more questions?"

Despite the guide's earlier pushback, Dmitri felt emboldened. "Have you ever broadcast a Beethoven symphony or a Verdi aria from underwater speakers during these recording sessions?"

Before the naturalist could reply, a gravelly voice shouted, "Hey, professor, what I heard was they played a Snoop Dogg recording, and the whales swiveled back and forth to the rhythm."

Greg responded to the deluge of raucous laughter. "As Cicero once observed, 'Nothing is more fickle than the favor of the crowd.'"

Dmitri, however, was lost in his own thoughts and paid no heed to the commotion. He raised a hand once again, arousing numerous groans. "Everything you've described suggests these are very intelligent creatures: their songs, the cooperative behavior of the bubble nets, their big brains, and their curiosity." He paused and exhaled a nervous chuckle. "Do you know if—?"

Before he could finish, the boat was jolted by another breach, this time by a three-ton calf.

"Sir," the guide interrupted. "I'm running behind on my presentation. If you have more questions, I suggest you consult with our director, Christopher Gorman, at the PICES office."

Dmitri tapped Greg on the shoulder. "Remember the screaming headlines in the morning paper about dead whales washing up on local beaches?"

"How can I forget?"

"The article was about Gorman. In our last email exchange, he mentioned he had big problems. I expect we'll get the straight scoop, since I'm invited to his office in a couple of hours."

Greg shook his head. "Like you just said, they're his problems, not yours."

Despite Greg's warnings, Dmitri remained resolute, keenly aware that destiny was quickening, moving him purposely toward some unknown destination.

"Jesus!" Greg's jolting cry mingled with an onslaught of chilling screams. Dmitri spun around, hard to starboard, guided by many outstretched arms pointing just a rod's cast distance from the boat. A blot of crimson, like the giant red spot on Jupiter, bubbled up from the depths, spreading away from its center like a biblical plague.

"Oh, my God!" It was the guide's megaphone-amplified voice.

A juvenile humpback emerged from a scarlet stain on the water, blood oozing from every orifice in its head.

A Cetacean Conversation

Kihei, Maui—early afternoon

WITH THE PICES tour boat back in port, Dmitri and Greg disembarked down a narrow gangway, swept forward by the crush of somber tourists.

"What caused that awful bleeding?" asked Greg.

"Your guess is as good as mine. Shark attack? I'll ask Gorman. You can browse the mall while you're waiting. Maybe you'll find a Hawaiian shirt to add to your collection?"

"I changed my mind." Greg's expression had turned sheepish.

"Huh?"

"After the sight of that poor humpback, I'm curious about Gorman's take on the recent whale mayhem."

"It would be great to have you along." Dmitri could not have been more surprised. Until this moment, Greg had consistently lobbied against "Dmitri's whale fixation." Greg accepted his offered fist tap.

The headquarters of the Pacific Institute for Cetacean Educational Studies was a short stroll away from the boat harbor. They approached a bustling waterfront shopping complex, an eclectic medley of tourist shops and small business offices. After passing through an arched gateway framed by the faces of hand-carved Tiki gods and jagged lava rocks, they entered a central courtyard.

"It's tropical geometry. It's gorgeous." Greg's voice gushed above the soothing sounds of a natural rock waterfall.

"Tropical geometry" was the mathematical basis of Google's search algorithms. Accustomed to Greg's esoteric puns, Dmitri's eyes imbibed the riotous colors of the equatorial landscaping. Lush beds of red and purple bougainvillea, white and yellow ginger, ferns and birds of paradise fringed the curving flagstone pathways. A grove of coconut palms cast wisps of shade upon a ring of benches and a chorus of merry mynah birds rained down from the branches.

As the enclosed courtyard blocked the ocean breeze, Dmitri wilted under the intensity of the early afternoon sun, his skin clammy beneath a flowery shirt. When he opened the PICES front door, the chilled air in the visitor's lobby washed over him. "What a relief." He sighed.

Dmitri approached the good-looking, fortyish woman seated at the front desk, her arms and face as bronzed as the models in tanning salon ads. "Why does everyone in Maui look so healthy and attractive?"

"It's the passion fruit," she replied.

At a loss for a clever comeback, Dmitri shifted to business. "We're here for a one o'clock meeting with Director Gorman."

"We're not very titular."

Dmitri stared blankly, making a supreme effort to maintain eye contact and not let his gaze drift down to her plunging neckline.

"To us locals, he's just Chris," she added with a wink, then ushered them through another door and into an inner office.

Gorman sat at his desk, pecking at a computer keyboard with a couple of fingers. "Just give me a few seconds," he mumbled.

Dmitri and Greg took the opportunity to browse the photographs of whales and dolphins decorating the walls. Gorman was a renowned undersea photographer. Dmitri scrutinized one photo with such intensity that his breath fogged the glass frame.

"Done." Gorman stood and walked up to them, offering his hand. "Thanks for waiting. Our fundraising season never seems to end."

Dmitri detected a military bearing in Gorman's posture and vise-grip handshake. Nearly six feet tall himself, he was impressed by the man's Nordic physicality. The PICES director towered at least four inches above him. Dmitri's own physical traits—swept-back, brown hair, prominent side-burns, and dark eyes—stood in stark contrast to Gorman's crew-cut and lantern jaw. Dmitri's pale complexion reflected the academic nature of his work. Gorman's skin displayed the imprint of the sun and the wind. He estimated the PICES director was of a mid-thirtyish, Gen X age similar to himself.

"These are extraordinary. How did you get so close?" Dmitri asked, pointing to a group of pictures of a humpback calf suckling her mother's milk.

"That was one hell of a memorable dive." Gorman faced the photos. "At first the mother didn't notice me. But after about a minute, I could see her barreling toward me on a collision course. I'll never know if it was an intentional act. Maybe she sensed I was a danger to her child. Anyway, my life started to pass before my eyes."

Gorman's recollection was so vivid Dmitri felt himself stiffen at the image of the charging behemoth. As Gorman reestablished eye contact, his irises were glimmering blue pools, like the ocean-filtered sunshine in the photo. They had a faraway look.

"At the last possible second, she adjusted course. Just missed me." The immediacy in Gorman's voice suggested he was anchored back in the present. "Her wake sent me tumbling, but I was fine. A warning. Nothing violent. I knew then and there I was the recipient of a message—from a highly sentient being."

"Whoa-ahhh." Dmitri's and Greg's harmonized response lingered in the air.

As the trio settled into chairs, a shorter, bearded fellow entered the office, approached Gorman, and whispered into his ear.

"I'd like you to meet PICES assistant director, Peter Hawkins," Gorman said. "He just told me about an incident during this morning's whale watch. I take it you were there?"

"Yeah," replied Greg. "It was a bad scene. Blood in the water . . . like *Jaws*."

"We're thinking it was a shark attack or a ship strike," said Hawkins. "These things do happen occasionally."

"It definitely shook everyone aboard," Dmitri said. "Yesterday at the airport, we read about the beached juvenile. Did you find out yet if there's a link to the Navy's sonar?"

"Peter and I visited Molokai two days ago." Gorman seemed edgy. "We were pretty disturbed by what we found."

"How so?"

"It's rare to find a fatally stranded juvenile with no obvious external injuries. The usual causes of death—predatory attack, accidental ship strike, or disease—weren't evident. Since whales don't have a swim bladder, most heavy cetaceans like humpbacks sink to the bottom when they die. Things just didn't add up, so we necropsied the skull."

"Why the skull?" asked Greg.

"Our sister organization in Australia has documented a number of fatal strandings of Cuvier whales. Their calculations indicate the Navy's sonar frequencies coincide with the resonance frequencies of the Cuvier's cranial airspaces. The sonar can therefore destroy the delicate tissues around their brains and ears." Gorman paused, crinkling his forehead. "Our examination in Molokai revealed extensive hemorrhaging of the brain sac and the inner ear cavity. This would clearly damage the juvenile's balancing and echo location abilities, which probably caused the stranding."

"That's grotesque!" Greg grimaced.

"But not unexpected," said Hawkins. "The power levels of the sonar pulses exceed two hundred decibels."

"The intensity of the sound pressure waves would dwarf the roar of a jet engine," added Gorman.

"Have you communicated your findings to the Navy?" asked Dmitri.

"I did. I served in the Navy, so I used my connections to remind them about the dangers of advanced sonar testing in Hawaiian waters." Gorman peeked at his wristwatch. "Time's tight right now, as you can imagine. Let's move on to the reason you contacted me."

"Yes, the whale songs," said Dmitri.

Gorman summarized the PICES research program, emphasizing their recent undertaking to record whale songs in Hawaii, Alaska, and Tonga. "Some researchers study the songs like musicologists searching for patterns of cadence and repetition. I'm more interested in correlating the phrase structure to social behavior such as feeding and mating."

"That's what I hoped to hear," Dmitri said. "As I mentioned in my emails, I've specialized in digital voice development for cell phone applications. I've analyzed speech waveforms to accurately reconstruct phonemes, the primitive units of spoken language. Using a similar approach, I'll analyze the microstructure of whale vocalizations, hoping to find similarities to the frequency patterns that characterize human language."

"Seems like a difficult task. What makes you think you'll find anything?"

"Human songs are a stylized expression of our spoken languages. Of course, we can whistle or hum a song purely for musical purposes. The real question is: Are these whales merely whistling a tune or singing a story? Since they've evolved twelve-pound brains rich in the convolutions of cerebral cortex, similar to our gray matter, why wouldn't they have responded to the same evolutionary pressures as humans to develop communications for purposes of cooperative hunting?"

"Like the bubble nets," replied Gorman.

"Exactly," said Dmitri. "I've a hunch whale talk is as expressive as English or French."

"You make a good case." Gorman's voice had become more animated. "Marine biologists, however, don't have the expertise to analyze waveforms. In fact, we hardly know anything about the physiology of sound generation in whales. There just aren't many opportunities to autopsy an intact humpback. However, we do know that there's a large laryngeal cavity, a laryngeal sac, and a series of valves between the trachea and the blow hole. The sac probably functions as a resonant sound chamber. We've also discovered a series of blind sacs branching off of the respiratory tract. They also might play a role in sound production, but we just don't know."

"Helmholz resonators," Dmitri answered. "You know, like blowing on a coke bottle." Gorman nodded. "It's a fascinating clue." Dmitri touched his Adam's apple. "Just like humans. We adapted our respiratory and digestive systems to harness sound and create language."

"Yes," replied Gorman, "but there's a recent discovery hinting at an even more intriguing adaptation."

"I'm all ears." Dmitri sensed that, beside him, Greg listened intently.

"Our Hawaiian humpbacks feed mainly in summertime while they're in Alaskan waters. They live off of fat reserves during their winters here in the tropics. The annual migratory round-trip is thousands of miles. A team in New Zealand recently published the results of an eight-year, satellite-tracking study."

As Gorman paused, Hawkins finished the thought. "They confirmed the humpbacks travelled up to twelve hundred miles in straight lines without deviating from course by more than a single degree."

"Like they're using GPS." Greg pointed at the ceiling.

"That's right," replied Gorman. "The Kiwi study concluded it's virtually impossible to achieve such remarkable navigational precision using only the sun or the earth's magnetic fields. We're forced to consider other alternatives such as tracking the stars or long-distance sounds."

Dmitri's mind burst into overdrive. "So, you're telling us they've adapted sound for feeding," he raised a thumb, "singing, and possibly even navigation." He counted to three with his index and middle fingers. "Given their big brains and their social behavior," he extended two more fingers, "it seems logical to assume yet another adaptation for purposes of communication."

"That's the mystery question," said Gorman. "I'd be happy to give you a CD with recent recordings for your waveform analysis."

"Sounds like a plan," Dmitri replied. They shook hands. "Thanks for your hospitality. It's time we left. I want to take Greg up to the mountaintop before sunset."

They were just standing up when Gorman's front desk assistant rushed through the office door, her face grief-stricken.

"Shelley, what's wrong?"

"We just received an urgent phone call from Ka'anapali . . ." She shook her head.

"And?"

"The Sheraton's reported a humpback washed up on their beach. It's still breathing."

The color drained from Gorman's face. "Damn the Navy." He spat the words.

Silence cloaked the room. Finally Dmitri said, "If there's anything we can do to help?"

Gorman faced Hawkins. "This puts a whole new spin on what happened this morning. It can't be the same whale. That's two incidents on the same day." He turned toward Dmitri. "Between you and me, I suspect the Navy's killing sounds are destroying Maui's whales. If you can find any proof of whale language, it could help to rally public opinion."

"I—"

But Gorman was already out the door.

Haleakala Sunset

Haleakala Crater Summit Lookout, Maui—midafternoon

NIBBLING ON BISCOTTI they had purchased at the PICES gift shop, Dmitri and Greg settled into their candy-apple-red Mustang GT convertible.

"Quite a meeting," said Greg. "This is a bad day to be a humpback whale."

"Gorman said a language breakthrough could help publicize the threats to their survival."

"There you go again. McPinsky, Part 2."

"Enough whale talk." Dmitri forced himself to sound upbeat. "This is our vacation . . . time to lighten up."

"Amen, brother. Let's pop the lid on this puppy." Greg released the latch securing the car's vinyl top.

Dmitri waved his hand with a flourish, as if he held a magic wand. "Expelliarmus!" He jabbed an index finger at the dashboard. "Reducto!" He waved and jabbed again. "Expecto patronum." Finally, he pressed a button on the control panel and watched the ceiling of the car gradually disappear, vanishing without a trace. He reached for the sky. "Let there be light."

"I didn't realize my stuffed-shirt engineering colleague minored in Hogwarts incantations. There's still hope for you, my older friend."

"Coming from the king of joie de vivre, I consider that a compliment." Dmitri genuinely felt better, despite Greg's reminder about their five-year age difference. "Considering my low-key social skills, I really appreciate your vitality."

"We're a good team." Greg slapped Dmitri on the shoulder. "I keep you loose, and you boggle me with your sense of wonder. However," Greg thrust an arm into the air like a rush-hour traffic cop, "your lust for discovery leaves you vulnerable to visionaries like McPinsky."

"Vulnerable! I think you've got it backwards, pal. He's given me a gift! It wouldn't hurt you to be injected with a dose of McPinsky-itis."

Greg didn't respond.

"Speaking of wonder, wouldn't it be wonderful to have a toy like this?" Dmitri brushed a hand across the leather-wrapped steering wheel. He gripped the wheel and shuttered his eyes. When the textured touch activated a region of dormant neural circuitry, he zoomed through a wormhole in his subconscious to the memory of a cold Christmas morning long ago. He was bundled in a toasty Pooh blanket. The room smelled like tangy evergreen, and the branches glittered with tinsel. Stroking the leather saddle of a shiny red bicycle, Dmitri's developing mind puzzled over a problem. How did Santa know that, during family shopping trips, he'd stopped to admire the very bike under the tree? On that Christmas day, he'd solved his first major mystery. It also was the day he stopped believing in Santa Claus, realizing instead something even more wonderful—that he would always be embraced by his parents' love.

"Hey, Dmitri, snap out of it."

Dmitri felt a friendly tug. As his eyes popped open, he beheld the sight of his hands clutching the steering wheel and Greg gazing at him with concern. "Really, Greg, wouldn't it be great to have a toy like this?"

"Dream on, Dmitri. We can't drive the L.A. fast lane on the vapor fumes of our academic salaries."

"It's what vacations are for, a vicarious life of luxury." He gunned the engine and accelerated from the curb, pinning them both back into their cushy leather seats. Like giddy teens, the two professors whooped and hollered down the road.

Dmitri hugged the coast highway for a while, sneaking an occasional glance at the spuming breakers crashing onto white sand beaches. He veered inland at the first crossroad, following the signs leading to Maui's geological raison d'être. Haleakala's massive shield volcano comprised more than 70% of Maui's surface. Zigzagging up the shortest paved road in the world between sea level and ten thousand feet, Dmitri felt as if he were flying a plane, climbing into the sky to reveal the contours of the entire island.

In two scenic hours, they'd traversed several distinct climate and vegetation zones, stopping twice at roadside sanctuaries to admire specimens of endangered species: the Nene goose, Hawaii's state bird, and the Haleakala silversword plant.

When they'd arrived at the chilly summit, Greg gestured toward the empty parking lot. "Is this the right place?"

"Yes, the tour groups are long gone. Most folks come here for the sunrise."

"And, as usual, you're au contraire?"

"You'll see why."

A gust of wind shook the car. "Good thing that ranger told us to raise the top," said Greg.

After they'd parked, they donned their airport souvenir-shop purchases, a pair of stenciled I LOVE MAUI hooded sweatshirts.

Dmitri couldn't wait. Ever since his first visit, nearly ten years before, an imperceptible force had drawn him back here again and again. "Last one to the lookout buys dinner."

They slammed the doors and raced across the parking lot, then hurtled down the sloping footpath leading to the summit's edge. Reducing speed as they approached the end of the trail, they grabbed the handrails of the protective barrier to prevent plunging into the abyss. Dmitri caught his breath and leaned into the stiff breeze.

As he stood at the edge of the precipice, he was enveloped by the gentle roar of the wind. The unceasing sound poured into both ears like the quavering drone of the harmonium in his favorite Ravi Shankar raga. In the Hindu tradition, this sustained resonance, or shruti, symbolized the universal soul of Brahma—the oceanic state of pure being suffusing all things. Entranced, he felt himself drifting in the tranquil flow of deep cosmic waters. The sound of the wind was a raga now, its shruti vibrations resounding as an all-encompassing essence while the emergent melody of the sitar sang the story of Haleakala's fiery creation.

"I'm feeling the biggest rush since my first trip to the Grand Canyon." Greg's voice broke Dmitri's spell.

Dmitri turned to enjoy the sight of Greg's exhilaration. "Haleakala means 'house of the sun.'"

"It looks like a geological Chartres," declared Greg.

"Very cool. I never tire of staring into this crater."

Like a compass needle compelled to yield to a greater power, Dmitri's focus swept back to the sight below. Sensing the late afternoon sun radiating his back, he saw their shadows spill onto the ground, cascade over the lookout's edge, and dissolve into the depression. As his eyes leapt beyond the arrows of their projected figures, he gazed three thousand feet down into a crater the size of Manhattan Island. The synergy of eons of oxidation and weathering had sculpted a Dali-esque landscape, a sea of ash strewn with islands of dormant cinder cones. Although the cones' various heights ranged between five hundred and twelve hundred feet, they were dwarfed in the vastness of the pit.

"It looks like the surface of Mars or an alien world like Dune, and the cones are like colossal anthills," whispered Greg.

Billowy puffs of luminous cloud drifted through the Ko'olau and Kaupo Gaps, two gaping wounds in the crater's outer wall chiseled by erosion and the relentless breath of the trade winds. The sun's slanting rays seeped through occasional breaks in the clouds, focused into intense beams. Like searchlights, they swept across the archipelago of cones to generate a dazzling spectrum of burnt oranges, yellows, reds, and ochers.

Dmitri recalled a mythic phrase he'd read on the Haleakala website. He stretched his arms, swaying back and forth, and imagined himself steering a glider. "'They soared with the Gods on the Kua Mauna—the land above the clouds.'"

"I truly feel it . . . like I'm floating above the ocean and the clouds."

"I'm glad you're here to share the good vibes. The locals believe Haleakala is the temple of the grandmother of the demigod Maui. They see it as a spot of power."

"Yeah, like the Native American traditions."

Feeling closer than ever to his friend, Dmitri scanned the crater with his prized possession, a pair of Swarovski binoculars. Although the last volcanic eruption had occurred over three hundred years ago, the force field here verged on the palpable, yet defied logical description. He offered the binoculars to Greg. "I'm inspired every time I'm here. This time it's about McPinsky's ideas for communicating with other species."

"Why am I not surprised?" Greg's voice was only mildly taunting. He peered through the precision-cut, crystal lenses, rotating through a full three-hundred-sixty degrees. "Love the bird's-eye view. Makes you realize this mighty mountain's just a speck in the vast blue Pacific." He drew a deep breath and then exhaled dramatically. "The renowned McPinsky Challenge," he announced. "I've memorized it verbatim by now: 'Find the biggest-brained being in the vicinity, identify and break the codes of their language, then build a bridge of symbols of light and sound and—'"

"Impressive, Greg," interrupted Dmitri, his neck tightening.

"So you want to converse with the whales? You heard what Gorman said. It's sad, but soon there won't be many left alive to have a conversation with."

"He also said that if someone can raise awareness about their intellectual potential, it'll be another compelling reason to lobby for their protection. Back at PICES, I thought I'd heard your concern."

"I do care." Greg's left eyelid twitched twice. "But who's gonna protect you and your job if you're spouting off about Mensa for whales? I don't want my friend to suffer the same fate as his mentor."

Dmitri interpreted Greg's familiar pleading tone like a guilt trip. "Simmer down," he snapped. "Let's not start a big argument up here on my favorite mountain." When Greg averted his gaze back to the crater, Dmitri instantly regretted his reaction. When a cloud drifted across the sun, an uncomfortable silence eclipsed the conversation.

Dmitri felt a pang of nostalgia for his old college thesis advisor and mentor. Three years ago, the renowned McPinsky had departed SoCalSci due to institutional resistance to his controversial theory that communications engineering and information science could address humanity's profound existential predicament.

A few months before McPinsky's departure, Dmitri had sat entranced in the front row during the landmark lecture when the professor looked directly at him and said, "For at least a few of you, this is the most important message you will ever receive." He'd held his breath until his mentor had issued his daring proposal. "Since alienation and isolation are the misbegotten stepchildren of fear and ignorance, humanity must be proactive if we are to escape the grip of solitude. There are no more excuses to justify our passive wait-for-the-ET's-to-contact-us mentality or our self-serving indifference to the fellow creatures who share our planet."

McPinsky's concluding remarks were seared into Dmitri's mind. After a tantalizing pause, he had pounded the podium with a fist and thundered, "Carpe diem! Find the biggest brained being in the vicinity, identify and break the codes of their language, then build a bridge of symbols of light and sound to initiate a conversation and begin to ask the questions that matter—before it's too late!"

McPinsky's message had resounded like a thunderclap in the progressive scientific arena. Christened the "Interspecies Communication Imperative" by the techno-cognoscenti, but more popularly known as the McPinsky Challenge, it was the reason Dmitri had scheduled this vacation. Beguiled by its philosophical appeal, he'd come to see the whales up close and to chat with the experts before he would begin to analyze their songs for a research paper. Now, with the additional impetus of Gorman's entreaty and the horrific memory of the hemorrhaging humpback, Dmitri had resolved to take an even bolder step to decrypt the mystery code. Why not take such a risk for the reward of a major communication breakthrough and the possibility of the first-ever cetacean conversation? He felt a buoyancy transcending the effect of the altitude.

Dmitri reflected upon his deep attraction to his mentor's philosophical narrative and to their bond. He knew that the links were rooted in childhood, when he'd been abandoned by both of his primary male role models.

Greg broke their prolonged silence. "Since the wind's died down, how about joining me for a quick hike?"

"No, thanks. I'll just hang out and enjoy the view."

After Greg disappeared beyond the crest of the trail descending into the crater, Dmitri ambled over to a nearby bench. As in all previous trips to this spot, the power of the mountain was soon upon him. Perched upon a ten-thousand-foot-tall platform in the middle of an immense sea, he was mesmerized by the refractions of the waning sunset. Eyes closed, he initiated his daily relaxation ritual. He visualized a ship's anchor drifting down into the depths of his consciousness. Shedding the stresses of the day, one at a time, he could control the rate of the anchor's descent, until it floated lazily in the void. A peaceful energy emanated from within. He visualized his mind as a perfectly shaped sphere, free of distorting forces, adrift in space and time, pure unfocused consciousness—

Crop Circle Conundrum

United States Satellite Imaging Agency, Maryland

MISSION SPECIALIST TAMARA Roberts's thoughts churned in a maelstrom of confusion when the klaxon's first shrill tones assaulted her eardrums. A knot of her colleagues had bolted up from their chairs. The alarm's rhythmic howl echoed throughout the auditorium-sized room, the command and control center of the United States Satellite Imaging Agency, better known by its acronym, the USSIA. A theatre-sized monitor suspended from an atrium ceiling flashed its warning beacon in blood-red letters: LEVEL THREE ALERT, bathing the brushed chrome and smoked glass interior in a pulsing, pink glow.

Seconds earlier, an RH-12 spy satellite had trained its eight-foot-diameter glass eye upon a region of the ocean near Hawaii. As sophisticated and complex as the Hubble Space Telescope, the outer-space magnifying glass extraordinaire could resolve the details of an object as small as a jackrabbit. After capturing the first surveillance images of the U.S. Navy's top secret maneuvers, the RH-12 beamed the electromagnetic incarnation of the digitized pictures through an invisible microwave downlink channel to a ground station in Guam. From there, the digital data stream flowed through an ultra-secure, worldwide communications network to the USSIA in Maryland. As more images arrived at the USSIA, a supercomputer had performed a preliminary pattern-recognition analysis, detected a suspicious object, and activated the alarm. In the ensuing milliseconds, the world's fastest video processing system sharpened the initial image, pixel by pixel, for brightness, contrast, and noise reduction via a complex correlation analysis of millions of data bits.

A collective clamor resounded throughout the viewing gallery when the first enhanced photo appeared on the threat monitor. The image revealed a vast array of concentric rings, frothy white against the backdrop of the blue Pacific, and hundreds of meters in diameter. The computers relentlessly crunched the numbers, enhancing each subsequent image, until a slow-motion video commenced on the big screen. The ring-shaped pattern changed with time, like a slowly evolving geometric construction, similar to time-lapse movies of flowers in bloom. When wisps of smoke emerged from the heart of the formation, all activity ceased in the USSIA control room.

Once the excitement had waned, Tamara and several of her colleagues settled down at their workstations to study the images of the enigmatic figures. If hostile forces dared to eavesdrop on the U.S. Navy's Hawaiian maneuvers, their job was to alert their superiors to the detection of such threats, but after an hour of expert analysis, no one could explain what it was or what might have caused it.

The anomaly reminded Tamara of the Internet photos of crop circle formations hewn into farmer's fields by ET hoaxers. The striking structure emblazoned on the monitor, however, had been photographed on the surface of the ocean, not in a cornfield. Her mind struggled to formulate a plausible explanation. Was it a naturally occurring event, possibly weather-related? But it didn't look like a spiral pattern with a central vortex, as would be expected if generated by cyclonic winds. Could it be an optical phenomenon similar to the halos encircling the sun and the moon? Those were caused by the diffraction bending and spreading of light waves around microscopic particles. Still, that happened up in the sky, not in the sea.

She typed "diffraction rings" into the laptop's web browser and found an intriguing post: "Specter of the Brocken ring patterns projected onto clouds and caused by the diffraction of light." Yet those only occurred at high altitudes, not at sea level. She kept on searching, but most of the results were crackpot theories about circular cloud formations generated by black-ops radar weapons. The design on the screen didn't look anything like a shadow projected from above. The ring shapes appeared whitish in color, suggesting they might have emerged from beneath the surface.

Stymied, Roberts decided to consult her colleague at the adjoining workstation. Once she'd finally captured his attention, he pocketed his cell phone and sauntered over. Mission Specialist Noel Harrison's face appeared baggy eyed, lacking its conspicuous, charismatic grin.

"How are you, Noel?"

"Just the usual money and kid problems." His voice bobbed with the cadence of a faint Appalachian accent.

Roberts sighed. "Sorry to interrupt, but I need a second opinion." She pointed at her monitor.

Harrison studied the image while scratching his head.

"Come on, Mister Recon Expert!" She nudged him in the ribs with an elbow. "Tell me what you see!"

Harrison gazed at the photo for another ten seconds, and then he sneered, "You playin' a practical joke on me?"

"Absolutely not."

"Is this photo linked to the surveillance of the Navy's operation near Hawaii?"

"Uh-huh."

"You're tellin' me crop circles are poppin' up in the middle of the ocean?"

The squeak of a nervous chuckle escaped through the tunnel of Tamara's windpipe. "That's what I thought too, but that's impossible."

"What about those rumors . . . that the Navy's testin' an advanced sonar weapon?

"You think that would cause these halo patterns?"

"Who knows," he replied. "And even if they did, they'd never admit it."

She sighed. "So do you think I should kick this up the chain of command?"

Harrison replied with an incredulous expression. "Ever hear what happened in the 1950's, to the Air Force pilots who swore their planes were being shadowed by UFOs? All endured psychiatric evaluations. They were never promoted, and some were even hounded out of the Force. Does that answer you?"

"I get the message."

As Harrison ambled back to his workstation, he turned around and drawled, "I need a good laugh. Why don't you copy that pic over to my workstation? I'll give it another looksee."

"Why not?"

A Message from On High

Haleakala Crater Summit Lookout, Maui—early evening

WHEN DMITRI OPENED his eyes, he saw Mercury and Mars gleaming in the twilight. Greg sat beside him, eyes closed and legs pretzeled into a lotus pose. An awesome silence, like shruti vibrations, filled everything. He braced his arms against the Haleakala mountain chill.

With the darkness intensifying, Dmitri's thoughts tunneled through the lingering scar of his father's untimely death, back to his first memorable experience of the night sky. To celebrate his eighth birthday, Dmitri had joined his father, Michael, and older brother, Paul, for an inaugural family camping trip. Experiencing a child's first-night jitters, he'd whined about the scary shadows and wailing coyotes. He'd known his dad would comfort him with a spellbinding story, and he was not disappointed.

Lying side by side in the blackness, he heard the reassuring sound of his father's voice. "David, want to see something cool? Reach your hand up to the sky." With a rush of anticipation, he'd lifted an arm. His dad grasped his wrist and said, "Now just let go and follow my lead." They'd begun with the Big Dipper. Michael Dmitri had guided David Dmitri's hand from star to star, drawing a connect-the-dots picture with David's pointed finger. Their hands journeyed across the heavens: Aquila the eagle, Cygnus the swan, Hercules the warrior, and Sagittarius the centaur. As they'd finger painted the firmament, Michael regaled his sons with tales about the ancients and their personification of the constellations' patterns into their mythology and stories. Enraptured by his father's narrative, David had imagined himself living during those olden times.

No longer afraid, David had wished the night would never end. When his father's deep breathing confirmed he'd fallen asleep, David had marveled at the Milky Way from the cocoon of his sleeping bag. So many stars, he'd thought, and every one a gigantic sun like ours. Maybe even with planets of their own, his dad had explained. As he'd felt his heart beat and tried to imagine the immensity of the universe, David thought his brain would burst. Then, from out of the void, he had heard the voice of God speaking directly to him, sounding like Oz booming from beyond the stellar curtain to proclaim the glory of His creation.

Years later, when Dmitri had shared the reminiscence with his mentor, McPinsky had a provocative explanation. "Your child's mind was hardwired to respond to its first glimpse of the infinite, thus evoking the auditory image of the divine creator."

Dmitri again shut his eyes and recollected the details of McPinsky's surprising response. The professor had told him about the sensory deprivation experiments pioneered by the neuroscientist and dolphin researcher John Lilly. "Lilly immersed his human subjects in a flotation tank of body-temperature water while wearing opaque eye patches and ear plugs. After a brief period of sensory starvation, many experienced auditory and visual hallucinations. Lilly hypothesized that the brain is so conditioned to process information, it generates its own 'lucid daydreams' to compensate for the absence of external sensations."

Dmitri was a trained skeptic, steeped in the empirical principles of the scientific method. "Sounds intriguing, Professor, but a single study isn't conclusive."

"Later researchers tested subjects in sensory deprivation rooms and confirmed Lilly's observations," replied McPinsky. "They concluded that the brain superimposes its own patterns when deprived of sensory stimuli from the environment. Depending on the circumstances, it's unable to distinguish whether the source is internal or external, real or imagined."

Shortly after their conversation, McPinsky had confounded the scientific community, going public with a journal article, "Cultural Psychopathology of Interspecies Communication Deprivation," about the profound impact of human existential isolation. "Humanity is achingly alone in the vastness of the cosmos. Just as nature abhors a vacuum, humans abhor the vacuum of isolation. Our intrinsic nature compels us to connect with others and to share our inner selves. Until now, however, our species has been unable or unwilling to have a dialogue with another intelligent species on this planet or from anywhere else in the universe."

McPinsky hypothesized that, in a manner similar to Lilly's experiments, the collective unconscious region of our minds fabricates the illusion of contact to substitute for the absence of interspecies communications. "This," he said, "gives rise to various paranormal phenomena such as close encounters with spirits and ET's and even conversations with God."

Dmitri had been galvanized by McPinsky's challenge to humanity's collective ego. It was part of why he still loved the professor: for his ultra, out-of-the-box mindset and the chutzpah to "stick his neck out" for his contentious theories.

"Over there!" Greg's voice shattered the silence.

Shocked back to the present, Dmitri saw a green bolt of light blazing in the heavens.

"It's erupting from those domes." Greg pointed up the hill.

"The LURE Observatory!" exclaimed Dmitri. "I've seen those domes before, but I never realized they could shoot laser beams into the sky."

"Hey, let's check it out. Maybe we can talk our way into a tour of the place."

"Absolutely! The Goddess of Fire is restless tonight. Pele's sending us a message—a beacon to guide us to new discoveries."

"Or a warning omen about the perils of a McPinsky-inspired quest."

"It's freezing out here. Let's go stargaze."

The Laser Ranger

LURE Observatory, Haleakala Summit—early evening

"WATCH OUT!" GREG gripped the passenger door safety handle.

Dmitri had nearly driven off the cliff when the flare of another laser arrow illuminated the stark volcanic moonscape. "Sorry. I feel like a fighter pilot in a dogfight." He fought with the steering wheel as he banked left and right up the winding road leading to the LURE Observatory. The car's high beams were as anemic as a glorified flashlight in the pitch black night.

Greg sighed with relief when they pulled into the observatory's parking lot. When they opened the doors, their faces felt the sting of the frigid mountain air.

"And I thought you were nuts when you suggested jackets for this trip." Greg followed Dmitri's lead and slipped a poncho-style windbreaker over his hoodie. "I'd feel even better in a down parka."

The two Californians stood shivering, their arms clutched to their chests. Dmitri glanced ahead to admire the floodlit, Kremlin-like profile of a single-story block building bookended by towering domed structures. Approaching the only illuminated door, he thought about the spiel that would hopefully gain them entrance into the facilities. Despite the warning sign posted on the door, ACCESS RESTRICTED TO GOVERNMENT PERSONNEL, they were undeterred. Greg and Dmitri never passed over an opportunity to engage other researchers, anytime or anyplace.

"Let's just stick to our standard SoCalSci introductions," Dmitri advised.

Greg pressed the button for the door entry buzzer. After a few impatient moments, he pressed it again. Dmitri felt the temperature plummeting and watched the swirling vapors of their breath vanish into the night sky. Greg began pounding on the door with his fists. Still no one answered. As they started to walk away, the door opened and Dmitri saw the faint crescent of an ethereal Asian face.

"Hello," said the face. "Welcome to the LURE Observatory." She poked her head further out the door, unveiling a Gioconda smile. "May I help you, gentlemen?"

Dmitri felt soothed by the gentle waves of her voice. She enunciated her consonants as melodiously as vowels, as if she were speaking English with a French accent. He'd dismissed his friends' stories about their love-at-first-sight encounters, but what about "love at first sound?" He'd always felt awkward in the presence of a beautiful woman, but a beautiful voice?

"I'm Dmitri, and this is my friend and colleague, Greg." He tapped a fist to his associate's shoulder. "We're from SoCalSci University on a whale watching vacation. We saw a laser flash from the lookout, and curiosity propelled us to your doorstep."

"Well." She hesitated. Still peeking out the door, her sober gaze scanned him top to bottom, and Dmitri held his breath. Her eyes shifted, ping-ponging over to Greg and back to him. At the conclusion of her due diligence assessment, she stepped into full view. "My name is Melanie. I'm sorry there are no whales here at ten thousand feet, but I do fire a mean laser." She flashed Dmitri a dimpled grin, then fished into a lab coat pocket and extracted a business card.

Dmitri read the inscription: MELANIE MARI, UNIVERSITY OF HAWAII, LASER RANGER. His eyes locked onto the last two words. "Laser ranger" sounded like some mythic hero in a Buck Rogers tale. "I do declare," he drawled. "I've met forest rangers and a Texas Ranger, but this is the first time I've ever even heard of a laser ranger. I'm actually just a humble associate professor of engineering."

"And I'm just a garden-variety mathematician," said Greg.

"I'm familiar with SoCalSci's reputation. You have more Nobel Prize winners," she tapped an index finger to her temple, "than any other university."

"We were wondering if you could give us a brief tour of the facility?" asked Dmitri. "Of course, if you're ever visiting our neck of the woods, we'd be more than happy to reciprocate."

"We're normally too busy to deal with tourists' special requests." Melanie's slender fingers caressed a silvery, oval-shaped, yin-yang pendant. "I suppose I could spare a few minutes to show you the duties of a laser ranger in exchange for some details about your professional credentials. Do you two have business cards?"

They whipped out their wallets and presented their cards for her inspection. "Well, that seems to be in order. It's cold. Come on in and take off your jackets." She waved them inside. "This is your lucky night."

Melanie whisked them into the central portion of the main building. Dmitri saw facilities akin to SoCalSci's Mechanical Engineering Lab. An array of cubicles, framed by four-foot by six-foot padded wall panels, formed the perimeter of a roughly forty-foot, square-shaped room. A cluster of computer workstations and a pool of ergonomic office chairs dominated the center of an open-plan workspace.

During a brief round of introductions to her two youthful colleagues, Melanie's take-charge attitude impressed Dmitri. She directed her guests' attention to a pair of stations adorned by a cheerful menagerie of stuffed marine animals. "We program and operate the telescopes and the laser from these two computers." She branched her arms and pointed left and right. "The domes for the telescopes are located at opposite ends of the control room. There are operational stations next to each of the telescopes." With a beckoning wave, she said, "Follow me."

The two professors trailed Melanie's echoing metallic footsteps up the stairs of a freestanding spiral staircase. They emerged onto a second-story platform which served as the observation deck in the seven-meter-diameter dome. The exposed girders, beams, and support structures reminded Dmitri of a giant erector set.

Melanie donned a wireless communication headset as if crowning herself with a high-tech tiara. She relaxed her back and leaned against the framework supporting the various gears, belts, and motors that controlled the telescope. "The transmitting telescope has been modified to accept the collimated beam from the laser as an input source to its forty-centimeter objective lens. Notice the laser is adjacent to the telescope." Her amplified voice reverberated throughout the room, enveloping Dmitri in its embrace.

"What a beautiful set of instruments." Dmitri gazed appreciatively, first at Melanie, and then upon the gleaming assemblage of black-and-white tube structures housing the array of large mirrors and electronic components. "I never expected an encounter with such sophisticated equipment here on the mountain."

Melanie stood center stage, her silver earrings and yin-yang pendant glistening beneath an intense spotlight. "I'll bet you didn't know the LURE

Observatory was built in 1974 and that LURE is an acronym for Lunar Ranging Experiment?"

"Not a clue," replied Greg, "but it'd be a great Jeopardy question."

"You SoCalSci guys don't miss a beat." Melanie pointed up at the sky. "With the LURE telescope, our UH scientists can measure the time it takes for the laser's light pulses to bounce back from reflectors on the moon."

"You're telling us there are laser reflectors on the moon?" Dmitri glanced over at Greg.

"Everyone remembers the grainy videos of Neil Armstrong and his merry band of Apollo astronauts doing kangaroo bounces on the moon. What people don't know is that they installed the reflectors just for the LURE experiment. We can measure the distance between the moon and the earth to an accuracy of less than two centimeters."

Dmitri fiddled with the touch screen on his iPhone. "Outstanding! That's a precision of one part in ten billion."

"Not too shabby, huh?" Melanie's smile accentuated her cheekbones. "Taking the measurements at different times of the day and month, it's just basic trigonometry to accurately compute the movement of the Earth's tectonic plates, to measure the length of a day based upon the rate of change of the Earth's rotation, and to calculate the precession of the Earth's axis."

"Answering another Jeopardy question, it cost the U.S. taxpayers twenty-five billion dollars to land on the moon," said Greg. "Considering that the reflectors went along for the ride, it's quite a bargain in return for the amount of science that's been reaped."

"Forty years later and they're still working," said Melanie. "My all-time favorite LURE discovery is the lunar orbit measurement accurate enough to confirm Einstein's prediction using general relativity."

"You reminded me of my all-time favorite Einstein quote," said Dmitri. "'Spend a week in Maui and it seems like a day. Spend a day at work and it seems like a week. That's relativity.'"

"That's special relativity," she replied. "But I can't picture Albert Einstein in a speedo." Melanie's laughter resonated with a distinct musical quality, delighting Dmitri.

Greg was in a more serious mood. "I recently read an article in *Scientific American* about the measurements of continental drift. I vaguely remember the mid-Pacific plate is moving in a northwesterly direction and dragging the Hawaiian Islands along with it." He motioned with his arm to illustrate the point. "Does the data from LURE confirm this?"

"Correcto, about five inches per year, moving toward Japan. This is really fascinating for us locals because it explains the formation and spacing of the Hawaiian Islands predicted by plate tectonics. Here, follow me." She paused and, with a dancer's grace, motioned them toward a freestanding whiteboard.

While Greg asked the questions, Dmitri's own visual tracking system scanned the contours of Melanie's East-meets-West fusion features, shaped, he surmised, by the merging of Asian, Pacific, and North American genetic tectonic plates. He was pleasantly distracted by the multiple images of her movements reflected back to him from the glass and metal surfaces of the telescope.

Melanie grabbed a marker pen and drew a schematic map of the Hawaiian Islands. "Geologists have discovered a huge column of upwelling lava that lies at a fixed location called the mid-Pacific Ridge. As the ocean floor moves over this hot spot at about five inches a year, the lava rises to the surface and creates a steady succession of new volcanoes."

"I'm picturing a gigantic conveyor belt of volcanic islands spreading away from the source," said Dmitri.

"The Hawaiian archipelago of nineteen islands was built by this lava plume over millions of years," she told them. "New islands are being born as we speak."

"Which is great for your tourist industry," interjected Greg. "Sorry to drift off of the subject, but we noticed the laser beam had a greenish hue—" He stopped in mid-sentence when Melanie started scribbling some esoteric numbers on the whiteboard.

"The YAG laser produces one-centimeter-diameter light pulses of 200 picosecond duration every 200 milliseconds," she said. "The wavelength of the light of a YAG laser is 5,320 angstroms, corresponding to the visible green light portion of the electromagnetic spectrum."

Dmitri cleared his throat and raised a hand like a schoolboy. "What's a YAG?"

"YAG is an acronym for yttrium, aluminum, garnet crystal."

Dmitri smiled. "Only a laser ranger could shed such a stimulating light on the optics of angstroms and picoseconds."

"Just think," she replied. "In the four-billion-year history of our solar system, no photon of light could make the 500,000-mile, round-trip trek to the moon and come back to the exact location it started from." Melanie extended her arms and twirled a full three-hundred-sixty degrees. "That is," she added, "until lasers were invented and the reflectors were delivered to the moon's surface. And I'm the lucky laser ranger operating all of this amazing technology, firing the zillions of photons heavenward."

When she arched her back and reached for the sky, Dmitri was mesmerized. He'd never imagined a planetarium show could combine astronomy with graceful dance movements.

"Even then," she continued, "only a handful survives the round-trip. We need a special amplifier to capture and detect those few photons so we can measure the time of their journey."

"Those photons remind me of the few salmon who survive the round-trip to spawn their species," said Greg.

"Very interesting," replied Melanie, looking thoughtful. "I never thought about it quite that way."

"So much for the conspiracy theory that the moon landings were a hoax," said Dmitri.

"Yes," she said. "We're an adaptable species, but it's also our nature to cling to the security of existing belief systems. There's been a status quo resistance to new ideas throughout history."

"Like the Creationists rejecting the theory of evolution," added Greg. "Although we're just a few DNA base pair degrees of separation removed from the genomes of our simian relatives."

Dmitri nodded his agreement. "It's unfortunately true. Humanity's vision is skewed. We filter objective awareness through the lens of our insecurities and ideological bias."

Melanie grasped her pendant. "That's interesting. I've been reading about the Indian philosopher J. Krishnamurti. He advocated that the ideal state of right thought is attained by awareness without judgment."

Dmitri's mouth was agape. "Simply amazing," he replied. "My college advisor and mentor quotes Krishnamurti."

"Great minds think alike." She tossed him wink. "Bet you didn't know that, in 1924, Joseph Campbell accidently bumped into Krishnamurti while sailing back from Europe. Although Campbell was only twenty years old, they discussed Asian philosophy and the Hindu and Indian belief systems."

"That I didn't know," said Dmitri, impressed by the breadth of Melanie's interests. "Their conversation probably influenced Campbell's ideas on the relationship of myth and the human psyche."

"Very cool," replied Greg. "We should all be so fortunate as to chance upon such an inspirational mentor." He winked at Dmitri.

"Here's my take on the photon round-trip," Dmitri announced. "It's a metaphor for the process of self-discovery. We learn about ourselves by building a bridge of symbols with others and reflecting upon information reflected back to us."

"I like that," said Melanie. "The earth will discover itself by reflecting information to and from its lunar brother."

Dmitri nodded and smiled. "Whereas the Hubble Telescope is harvesting one-way photons emitted long, long ago and far, far away so we can discover the mysteries at the edge of the cosmos."

"Did either of you ever read the *Sirens of Titan*?" asked Greg. Melanie and Dmitri shook their heads.

In SparkNotes-like fashion, Greg summarized Vonnegut's story of an intergalactic explorer stranded millions of years ago on Saturn's largest moon because a critical component of his spacecraft had broken. The raw materials for this component didn't exist on Titan, but they did on Earth. "The ET's used their quasi-omnipotent powers to manipulate human evolutionary history to produce a civilization capable of developing such a part and, after inventing space travel, Fedexed it back to Titan," he said.

Dmitri knew what to expect: an eccentric but brilliant conclusion.

Greg finished the thought. "So, putting a Vonnegut spin on the Gaia Principle, which postulates that our biosphere is a single complex organism, maybe the Earth has evolved creatures like us to invent technologies that enable Earth consciousness to expand its self-awareness. You, Lady Melanie, as the appointed laser ranger, are the enabling agent for the Sirens of Earth Gaia. You were created by the Gaia to ascend the holy mountain and to shine the light of illumination upon planetary consciousness."

This one tops them all, thought Dmitri. He sincerely hoped Greg's celestial, time-travelling romp hadn't weirded out Melanie.

Her eyes opened wide, like a child experiencing her first rainbow. When she'd begun to whistle the theme song from the *Twilight Zone*, her guests joined her in moaning their version of scary ghost sounds. Melanie raised both arms, and the spirit sounds ceased.

"Oh, guys," her tone playful, "by the way, this is my part-time job. I also have a day job as a speech therapist. After all, what's the use of this high-tech stuff if it can't help improve the human condition? You'd be impressed how technology has revolutionized language training programs for the hard of hearing. If you have some free time, why not come by the University of Hawaii Speech Lab in Kahului and I'll give you another tour?"

Greg looked both amazed and eager. "Absolutely."

Dmitri couldn't have been happier if he'd won the lottery. "Melanie, you sure know how to entice a couple of techies. We're totally booked tomorrow, but the following morning we'll be finished with the snorkel cruise to Molokini and Turtle Town by 10 a.m. and then returning to Kihei."

Melanie responded with a charming tilt of her head. "Ooh, that's a great dive, and say hello to the giant sea turtles. The drive from Kihei to Kahului can take thirty minutes, so let's rendezvous at about eleven." She jotted on a yellow Post-it. "Here's the address. But before you leave, how about a light show?" Her index finger hovered tantalizingly above the telescope's control panel. "Did you know there are more UFO sightings on Haleakala Mountain than practically anywhere else on the globe? Want to know why?"

With a flick of her wrist, the laser ranger unleashed another flaming emerald bolt into the Hawaiian night.

Speech Lab—A Bridge of Light and Sound

University of Hawaii Speech Lab, Kahului, Maui—two days later

THE DRIVE FROM Kihei to Maui's largest retail and population center, Kahului, was one of Dmitri's all-time scenic favorites. He assumed, therefore, that the leisurely trip through the idyllic countryside would allay his jitters about seeing Melanie again.

"This is the life!" Greg howled above the roar of the wind. "Never thought I'd play tag with giant sea turtles."

Dmitri turned to look at Greg. "What's your take on the laser ranger?" he shouted before focusing his attention back to the highway.

"A Renaissance woman," replied Greg. "Brains, beauty, and multiple interests—the feminine ideal you've long sought. Back home, guys would be lining up around the block to date her."

With a sideways glance, Dmitri caught his chum's broad grin. Greg's assessment about Dmitri's "perfect woman" confirmed the real reason for his anxiety. Why would she be interested in someone labeled an engineering geek by more than one ex-girlfriend? He realized he had better enjoy the scenery if he hoped to unwind.

In the open-air vehicle, they were surrounded by a lush valley of sugarcane fields. Rows of cane rose from the valley floor, gradually ascending the lower slopes of Haleakala to the east and, more dramatically, climbing the jagged contours of the Maui Mountains to the west. The stalks swayed like a hula in the ocean breeze to the accompaniment of the rolling, steel-guitar rhythms of "Harbor Lights," the Hawaiian favorite, playing on a local radio station. As the warm wind massaged his face, Dmitri stole an occasional glance at the towering, cloud-crowned summit of Haleakala. By the time they'd pulled into the University's parking lot, he felt more relaxed.

"Where to?" asked Greg.

"This is a college campus," replied Dmitri, leading Greg down a sidewalk shaded by acacia trees. "Someone's gotta know about the Speech Lab."

"The place reminds me of my small-town community college," remarked Greg, "low-rise and compact."

"It's definitely not as glitzy as SoCalSci, but this is laid-back Hawaii. Very cool roof designs."

"Polynesian inspired."

Dmitri and Greg were attired like any of the students scurrying off to their classrooms, having changed into shorts, sandals, and DIVE MOLOKINI souvenir T-shirts at the conclusion of their cruise. Stopping to examine an artsy, oversized campus map, hand painted onto the side wall of a two-story, white stucco structure, they followed the directions to a modest, white-washed bungalow. A plaque mounted on the front door indicated it was the University of Hawaii's Experimental Speech Lab.

Melanie's face brightened with delight when they entered the lobby. "You're right on time," she said, greeting each of them with a spirited handshake.

Dmitri hoped this first contact wouldn't be the last time he'd feel her touch. Framed by a window overlooking a tropical garden, she looked even lovelier in the daytime.

"So how did you enjoy your Molokini cruise?" she asked, eyeing their T-shirts.

"As awesome as the PICES whale watch," replied Greg.

"I try to do it every year." She smiled at Dmitri. "How was it for you?"

Mildly bemused, he wondered if she intended the double entendre. "We thrilled to the giant cetaceans rocketing from the deep blue sea."

"So poetic," Melanie replied with that signature tilt of her head.

"Really, we were so inspired by the humpbacks we decided to visit PICES headquarters. We might be analyzing whale songs. I'd like to tell you about it."

"Sounds intriguing. It's possible we have something in common. Let me show you how we analyze the voices of children with hearing loss."

The night before last, Melanie had been cloaked in a plain white lab coat. Following her down a short corridor, Dmitri cast more than one admiring glance at her hip-hugging jeans and silky, floral blouse. In her wake, he inhaled a distinctive essence, like a subtle lavender and sandalwood potpourri.

They entered a classroom bustling with activity yet surprisingly silent.

With a sweeping gesture of her arm, Melanie said, "So here we are. We're very proud of our modest UH Experimental Speech Therapy Lab."

Dmitri surveyed the utilitarian chamber. A gallery of black-and-white photos of smiling children's faces graced the cream-colored walls and suggested the room's personality. An unusual scene at the front of the room attracted his attention. A bobbed brunette, tastefully tattooed, and about the same age as one of his graduate students, stood in front of a wall-mounted whiteboard, semi-encircled by the desks of eight elementary-school-aged pupils. As her head arced back and forth, her shoulders swayed and her hips undulated, her hands danced a pas de deux, and her fingers embroidered an intricate web of shapes into the fabric of the air. Her deftly coordinated movements, intermingled with occasional darting gestures to drawings on the whiteboard, spoke to her students as meaningfully as any lecturer.

Language as choreography, thought Dmitri. As the room pulsed with her silent intensity, he was startled by a chorus of children's laughter, like joyous music, erupting from the void. The youngsters' eyes were riveted to their teacher, whose movements had become more percussive. Like a boxer, she bounced, dipped, and jabbed her visual communiqué. The students chortled in response to each dramatic thrust. Melanie laughed along with the children.

Once the room had quieted down, Melanie motioned to her right, toward the near wall. Dmitri observed two brown-skinned boys, pre-teens who looked like brothers, and a younger bespectacled girl with long, blond hair. The three youthful subjects wore headset microphones and sat in front of computer workstations. They spoke into their microphones and peered intently at their monitors as figures were plotted in real time. To Dmitri, the shapes on the screen looked like the innocuous scrawls of a child.

"This brings back memories," said Greg. "I was trained in pronunciation using a similar but more rudimentary program."

"I didn't realize you were hard of hearing," Melanie replied. "Your pronunciation is extraordinary."

Greg's tanned face glowed with an ivory grin. "I'm pretty fortunate to have some residual auditory function, so it's only a problem in a noisy setting. Luckily, my training began when I was even younger than your students."

Dmitri scratched his head. "Will someone please clue me in?" His words were muted.

"You don't have to lower your voice in here." Melanie waved a thumb, hitchhiker style, toward the children. "Let me show you."

She brought them over to one of the training consoles, surprising the boy there by patting him on the shoulder. He glanced up, his eyes brimming with affection. "Hi, Ms. Mari. I'm ready for my lesson." His voice sounded labored and off-key.

"I'd like to introduce you to Javier. He's one of my best students." Melanie deliberately shaped each word for lip-reading purposes and simultaneously gestured with both hands. She extended an arm toward her adult guests and then resumed signing. "Javier, this is Dr. Dmitri and Dr. Bono from California. Would you believe Dr. Bono was trained using an early version of the Speakeasy system and now teaches mathematics at a famous school?"

Javier stood, greeting them with brown eyes full of curiosity. He seemed shy and self-conscious. He addressed Greg in a mumbling voice while he signed. "I want to be a teacher like you someday. I know it takes lots of practice, but Ms. Mari has spent major time with me."

"Javier," said Melanie. "Let's show Dr. Dmitri how we use Speakeasy to train for correct pronunciation." As the boy settled down in his chair, Melanie pointed at Javier's computer monitor. "The figure displayed on the screen is called a target word gram. It's a visual representation of the primary frequencies of the unique sequence of vowels and consonants comprising an English language word. Each word gram picture corresponds to a different word."

"Except for homonyms?" said Greg.

"Yes, very good," she replied. "Words that sound alike, such as 'to,' 'two,' and 'too' have the same shaped word grams. The word gram currently displayed on Javier's monitor shows the target frequencies for the correct pronunciation of the word 'you' that, as you just mentioned, would look the same as the word for a female sheep."

"It's just a straight line," said Greg.

"Correct," said Melanie. "'You' only consists of two vowels, 'ee' and 'oo,' which are connected by a straight line on the plot. Words consisting of many vowels and consonants have more complex word gram shapes."

"I'd love to see the shape for 'antidisestablishmentarianism,'" said Dmitri, his tone roguish.

Melanie gazed up at the ceiling, mouthing silently while she counted with the fingers of both hands. She stared at him with a look of triumph. "That's twenty-seven vowels and consonants. More than a match for Dr. Bono's mathematical expertise."

"Touché!" replied Dmitri, wowed by the speech therapist's cerebral savoir faire. She answered with a playful bow. "By the way, just call us Greg and Dmitri."

He cast a knowing glance at Greg. "We're not titular. Please continue."

"No problem." Melanie smiled and rested her hand on the student's shoulder. "As Javier speaks into the microphone, the computer will analyze the frequencies of his voice in real time and plot those as it draws the shape of his spoken word gram. When Javier's word gram shape finally matches the target word gram, he'll know his pronunciation is correct. Since he can't hear his own voice, he doesn't receive the audio feedback cues that allow hearing-enabled speakers to make instantaneous adjustments for correct pronunciation. Visual feedback, however, provides the deaf with virtually the same information."

Greg raised a hand. "What are those icons displayed around the borders?"

"These correspond to simpler training tasks, stepping-stones to the more sophisticated word-gram-based program. Javier can select these training options with a click of the mouse. For instance, he can initiate a video close-up of a person's face pronouncing the same word. He can zoom in to observe facial features such as of the lips or jaw."

"What about the rest of the vocal tract?" asked Greg.

Melanie reached for the desktop mouse and clicked on one of the icons. "This diagram shows the varying positions of the teeth, tongue, lips, velum, jaw, and the vocal cords. Javier can freeze the frame to study the details for positioning his own vocal tract articulators."

Melanie signaled to Javier with the traditional Hawaiian "hang loose" shaka sign, her thumb and pinky finger extended and the three middle fingers curled. Javier scrunched up his face, uttered his first muffled attempt, and then sighed. The plot of his vocalization, as it appeared on the monitor, clearly didn't match the target shape. It pained Dmitri to see the boy's mask of frustration. Javier took a deep breath and spoke again. The boy's smile and the shape of the word gram confirmed the results. Two successive attempts resulted in improvements of pronunciation and shapes that converged more closely to the target word gram.

As the Speakeasy system translated the youngster's thoughts into images on the display, Dmitri was reminded of the speech bubbles and thought balloons hovering above the heads of the characters in the comics. When the shape of Javier's next word gram looked nearly identical to the target, the display lit up like a pinball machine, flashing a colorful smiley face. The boy turned to face Melanie, his face radiant. She squeezed his shoulder.

"Excellent, Javier."

Dmitri congratulated Javier with the mainlander's version of the thumbs-up sign and then turned to Melanie. "That was a very impressive demo, Ms. Mari. The visual representation of the target frequencies is very clever. Do you have the time to describe some of the technical details of Speakeasy's translation from audio to visual mode?"

"I anticipated your question." She waved across the room, and her young colleague approached them. "I'd like to introduce my associate, Erika. I'm sure you noticed she's a dynamite speech teacher. Erika, these are the SoCalSci professors I told you about, Dmitri and Greg."

Dmitri immediately recognized the signs of Greg's interest in Melanie's associate, as his gaze fixated on the colorful tattoos of flowers, birds, and butterflies gracing her bare arms and shoulders. The golden ring embellishing Greg's left ear struck Dmitri as a faint echo of Erika's sparkling, silvery ensemble: treble-pierced, hooped earrings accented by diminutive lip and nose rings.

"Melanie's right about your teaching technique." Greg's voice bubbled with congeniality. "Your body language is extraordinary. What's your secret for tickling the children's funny bones?"

"Humor is a matter of trust." Erika's tone was surprisingly businesslike. "They respond when you're open, not afraid to make yourself vulnerable."

"How so?"

"I recited examples of embarrassing gaffes I've committed when signing."

"Erika's going to sub for me with Javier and his group while we have that talk about Speakeasy," said Melanie. "Thanks, Erika."

"Nice meeting you." Erika waved goodbye.

Greg and Dmitri followed Melanie across the room. They stopped and stood in front of a whiteboard mounted on the opposite wall. With Melanie in the center, the two men flanked her with elbow room to spare, close enough for Dmitri to appreciate the fragrant breeze when she shook the tangles from her lustrous, black hair.

"Since you gentlemen are tech-savvy, let's review the rules for constructing a language. It's the best way to understand the principles of the Speakeasy system." With a big smile, Dmitri handed her a marker pen. "Thank you, and please tell me if it's too tedious."

"Not at all," said Dmitri. "It's been years since my Linguistics 1A course, and I've completely forgotten the material. A refresher course is much appreciated."

"Same for me," said Greg.

"Okay. The symbols for both written and spoken languages have similar structure and function." Melanie shook the pen as she punctuated each point.

"If we examine the written word first, we can gain insight into the foundations of spoken language. You probably know the human brain processes about twenty times more visual than auditory information?"

Dmitri perked up. "Hey, I know where you gleaned that factoid. Dolphin researcher John Lilly cited the same ratio for dolphins, except the roles are reversed. They process about twenty times as much sound information as visual."

"Actually, I didn't know that. It's curious, isn't it?"

"Yes. Those ratios indicate that sounds play the same primary role in whale and dolphin communications as visuals do in our own culture."

"Quit interrupting." Greg's tone wasn't very collegial. "I thought I signed up for Melanie's Linguistics 1A class."

Dmitri felt his face flush. Greg's ultra-arched eyebrow confirmed that he considered whale communications a taboo conversational topic. "Greg's right." Dmitri shrugged. "A lecturer's bad habit. Please continue."

Melanie hesitated, looking first at Greg, then Dmitri. "Okay. So the building blocks of language are words. These, as you know, are the abstract symbols representing our thoughts about things and ideas. In our written language, we assign a unique symbol to each word. There are two options for encoding these written word symbols. One approach is pictorial, like the ideograms of the Chinese written language." With confident strokes, she drew a Chinese character on the board. "There's a relationship between the shape of the symbol to what it represents. Can you guess this one?"

"Looks like wavy lines to me," said Greg.

"Is it a stream?" asked Dmitri.

"You're both right," replied Melanie. "It represents 'water.'"

"By the way," said Dmitri, "is Chinese script another of your many talents?"

"I only know a few characters. There are so many. This one-to-one correspondence between each ideogram and the thing or idea it represents requires thousands of different symbols and demands a steep learning curve to master each and every image. One virtue, however, is that written language is influenced by personal artistic interpretation. Think about the art of calligraphy."

"You're right," said Dmitri. "In Japan, I was struck by the artistry of the Kanji characters on the signs and billboards."

"I wouldn't be surprised if the bonsai sculpting of trees and bushes is also rooted in the pictorial forms of their written language," said Greg.

A subtle smile played at the corners of Melanie's lips. "Your insights never disappoint."

"Let me guess," said Greg. "The word gram shapes in the Speakeasy program are the audio equivalent to the pictorial symbols used in written language."

"Like the Chinese ideograms," added Dmitri.

Melanie flicked her arm, as if banging out a rim shot. "Precisely. When we learn the written language, we memorize the patterns of the ideograms with the visual memory region of the brain. For spoken language, we store the shapes of the frequencies of individual words using the auditory memory region."

Dmitri snapped his fingers and thumbs. "So we literally maintain separate dictionaries of both visual and spoken symbols in our mental database. While we're reading, we instantaneously perform a search-and-match procedure for each word."

Melanie nodded. "We're on the same page. Likewise, when listening to a speaker's words, our brains first draw the frequency shape of the word gram in the auditory processing center."

"And then we scan the memorized database of target shapes for a match," added Greg.

"And this all happens, word for word, in real time," she said. "It's amazing."

Dmitri smiled and stroked his chin. "I'm still puzzled by the exact relationship between these frequencies and the shapes of the word grams."

Melanie looked up at the wall clock. "How much time do you have?"

"Whatever it takes." Dmitri shifted closer to her.

"Let's review the rules for constructing the word grams," she replied. "It'll help if I introduce you to the representational form of written language, based on an alphabet of written symbols, such as the letters in the English alphabet."

As an alternative to pictorial ideograms, she explained how each word can be represented by a unique string of primitive, alphabetic characters. "Similarly, each word in a spoken language is represented by a unique string of primitive units, called phonemes. Phonemes are the vowels and consonant sounds of spoken language."

"Slow down," said Greg. "Phonemes are the building blocks of the spoken language. So, there are layers of symbols. Words are the big thought symbols composed of primitive written alphabetic or spoken phonemic symbols."

Melanie nodded. "Let's get back to your original question, about the relationship between the frequencies and the symbols. Here, look at this."

She swiped the marker pen vertically down the center of the whiteboard, made a sharp right turn, and continued horizontally. The finished figure resembled the two legs of a right triangle bereft of its hypotenuse.

"On this x,y plot," she marked the horizontal line with an 'x' and the vertical line with a 'y', "the x and y axes represent the range of frequencies for a pair of tones. Each x,y point on the plot represents a unique pair of tones." She peppered the plot with a sequence of points that reminded Dmitri of a constellation of stars. "I'm plotting the points representing the first two resonant frequency tones for each of the ten primary English language vowels. The x-axis represents the range of possible frequencies of the lowest frequency tone and the y-axis is the frequency of the second tone. We can generate the different combinations of tone-pair frequencies by changing the shape of our vocal tracts."

"Wait, something just occurred to me." Dmitri stepped up to her and extended his arm. "May I?" Their arms lightly brushed when she handed him the marker pen. "In your plot, the points representing the tone pairs for the ten English vowels are arranged in a triangular pattern and equidistant from one other." He drew a triangle whose perimeter circumscribed the outer boundary of the points.

A jumble of lines appeared on Melanie's forehead. "Uh-huh?"

"It's a modem constellation." Dmitri sounded triumphant. "The vowels are communication symbols, similar to the optimal arrangement of symbols used by engineers in the design of communications devices. There's a fundamental principle of communications theory called the Shannon theorem. A noisy communication link, like a phone wire or the air between two people talking, has a limitation on the maximum number of frequency-dependent symbols that can be transmitted without errors. As the noise level increases, you'd have to reduce the number of phoneme symbols to prevent the error rate from increasing."

"And since conversations need to be error-free over a wide range of background noise levels, this explains why the English language evolved to have no more than ten primary vowels." Melanie grinned. "That's so cool. I never realized the evolution of language is shaped by a universal principle of communications engineering."

"Now you know why I love my job." Dmitri suddenly realized that the Shannon Theorem also applied to the effect of the Navy's sonar blasts on the whales' ability to communicate.

"Me too." She surprised Dmitri with a playful high five. "Let's revisit the relationship between the frequencies and the word grams. When we say a word, we generate a continuous series of tone pairs which, when plotted in x,y frequency space, look like a picture or shape similar to an ideogram in a written language. Every different spoken word therefore has a different pictorial representation."

"The word gram shapes," said Greg.

"Yes."

"As with a child's coloring book," said Dmitri, "I can sketch a shape by connecting the series of dots along the path of each shape." He connected Melanie's dots into the shape of a cloud.

Melanie grabbed her own marker pen and started to scribble. "In the case of spoken language, the guiding dots are the tone-pair frequencies of the phonemes, the vowels and consonants. They are the primary frequency targets we need to connect in order to correctly pronounce words. The vowel tone pairs correspond to the points I've already plotted in the middle of the graph." She started to scribble around the edges of the graph. "Now I'm adding the points corresponding to the low, medium, and high-frequency consonants around the borders. This is the plot that finally answers your earlier question, Dmitri. It's the underlying principle for learning speech. The mastery of the phonemes is the basis for learning a language and the basis of the Speakeasy system."

"It's ingenious," said Dmitri. "The Speakeasy word grams also provide the visual insight as to how our brains recognize the words of language. Every spoken word corresponds to a particular shape, or word gram, resulting from connecting the dots of the different phonemes in frequency space."

"The language region in our brains processes the continuous sequence of phoneme frequencies," said Greg, "searching for a match to the sequences of phoneme frequencies corresponding to each word we've stored in our learned database."

"By George, you've got it!" Melanie laughed. "I tell my students to imagine they've entered a magical soundscape where they can exchange their thoughts by shape writing and shape matching."

"Now you're the poetic one," said Dmitri.

"When you mentioned shape writing, I thought of something cool," said Greg. "Speakeasy's shape-matching concept is similar to the Swype texting app on my Android phone. It's also based on a shape-matching algorithm literally called shape writing. Instead of typing in the text, you can drag your finger over the touch screen keypad, from letter to letter, to spell each word. The shape of the path your finger traces is compared, word for word, to a dictionary of stored shapes."

"Spoken language is shape writing by sound," said Dmitri, "and the keyboard is the map of phonemes stored in the frequency processing region of our brains."

"And it's all based upon a universal principle of communications engineering called the Shannon Theorem." Melanie nodded rhythmically as she spoke.

"Better be careful," said Dmitri. "You're talking like an engineer."

"Resistance is futile." Greg's voice sounded robotic. "Welcome to the Borg."

As the trio shared a laugh, Melanie led the men back to Javier's workstation where Erika still tutored the boy. "Thanks for helping me out, Erika. One more favor. Please set up the Speakeasy to display the word 'sky.'"

"Sure enough." Erika sat down next to Javier, sliding the keyboard over to her side of the desk. Her garden tattoos fluttered in an imaginary breeze when she started typing a series of commands. Greg appeared spellbound.

Melanie faced the boy, her fingers dancing. "Javier, let's do another demo for our guests. Let's pronounce the word 'sky.'"

When Javier nodded, the bright red target word gram for the word "sky" appeared on the Speakeasy display. To Dmitri, its shape resembled a puffy crimson cloud.

"'Sky' is a sequence of four phonemes." Melanie placed a finger upon the display. "The word gram for 'sky' is formed by connecting the tone-pair points for the frictional consonant 's' followed by the plosive consonant 'k' followed by the vowel 'ah' followed by the vowel 'ee.'" She traced her finger from point to point. "In addition to hitting the four target points, Javier must also stay on the correct frequency path that connects the points. Otherwise, it'll sound like a mispronunciation. Did you realize a foreign accent is a consistent mispronunciation, a bias induced when the word gram targets of the native language are overlaid on top of the phonemes of the learned language?"

"*Oui, cheri.*" Dmitri delivered his brutish Bronx accent with a smirk.

Melanie grimaced. Her "Oy vey!" sounded as if she'd pinched her nose shut. "Go ahead, Javier."

When Melanie double-tapped Javier's shoulder, he grasped the edge of the desk, took a deep breath, stiffened his spine, and mumbled a first attempt. Just as Dmitri expected, the plot of the boy's word gram was a far cry from the target shape. Nonetheless, a new idea, as yet elusive, lurked at the periphery of his awareness.

Javier's next attempt sounded much better. During the span of three more iterations, as the boy's pronunciation improved and the shapes traced onto the display converged to the correct version, Dmitri's amorphous vision was coming into focus. He became aware of a powerful force emanating from the shapes on the screen. On Javier's final attempt, the monitor erupted with colorful videogame-like special effects. At the same moment the boy cried, "Yeah!" and thrust his arms into the air, the welling realization breached the barriers of Dmitri's consciousness.

As the symbols of the boy's thoughts emerged from the display, Dmitri felt himself directly experience the creative process of the human mind. The medium that conveyed the symbols of language—sight, sound, touch—suddenly seemed immaterial. He felt liberated to perceive the process in its elemental form, freed from its bonds to matter and energy. This, he realized, was a new gateway for connecting with the minds of other sound-based creatures, human or otherwise.

"Are you still with us?"

Melanie's voice roused Dmitri. He blinked three times. "Sorry. I just had a fantastic revelation about the Speakeasy."

"Yes, it's a remarkable breakthrough. It simulates how the auditory region of our brains interprets each word as a unique shape in frequency space, a word gram."

"Just like each word in the Chinese language is written as a unique pattern or ideogram on the printed page," remarked Greg. "And don't forget, the computer plotting the word grams has to do hundreds and thousands of computations per second to analyze the continuous stream of sound for the correct frequencies."

Dmitri smiled at the boy. "Javier's brain also performs umpteen calculations per second in order to trigger the vocal tract adjustments to hit the phonemic target points in frequency space."

Melanie tousled the boy's hair. "You see, Javier, your brain is more powerful than any computer. Good work." Her hands spoke the same words. "Go ahead and practice your verbs for a while. I'll be back to test you in twenty minutes."

Dmitri was struck by Melanie's rapport with her student. She showered him with affection, and the boy's face was luminescent as he gazed up. She turned back toward Dmitri. "It's a miracle," she said. "The Speakeasy's like a voice-activated videogame. The children can't wait for their next lesson."

"In your own words, Melanie," said Dmitri, "science and technology help the disadvantaged bridge the worlds of silence and sound."

"I think I mentioned some of those things, but it's nice of you to express them poetically."

Dmitri felt a rush and decided to go for broke. "After yesterday's whale watch, Greg and I met with the Director of PICES. I volunteered to analyze a recording of humpback whale songs. Your fantastic demo with Javier has given me a new inspiration. I'm intrigued by the idea of using Speakeasy to search the songs for phonemic patterns. How about it?"

Dmitri held his breath. Melanie's face was inscrutable as she paused for a few seconds. "Tell me more, Dr. Dmitri."

"I propose we meet for a drink to discuss the details."

She did not hesitate. "It's a deal. Why not meet me for a late lunch, about an hour from now. I'll treat both of you at the local bar and grill." She scribbled on a Post-it and handed it to him. "Here's the address. Just wait for me at the bar in case I'm running behind."

As Javier smiled and Dmitri placed a congratulatory pat on the boy's shoulder, Greg leveled his friend with an unsettling stare. Thinking about the TV show *Whale Wars*, Dmitri braced himself for yet another cetacean conversation with his best buddy.

TABLOID MYSTERY

United States Satellite Imaging Agency,
Maryland—early afternoon

IT WAS NOT unusual for USSIA Mission Specialist Tamara Roberts to be summoned to her supervisor's office to discuss the status of her latest assignment. What was startling, however, was Lieutenant Nina Davis's syrupy tone and abrupt exit once Tamara had taken her customary seat. During the nerve-wracking wait until her supervisor's return, Roberts admired the Davis family photos perched on the Spartan desktop. She had always been beguiled by the images of her superior's attractiveness at an earlier age, before life's cumulative stresses had stamped their imprint on her face and grayed her hair.

Despite the lieutenant's no-nonsense approach to her job, she was highly respected by the members of her staff. In a world of gender-biased glass ceilings, Tamara totally understood the reason Davis had encapsulated her private life inside a persona of hard-core professionalism. That's why Davis's sympathetic demeanor, before she'd excused herself, had unnerved Tamara.

When Noel Harrison opened the door and glided into the room, Tamara's nagging unease flared up into full-blown fear. "Any idea what this is about?"

"Not a clue." Harrison sounded as cavalier as ever.

"Where's Lieutenant Davis?"

Harrison sat in the chair next to her and pointed toward the door. Davis entered the office holding an oversized manila envelope. With her grim-faced supervisor staring directly at her, Tamara felt a sickening sensation in her gut. She shifted her gaze to her colleague, but his face exuded its usual nothing-fazes-me expression.

Still standing, Davis faced her subordinates from behind the desk. She reached inside the envelope to extract what looked like a news magazine and, with a dramatic flourish, slapped the copy of a popular supermarket tabloid onto the table. The two-inch headline screamed: OCEAN CROP CIRCLE MYSTERY.

"Have either of you mission specialists seen this photo?" Davis pointed to the image below the headline. Like a scolding school principal, Davis leaned across the desk, appearing to hover directly above Harrison and Roberts.

As soon as Tamara recognized the picture, her heart palpitated with an electric chill. Neither she nor Harrison uttered a sound.

"No?" Davis stared accusingly first at Noel Harrison, then at Tamara. "Well, the encryption codes embedded in the photo indicate it could only have been taken from one of our birds, exactly two days ago. I think you two might have some explaining to do."

Tamara turned, shocked to see Harrison's deer-in-the-headlights expression. Two days too late, she realized she'd made a huge mistake to follow his advice. A single thought throbbed like a migraine in the center of her skull. What has Harrison done?

Change of Plan

Island Fish Restaurant, Kahului, Maui—early afternoon

"EVERYTHING WILL BE fine," said Greg. "She's definitely taken a shine to you."

Amidst the laughter, the chatter, and the mouth-watering aromas of grilled fish, roasted garlic, and draft beer, Greg had been waiting along with Dmitri at the bar inside of Kahului's most popular watering hole. Greg had agreed to keep him company until Melanie's arrival.

"I really hope so, pal." Dmitri channeled his jitters into preening the curly edges of his sideburns. "She's cast her spell upon me, for sure."

"I haven't seen you so smitten since the Swedish particle physicist two years ago in Vienna."

"I'm definitely attracted to brainy women, and I guess I'm more receptive to romantic interludes on foreign shores."

"Maybe the risk of rejection is less brutal when it's just a vacation fling."

Dmitri frowned. "It's not that."

"Well anyway, it doesn't hurt that Melanie's a knockout babe. By the way, I'm assuming you aren't serious about analyzing whale songs. It's just your clever way to connect with her. After your fling, you can forget all about the whales."

Dmitri wasn't in the mood to start another argument with his friend, especially since Melanie could appear at any moment.

"Dude, what'll it be?" asked the brawny bartender, sizing Dmitri up as an outlier. "You look like you could use the house special."

"Which is?"

"A tribute to James Bond. Mango martini, shaken not stirred," he replied with a dab of the local accent. "Since you're wound up pretty tight," he grinned, "just hold the drink a minute and save me the trouble of mixing it."

"I'll pass on the drink."

"By the way, who is she?"

"Is it that obvious? Well, maybe you know her, Melanie. She's a speech therapist at the community college."

"Wow, everybody knows Melanie. You might need some of them Agent 007 moves to get to first base. She's made it perfectly clear to us local guys we're not in her league." He left to attend to another customer.

The bartender's comments stoked Dmitri's anxiety. He was an engineer, a professor, and a stickler for scientific rigor, yet he felt like a nervous school boy waiting to meet a blind date. Over the years, he'd endured teasing from friends and colleagues about his techno-geeky tendencies, and even he had to admit he was no Casanova. He'd dated occasionally. He'd even enjoyed a couple of year-long, live-in relationships, but after a while, his partners had realized he wasn't attuned to a lifestyle of domesticity. During his college days, he'd buried himself in his studies and sports activities, and now he was married to the intricacies of work. Yet here he was, waiting in a Hawaiian bar, pursuing an impossible dream.

Many of the women drifting by were as attractive as Melanie, but probably none of them were as intelligent, motivated, and articulate as she. Dmitri practically tipped over in the barstool when a hand tapping his shoulder rocked him from his musings.

"Aloha." Melanie waved a hand in front of his face. "Sorry I startled you, but you didn't see me standing here."

Greg just laughed. "Don't know how my mate could not see such a dazzling vision approaching from miles away."

Melanie smiled and waved him off.

Dmitri was crimson-faced. "M-many apologies," he stammered through a nervous grin. "Greg's right. I must have been daydreaming about the whale songs."

"Totally understandable," she said, "which is why there's been a change of plan. How'd you guys like to do some community service? Maui style?"

"What's up?" queried Greg.

The bartender's frantic arm waving stilled all nearby conversation. He cranked up the volume on the TV, and everyone seated at the bar focused their attention on the sixty-inch flatscreen mounted on the wall. After a chain reaction of shushing, the merriment throughout the restaurant evaporated into silence. The voice of the female news correspondent shouted from the set. Dmitri saw her standing on a beach, dwarfed by the body of a beached humpback whale.

Melanie pointed up at the TV. "That's where we're going—to help rescue that whale. Let's get some food for the road." She signaled to the bartender. "Hi, Jimmy. We'd like three mahi-burger specials to go. Pronto, please."

While waiting for their order, the trio focused their attention on the compelling images and words streaming from the TV broadcast.

"Ladies and gentlemen, this is unprecedented," bellowed the Eyewitness News correspondent. "Yesterday began as another blissful, tropical winter day in West Maui. It's the reason that tourists from around the globe flock to the mega-resorts fronting the beaches of Ka'anapali. Now the specter of death stalks our shores. A juvenile humpback whale has mysteriously washed ashore. The incident has shocked the beachgoers at one the island's most pristine stretches of sand, Black Rock Beach at the Sheraton Resort.

"The pattern of the strandings is unmistakable to marine biologist Christopher Gorman, founder of the PICES organization. This week alone, Gorman's witnessed a second seemingly healthy juvenile humpback stranded upon a shore fringing the Auau Channel. Right behind me you see the frantic rescue effort he's organized, now entering its second day."

"Gorman must be going crazy." Greg spoke directly into Dmitri's ear, startling him.

"He was already grim the day before yesterday," said Dmitri. "No doubt about it. It's as if the black plague has been unleashed on Hawaii's whales."

The broadcaster's voice echoed from the multiple TVs throughout the bar. "Is this unfortunate marine mammal doomed to a lingering death? Its labored breaths sound like a mournful dirge to the hundreds of gawking seaside vacationers. Let me point the microphone back toward the humpback so that you can all listen."

The restaurant patrons within earshot of the TV heard the desperate gasps and hisses of a very large marine mammal trying to squeeze the oxygen from the air. Many squirmed in their barstools and grimaced in reaction to the unsettling sounds.

Melanie pointed up at the television. "So now's your chance to help Gorman and the whales." The bartender handed her a large brown paper bag. "It's time to go, guys. We'll hook up with the other PICES volunteers in Ka'anapali."

The Killing Sound

Ka'anapali, Maui—midafternoon

THE SWEEPING ARC of Maui's northwest coastline was shaped long ago, when two mighty volcanoes rose from the ancient seabed and merged to form the island. Maui's main population center and the University's speech lab were nestled in the northern section of the lowland valley where the two mountains joined flanks. After a whirlwind drive south through the lush valley, then arcing northwest along the breathtaking coastal road encircling the island, they arrived at their leeward Ka'anapali destination in under an hour. Dmitri parked in the Sheraton's overflow lot.

"Wow," said Melanie. "I've never, ever had to park so far away." At her prompting, the trio rushed along the flagstone path skirting the tennis courts and leading down to the beach.

"What a coincidence." Dmitri panted like someone not used to talking and jogging at the same time. "We're close to our hotel."

"I can already hear the crowd noise," Melanie replied. "The beach must be a zoo."

When they had reached the serpentine promenade demarcating the boundary between the beach and the resorts, Dmitri stared in disbelief.

"This is unreal," said Greg. "I went for a peaceful swim on this beach two nights ago. Now look at it."

Instead of the usual tranquil setting of sunbathers and body surfers, the beach swarmed with tourists and locals. At the shoreline, the inert body of the giant cetacean loomed above the frenetic crowd. From his distant perspective, the scene evoked Dmitri's childhood memory of a drawing of Gulliver and the Lilliputians. Just a couple hundred feet up the shoreline, however, he observed the ever-present, young daredevils cliff diving from the thirty-foot-tall, lava-sculpted promontory called Black Rock. It was a risky business, since the water below was a favorite snorkeling spot for close encounters with giant turtles, rays, and schools of tropical fish.

Melanie pointed toward the beached behemoth. "The sand's blazing hot, so keep your sandals on and follow me."

They threaded a path through shifting currents of beachcombers to approach the huge body, ringed by a surging crowd held at bay by hotel employees. Dmitri's first sensory impression of the beast was its fishy odor. The whale rested on its belly, its head facing inland with its fluke partially submerged in the surf. An unending procession of waves lapped against the rear portion of the body.

"Hi, Kirby." Melanie addressed a pony-tailed security guard, his name stenciled across the front of his T-shirt. "My partners and I are here to help."

"Okay, Mel. Thanks for coming." The sun-scorched Hawaiian waved them through.

Melanie spearheaded the trio through a momentary gap in the human chain. With his view unencumbered, Dmitri observed the skillfully coordinated teamwork of dozens of volunteers supervised by Chris Gorman. One energetic team culled bed sheets from a mound stacked upon the sand. They'd draped the linen onto the creature's back in a patchwork quilt pattern. Another group comprised a bucket brigade. As some dipped children's sand pails and hotel ice buckets into the water, their mates passed them on down to the end of the line, where they were emptied onto the sheets. Other volunteers circulated, dispensing granola bars and bottled water.

Following Melanie's lead, Dmitri and Greg tossed their sandals into a cordoned area jam-packed with footwear. Then they hot-footed back to the surf, and merged with the section of the bucket brigade closest to the leviathan. Melanie handed the pails directly to the SoCalSci professors. Reaching high, they spilled the contents onto the whale's linen-covered back.

"This is amazing, pal." Greg lifted his voice above the roar of the breakers. "I never imagined getting so close to such a large animal. Look at the size of these fins. More than double our height."

"It's too bad we're here under such crappy circumstances." Dmitri fought to keep both legs steady in the churning surf.

Gorman walked the line of volunteers. "Okay, folks!" he yelled. "Listen up. Keep those sheets moist. Just keep dousing them."

"Hi, Chris." Melanie's greeting captured Gorman's attention. "You look like you need some sleep."

Gorman approached her. "Hiya, Mel. Yeah, duty calls. We've been going nonstop with rotating shifts for almost forty-eight hours. Thanks for being here."

She nodded in the direction of the two SoCalSci professors. "I brought some friends along to help."

"I know these gentlemen. Thanks for interrupting your vacation. Now you see for yourselves what I was venting about the other day."

"What are its chances for survival?" asked Dmitri, after he'd dumped his bucket onto the victim's back. He winced in reaction to the asthmatic brew of wheezing and moaning noises.

"To be honest with you, I don't think this poor little guy can survive much longer." Gorman spoke in listless tones as the creature's body convulsed in the struggle to capture each life-sustaining breath. "If it was healthier, we could hope it would ride out with the next high tide. Sad to say, its breathing has become more labored and irregular."

"Like a person in a comatose state," Dmitri replied. A wave of melancholy overtook him, the memory of a bedside vigil during his mother's final hours.

"So what's the use of continuing to douse the sheets?" The contemptuous voice belonged to a spiky-haired teen. His arms and shoulders were tattooed with the distinctive comic book scenes of Japanese manga art.

Gorman scanned the teen's body before answering. "You've got to realize, even though marine mammals can still breathe when they're out of the water, their massive bodies aren't designed to survive on the land. Their internal organs can be crushed by their own weight. Nothing we can do about that, but we can reduce its suffering and prolong its survival by lowering the body temperature. Think about it. The thick layers of blubber that insulate in the water trap the heat inside the whale now that it's exposed to the warm air. That's why we're keeping it moist. The sheets also protect its skin from the sun's ultraviolet rays."

"He certainly doesn't look like a 'little guy' to me," said the teen. "These fins are huge. They look like dragon's wings." There was a touch of awe in his voice.

"Even a juvenile can be thirty feet long and weigh twenty-five tons like this specimen," replied Gorman. "If he lived to maturity, he could grow to nearly fifty feet and weigh fifty tons."

"This is definitely a labor of love." Melanie pushed out the nasal-toned words through tight lips. "The odor of its breath is pretty foul."

"That's the way it is with humpbacks." Gorman sighed. "We think it's the bacteria in their digestive or respiratory tracts. After a while, you get used to it."

Dmitri crinkled his nose and inhaled very shallow breaths. "You're a better man than I."

"Wait," barked the tattooed teen. "Did you hear that? The breathing's changed. It sounds even more depressing."

Gorman angled closer to the whale's head and peered at his wristwatch. In a few seconds, he shook his head and muttered, "You're right, the rate is slowing down." The marine biologist's entire body appeared to sag. "I gotta go check on the other volunteers." A veil of resignation settled upon Gorman's face. "Carry on."

Dmitri stopped what he was doing and approached Melanie. "I didn't realize you knew Chris Gorman."

"Everybody knows everybody on the cozy island of Maui," she remarked blithely. "Which means that no secrets are safe around here."

"Stop that kid!" Chris Gorman's voice eclipsed the ambient chatter.

Heads turned as the blur of a pixie-like figure dashed across the field of Dmitri's peripheral vision. The intruder, a small blond girl, had somehow evaded detection and breached the barrier of humans. She made a beeline to the humpback. Adorned in a striped bathing suit, and with her arms, legs, and face caked with wet sand, she looked like a motley-colored doll. She knelt on the sand and placed a cuddly, stuffed-animal whale next to its mammoth head. It reminded Dmitri of a scene in a fairy tale, with a munchkin huddled next to a giant. The child clasped her hands together, stared directly into the whale's eye, and moved her lips as if in silent prayer. While she paid tribute to the creature, a pair of volunteers crept up behind her, then froze like statues as many gasped.

"Quiet! Do you hear it?" Gorman called.

Dmitri heard a familiar haunting sound. The humpback had begun to sing its ethereal aria, a song heard only in the ocean depths. He held his breath as successive waves of low, mournful tones ebbed away into muted sadness. But as the whale's voice comingled with the air, Dmitri thought he heard faint threads of something new—emotionally uplifting filaments embedded in the fabric of the lamentation. Straining to hear every sound, he realized he wasn't mistaken. An ornamentation of new phrases had blossomed from the elegiac. Like the sliding tones of a tenor's portamento, each brief passage climbed a staircase of brightening frequency. A richer texture emerged, woven into a perfect harmony of joy and sorrow, music as sublime as Brahms's *Requiem*.

Dmitri observed his own amazement mirrored in the sea of faces around him. Melanie's eyes glistened with moisture.

More gasps cracked the panes of human silence. One of the whale's gigantic pectoral fins lurched sideways like a stilled heart reanimated by a defibrillating spark. As the humpback continued to sing, its fin began to rise up, at first almost imperceptibly, from the sand. Dmitri saw the girl and the two volunteers stumble backward, their mouths agape, as the giant wing inched toward the sky. Pausing briefly at the zenith of its ascent, it reversed course and began a gradual descent. About halfway down, the fin made a sharp right turn and swept laterally in a wide arc, back and forth, parallel to the ground. Then, like a puppet whose strings had suddenly snapped, it fell to the earth with a thunderous thud.

"That was spooky, pal." Greg slapped himself gently on the cheek. "Am I crazy, or did that whale just make the sign of the cross?"

Too perplexed to respond to Greg's question, Dmitri noticed the couple next to him wave their arms in a familiar ritualistic gesture. Seeing the same devotional proliferating all around him, he realized that Greg's observation was shared by many. Like a wave of falling dominoes sweeping through the multitude, many knelt upon the sand, closed their eyes, and clasped their hands in supplication. A scientist, Dmitri was completely baffled by the inexplicable events unfolding around him.

A ghastly noise assailed Dmitri's mind, triggering an adrenalin surge and the sight of Melanie's pained reaction. She squeezed her hands to her ears as a sputtering and gurgling cacophony spewed from the giant's mouth and blow hole.

In a few seconds it was all over. The familiar sounds of the whale's breathing were no more. A suffocating silence and a dreadful stench filled the void. Wherever he turned, Dmitri saw ashen faces and vacant stares. He felt a bit queasy and experienced the unsettling sensation of his pulse throbbing inside his skull. Punctuated bursts of "Oh, my God!" and "Oh no!" pierced the veil of his shock.

"This . . . this is terrible," Melanie choked through quivering lips. "I . . . I . . ." Tears cascaded down her cheeks.

Although he had just witnessed a death rattle of epic proportions, Dmitri's main concern was for Melanie. He inhaled a restorative breath, dropped his bucket, and wrapped both arms around her shoulders. When she'd begun to convulse with sobs, he felt the full intensity of her grip. Squeezing her tenderly, he could not have imagined a more unlikely set of circumstances for their first embrace. In fact, it was like no other first hug he'd experienced in his adult life, more bonding than romantic. Yet it felt so good; it felt so right. He desperately yearned to comfort her.

While she quaked in his arms, he wondered if this was what fate was all about, the remarkable chain of events culminating in this moment. He'd discovered her on a sacred mountain by following a light in the night sky. Her devotion to her hearing-challenged students had kindled his attraction to her. And now they shared this moment of communion. They'd been hurled together by a mysterious force emanating from the spirit of a dying humpback whale. Maybe she was the "one?"

As she pressed against him, Dmitri's eyes panned the crowd. He saw grief-stricken faces comforted by similar embraces and the clasping of hands. Some, like Melanie, emoted the full intensity of their heartache, including the little girl who had been reunited with her mother. The familiar figure of the TV newscaster suddenly barged into the assembly of mourners and careened into Dmitri and Melanie. After a perfunctory apology, she marched over to the youngster, signaled to the cameraman, and shoved a microphone in front of the girl's face.

"Tell us, sweetie, what did you say to the poor whale?"

At first bewildered, the child looked directly into the camera, flooding it with the tears pouring from her eyes. "I told the whalie to take my gift to heaven." Her words were punctuated by rasping sobs. She turned to face her mother. "Mommy, where do the whales go after they die? Is there a whale heaven?"

Dmitri tapped Greg on the shoulder. "Wow. That girl just delivered the most poignant plea in the history of any save-the-whales campaign. It'll go viral by nightfall on YouTube and every newscast."

"You got that right. Uh-oh, look who's coming."

They saw Chris Gorman looming large and heading directly for the newscaster. Upon arrival, he reached for the microphone. She handed it over without hesitation, and Gorman turned to face the cameraman.

"Ladies and gentlemen." Gorman's voice conveyed both calm and conviction. With his sand-encrusted hair and weathered face, he looked like a proverbial holy man back from a desert pilgrimage. "Write to your congressman. Tell them to stop the Navy's sonar experiments. They're slaughtering Maui's young whales. Probably at this very moment, a Navy research vessel is blasting the bodies of humpbacks for target practice to test the latest version of their equipment." He returned the microphone and loped away.

A man standing upwind from Dmitri uttered a barrage of anti-military epithets laced with garlic fumes. Sympathetic protest slogans erupted from the crowd. Engrossed in interpreting the clot of vehement remarks, Dmitri was startled by the sound of fingers snapping directly in his face. It was Greg.

"Hey, D&D, good buddy. As hard as it is for me to admit, I humbly apologize for giving you grief about the whale song work. After the catastrophe we just witnessed, the humpbacks need all the help they can get. I'll do anything to assist." Greg surprised Dmitri with a bear hug and then excused himself. It was time for his daily five-mile run.

Dmitri, still shaken, stood by while Melanie engaged in a whale-related conversation with the devout couple who had crossed themselves minutes earlier. Impressed by their camaraderie, Dmitri's heart and mind agreed that all who had witnessed the tragedy on the beach had been bonded together by a life-altering experience. He realized now, more than ever, that the existential crises of humans and whales were inextricably intertwined. A sense of urgency infused his desire to resolve the McPinsky Challenge. If he could somehow decode the signals in their songs, gain even the briefest glimpse of their language, he could raise public awareness about the plight of humpbacks and address McPinsky's goal of ending our species isolation.

Dmitri felt the tug of an arm and heard a familiar voice.

"We've done all that we can do here." Melanie sounded wistful. "Let's go to the Island's best sushi house and discuss your plans to study the whale songs."

For the first time all afternoon, Dmitri smiled.

Sharing a Passion

Sansui Sushi Restaurant, Kapalua, Maui—5 p.m.

THIRTY MINUTES LATER, Dmitri followed Melanie into her favorite restaurant. They waited, silently, in front of the hostess stand. He observed an eclectic crowd of tourists and locals, families and couples, engaged in subdued conversations and savoring the generous portions of their early-bird dinners.

"Oh, my God," Melanie moaned, "what a day."

Dmitri felt relieved. Except for giving directions to the restaurant, those were the first words she'd spoken since they'd left the beach. "I'm still in shock, too." He tapped his chest. "That was a terrible scene."

"Which might explain why this place is so quiet."

"Let's grab a table and talk about cheerier subjects."

When they'd been seated in their cushioned, koa wood chairs, he ordered a bottle of his favorite California wine. Now that they were alone together for the first time, he noticed that Melanie's grief and the candlelight had softened her face. She looked luminous, like the first time he had seen her on Haleakala Mountain.

"Let's at least try to lift our spirits," he said, buoyed by her sympathetic glance.

The bottle of sparkling wine and an ice bucket soon arrived. The waitress filled their flutes, and after Melanie had requested two orders of her favorite catch of the day and a Rock-N-Roll sushi appetizer, they were alone once again. Dmitri had a great deal to say but, as usual, with a woman of this significance, he grew tense. Ordinarily, when confronted with a similar challenge, he relied upon a cheery toast to kick-start the evening. In the aftermath of the appalling scene on the beach, however, such a scenario seemed absurdly inappropriate. Tongue-tied, he began to fidget, and when she stared at his nervous hands, his embarrassment peaked. But then she reached across the table and held them still.

"It was really thoughtful of you to support me on the beach." She rewarded him with a deep and steady gaze. "Thanks."

Dmitri was grateful she'd initiated the conversation and the contact. Her touch felt velvety soft. Despite the pleasant tingling sensation coursing up his arm, he tried to look composed. "Chivalry is one of my better traits." Still nervous, he decided not to mention how much he had enjoyed their earlier embrace.

She gave him a curious look. "So why didn't Greg join us? I've only known you two as a team." Her hands retreated to her wine glass.

"Greg sends his regards, but he's not as enthusiastic as I am about the whale song proposal. In fact, until he experienced today's stranding, he actually tried to discourage me."

"That's strange. Why so?"

"He's worried about the backlash from the skeptics at our venerable institution."

"Well, in my humble opinion, I hope you proceed with your plans." Dmitri was distracted by the subtly pouting shape of her lips whenever she pronounced the letter "p."

"Maybe you can be the one who makes a difference for the poor humpbacks," she said, raising her glass. "I therefore propose a toast to christen Dr. Dmitri's new project with the Whale Institute."

"Thanks, Melanie. That's the way I feel too." They clinked their flutes together and tasted the varietal.

"*Trés bien, monsieur*, an excellent choice."

"*Merci*," he replied with a gallant nod. "Now it's my turn to salute your work with the children." After another nervous sip, Dmitri's temples tingled with the first rush of the alcohol. "Your Speakeasy tutorial and demo were terrific. I experienced language in a whole new light. When you speak to me, I imagine the shapes of the word grams floating from your mouth and hovering in the air." He rounded his lips and pantomimed puffing smoke. "As if you're blowing word-gram-sculpted smoke rings, like the smoking caterpillar in *Alice in Wonderland*."

Resting both elbows on the table, Melanie cradled her face with her hands. She leaned forward and gazed directly into his eyes. "My, my, Dr. Dmitri.

You're one trippy professor, and definitely a quick study. Is that why you keep staring at my lips?"

"Am I?" His face suddenly felt like he'd leaned too close to a blazing fire. "I apologize. That must be the reason." Melanie seemed to be warming up too. She smiled again so Dmitri pressed on. "It dawned on me that Speakeasy could be very useful in the analysis of the whale songs. Compared to the massive amount of frequency data cluttering a spectrogram, it really simplifies visualizing the symbols of language."

"That's a fantastic idea!" Melanie's whole body perked up and her onyx eyes sparkled. "I'd be happy to provide a copy of the Speakeasy program, for lab use only. However, since it is proprietary, you'd have to purchase your own copy if you want to publish any Speakeasy-generated data."

"Agreed! I'd also like to deputize you as a SoCalSci research consultant. You could start by Skyping a Speakeasy training session with my grad students. It would help them understand how to adapt the program for the whale song analysis."

"Why Dr. Dmitri, this is certainly the most scintillating beginning of a business meeting I can ever remember."

Dmitri couldn't mask a contented grin. He sincerely hoped that this was more than a business meeting. "I think we make a pretty good team." He reached for his wine glass. "I propose another toast to launch the research collaboration in the quest to discover cetacean phonemes."

A sharp bang jolted him, followed immediately by the sight of Melanie propelling up and away from the table. Liquid dripped from her blouse and jeans. In a flash, Dmitri realized that in his toastmaster's zeal, the ascending arc of his champagne flute had intersected the space occupied by his water glass, unleashing a mini flash flood onto Melanie's side of the table. In futility, she sponged the lap-sized wet spot with the dry corners of her dinner napkin.

"I'm so sorry!" He stood, gawking at her, too bewildered to react. He finally offered his own napkin, presenting it like a bouquet of flowers. He scanned the room. The stares of some patrons were accusatory, and the teens at the next table giggled into their cupped palms.

"I'll live. It's only water . . . just an accident." A dry towel appeared and, while the waitress changed the tablecloth, Melanie swabbed her waist. After she returned the towel to the waitress, they sat back down. "By the way, you've seemed edgy ever since we met at the bar. Don't worry, I don't bite. In fact, I was somewhat anxious about meeting you too, an illustrious SoCalSci professor."

"Really?"

"Yes, really. So now that we've been formally introduced," she said, grinning as she glanced down at her sopping lap, "I'd like to ask you a personal question. How did you acquire such a unique name?"

"My parents are of Russian heritage, but the truth is, Dmitri is both my surname and my chosen nickname. My legal first name is David."

"A man of mystery with an alter ego?"

"No, a personal identity crisis during my childhood and teen years."

"Really? Self-doubts?"

"I wasn't exactly the most popular kid in school. I've always been a bit of a loner. My dad died when I was nine and, after that, my family had . . . well . . . problems."

"Problems?"

"After he finished college, my older brother unexpectedly fell apart."

"How's he doing now?"

Dmitri stared at the table. "I see him about once a month, but he's been alcoholic for years."

"That's so sad." She cupped his right hand. "What about your mom?"

"His emotional collapse took a toll on her." Dmitri paused, staring at the wine glass. "I made it a point to try to support her. We were always close. Unfortunately, she passed away five years ago."

"You were a good son." Melanie's gaze tempered Dmitri's angst. "God gives us our family; thank God we can choose our friends."

Dmitri sighed. "How true," he replied. Although he acknowledged her adage with a half-hearted smile, he felt ashamed to admit he both loved and partially loathed his brother, who was now a shell of a man. Paul was six years older and would have been the ideal substitute father figure in his life. Instead, Dmitri remembered years of Paul's frightening temper tantrums, his blaming of their mother for all of his problems, and how he drank himself insensate every night. He knew it wasn't fair to hold his brother responsible for his own self-esteem issues. Because Paul obviously suffered from a severe psychological affliction, Dmitri had forgiven him years ago. But he'd always wondered what might have been if he'd not been traumatized at such a young age.

Melanie's pendant, sparkling in the candlelight, caught his attention. She grasped the silvery object between her thumb and forefinger. "It's a gift from my mother—my good luck charm."

Dmitri gazed, captivated by the sinuous, figure-eight gyrations of Melanie's thumb circumnavigating the filigreed curves of the yin-yang mandala. "I'd like to hear about your family," he asked.

Melanie's sympathetic expression vanished. "It's a classic outer-island story. After high school, my mom married her childhood sweetheart because she was pregnant with me. My dad drifted to Oahu after a few years to pursue better job prospects. The distance separating them finally resulted in the end of the marriage. Like mother, like daughter, I repeated the same sequence of events. I have a nine-year-old son. His name is Mark. After my husband left us, I attended night classes at UH for my speech therapist credentials. Last year, my ex-boyfriend set me up with the connection for the night-shift job at LURE for the extra spending money."

"So you're a single mom raising a child. Not the daunting personification of a Hawaiian mountain goddess, laser ranger, and speech therapist."

"I don't know whether to be flattered or wigged out by that remark."

"It's definitely a compliment. How's your mom?"

"She got lucky. Five years ago, she remarried and moved to Florida. Still, that's enough about me. The other night you mentioned that you were inspired by your college mentor. Tell me more about that."

Dmitri briefly recounted the profound influence of Professor McPinsky. "I think our relationship is partly based on my need for a father figure. He's a complex, brilliant, and inspirational force who provokes strong reactions from his admirers and critics. However, since he's my numero uno role model, to me he can do no wrong."

"I'd say you were pretty fortunate to have someone like that in your life."

"Yes. He has my complete admiration because, like you, his goal is to enlist science in the service of humanity which, in McPinsky's case, is nothing less than the solution of mankind's existential crises. Let's face it. Because of fear and ignorance, Homo sapiens are out of control. We're raping and pillaging the planet—"

"Not to mention slaughtering the whales and each other," interrupted Melanie. "And you say McPinsky has a plan to deal with all of this?"

"Yes, and it's as straightforward as employing the scientific method, instead of some metaphysical hocus-pocus. Can you believe it? He recently issued a challenge to the scientific community to break the interspecies communication barrier and end our group isolation. Amazingly, the events of this trip have inspired me to take the plunge and—"

"Dmitri," Melanie interrupted again, "you're coming on like a freight train. Slow down for a sec and tell me more . . . slowly."

"You're right. I apologize." Why couldn't he just be more relaxed, more natural, with her?

Making sure to pace himself, Dmitri went on to summarize the wave of events he considered fateful during his brief sojourn in Maui: the whale watch, their meeting on Haleakala, her Speakeasy demo with Javier, and the fatal stranding of the juvenile humpback. "I'm saying the cetaceans, too, are threatened with an existential crisis. We've hunted them to near extinction. There's no guarantee that the whaling nations will continue to honor the international moratorium. We're killing them! Given their potentially high level of intelligence, humanity needs a wakeup call ASAP."

"As a teen, I was inspired by Helen Keller's amazing autobiography. It's probably why I opted to study speech pathology. Just as speech therapists strive to give mute children a voice, maybe you can give the whales the means to express themselves to our species."

"It's definitely a worthy undertaking that justifies the pushback I'm gonna get from peers and higher-ups."

"I'm glad I signed up!"

Their gazes briefly merged, and then they each looked away to admire the candle's dancing flame.

"Hey," she whispered, gently breaking the spell. "I know you'll love tonight's dinner. It's grilled, coconut-milk-infused opakapaka smothered in caramelized Maui onions."

"Sounds delish," Dmitri licked his upper lip, "and it reminds me of another important reason to assess the communication potential of the cetaceans."

"What's that?"

"As you said, eating them is the reason we continue to slaughter whales."

"Right, whaling." She paused. "My mom's family is Japanese, and Japan still engages in whaling. After World War II, whale meat kept people from starving, but that's obviously no longer justified."

He nodded. "My dad's Russian ancestors decimated Pacific whale populations and continue to do so. More than any dramatic protests by Greenpeace and Sierra Club advocates, a verifiable confirmation of their language could be the tipping point in winning the argument to protect them."

"Is it possible, Dmitri?" Her eyes seemed wider as she asked the questions.

"Not unless humans take the first step. I'm supervising a couple of research assistants who're going to be awfully surprised when I present them with their new assignment. Speaking of which, what do you see in my glass?"

"I see beautiful bubbles rising in a glass of champagne."

"I see a bubble net, the catalyst for me to realize there's something significant happening in these Maui waters."

"Bubble net? It's a whale thing, right?"

He summarized the description he'd heard during the whale watch and was delighted to see Melanie's eyes, sparkling with the reflected light of the candle flame, open even wider. "That is so cool."

"That was my initial reaction too. Then I thought about it and realized it might be more than just cool. One could conjecture it's a fantastic innovation of a mind that weaves the principles of math together with physics."

"Okay, but what's the difference between a wolf pack that stalks and herds its prey and the bubble net social behavior?"

"Excellent question. Although there are similarities, there's a dramatic difference in the mechanism for achieving the intended result. Since the prey move in response to their fear of the predator, the stalking by the wolf pack is instinctual. The wolves react in a stimulus-response fashion as they observe that their movements are correlated to the prey's movements."

"I can tell you're a college professor. Sometimes you speak like you're lecturing to me."

"Mea culpa. It's a bad habit. Please stop me if it happens again."

Melanie patted Dmitri affectionately on the hand. "Good answer. There's hope for you yet. Okay, so you were saying the wolves act instinctively. What about the bubble net?"

"The generation of the bubble net could be one level of mental abstraction removed from purely conditioned behavior. Think of it as a tool that has been fashioned, like the club or the spear, for the express purpose of capturing food."

"But like the wolves, the whales could have instinctually observed that the fish became scared whenever they released their bubbles."

"Yes, but that's only the first step in the process. Are you familiar with the movie *2001: A Space Odyssey*?"

"Yeah, I saw it with my parents long ago."

"Do you remember the opening scene? One of the protohumans observed that he could use an animal's femur bone to crack other bones. Then he abstracted the concept into his internal thought process to make the conceptual leap to the bone as a killing tool."

She nodded. "Ah, I see. The humpbacks fashioned a tool, a net of bubbles, after making the conceptual leap from their initial observation. QED: tool-making and high-level intelligence are synonymous."

"And not just any old tool, such as discovering a bone lying on the ground," he said, his voice animated. "The protohumans improved the bone tool concept using simple geometric reasoning. They sharpened the end of the bone or tree branch to create the more lethal spear. Likewise, the team of Megapterans organized a precise, geometrically shaped structure from the rudimentary bubble concept."

"Who are the Megapterans?"

"Oh, sorry, Melanie. It's just my personal tribute to the humpback species Megaptera novaeangliae."

"That's brilliant," Melanie merrily intoned in a faux-British accent.

"Jolly good," Dmitri replied in kind.

"You know what?" she said. "I just thought of one more reason why the bubble nets could be linked to purely instinctual rather than to toolbuilding behavior. I read in a recent *Scientific American* article that the complex flight patterns of large flocks of birds are governed by the response of any one bird to its two nearest neighbors. Likewise, a single whale's movement is possibly influenced by the reaction of the fish and by the motions of its two nearest whale companions."

"Hmmm." He thought about the analogy. "You're proposing that the whole process was perfected after many generations of refinement and repetition?"

"Possibly. We humans think of toolbuilding as the exclusive province of the opposable thumb. This gives us permission to maximize our own importance and to downplay other species, maybe even the significance of the bubble nets. Look no further than religious doctrine, which places mankind at the apex of the pyramid with dominion over the planet."

"You're right!" Dmitri said it so resoundingly that Melanie leaned away from the table as if blown backward by a blast of wind.

"Thanks for the approval, professor." She gave him a mischievous smile. "So you were saying?"

"I've encountered this prejudice in academia," he told her. "Remarkable discoveries about ourselves blind us to other possibilities. It's the reason I support McPinsky's trans-species theory about the 'continuum of intelligence.' I suspect the humpbacks' inventiveness and cooperative behavior are clues of a higher-order intelligence that utilizes communications. It's all conjecture, of course, unless someone can find concrete evidence of language in their songs."

"I'll toast again to that." They tapped their flutes together and took another sip.

"You're remarkable, Melanie. Outside of the university, this has been the most engaging discussion I've had in ages."

"Flattery will get you everywhere, Dr. Dmitri."

"If this bubbly has had the same uplifting effect on your cognitive centers as mine, would you indulge me in yet another bubble-net-inspired flight of fancy?"

Melanie hiccupped and laughed. "You could characterize that hiccup as an upliftingly inspired phoneme. Go ahead. I'm all ears."

"Are you familiar with Frank Herbert's *Dune*?"

"Sure. We math and science geeks consider *Dune* one of the top sci-fi books of all time."

Dmitri suppressed a chuckle at the preposterous notion of Melanie as a geek. "Do you remember the Guild Navigators?" Melanie nodded. "They mutated over countless generations by ingesting the spice melange. The mutation gave them the ability to fold space so that spacecraft could travel instantaneously to anywhere in the Galactic Empire. I'm visualizing an image of the Guild Navigators, the Gatekeepers of the galaxy who, by the way, bear a faint resemblance to small whales floating inside of the ship. They hypnotically weave their holographic web, which eventually causes the space surrounding the craft to fold. They suddenly disappear and reappear at Arakis."

"I remember that scene in the movie. It just blew me away. I think I might have been stoned at the time."

Dmitri arched his right eyebrow, and Melanie appeared delighted. "That's a very good imitation of Mr. Spock."

He lifted his left eyebrow. "Now I have this vision of a pod of Megapterans collectively weaving their geometrically structured bubble net, folding their own aqueous domain of space, to herd their meal. And I'm thinking, wow—"

Melanie completed his thought. "A gang of highly evolved, big-brained creatures folding space by weaving a bubble cloud and their favorite sushi suddenly materializes at a single point in space, where their buddies are waiting with open mouths."

They both paused to reflect on the possibilities.

"Speaking of sushi," said Dmitri, "I just realized I'm ravenous. Where's our food?"

"I have a suggestion. Let's close our eyes and try to visualize the steaming plates of fish appearing inside of a bubble net."

"What an ingenious suggestion." Dmitri shut his eyes and imagined himself kissing Melanie inside a cloud of bubbles.

Top Secret

United States Satellite Imaging Agency—Maryland

LIEUTENANT NINA DAVIS'S manager, Glen Welch, had requested an immediate status update after her interrogation of Mission Specialists Tamara Roberts and Noel Harrison. Now Nina sat in her USSIA headquarters office, listening to Welch's husky voice on the secure speakerphone.

"How did you get them to admit it?"

"I threatened them with violation of the National Security Act with a chance for leniency if they made a full disclosure. Then Harrison caved and admitted the breach after Roberts had sent him the photo."

"How'd he dare think he could get away with it?" asked Welch.

"In the first place," she replied, "no one's to know, not even our mission specialists, that every satellite image has a unique identification code embedded in the digitized photo."

"Like a watermark?"

"Something like that. Our geniuses have devised an algorithm to recover that code even if the image has been photocopied."

"That's amazing, Lieutenant."

"Even more amazing are the recent advances in continuous monitoring technology in the RH-12 satellites. We could never have detected the anomaly without them."

"What's going to happen to your mission specialists?"

"Just a slap on the wrist for Roberts. A temporary transfer to another facility."

"And Harrision?"

"Harrison's a cocky dude, but he said he needed the ten grand for his kids, and I believe him. He thought if he sold the photo to an anonymous middleman, he couldn't be directly implicated. Unfortunately for him, justice will have to play itself out."

"Tell me Lieutenant, what else are we going to do about this? We caught them red-handed."

"Deny it, of course."

"But Harrison's on the record. You say he's admitted the breach, got ten thousand for it. What I'm actually saying is, beyond strategizing, we can't deny it to ourselves. This artifact has been captured in living color by the most sensitive camera ever invented and rendered picture-perfect by the world's best image enhancement software. It's real, but what is it?"

"We're still working on it, Glen, but based on some late-breaking developments from my analysis team, something very peculiar is occurring in the sea near Hawaii."

"Which means?"

"Like I said, the results are preliminary. I'll keep you informed."

Davis stared at the folder stamped TOP SECRET resting on the desk, knowing she dare not disclose the startling nature of its contents. There was one more person to contact before she could bury the incident. Though she'd never met the Navy officer in charge of the maneuvers in Hawaii, she'd love to see his expression when he read her report.

OCCUPY PEARL HARBOR

Pearl Harbor, Oahu—mid-January

"SAVE THE WHALES! Save the whales! Save the whales!"

Christopher Gorman's eardrums throbbed as he gazed out at the massive turnout, a veritable sea of humanity by Maui standards. Three thousand ardent citizens chanted the nonstop refrain. Behind him, OCCUPY PEARL HARBOR screamed loudly from the hand-painted banner attached to two poles rising above the speaker's platform.

As he waited at the edge of the stage, their roar buffeted him like a gale-force wind. He heard the crowd's grief and anger, mirroring his own emotions on the day, two weeks ago, when he had endured the forty-eight-hour deathwatch of the juvenile humpback in Ka'anapali. The PICES director was deeply moved by the presence of so many kindred spirits. When a surge of tears filmed both eyes, he closed them, briefly, and concentrated as his mind raced through a dry run of his prepared talk.

The mounting cetacean death toll during the past month had provoked pervasive public outrage, spawning numerous protest rallies throughout the Islands. Oahu was at the epicenter of the eco-fervor, and this was the biggest rally yet. They had assembled in an open field about a mile down the road from the main entrance to Pearl Harbor Naval Station. As an expression of civic support for freedom of speech and for the event's publicized goals, city officials had promptly approved the requisite permits for the mass rally. From his offstage perch, Chris was relieved to see a minimal presence of law enforcement officers.

Although many in the crowd brandished VIVA THE BLOCKADE protest signs, the politically charged atmosphere scintillated with vintage Hawaiian zest—"the spirit of Aloha." Interspersed amongst the scheduled guest speakers, local rap and rock bands performed on the temporary wooden stage. The air suddenly quaked and the crowd came alive when a featured group's popular recording began to blast through the portable public address system donated by a Green do-gooder. Youthful guys in tank tops grooved with svelte, halter-topped gals in front of the makeshift stage. Frisbees were as ubiquitous as sandwich board slogans. Scarlet-scarved Labradors scurried after lei-bedecked youngsters kick-stepping their Razor scooters around in figure-eight patterns. Some of the locals had dug a pit in the open earth, much to the consternation of the local authorities. The aroma of roast suckling pig permeated the air, intermingling with the sweet scent of weed.

The profusion of protestors spanned the Green spectrum from mainstream to extreme activist. Advocates for agenda-driven groups as diverse as the NRDC, Greenpeace, RUSH, and the Sierra Club congregated with hundreds of others to express their unique brands of marine mammal protectionism. Chris was normally turned off by partisans fulminating about their just causes, but this felt different. They'd now allied with his cause. He'd come here to remind every one of them about the scourge of juvenile humpbacks still washing ashore. Feeling itchy beads of perspiration dripping down his forehead, he envied the happy campers who had erected colorful canopy and dome tents, Edens of shade strewn across the field.

When the music stopped, the amplified, histrionic voice of Chris's friend Joe reverberated in the air. "The next speaker on the Occupy Pearl Harbor program, from our neighbor island of Maui, is none other than the Director of PICES, Christopher Gorman." Joe, the president of the Oahu chapter of Greenpeace and the event's master of ceremonies, extended his arms in a welcoming gesture.

Wearing a white PICES T-shirt, his head shaded by a billed cap, Chris stepped up the risers and onto the platform. Upon his arrival at the guest speaker's rostrum, he waved a paperback book aloft to acknowledge the thunderous applause. He would express his gratitude the way he knew best.

He leaned into the microphone mounted on the speaker's table. "Aloha, everybody." He doffed the cap and forced himself to smile. "I want to thank you all for being here today. It's very important, because your presence and your energy can help save lives." Drowned out by the raucous rejoinder of three thousand sympathizers, he waited until the group's temperature had cooled. "I'm not gonna belabor the obvious. You've heard it all before. The Navy has undeniably resumed sonar testing, and now, suddenly, we have the deaths of many young humpbacks. I've seen the results in Maui, and it's not a pretty sight."

Vociferous outbursts of anti-military obscenities and a menacing display of protest-sign saber-rattling forced Chris to pause. He waved his arms to no avail, waiting for the audience to discharge its frustration. Despite the uproar, the sight of so many engaged young people brought back memories of his globe-trotting childhood as a military brat.

Once the seething spectators had settled down, Chris continued. "Now I'll tell you all a little secret." He reconfigured his sober visage into a tantalizing grin. The crowd grew hushed. "I spent some time in the Navy—" he heard the booing, "—and I want to thank the Navy for giving me the opportunity to discover the amazing mammals thriving in our oceans. The first time I experienced a humpback's underwater song, it felt like a baptism in a font of liquid vibration and sound. In that very moment, I knew I'd devote my life to their study and to marine mammal education."

Taking a deep breath, he said, "I'm simply hooked on humpbacks." Wisps of laughter stirred the air. "I'd like to read an excerpt from an essay I co-authored in a recent PICES publication. It's written in rather formal language, so please bear with me." He thumbed to a bookmarked page in the paperback he grasped. "By the way, these books are informative and the proceeds pay for PICES research."

"Go, Brother!" The husky, Island-accented voice emerged from the background buzz.

Chris replied with his hand raised in the shape of the shaka sign. In a calm and measured cadence, he began to read. "'Of the thousands of mammalian species that ever existed, only a handful has completed the evolutionary round-trip from the watery womb, to the world of land and sky, then back. About fifty million years ago, the land-dwelling ancestors of modern whales perplexingly reversed course and boldly returned to their ancestral home. Although today's hydrodynamically sculpted whales are able to cruise the oceans with elegant efficiency, the lineage of these giants is more closely related to the camel and the hippo, and their anatomies retain vestiges of their four-legged forebears. By their irrevocable action, their descendants are compelled to surface every fifteen minutes of their waking lives to sustain the oxygen of life. They must have achieved an enormous selective advantage to justify a plight akin to the emphysema patient forever tethered to the oxygen cylinder.'"

As he paused to let his remarks register with the listeners, Chris sensed a barometric shift in the mood of the crowd. The aura of a tranquil hum had enveloped the multitude. Many of the children had stopped playing and were nestled into their parents' laps.

"'Evolution continued upon its merry course, and the limbs so useful on land transitioned into fins and flukes better suited to propulsion in the water. The fin of the humpback whale is the largest pectoral appendage in the animal kingdom.'" He branched both arms. "'Biologists, inspired by its remarkable proportions, named the humpback species, in the lingua franca of the Linnaean classification system, Megaptera novaeangliae, the giant-winged New Englander.'"

Since he was about to embark upon more sophisticated concepts, he shifted to a more leisurely pace. "'On land, creatures of this immensity would be mired in a gravitational well. Their act of repatriation, back to their pelagic origins, was a masterstroke, since their massive bodies could literally defy gravity. The synergies of buoyancy and a bountiful food supply enabled an evolutionary positive feedback loop of burgeoning body size, a bigger skull, and an ever-expanding brain. Humankind is conditioned to view the culture of the sea from our anthropocentric fishing-for-primitive-creatures perspective. The big-brained humpbacks, however, have behaviors similar to their sapient terrestrial counterparts: children to raise, food to catch, and songs to sing.'"

Chris paused again as the song of the humpback whale streamed from the speakers and resonated in his ears. Many in the audience closed their eyes, their faces expressing rapture. Some of the children bounced up and down, spread their arms, and whirled like dervishes.

He resumed reading. "'The evolution of humans and whales proceeded to bequeath another distinguishing advantage: brain tissue sheathed in intricate convolutions of cerebral cortex that, for humans, has enabled the creation of symbols useful in thought experiments and communications. For Homo sapiens on the land, this process has transpired for less than a million years and has generated the self-proclaimed 'extraordinary' three-pound computer brain we know and love so well. For Megaptera in the sea, the evolutionary recipe has simmered for a span of thirty million years, spawning the massive cranium that encases a fourteen-pound brain endowed with a copious quantity of gray matter. One can only wonder what capabilities nature has bestowed upon the cetacean mind.'"

"One can only wonder," swirled throughout the audience like a ceremonial chant.

Chris was taken aback, pausing until the repetitions had faded in intensity. He signaled to someone off stage, and the song of the humpback infused the air once again. "Let's imagine the possibilities while meditating upon their mesmerizing songs."

He'd waited until the song had played for a full minute. "Thank you." Gorman's quiet finale caught many by surprise. Their delayed reaction crescendoed into a torrent of applause. He bowed repeatedly, then announced above the din, "Please log into the PICES website and sign the petition to halt all sonar testing in Hawaiian waters! Mahalo!"

While waving a goodbye, the master of ceremonies reappeared and grabbed Chris's arm, raising it in a linked salute. With the crowd still in an uproar, Joe shouted into the hand-held mike, "Thank you, Christopher Gorman! The next speaker on the program is RUSH activist Bill Baldwin!"

Once Gorman had disappeared, slender William Baldwin jumped up onto the stage, pumping a fist with the gusto of an athlete's victory celebration. In stark contrast to his purple, tie-dyed T-shirt, his carrot-top hair flamed in the harsh sunlight.

"It's an honor to ride Brother Gorman's wake. He's not only a dedicated researcher and educator; he's one of the quintessential secular humanists of our times. His poetic portrayal of the majestic humpbacks is pure inspiration. Excuse the pun, but I get a rush at every one of Christopher's talks. However, words can only take us so far. I represent RUSH, the Radical Ultra-Secular Humanist movement, and we put words into action! We're dedicated to stopping government and corporate exploitation of earth's most magnificent creatures." He belted out the phrases like a seasoned politician. The crowd bellowed its approval.

With sleight-of-hand proficiency, Baldwin lofted a shiny, white canister into the air, and then pointed it toward the microphone. "Hear for yourselves what the Navy's doing to the whales." Like the blast of an eighteen-wheeler's horn, a mind-numbing howl exploded from seemingly everywhere. A thousand souls reacted instinctively with hands pressed to ears and faces contorted in pain. After five interminable seconds, Baldwin mercifully doused the sonic inferno. His voice penetrated the ear-ringing silence. "I'm sorry to have discomforted you. This sports air-horn generates 115 decibels of sound energy. Yet the Navy's pulses of underwater sonar are hundreds of times more powerful. Need I say more?"

The crowd replied with an angry roar.

Baldwin shook his arms and shouted into the microphone. "RUSH leadership stands united with the other eco-movement representatives to express our outrage! It's time to put an end to anthropocentric fascism or, in other words, our species ego trip. Did you know the blue whale, the largest creature that has ever lived, was driven to the edge of extinction by whalers? Did you know humans killed over two million whales during the twentieth century?" In this rhetorical fashion, Baldwin besieged the audience with a litany of sobering accusations. Like the chorus of the faithful at a religious revival, the crowd answered back after each question, delirious with indignation.

"Greenpeace protests aren't getting it done," he continued. "The eco-enemies need a fist-in-the-face reminder of their role in the slaughter of earth's endangered marine mammals. Now is the time to show the whole world what's really going down. Let's link hands and march to the gates of the oppressors! Our symbolic blockade will tell them to cease their killing ways. Save the Whales! Let's move out!"

With the bravado of a hang-glider pilot launching from the edge of a cliff, Baldwin leapt from the stage and was snared in the net of his front-row devotees' linked arms. His prostrate figure was borne aloft and then passed overhead from person to person. Soon back on the terra firma, Baldwin cranked an arm forward and shouted, "Follow me!" The mob resounded with a fierce cheer.

A lone drummer beat the solemn rhythm heard at military funerals while the parade of humanity marched resolutely toward its destination. At least two hundred RUSH loyalists trailed in Baldwin's footsteps, chanted protest slogans, and screamed for justice. A phalanx of security guards waited to greet them as they approached the main gate to Pearl Harbor Naval Station. With the crowd surging forward, their shiny shields, helmets, and batons broadcast an intimidating warning.

Baldwin shouted into a bullhorn, "Everybody stop here." Once everyone had settled in, he cried, "Now let's link hands and form a chain! Nobody gets into this base until the Navy ends the sonar experiments!"

After several rounds of solidarity songs, and as the temperature climbed, the mob grew restive. When someone cried, "Let's make fruit salad!" front line provocateurs began to hurl squishy ripe guavas and mangoes.

"Yeah! Let's give 'em Hawaiian punch!"

Ruby red and yellow splashes of fruit pummeled the linked array of transparent plastic shields. As their body armor began to resemble a Jackson Pollock canvas, the guards' friendly faces turned angry.

"Viva the whales!" a young woman shouted.

"Yeah! Let's get 'em," screamed a disheveled youth wearing a RUSH T-shirt. Then, beer bottles propellered through the air, crashed into shields, and shattered into glistening shards like Hawaiian shave ice. The sprays of spittle, the showers of glass, the rain of curses, and the clashing of bodies—these were the primal elements precipitating the tipping point in human relations. Billy clubs answered back, battering human flesh, and the blood of one species was shed in protest against the bloodshed of another.

THE BEST AND THE BRIGHTEST

SoCalSci University, Department of Engineering, Los Angeles, California—mid-January

"GOOD MORNING, SEEMA and Andrew," said Dmitri. "It's great to be back home." SoCalSci was his home, he thought. His students were his family. "Grab some chairs."

Southern California's mid-winter, morning sunshine poured through the floor-to-ceiling windows of Professor David Dmitri's second floor office, illuminating the faces of his two stellar graduate students. Seema Roy and Andrew Chu removed the piles of paper gathering dust atop two ergonomic guest chairs and settled down for their weekly advisory session. It was their first meeting in nearly a month, since before the winter break campus shutdown.

"Hey, boss," said Andrew, "seems like your vacation paid off. You look tanned, rested, and ready to go for our next handball match." He flexed an arm in a muscle-man pose.

Dmitri shook his head in feigned exasperation. Today, more than usual, he enjoyed Andrew's playfulness as a counterpoint to the usual academic chitchat and to his own darkened thoughts about the whales still perishing in Maui.

"I adore your shirt," said Seema, referring to the floral-red, silk-print shirt Dmitri had found in Lahaina. She touched a finger to her temple. "My sixth sense also tells me that you had a transformative experience in the Islands, possibly even a romantic encounter."

Seema's teasing smile and lilting voice delighted peers and colleagues alike. Her willowy figure reminded Dmitri of a classical dancer's, and her large, dark eyes revealed an innate curiosity. Seema's calming British-Indian accent relaxed him during their meetings. Her accurate hunch, however, reignited his concern about Melanie. He knew she'd be shaken by the news of the mounting humpback death toll. He willed himself to appear at ease.

"I was going to inquire about your holidays, but since you mentioned it, I did indeed have a transformative series of encounters. Since I've returned with materials for a new line of inquiry, let's temporarily suspend your current research activities. I'd like you to conduct a brief investigation for me."

Dmitri's students exchanged expressions of concern. Andrew spoke first. "But, boss—"

Dmitri interrupted. "I apologize for the sudden shift of priorities. Do you remember our discussion last year regarding Professor McPinsky's ideas about interspecies communication?"

"Of course we remember." Seema replied in crisp, enunciated tones. "You're referring to his challenge to the scientific community to break the linguistic codes of other sentient species like whales and dolphins and engage them in dialogue."

"But it's already been done," said Andrew. "Koko the gorilla has learned to communicate using sign language gestures."

"Touché," replied Dmitri. "Over a thousand signs, in fact, but that's just scratching the surface of human potential. Koko's gorilla brain is just one-third the size of a human's and her measured IQ barely tops eighty-five."

"And the whales?"

"Their brains are at least four times bigger than ours with gobs of cortex. Think about the possibilities."

"But surely you don't think our team can attempt such an ambitious task?"

Dmitri rocked in his chair. The swaying motion helped to moderate his heartbeat and focus his thoughts. "A week ago, I would have agreed with you. While in Hawaii, however, I discovered both the means and the motive for pursuing such a controversial research project." Andrew furrowed his brow. "Riddle me this. Why would a fifty-ton, fifty-foot-long, fourteen-pound-brained whale leap completely out of the ocean with such reckless abandon?"

"Why do seemingly intelligent people jump from airplanes?" replied Andrew.

"Exactly!" When Dmitri slammed his palm on the desk, both students recoiled. "It could be a leap of the imagination, by a mind that's evolved over thirty million years. To experience novel forces: the weight of their bodies, the deceleration and acceleration through the ether, the thrill of the wind, the chill of evaporative cooling on their skin, and finally the jolt of the impact."

"Like a roller-coaster ride," said Seema.

"More than that," replied Dmitri, his voice rising on an updraft of emotion. "Just as humans seek to explore other worlds, the curious humpbacks thrust skyward for a kaleidoscopic vision of the world above—brilliant light, intense colors, mountains, clouds, and alien craft."

"Sounds like you had a great time in Maui, boss."

Dmitri, seeing his students' tentative expressions, realized he'd better dial down on the intensity. "The more I directly observed and learned about the behavior of the humpback whales, a common thread emerged, a level of intelligence meriting further investigation. And thanks to the marine biologists at the Pacific Institute for Cetacean Educational Studies, I've brought back recent recordings of whale songs we can scrutinize."

Seema swiveled slowly, back and forth, in her chair. In the same rhythm, she stroked a lock of jet black hair between her thumb and forefinger, as if she were bowing a string instrument. Dmitri recognized the telltale sign of an impending question.

"I'm sure I will appreciate the humpbacks' songs," she said, "but how do you propose we make the conceptual leap from music to the identification of linguistic symbols?"

"Do I detect a glimmer of interest?" Dmitri knew damn well his students couldn't resist the challenge. He considered Seema Roy and Andrew Chu the most exceptional of the many outstanding graduate students he'd advised in SoCalSci's Engineering Communications Program. After graduating at the head of her class from the Bangalore Institute of Technology, Seema had applied to some of the world's top graduate engineering schools. Since it had been her dream to experience California's rich tapestry of academic, cultural, and scenic attractions, she had not hesitated to accept SoCalSci's generous offer of a stipend and research assistantship.

Seema was a gifted musician, a violinist, who nonetheless realized the advantages of an advanced degree in an income-generating profession. She'd confided in Dmitri the hope that, with a mechanical engineering diploma in acoustics, she could one day design improved or even new types of musical instruments. Currently, she was investigating the properties that defined the superior tone quality of notable stringed instruments such as the Stradivarius violins. Dmitri knew she appreciated his support of a project that other professors would dismiss as too conjectural.

Andrew, an upbeat and competitive, second-generation Chinese-American, was also stellar. He had graduated summa cum laude with a Bachelor of Science degree from SoCalSci. Despite Andrew's wisecracking facade, Dmitri understood this young man was, like himself, passionately devoted to the fields of digital voice and signal processing engineering. During their joint research activities, Andrew had marveled aloud about the deep-space probes that could transmit pictures and data from Saturn, Neptune, and beyond. Dmitri took pride in the work of the brilliant SoCalSci colleagues who had designed the sophisticated error-correction codes to repair the data waveforms damaged by radiation.

Andrew frequented the university athletic center's handball courts, and like many of the serious student athletes, he sported a buzz cut. Dmitri admired the young man's disciplined workout regimen and his impressive physique. It was obvious that Andrew relished their weekly handball matches.

As rising stars, Seema and Andrew had earned a virtually guaranteed first choice in the selection of a major field advisor. Independent and adventurous, they had wanted more than a secure roadmap toward the pursuit of their advanced degrees. During their due diligence survey of the engineering faculty, some of their more senior schoolmates had spoken in superlatives about Dmitri. They reported that he treated his students like peers, and that he encouraged them to develop proposals based upon their own interests rather than coercing them into accepting pre-formatted research projects. Most importantly, Seema and Andrew were well aware that Associate Professor Dmitri had himself been mentored by the illustrious and iconoclastic Professor Theodosius McPinsky.

"Okay boss," said Andrew, cupping his hands behind his head. "As usual, you've piqued our interest. What's the history and current status of whale song research and how do we fit into this picture?"

Dmitri stood. "It's a remarkable *National Geographic* story." He started to pace slowly, his eyes studying the wavy patterns woven into the carpet. "Over forty years ago, marine biologist Roger Payne and his colleagues pioneered the acoustical analysis of humpback whale vocalizations. He discovered that, unlike bird songs or the utterances of any other species, these particular vocalizations exhibited a rudimentary linguistic structure. Using pre-digital technology, Payne identified about a dozen different types of discrete sound elements called 'units.'"

Dmitri stopped pacing. He reached down and rotated his laptop so that the screen faced his guests. "Here's a time and frequency plot from Payne's original research paper." He touched the screen, pointing to alternating sequences of squiggly lines and blobs, arranged somewhat like sheet music. "You can see each unit has an average duration of about 2.5 seconds, separated by intervals of silence. Payne classified these sound units according to their acoustical attributes. Some, like our vowels, contained elements of frequency- and amplitude-modulated harmonics. Others had a broadband frequency character like our consonants and sounded like rumbles, grunts, and gurgles."

Seema pivoted her chair toward Dmitri. "So you're saying these sound units are similar to the phonemes of our spoken language?"

"On the surface, yes, but it gets better than that. Look at the next slide." Dmitri clicked his mouse to refresh the screen. "Payne also proved that these units were organized into repeating and varying patterns of short and long duration, similar to the short phrases and longer themes in human songs. Each song can last up to thirty minutes and sometimes for many hours. Even more fascinating, Payne's wife Katy discovered that a humpback population's song constantly evolves during each season and from year to year. The Paynes became environmental heroes. Their findings were persuasive evidence of whale intelligence and instrumental in the U.S. Congress's passage of the Marine Mammal Protection Act in 1972. They also influenced the International Whaling Commission's 1986 moratorium on the commercial whaling of endangered species like humpbacks."

"Okay," said Andrew. "So he's a Payne in the fluke to the whaling nations."

Dmitri groaned. "I'll ignore that."

Andrew raised a hand. "Has anyone else used more sophisticated techniques and advanced computing power to study the songs?"

"Bingo. In fact, as recently as three years ago, an engineering team at Columbia applied information theory. They measured the information content of the whales' lexicon in the context of their song. They also confirmed Payne's observations that whale songs are hierarchical in structure, similar to the way human language is organized into clauses and sentences."

Seema sighed. "I realize you're both familiar with communication theory but as an acoustics major, I just signed up for this semester's Engineering Communications 101 class."

Dmitri smiled at her. "Then let me explain." At the whiteboard behind his desk, he sketched out the interconnected rectangular, circular, and diamond shapes representing a system block diagram. "Think about a message such as a book, an email, or a song. In this context, the information content of the message is proportional to the number of words in the dictionary of the message's native language. The units of measurement are called 'bits,' representing the exponential powers of the number 'two.'"

"Can you give a simple example?" asked Seema.

Dmitri nodded and wrote the numbers 4 and 2 in the middle of the diagram. "If you have a simple language which consists of four words, then two times two equals four, so the information content is two bits. If you double the number of words in the language from four to eight, then two times two times two equals eight. So any message written in that language contains up to three bits of information."

"Got it," replied Seema. "Every time you double the number of word entries in a language's dictionary, the information content measured in bits increases by one. It's a base two logarithmic scale."

"Yes, good. It's similar to the way earthquakes are measured on the Richter Scale."

"Except that's a base ten logarithmic scale," said Andrew. "A magnitude seven earthquake is ten times more powerful than one that registers magnitude six."

Dmitri wrote the numbers 8,000 and 13 on the board. "So, for the English language, nearly all messages can be expressed using 8,000 of the most commonly used words." He tapped the number 8,000.

Seema reached for her iPhone and played with the touchscreen. She touched her palm on the whiteboard where Dmitri had written the number 13. "According to my calculator, if you multiply the number *two* thirteen times, it equals 8,192, which is the power of two closest to 8,000."

"Exactly," replied Dmitri. "The information content of messages sent in the English language is therefore thirteen bits." He gestured toward Andrew. "Why don't you continue?"

Andrew nodded. "However, that's the maximum possible amount of information in the source message, assuming that all of the words are equally likely. But in fact we know that many English words are used more frequently than others. The probability of each word is also dependent upon syntax, its placement in a sentence, and the context of the neighboring words." He paused. "Engineers exploit these statistical dependencies and redundancies to design more efficient sets of code words that compress the amount of data required to transmit or store a message. It's so cool, like freeze-dried food. Just remove the water and add it back later."

"'Freeze-dried food.' That's a good one, Andrew. Can I borrow that gem for one of my lectures?"

"Sure, boss, just remember to give me credit."

Andrew's smile reminded Dmitri of the tooth-whitening ads gracing the walls of his dentist's waiting room.

"So, to finish up, Seema," Andrew continued, "these data compression formulations are essential to all types of digital communication technologies such as Internet file transfers, wireless iPad and iPhone transmissions, and the storage of audio and video information onto CDs and DVDs."

Despite his own tension, Dmitri cast a smile of satisfaction in the direction of his protégé. "Because of these redundancies, the actual information content of the English language can be compressed from thirteen to ten bits per word." He crossed out the number 13 on the board, writing a 10 directly above. "So, the Columbia team used similar techniques to compute the redundancies of the periodic units in the whale songs. Interestingly, they measured the information content of the Hawaiian whale songs to be a measly one bit per sound unit."

"Jeesh," said Andrew. "There's no comparison. That's one bit for whales compared to ten bits for human speech, measured on a logarithmic scale."

"Exactly," said Dmitri. "They concluded that human language conveys hundreds of times more information than humpback language. The implication is that, although the whales sing a pleasant tune, they don't measure up to the higher standard of human intelligence. But, and this is vitally important, like a self-fulfilling prophecy, the stigma implied in their findings might discourage others from investigating cetacean languages."

Andrew sighed. "So it sounds like all the work's been done before and the answer is *nada*. Doesn't that leave us out in the cold?"

"Well, let me repeat. They're comparing their measurement of the humpback's phonemic-like alphabet of about a dozen symbols to the entire lexicon of the 8,000 most commonly spoken English words. Does that seem reasonable to you?"

Andrew exclaimed, "You're right! You get it, Seema? Like apples and oranges, they're comparing the amount of information in a dictionary of 8,000 words to the information content of the twenty-six letters of the English alphabet."

"Which is only about one to two bits per letter, about the same as the whale songs," replied Dmitri.

"What a crock," said Andrew. "How'd they decide that the basic acoustic units of whale songs are similar to human words instead of letters or phonemes?"

"That's the point! They just assumed that each 2.5-second vocalization was a distinct acoustic entity, regardless of the details of the frequency modulations within each unit. Heck, an entire human sentence averages about 2.5 seconds and consists of numerous words and many more phonemes." Dmitri's gaze intersected Andrew's, and then Seema's. "That's why our team should focus on analyzing these units for phonemic changes, similar to human speech, on a much smaller timescale."

"It's beginning to make sense," said Seema. "Nevertheless, we can't ignore the fact that these songs contain a very limited set of acoustic symbols grouped into repetitive patterns."

"Seema, you've hit the nail on the head." Dmitri's face registered his approval. "So here's the thing to know. Only the male humpbacks sing these Aquarian shanties and they stage their productions almost exclusively during the breeding season in Southern waters like Hawaii, Mexico, and Bermuda. Since marine biologists hypothesize the songs serve a mating function, who are we to argue? So, if you're trying to analyze a humpback vocalization for linguistic codes and information content, which source data are you going to use? A mating song or vocalizations linked to communal behavior during the feeding season?"

"I get it, boss. It's like comparing the conversational IQ of a couple at the dinner table versus when they're trying to make a baby. What's the information content of oohing, aahing, and moaning? Not even one bit per symbol."

"Exactly, Andrew. Imagine extra-terrestrials evaluating human intelligence from the satellite-television transmission intercept of a porn video."

"No wonder we haven't been contacted by the ET's," said Seema.

"Correctamundo!" Dmitri punched a fist at an imaginary foe. "So although the researchers acknowledge that the linguistic structure of humpback songs is a barometer of their intelligence, the information measurements decree it to be a low-level intellect. Since the medium is the message, the results are a fait accompli, conditioned by anthropocentric bias."

Seema stared directly at Andrew. "I'm surprised there's even one bit per symbol considering how puerile guys are when they're showing off."

When Andrew rolled his eyes and made a silly face, Seema laughed and poked him in the ribs. Dmitri wondered, not for the first time, if the nature of their relationship was more than academic.

"Maybe the whale mating song is more like a rap song or a Twitter post to lure groupies?" Seema uttered a series of high-pitched tweets. "Something like, 'Meet me at the Fluke and Fin for a breach.'"

Dmitri smiled, glad that she too felt free enough to be playful in his office. "Precisely. Just as you'd expect for a mating ritual, their songs are stylized communications with low information content. But maybe this is just the tip of the iceberg of an information-rich language. There's bound to be more dense and meaningful dialogue when the humpbacks are engaging in a moveable feast."

"Or if the pod is planning this season's bubble-net, fashionista designs," added Seema.

"So I take it we're gonna be research contrarians?" Andrew asked.

"Absolutely! Instead of a Masters and Johnson study, we'll focus our analysis on the less melodic vocalizations in the Alaskan recordings when they're not in the breeding mode and their communications are hopefully more diverse. And we'll analyze their microstructure for the more fundamental phonemic units of language, not just these big stylized units in the songs."

"Aw," Andrew moaned, "that's too bad. I was hoping to pick up some pick-up lines from the big boys."

Seema groaned. "Sorry to inform you, Andrew, but the information content of your jokes can be measured in fractional bits."

Andrew chuckled with the percussive dots-and-dashes rhythm of Morse code.

To stifle his own laughter, Dmitri bit his cheek. "Okay, let's get back to Seema's original question. How do we identify acoustic symbols in the vocalizations? As Andrew knows from our voice codec work, there's the traditional technique of correlating the shifting frequency patterns in a spectrogram to likely phonemic units."

"And as we previously discussed," replied Andrew, "adapting speech recognition techniques to this task could be our full-time occupation for weeks on end."

"Ah, so now I have to reveal my second transformative experience in Maui," Dmitri said. "Thanks to a speech therapist, who will be nameless," he winked at Seema, "and a deaf twelve-year-old boy, I believe we have another exciting option for attacking the problem. Have either of you heard of the Speakeasy speech-therapy computer program?"

"Nope," replied Andrew.

Seema shook her head.

"Until recently, I hadn't either. It was developed by a research team in New Zealand to correct the pronunciation of people with hearing loss. They cleverly exploit a visual representation of the primary frequencies of the consonant and vowel phonemes." Dmitri drew an example of a Speakeasy word gram on the whiteboard and briefly described the relationship between the tone-pair frequencies and the shapes. "Are you with me?"

Both students nodded. "We're chill, boss."

Dmitri continued. "It's designed like a videogame to provide real-time visual biofeedback. Compared to all the data in a spectrogram, it calculates and depicts a concise set of variables in the frequency domain. Speakeasy is the optimal tool to determine if the whale's language is frequency modulated like our own. I brought a copy of the program back from Maui. I'd like Andrew to preview and prep the whale song data using the spectrum analyzer. Then Seema can massage the data for the Speakeasy analysis. Any questions?"

Andrew raised his hand again. "Have you booked our flight to Stockholm for the award ceremonies?"

"Very funny." Dmitri kept a straight face while opening a jewel case and removing a CD. "This disk contains all of PICES's recent digitized whale vocalizations." He held it aloft, hummed the first four notes of *Beethoven's 5th*, and considered their symbolic meaning—Fate knocking at the door. "Think positively since, for all we know, it could be the cetacean Rosetta Stone."

Andrew grabbed the CD case, and the two students waved their goodbyes. Dmitri reflected upon his good fortune, happy to be the mentor of two such delightful and competent individuals. Their team chemistry was superb.

It had taken all of his self-control, however, to appear cheerful during their discussion. Prior to their meeting, he'd scanned the online edition of the *Honolulu Star-Advertiser*. Now he clicked on the window he'd previously minimized and glanced again at the headlines: MORE WHALES STRANDED IN MAUI . . . DEATH TOLL MOUNTS. Dmitri hadn't wanted his students to be spooked by his anxiety over Melanie's peace of mind or his desperation for a language breakthrough. He required every ounce of their talent. They'd need to be as relaxed and upbeat as possible during their investigation of the whale songs. Maybe, with their creativity, their help, he could actually break the codes to unlock the gates that guarded the interspecies *Tower of Babel*. It could be the whale's best hope for survival.

Tell Me I'm Not Crazy

SoCalSci University, Los Angeles, California—the next day

DMITRI WHISTLED GERSHWIN'S *Rhapsody in Blue* as he approached the Engineering Department's Signal Processing Lab. He was in a much better mood now that he'd finished the early afternoon lecture for his undergraduate signal processing class. The intellectual challenges of his work and the stimulating interactions with bright young minds often helped to balance his emotional swings.

He swiped his magnetic card, punched in the security code on a wall-mounted keypad, and entered a dimly lit, windowless anteroom. The lonely space was jam-packed with rows and racks of electronic equipment. Banks of gizmos and gadgets, studded with garish chorus lines of pulsating LED status lights, oozed waves of electromagnetic radiation. The mind-numbing roar of an army of cooling fans besieged him. He'd worked in rooms like this before, sometimes experiencing headaches and disorientation.

Dmitri hurried through a central corridor, flanked by columns of hardware, and parted a pair of double-swing doors. He found Seema and Andrew huddled together at a computer workstation crowded with test instruments, their faces masked by a fluorescent blue glare. They gazed at two video screen displays of various frequency plots, presumably from one of the whale song recordings.

Dmitri tapped Andrew on the shoulder. "How's it going?"

"Look at what we found." Andrew pointed at the monitor.

Dmitri recognized the peaks and valleys of a waterfall plot, a way to represent time-varying, two-dimensional information in three dimensions. The sequence of two-dimensional frequency plots, each resembling the rising and falling of a mountain range, receded into the depth dimension of the monitor like a series of cascading waves. He studied the peaks and valleys of the power levels across the spectrum of frequencies. "This section over here," he pointed, "looks like amplitude modulation of three fixed frequencies."

"As if playing multiple organ pipes of different lengths," replied Seema.

"But this section on the right looks like the inter-frequency modulations of vowels," added Andrew.

"Like the human vocal tract." The words surged through Dmitri's lips on a wave of rising pitch. "The anatomy and physiology of their vocal system could be even more complex than our own. Seema, since you're interested in the design of novel musical instruments, how about a project to reverse engineer a model of the humpback's vocal tract from these waveforms?"

"Very interesting," replied Seema. "Like a whale French horn or bagpipes."

"Don't do it," said Andrew. "The whaling nations could use that thing like a duck call to lure the whales to their doom."

Seema glared at Andrew and then faced Dmitri. "By the way, you were right. There's nothing above four thousand hertz in these frequency plots."

"Curiously in the same range as human speech." Dmitri leaned over Andrew's shoulder to peer at the monitor.

"I applied more than the usual amount of pre-emphasis to the higher frequencies," said Andrew.

Dmitri backed away. "Not that easy to position a microphone close to a whale."

"Ahh, so that's why the high-end frequencies are so attenuated." Seema tapped the screen.

Andrew rotated his chair to face Dmitri. "We decided to test-drive the analyzers by comparing the Maui whales to the Tongan humpback data. The grouping of the resonance peaks is of a different pattern. We think their songs exhibit a dialect unique to their region."

Seema laughed. "It's so cool, as if the Tongans have an Oxford English accent and the Hawaiians speak American English."

"Intriguing," said Dmitri, "but remember, we're here to decode discrete phonemic units from these frequency patterns, not to discover the next great whale rapper for *American Idol*."

"How about a trip to Maui?" suggested Seema. "We could drop some speakers into the ocean, play back the recordings, and just lay back and listen for feedback."

"Don't forget the mai tais." Andrew lifted an imaginary glass to his mouth.

"Nice try." Dmitri glanced at his watch. "In fifteen minutes, Melanie's calling us from Hawaii." He saw their quizzical expressions. "The speech therapist, right? She'll instruct you in the operation of the Speakeasy interface. I've committed to a workshop in Santa Barbara tomorrow, so let's reconnect in a couple of days. If Speakeasy reveals anything interesting in the Alaskan vocalizations, don't hesitate to text me. Right now, I've got a meeting in the dean's office. Goodbye and good luck."

Seema stretched and Andrew yawned. It was early morning, and they were still camped-out in the Signal Processing Lab, their workstation cluttered by Styrofoam cups and Chinese take-out boxes. All night long, they'd tried to make sense of the Speakeasy images and the captivating relationship between the humpback's vocalizations and the word gram shapes on the monitor.

Seema pointed at the screen. "As Dmitri suggested, these sharp turns are the most likely regions to find cetacean phonemes." She mumbled through a blanket of fatigue.

"Pretty ingenious suggestion," replied Andrew. "Like the discovery of super-massive black holes from the time-lapse pictures of stars orbiting around them."

"Unfortunately, we'll need more persuasive evidence than visual observation."

"We'd have to do a statistical analysis of the Speakeasy data. It'll take at least a week to code and test."

"Let's discuss it later." Seema slumped over, resting her head on the table top. "It's almost morning, so let's get some sleep."

"Give me just a few more minutes," said Andrew. "We've focused our attention on these dense episodes of frequency modulation that Dmitri's interested in." He indicated a second monitor that displayed the non-Speakeasy, time-varying waveforms. "We've totally ignored the other sections of the recording. What about this?" He pointed to a sparse region of sound blips separated by many seconds of silence. "Let's analyze this segment before calling it a night."

"Oh, what's the use? It looks like noise to me." Seema lifted her head, leaned back in the chair, and stretched like a feline.

"Please, just bear with me." Andrew steepled his fingers. "My grandfather was a Zen Buddhist. He told me that patience was a virtue and the search for meaning is revealed in the silent corners of our minds."

Seema muttered, "Sounds like you're quoting from last night's fortune cookie."

"Have you no respect for cultural values other than your own? Anyway, I got a much more clever fortune. 'Fu-Ling-Yu say: eunuch—man cut out to be bachelor.'"

Seema responded with a dramatic groan. "My Hindu grandmother once said, 'Early to bed, early to rise, makes a Brahmin healthy, wealthy, and wise.'"

"Let's make a deal. I'll exchange my world-famous, five-minute shoulder massage for another fifteen minutes with Speakeasy."

Seema rotated her head and shoulders. "They *are* kinda tight. Okay. How can I refuse such a noble offer?"

Andrew stood, positioning himself behind Seema's chair. "Close your eyes and relax." He began to knead both thumbs into her neck and shoulders. "You've definitely got some huge knots here."

"Ouch, be gentle. Yes, that's much better."

"I'll have these knots untied in five."

Seema sighed with relief as Andrew worked his hands and elbows into the crevices of her upper back. "Ooooh, that feels so good. I never realized you had talents outside of engineering."

"Anytime you want, these hands are for hire."

"I just might take you up on your offer." Seema purred as Andrew's elbows sank into the taut regions of her trapezius and deltoid muscles. "Oh, God, I'm starting to feel like a new person."

"Good, then we can work some more." Andrew sniffed the air. "By the way, your hair smells great."

"It's a family-secret hair conditioner made from cinnamon, cardamom, and cloves."

"Like my favorite herbal tea." Andrew kneaded silently for five more minutes. When he released his grip, Seema turned around and flashed a huge grin.

"That was wonderful." She stood and surprised him with a hug. "Thank you." She pecked him on the cheek.

Andrew hesitated. Although their relationship had been full of friendly banter, it was more collegial than personal. Now, for the first time, they were cheek-to-cheek. Sensing the warmth of her breath, he reciprocated the hug and gazed into her eyes. The brief spell lingered.

"Time to work," they uttered simultaneously and then laughed. With some hesitation, they disengaged.

Andrew settled into his chair, typed some commands, and stared at the blank screen. To his surprise, a small, circular shape materialized in the middle of the Speakeasy display. Thirty seconds later, after the screen had auto-refreshed, a similar form appeared in a different region of the plot. The sequence of curious shapes persisted over a span of several minutes.

"What the heck." Andrew stared and pointed. "These ring figures seem to be popping up in locations all over the frequency plot."

"We never saw shapes like these with human speech. It sounds like a barking seal and looks kind of like a bubble. Maybe they're like whistles."

Andrew whistled. "We're definitely making progress," he said, "but my brain has finally hit a wall. Let's call it quits for now, get some sleep, and show this to Dmitri when he's back from Santa Barbara."

"Finally, we agree." As Seema began to shut down her workstation, her entire body went rigid. She stared straight ahead.

"What's wrong? You look like you've seen a ghost."

Seema raised an arm in slow motion, like a mime, and pointed at the monitor. As the whale squealed through the speakers, the Speakeasy translated its vocalizations into familiar shapes embedded in a very unfamiliar setting.

"If you're seeing what I'm seeing," Andrew gulped, "please tell me I'm not crazy."

Seema faced him, wide-eyed. "You're not crazy."

Andrew turned back to gaze at the figures painted on the computer monitor. "So what are we gonna do about this?"

"Get some sleep."

HITTING THE BULL'S-EYE

SoCalSci University, Los Angeles, California—one day later

DMITRI SAT AT HIS desk, studying the lecture notes he'd prepared for his afternoon class when Andrew and Seema appeared in the doorway. They seemed tense, and he wanted to put them at ease. "How was your Speakeasy tutorial with Melanie?"

"She was very nice, very professional." Seema had a gleam in her eye. "She had us up and running in less than an hour."

"She also has a very nice voice." Andrew accentuated the word "very."

"I couldn't agree more," replied Dmitri. "What's the scoop on the whale song data? By the way, you both look exhausted."

"We pulled an all-nighter." Seema's voice sounded dreamy. "But it was worth it. You'll see."

"There's an intriguing development," said Andrew. He looked punch drunk with puffy eyelids. "Before we get to that, you should Google this link."

Dmitri stared at the sheet of paper Andrew gave him. "What the—"

"Just enter the link into your browser, boss, and all will be revealed."

"Okay, I'll humor you, but this better be good." As Dmitri typed, Andrew and Seema circled his desk and stood behind him.

"That's it." Andrew pointed at the picture displayed on Dmitri's monitor. The headline above the photo read, CONTROVERSIAL OCEAN CROP CIRCLE PHOTO MAY BE LINKED TO WHALES. "Just read the first two paragraphs."

Dmitri scanned the article, pawing his hair, squinting at the screen. "What am I supposed to be thinking? It says that an Australian marine biologist studying a satellite photo, allegedly taken in the vicinity of Hawaii, discovered geometric patterns that might be linked to humpback whale activity. 'Alleged' and 'might' don't instill much confidence in the credibility of the guy's theory."

"But if you read the fine print," said Andrew, "he also states that the concentric patterns could be related to humpback bubble-net behavior."

"And that's supposed to prove—"

"We found a similar pattern in the whale vocalizations," Seema interrupted.

"What?" Dmitri heard Seema's words but they made no sense.

"We're as surprised as you are," replied Andrew.

"We found a baffling geometric pattern embedded in the Speakeasy translation," said Seema, "but didn't know what to make of it. When Andrew stumbled across this Internet story, we thought there might be a connection."

"Just come with us, boss."

Five minutes later, Dmitri, Seema, and Andrew stood before a bank of three display monitors in the Signal Processing Lab. Andrew initialized the Speakeasy program.

"Check out the display." Andrew directed his "first-down" gesture at the central monitor. "The figures being drawn sometimes take sharp turns, just as you'd predicted."

"That's great news." Dmitri touched the curlicue pattern on the screen. "If you could automate the detection of these inflection points, we could build a statistical database of frequency-pair targets."

"We're way ahead of you, but it'll take at least a week to launch."

"The real reason we called you back," Seema gushed, "was because of Andrew's idea to analyze another section of the recording."

Andrew replayed the video depicting the circular patterns. "We were pretty surprised to see these small ring shapes appearing at a rate of about once or twice per minute. They seem to be distributed uniformly throughout the plot, over a range of frequencies between 100 and 4,000 hertz."

Dmitri studied the screen and massaged his scalp. Finally, he said, "Not the patterns you'd expect for the symbols of the language of a sentient species. My guess is these frequencies correspond to the sounds of whistling." He strafed the air with a percussive sequence of high-pitched whistles. "Good try, though."

"That's what we thought, too, until we observed the anomalous event. Wait just a few more seconds. There!" Andrew punched a fist toward the monitor.

Dmitri leaned forward and stared as the Speakeasy translation emerged. An invisible hand, guided by an anonymous cetacean voice, rendered the perfectly round figure of a large circle, followed shortly thereafter by a smaller circle, and finally, by an even smaller one. He could not deny the reality of the image stamped on the screen. A bull's-eye pattern of three, perfectly concentric circles hovered before his eyes. Before he could speak, the process was repeated with the same implausible detail. The second bull's-eye was nearly identical to its predecessor and overlaid on top of the first.

Dmitri gazed without blinking for nearly a full minute, his mind unable to process the data revealed by his own senses. He turned around to face both students. As his eyes darted back and forth, the expression on his brow shifted between skepticism and wonder. He eventually fixed his gaze upon Andrew. "You know, this really isn't the right moment for a practical joke."

Andrew clasped both hands over his face. "Nooooooo!"

Seema laughed.

"What?" Dmitri sounded impatient. "I'm right then?"

Andrew yanked a wallet from his pocket, extracted a ten-dollar bill, and slapped it onto Seema's waiting hand. Dmitri was befuddled by her triumphant grin.

"No, boss, you're dead wrong, but Seema predicted your skeptical response. We placed a wager on it."

"Wait a second. You're telling me this is legit?" He pointed at the screen.

"We're as stunned as you are," replied Seema.

"Let's pinch ourselves for a moment." Dmitri's voice flowed like molasses. "This *could* be an acoustic artifact. Since our analytic minds coexist with our imaginations, we're tempted to perceive patterns where none exist."

"Like those old NASA pictures of the giant face on Mars?" offered Seema.

"That's a good example. We're trained from birth to compare patterns we observe to those we've stored in our mental databases. Recognition of our mother's face is our first such experience."

"Sometimes, however," replied Seema, "like the face on Mars, we're deceived by a pattern that's a close match to the ones in our memory."

"I remember that," said Andrew. "After NASA examined the same region from different angles and lighting conditions, they realized it looked less like a face and more like an erosion pattern."

"Precisely." Dmitri uttered each syllable with equal emphasis. "Engineers and scientists are trained to use math, logic, and the scientific method to avoid coming to false conclusions. A single, circular pattern has a distinct geometric quality, but we cannot logically infer that this was the intention of the whistler. What we've got is a complex form: the frequencies of three highly correlated whistles in a linked geometric relationship. And it satisfies the math criterion. This does not appear to be random. In *my* mind, there's a higher probability of the whale's intention to define some sort of geometrically based symbol. Congratulations on your great detective work."

"Not to mention the concentric circular patterns in the water near Hawaii," murmured Seema.

"Touché," replied Dmitri. "The patterns are similar, and if they're both related to the humpbacks, it could be a real breakthrough. "I say we should investigate further."

Dmitri hugged each of his students. Despite their exhaustion, the two were clearly proud. It struck him that they seemed different with each other, but he couldn't pinpoint how, and in his excitement, he put it out of his mind.

"So, what's our next move?" Seema asked.

Dmitri reached for his cell phone and pressed the speed-dial button. "Good morning, Greg. Are you in the office yet? Good. We need a math expert in the Signal Processing Lab, as soon as possible. There's something intriguing for you to ponder. *Arigato.*"

"Calling in the big guns, boss?"

"We need a pattern recognition expert, and Dr. Bono is, after all, the mastermind of the geometry of eleven-dimensional hyperspace."

"Oh, yeah," replied Andrew. "Dr. Bono's recent article in *Science* . . . his new slant on the mathematics underlying string theory."

"Exactly," said Dmitri. "I'd like a quick resolution to this project, so please don't take it personally. You two are more than welcome to participate. While we're waiting, let's examine some of the other plots."

Three minutes later, Greg burst through the lab's swinging double-doors. He wore a blue and gold L.A. Lakers Championship cap.

"Professor Bono, I presume," said Andrew, his tone respectful despite the joking words. "Did the Lakers win last night?"

Greg mimed a jump shot. "Yep, a Kobe buzzer-beater from beyond the arc. Swish!"

While Greg examined the circular patterns, he received a ten-minute briefing. "I agree with you," he finally said. "This could be a significant development. You can count me in, but I'll need a Speakeasy tutorial."

"Absolutely." Dmitri and Greg sealed the agreement with a fist bump. "Since Seema and Andrew need to catch up on their sleep, let's all meet here tomorrow at 9 a.m. I'll rearrange my schedule to work with you."

ENGINEERING KARMA

SoCalSci University, Los Angeles, California—late afternoon

IT WAS NEARLY 5 p.m. and Dmitri was back in the office after teaching his afternoon class. "Fred, I've attached the PowerPoint files for both lectures to the email. Thanks so much." With the cursor on the email SEND button, he clicked his mouse, pleased that a department colleague had agreed to substitute teach both of his undergraduate courses on short notice. He had bought two days of freedom to assist Greg in the analysis of the recordings.

Grabbing a pencil, Dmitri beat the rhythm of a favorite jazz riff against a coffee mug, swiveling and rocking in his chair. The thought of Seema's and Andrew's startling Speakeasy observation triggered a familiar tingling sensation in his chest. Even Greg, an inveterate skeptic, had been intrigued by the cryptic bull's-eye pattern. Was this the proverbial smoking gun of a breakthrough discovery or another false lead in the labyrinthine pursuit of the scientific method? He couldn't think of anyone more qualified than Greg to help him deduce the significance of the geometric figures in the whale song.

Dmitri closed his eyes and reflected back to the childhood memory of lazy summer mornings when he could sleep in undisturbed by an alarm clock. He remembered pulling the sheets over his head to create a private sanctuary and listening, spellbound, as the neighbor's parrot alternately squawked and enunciated perfect Spanish phrases from a backyard cage. At the time, he wondered how a bird could speak a foreign language better than anyone in his fourth-grade Spanish class. This linguistic revelation had been indelibly etched into his young mind, launching a lifelong fascination with sound and language.

During his father's final year, Dmitri had grown quite fond of a pair of blue and yellow talking parakeets at the local pet store. A few months after Michael Dmitri's death and with the onset of her son's spells of loneliness, Dmitri's mother purchased the birds as a tenth-birthday present. Just as she had hoped, his devotion to the loquacious budgies had sparked her boy's emergence from his doldrums.

Inspired by the neighbor's parrot, Dmitri had a brainstorm about show-casing his birds' vocal talents as a school science fair project. After a year of training, the budgies had finally learned to speak the same two phrases in three different languages—English, Spanish, and French. During the fair's public session, his avian subjects' multi-lingual pronouncements and the title on his poster board, BIRD BRAIN TRANSLATORS, had delighted the attendees.

Dmitri's parakeets often brushed their beaks together in the fashion of kiss-ing. When performed to the squeaky-pitched accompaniment of *"Je t'aime, cheri,"* the love dance had proved irresistible to his prettiest and most popular sixth-grade classmate, Joanna Barnes. Since the precocious Joanna had never previously sought his attention, Dmitri willingly acquiesced to her request for an encore performance.

On the following afternoon, Dmitri had felt the tickling of "butterflies" in his stomach as he'd escorted the unusually chatty Joanna to his modest ranch home. With his parents at work and his brother still in school, Dmitri, the son of an ice cream man, served up hot fudge sundaes. In the ensuing sugar rush of a second helping, he'd meekly surrendered to Joanna's maternal play instincts while she'd force-fed him globs of goo and giggled unabashedly as they dribbled down his chin.

Hearing the sounds of budgies nearby, Joanna had announced she was ready for the show. Dmitri toweled his face, led her into the living room, and prepped his pets for their language lesson. As soon as the birds had commenced their French-kissing ritual, Joanna cooed a melodious refrain of *"Je t'aime, cheri, Je t'aime, cheri"* and danced around him in an ever-tightening circle. Inching closer and closer, Dmitri would forever remember the moment their noses touched, the sensory rush of Joanna's rosebud scent mingled with her warm cocoa breath, and her elfin grin as she poked his cheek and whispered, "You missed a spot." When Joanna licked the creamy residue from his cheek, his entire body quivered like Jell-O. In ultra-slow motion, her lips had glided across his face and down to his mouth, leaving a moist trail and a pleasurable tickling sensation in their wake. When her tongue grazed his lips, Dmitri had experienced a shocking revelation: language wasn't the only adaptation of the mouth's primary taste-sensing organ.

As it turned out, it was the first and last time Joanna would grace him with tactile affection, with the single exception, years later, of a polite handshake as his high school's homecoming queen. However, he had learned an important lesson on that long-lost afternoon. Science was more than just interesting. Science was way cool, yielding discoveries as unlikely as his first romantic encounter and the enduring, up-close vision of Joanna's dazzling smile.

Pleased that his feathered friends had performed so admirably, Dmitri had devised an even more ambitious project for the following year's fair. In an attempt to assess their mental abilities and rekindle Joanna's favor, he had taught them phrases for simple addition such as "one plus one is two," "one plus two is three," and "two plus two is four." Once they had mastered those sentences, he'd tested their responses to partial phrases such as "one plus one is" or just "two." For hours and days on end, he'd prompted them with these test questions but, to his disappointment, their replies were limited to mere mimicry.

Joanna's stinging rebuke on the night of the fair compounded his frustration. "It's fiendish," she had snarled. "You've turned your love birds into math geeks." After she'd stalked away, Dmitri had nearly cried, feeling like a failure.

Advised the next day of a grade of A+ and a special award for his endeavor, a perplexed Dmitri had queried his science teacher. Mr. Garcia's reply resonated throughout Dmitri's lifetime. "It's the nature of the scientific method. An experiment's success doesn't only depend on proving its hypothesis. What's most important is that the results should lead to an improved hypothesis. The questions you pose are just as important as the answers you seek."

His teacher's advice, however, had only partially helped to disentangle his jumbled feelings about the project and Joanna's reaction. Why was life so complicated, so unfair? In less than two years, he'd lost both his father and Joanna. The memory of his parakeets had always evoked strong emotions about life's bewildering stew of intertwined dualities: discovery and loss, success and failure, love and hate. He'd eventually learned to minimize the confusion, to build a firewall around his feelings, by immersing himself in schoolwork, hobbies, and sports.

With the passing years and the accumulation of more science awards, it was not surprising that, as a college freshman, Dmitri would pursue a joint engineering major in acoustics and signal processing. If he were more of a true believer than a seasoned skeptic, he would have sworn that the intersection of his world line with McPinsky's was preordained. After enrolling in SoCalSci's Graduate School of Engineering, his new mentor had not only rekindled his childhood fascination, he had inspired its transformation into near reverence for the mathematical and scientific foundations of speech and language.

There was no better example of this than in Dmitri's field of specialty, digital speech engineering. Digital signal engineers had developed mathematical formulas which, when coded into a mobile phone's microprocessor chips, transform the speaker's voice into a compressed string of binary digits—ones and zeros. These compression techniques enable the bandwidth-limited cell phone infrastructure to support increased levels of traffic for a fixed cost. Once this information flows through the network, the inverse set of transforms at the receiving phone reconstructs a facsimile of the speaker's voice. The quality of the resynthesized voice, he had learned, is amazingly good enough to convince most mobile phone users of the speaker's authenticity.

Dmitri had been blown away by his first glimpse of the international voice coding standard, called a "speech codec," used in the early cell phones. As thick as a small phone book, it contained pages of complicated equations, codebooks, and sophisticated detectors of periodicity and randomness, all to determine the shape of the speaker's vocal tract, the vibrations of their vocal chords, and most importantly, to capture the essence of personality in the medium of sound.

Nothing, he had thought, could be more compelling than to reduce the pitch and timbre of spoken words to their primitive mathematical elements as dictated by signal theory, to reconstruct them according to the same rules, and to hear the results: the immediacy and poignancy of a human voice. Thanks to his mentor's inspiration, the realization that speech, the acoustic vessel that conveys our thoughts, emotions, and identities, could figuratively be dissected into little pieces and then reconstituted into the reanimation of the original utterance was a moment of satori.

Dmitri had experienced this revelation first hand, many years ago, during a college summer internship. He'd been hired by a Fortune 500 cell phone manufacturer to test the voice quality of their product subject to a variety of challenging situations, such as noisy acoustic and electronic environments, networks saturated by high volumes of traffic, and even for speakers with pronounced accents. Remembering the emotional impact of hearing his father's voice when watching old videos, he'd fed a precious family recording into a computer simulation of the company's speech codec prototype. He wasn't at all surprised that the program's resynthesized version, a mathematical abstraction of his father lovingly calling out to his mother, "Sylvia, honey," still held the power to move him to tears.

With the passage of years, McPinsky's challenge had set Dmitri upon a path which ultimately led to PICES, Chris Gorman, and Melanie. His life had done a full circle, and all the significant threads had comingled. His world now encompassed a convergent mix of sounds—the sounds of language, the sounds of songs, and tragically the sounds that kill. Thinking about tomorrow's hope for a breakthrough, the familiar tingling sensation returned.

Eureka, Eureka

SoCalSci University, Los Angeles, California—two days later

"GIVE IT UP, pal. Get some rest." Dmitri's voice was hoarse with fatigue, his tone apologetic. "Your face looks like a slept-in suit."

"Your eyes look like Bloody Mary's." Greg stroked his face, measuring the lengthening stubble for the twentieth time. "It's just no use. We've scoured every second of the data in all three of the recordings. Just the random circular loops and that single bull's-eye in the Maui data. There's nothing at all in the other two recordings, just burbles and bleeps. No interesting shapes or patterns."

"And I was hoping for more instances of inflection points where the symbols might be likely. The humpbacks guard their secrets well." Dmitri's pale face wore an amused grin. "Never say die. I'll ask Gorman for more data."

Greg's lips sputtered like a motorboat. "Just label me a skeptic."

It was late afternoon, and Greg and Dmitri had toiled for two sixteen-hour days in SoCalSci's Signal Processing Lab investigating the whale song data. With no breakthrough in sight, Seema and Andrew had resumed their own research projects. Dmitri had occasionally excused himself to attend office hours and meetings while Greg, who had no other commitments, spent the entire time in the lab. They'd experienced fleeting moments of inspiration, only to be disappointed as the mirage of discovery evaporated into the recesses of the LCD monitor.

Greg counted the empty cans of Red Bull strewn across the desk. "I'm done. I need a shower and a quickie nap. Got a big date with Michelle tonight."

"Go for it, pal. I'm late for my 4 p.m. lecture. We'll talk tomorrow." Dmitri vanished through the double doors.

After the drive home, Greg entered his sparsely furnished bachelor flat. He checked his voicemail, changed out of his jeans, and slipped into his favorite garment—a silk, "thousand cranes" motif, jujitsu kimono he'd acquired on a recent trip to a Japanese university. He completed his daily regimen of yoga exercises and then sought relief in the shower. As he lathered up, he tried to shift his attention to the pleasant prospect of his date. Yet he couldn't shed the suspicion he had glimpsed a fatigue-masked clue lurking somewhere in the song data.

Greg's most creative thinking sometimes occurred while luxuriating in a shower, as the pulsations of liquid heat stimulated his nervous system. He had surmised that the tactile white noise induced alpha brainwaves, those resonant frequencies revered by mystics who believe their rhythmic contractions birth visionary moments. Now, thoroughly relaxed by the cascading spray, he dreamily pictured the stream of water droplets morphing into a helical pattern of sparkling bubbles rising to the surface of the ocean. Some of those bubbles looked vaguely like the whale song circular patterns and shimmered more brightly than others. He imagined a constellation's pinpoints of starfire rising toward the zenith of the night sky. When the parade of stars burst through the water's surface like a fountain of supernovas, his conscious mind was jolted by a revelation.

"Eureka!"

He exited the shower, toweled himself dry, and phoned his date to say he would likely be late. He donned a sweat suit, grabbed his wallet and keys, and dashed out the front door. In fifteen minutes he was back in the lab, typing commands into the Speakeasy computer workstation.

Since Speakeasy's user interface had been designed for interactive sessions, the GUI featured several options for displaying the data. In order to prevent screen clutter for the streaming whale song data, Andrew had changed the default setting to refresh the display every thirty seconds. Greg disabled the setting so none of the symbols would be erased. This would allow him to observe if the symbols were correlated over a longer period of time, something he'd not done earlier.

He cued the Speakeasy to the beginning of the section of ring-like figures. Despite his anticipation, nothing noteworthy appeared during the initial phase of the analysis. His disappointment grew as these new observations only confirmed his earlier finding: the random arrangement of the circular shapes, distributed uniformly, throughout all regions of the plot.

As he stared at the screen, his heart started to pound. A pattern began to emerge. For the first time, he noted that symbols were sometimes "drawn" in a clockwise direction and at other times, counterclockwise. Subsequent symbols eventually appeared in clusters, their positioning limited to specific regions of the tone-pair frequency space. Their placement also seemed correlated with the location of the preceding symbol.

"Could it possibly be?" he whispered. He snatched his mobile phone and punched in the speed-dial code for a math colleague. Despite the late afternoon hour, Joel Spelvin answered.

"Hi, Joel. Greg here. I'm trying to solve an interesting problem, and I need a specialist. I hate to bother you on such short notice, but can you meet me in the Engineering Signal Processing Lab?" As was his habit, he maxed out the handset's volume control setting.

"Sure," replied Spelvin, "but you're going to owe me a dinner."

Greg pressed the phone tightly to his ear. "Absolutely, pal, but not tonight. Don't forget to bring your laptop." While he waited, he silenced the room's loudspeakers so Spelvin wouldn't be distracted by the whale songs.

The graying mathematician arrived ten minutes later. "What's up?" he asked as he booted up his laptop.

Greg replayed the Speakeasy video while he summarized the nature of the problem, deliberately omitting any references to the source of the data. They worked in tandem to transfer the data coordinates of the circular figures from the Speakeasy program to Spelvin's laptop.

Ten minutes later, Spelvin ceremoniously waved a hand and poked the ENTER key. "The correlation analysis program should be completed in just a few seconds. Ah, there are the results." He traced his fingertips across the contours of the plots of some squiggly lines that the application had painted onto the display. "Just as you hypothesized, it's a classic correlation profile in both space and time coordinates. Initially the data is randomized. Eventually, however, both the auto- and cross-correlation coefficients monotonically increase through a transitional phase until the symbol-location profiles asymptotically approach 100% correlation. By the way, Greg, what's the nature of the data we're examining here?"

Greg jumped up from the chair. As he rushed toward the lab's exit doors, he shouted back at Spelvin, "Joel, just hang in there while I go fetch Dmitri!" He bolted through the double doors.

Lacking the patience to wait a few seconds for an elevator, Greg raced up the three flights of stairs and sprinted down the empty hall to the front door of lecture room 300. Pausing to catch his breath, he peered through the peephole window, and saw Dmitri lecturing at the whiteboard. Greg knocked on the door, cracked it open a bit, and waved. Dmitri eyed his colleague with a quizzical expression. Greg pointed at the wall clock and then, with a slashing motion, waved an index finger across his throat. Dmitri responded immediately. He surprised his students, copying their next homework assignment onto the board and dismissing them ten minutes early.

After the last of the students had filed out into the hall, Greg approached his colleague. "I can see from your expression you're annoyed, and I don't blame you."

"It's more like perplexed. What's this all about? I thought you'd gone home for your date."

"You'd better come with me. Spelvin is waiting for us in your lab."

Dmitri sighed. "But Joel Spelvin's a game theorist. Why would he be involved?"

"Because it turns out we needed to look not just at the shapes themselves."

"Huh?"

"It's really about the relationship *between* the symbols, Spelvin's specialty. Brace yourself, pal. You're not gonna believe it."

"Believe what?" Dmitri fidgeted while he waited for an answer. "Tell me already."

"It's . . . a . . . game." Greg pronounced each word, incredulously, with equal emphasis.

"A game?"

Greg grasped him by the shoulders and shook him gently. "It's the bloody whales. They're playing a game!"

Dmitri stared at the ceiling. "It's not possible."

Greg held his friend's arm and led him to the door. Dmitri's later recollection of the subsequent events was vague. He barely remembered the trip back to the lab.

Spelvin was flipping a coin into the air when the pair rushed through the doors. "Okay, gentlemen. Please keep me in suspense no longer. What's the significance of the data I've been number crunching?"

Greg glided over to the computer console and turned up the speaker volume. The hypnotic song of a humpback whale reverberated throughout the room.

Spelvin crossed his arms. "Greg," he said, "it's awfully kind of you to entertain me with elevator Muzak, but I don't believe you've answered my question."

Dmitri's laugh was maniacal. Spelvin frowned and stared, openmouthed, as Dmitri convulsed with laughter. When Dmitri calmed himself enough to speak, he said, "Joel, this is Greg's inimitable way of saying that you're actually listening to the data right now."

Spelvin sounded annoyed. "Give me a break, guys. I don't believe its April first, so what's the gag here? All I know is that the results of the data I just analyzed fit the statistical profile of the strategy employed in a classic, two-player board game."

Dmitri approached Spelvin and murmured, "Please elaborate."

"Think of games like checkers, chess, or Go," Spelvin answered. "There's very little correlation at the beginning because players are cautious, not wanting to reveal their strategy. The initial moves appear random and are used to progress to empty spaces of the board to prepare for attack. Inevitably, there's a transition period of gradual engagement marked by an increasing correlation between the attacker and defender. Finally, when the attack and defense begin in earnest, moves are highly correlated in space and with respect to the attackers' and defenders' preceding moves. So, are you saying I just confirmed that this matches the correlation profile of data from a whale song?"

"I'll show you." Greg fiddled with the computer. "I'll rewind to the beginning of the recording. Now listen and watch carefully." He waited a while. "Don't you see? The ring-shaped symbols plotted on the display, the data we just transferred to your laptop, correspond to the sounds we're listening to!"

The three men stared at one another. After another full minute of silence, Dmitri slid open the top drawer of a filing cabinet and removed a bottle of Scotch and three crystal tumblers. "Gentlemen, join me in a toast."

Spelvin stammered, "But, but—"

"'But, but—' nothing," insisted Dmitri. "I'm as flabbergasted as you are, but I can say with a hundred percent confidence we should pause to celebrate." He poured the drinks. Raising their glasses in a toast, he announced, "The genie's out of the bottle."

Greg slapped the side of his head. "Ouch. I forgot I have a date with Michelle tonight."

"And I need to phone Seema and Andrew to share the news," said Dmitri. "Let's meet tomorrow in the conference room at 9 a.m. sharp. Oh, and by the way, let's keep this development under wraps for now."

Spelvin gasped, "But how—"

"Tut-tut, Joel," Dmitri interrupted. "I believe you need to loosen up with another drink." With a Cheshire Cat grin, he refilled Joel Spelvin's glass.

MEETING OF THE MINDS

SoCalSci Department of Engineering, Main Conference Room—the next morning

THE BRACING AROMA of French Roast permeated the air, and exhilaration tinged by a halo of exhaustion charged the atmosphere of the SoCalSci Department of Engineering conference room. Less than twenty-four hours had elapsed since the electrifying discovery.

The three professors huddled together in the center of the long, oval-ended conference table dominating the walnut-paneled room. Spelvin appeared pensive while Dmitri chatted with Greg. Facing them from the opposite side of the table, Seema and Andrew sipped the coffee Dmitri had brewed expressly for the occasion.

Dmitri peered at his wristwatch. "I want to thank all of you for being on time. I phoned Seema and Andrew last night to brief them about our findings."

"When Dr. Dmitri phoned me with the news, I thought he was pulling my leg. Like a sorority initiation ritual." Seema sounded giddy.

"I'm embarrassed to admit I felt the same way." Spelvin paused. He flipped a quarter into the air, swiveled his chair, and caught it behind his back to scattered applause. "My logical mind is screaming it can't be true. Any minute now, I'm expecting to wake up from this dream."

"Look," said Dmitri. "Even I need someone to pinch me, but we really need to come to grips with the situation. Joel, how about a recap of last night's session?"

Spelvin extricated his gangly frame from the chair and sauntered up to the whiteboard hanging from the wall behind Dmitri's chair. His Dilbert-like appearance and techie fashion statement—Coke-bottle glasses and a rumpled, white shirt with a plastic pen holder clipped to the front pocket—was no doubt responsible for the amused expressions of Dmitri's students.

Spelvin proceeded to draw an x,y plot containing two curves. "For the dataset I analyzed, the bottom plot is the correlation profile for the spatial coordinate, and the top curve is the correlation profile of the spatial coordinate with respect to the previous symbol. The profiles derived from the whale song data are nearly identical to the profiles that characterize a classic two-player board game. Are there any questions?"

Spelvin's query was greeted by stunned silence. What could anyone say, thought Dmitri? The arc of their careers and their lives had collided head-on with the perplexing proposition that they'd decrypted a game in the middle of a whale song. This was uncharted territory. Knowing his students needed more background information, Dmitri decided to jump-start the discussion.

"Last night after Greg left, Joel and I worked until midnight to examine the data with a fine-tooth comb. The more we learn, the more certain we are that this is indeed a game."

Greg's face appeared puffy. He mumbled, "Sorry, I'm a bit hung over after a late night celebration with Michelle, but the suspense is killing me. What else did you discover?"

"In the beginning of the alleged game," Spelvin said, "we confirmed that the circular symbols were drawn in an alternating clockwise and counterclockwise fashion."

"As if the two players were identified by the direction of the spin," added Dmitri.

"You say it's a classic two-player board game. So where's the board?" asked Seema.

"Ah," answered Dmitri. "To quote Churchill: 'That's a riddle wrapped in a mystery inside an enigma.' However, the most likely conclusion is that the board is some kind of a template synthesized in the auditory processing region of the whales' brains. Their minds draw and memorize the symbols acoustically. It's similar to the way we visualize the Speakeasy word grams in the frequency domain on our computer monitors."

Andrew raised his arms chest high. "Look ma, no hands. Want to play a board game? Then let's just use the one inside our heads." He was greeted by groans.

"As incredible as that sounds, it's not far from the truth," interjected Dmitri. "However, we need to wrap our minds around the ultra-precise control required to generate and image these acoustic shapes. It's almost unbelievable that—"

"And think about the memory capacity required to retain the image of all the symbols generated during the game," interrupted Greg. "Like chess masters who can play single or multiple opponents while blindfolded."

Spelvin frowned. "Greg, your notion strains the bounds of credulity. We'd better be certain we're not diving off the deep end."

"Greg's chess-master metaphor is not implausible," Dmitri responded. "The human brain is hardwired to process twenty times more visual- than sound-based information. John Lilly's dolphin communication experiments confirmed the cetaceans process twenty times more audio information than visual. QED: Their big brains have evolved to process sound with the same level of sophistication as our brains have evolved to process images. Human chess masters play blindfolded as a challenging novelty. Our fingerless cetacean friends have no choice but to image a version of the game board in the frequency portion of their brain's audio processing region. Oh, and by the way, Joel, tell everyone about our other breakthrough observation."

"Oh, yeah, I forgot to mention that the signature three-concentric-circle, bull's-eye pattern occurred at the point in the profile corresponding to the end of the game."

"Checkmate," Dmitri exclaimed triumphantly.

"So what kind of a game is it?" asked Seema.

"Well, once you realize you're looking at a two-player game format, the patterns look eerily similar to the strategy of the game called Dots and Boxes," answered Dmitri.

"I used to play that with my kid brother," Andrew grinned. "I didn't realize it was such a whale of a game." His remark elicited another chorus of groans.

"I may know this game. How is it played?" asked Seema.

On the whiteboard, Dmitri drew a diagram depicting the principles of the Dots and Boxes game. "Starting with an empty grid of dots, players take turns adding a single horizontal or vertical line between two adjacent dots. A player who completes the fourth side of a box earns one point and takes another turn. The game ends when no more lines can be placed. The winner of the game is the player with the most points. Beginners play more or less at random until all the remaining boxes are joined together into chains of varying lengths. If you're not careful, a bad move can give an opponent the opportunity to build a long chain." He drew an example of boxes in a chain.

"Yes, that's the game I'm familiar with," replied Seema. "So in the whale's version, the circular squiggles are the dots, and they are acoustically drawn onto an imaginary grid of dots?"

"And in their version of the game, they don't draw any lines," interjected Greg. "Instead, a box is completed when all four corners on the imaginary grid are occupied by their sound-generated symbols."

"Remember, we're not literally saying the grid is square or rectangular," replied Spelvin. "Only that we measure a geometric correlation between the placement of the symbols. Human versions of the game are played on triangular and hexagonal grids. There's also a variation in Bolivia played on an Incan Cross grid. Think about how challenging *that* would be."

"Joel, your knowledge never ceases to amaze me," replied Dmitri. "So, everyone, according to Joel's calculations, and by our own biased visual interpretation of the Speakeasy plot, we aren't certain they're literally playing Dots and Boxes. Just that it's game-like and similar."

Joel addressed Dmitri's graduate students. "Game-like in that we measure maximum randomness at the beginning, followed by a series of increasingly correlated maneuvers," he explained. "I have to admit I was so shocked by the initial implications of the patterns, I spent half the night investigating other alternatives."

Dmitri laughed. "Despite your cynicism, Joel, I knew you couldn't resist the challenge."

Spelvin arched his thin lips into a sheepish grin. "Of course, you're all familiar with the Nobel Prize-winning game theorist, John Nash."

"Yeah," replied Greg, "*A Beautiful Mind*. A stimulating portrayal of the fine line separating genius from madness in brilliant mathematicians, present company excluded." He cocked his hat at a sideways angle.

"Of course," said Dmitri, suppressing a grin.

"I loved the movie." Seema sighed. "Especially with Russell Crowe as Nash."

"Such credible character casting," replied Andrew. "Gladiator morphs into a brilliant, bumbling mathematician. If there's ever a movie based on *A Brief History of Time,* I expect the director to cast Brad Pitt as Stephen Hawking squawking about black holes."

The room erupted with laughter.

"Okay, folks, let's get back to business," interrupted Dmitri. "Joel, you were saying . . ."

Spelvin flipped another coin. "Nash's theories were instrumental in the field of economics. Nash himself was inspired by the first great game theorist of the twentieth century, the German Ernst Zermelo. In 1913, Zermelo's theorem proved that, for every two-player game with clearly defined rules, a winning strategy always exists for one of the players, as long as both players know all the preceding moves. To understand this theorem, it's helpful to illustrate how the moves of the two-player game correspond to a tree structure with many branches." He began to draw a branching structure on the whiteboard. "Each branching path in the tree corresponds to the range of options available on the player's next move, as defined by the rules. The theorem applies to games like tic-tac-toe, checkers, and even to chess."

Dmitri pointed at the whiteboard. "So, according to the theorem, a computer like Deep Blue should always win a game of chess when pitted against a human. Some of us know, however, that the 1997 world champion won a few of those games."

"Touché, Dr. Dmitri," exclaimed Spelvin. "Yes, according to Zermelo's theorem, a computer should be able to trace through all of the alternative paths to converge upon the optimal winning path. However, a tree structure for the game of chess would have on the order of 10^{120} branches to consider. In comparison, according to the Standard Model of physics, there are only 10^{80} particles in the known universe."

"Okay, Joel," said Greg, "so even the universe's most powerful supercomputer can't play the perfect game of chess. How did you apply Zermelo's theorem to the whale song data analysis?"

"I just assumed, a-priori, that the rules of the game were the same as for Dots and Boxes. I programmed my laptop to build a set of tree structures based upon the actual whale song symbol locations. I then constructed an alternative set of trees based upon the current position in the actual game and generated the next set of branches according to the rules for Dots and Boxes." Spelvin scribbled two sets of tree structures, appearing side by side, onto the whiteboard. "I then compared the theoretical best solution tree to the tree corresponding to the actual moves in their game and, bingo, I calculated with 85% confidence that it's Dots and Boxes."

"Amazing!" Andrew shook his head.

Although both Seema's and Andrew's faces were wan with fatigue, Dmitri saw their mouths agape, dazzled just as he was by Spelvin's expertise and findings. "That's pretty impressive, Joel. It confirms your initial correlation measurements."

The hyper Spelvin drummed his fingers to his temple. "It's highly suggestive but still not definitive enough to publish. We need more conclusive proof."

"If this is indeed the type of game we suspect it might be, we have a duty as scientists to confirm the discovery," said Dmitri. "If these beings participate in games as a form of social engagement, that's irrefutable evidence of a highly evolved intellect. Since the game requires a prodigious memory and precise control to generate the game-symbol frequencies, it's probable they've adapted the use of acoustical symbols to other forms of communication."

Seema leaned forward in her chair and peered at Dmitri, her eyes wider than he'd ever seen.

"Dmitri, buddy, you're preaching to the choir." Greg laughed. "Where do we go from here?"

"I have a plan for obtaining the irrefutable proof that Joel demands."

Spelvin responded with crossed arms. "And how do you propose to do that?"

Dmitri paused for a few seconds, the glimmer of his smile gradually growing more playful. "We challenge them to a match, of course."

The room exploded in a tumult of gasps and groans.

"No, really." Dmitri pounded the table. "I've already given this some thought. During our recent trip to Maui, Greg and I discussed this issue with Chris Gorman. He wanted to be informed if we found new evidence about language in the songs. Once we brief him, I'm confident he'll cooperate in a follow-up experiment in Hawaiian waters, particularly since whales are still dying in Maui."

"What kind of experiment are you proposing?" Andrew asked.

Dmitri replied without hesitation. "We configure a research vessel with underwater hydrophones and speakers. Given their ongoing whale song recording program, Gorman's institute probably has the equipment. We sample the game portion of the sound track of our whale song recording and rebroadcast the symbols, one at a time. We select the particular frequencies that are appropriate to the context of the game."

Spelvin grimaced. "Problem number one: How do we entice a forty-ton grandmaster to sit down for a game with a research vessel? Problem number two: How do we ensure that the game develops according to the strategy we're hypothesizing?"

Spelvin clenched his arms to his chest, telling Dmitri he'd need to be more convincing. "Let me address your first challenge, Joel. Since we would rebroadcast recorded samples of actual Maui whale vocalizations, they are more likely to respond."

"Right," said Andrew. "They'd think it's one of their own that's communicating."

"That could be a problem," said Greg. "Our current knowledge is based upon the few symbols whose frequency combinations we discovered in the only game in our possession."

"Okay then." Dmitri paused and gulped some coffee. "We can sample the current data and then build a special synthesizer that generates the tone pairs corresponding to any possible symbol in the game."

"Like a musician's sampling keyboard, a whale synthesizer." Seema placed her hands on the table and mimed a keyboard solo. "That's right up my alley. It also reminds me of my music professor's definition of music as 'sound-sculpted time.' The whales are using sound-sculpted time to represent images in space—frequency space, that is."

"That's an interesting analogy, Seema." Dmitri's fingers appeared to tap out a tune. "Okay, so assuming we have a synthesizer of prerecorded samples that sound whale-like, we would broadcast a sequence of tones every thirty seconds, corresponding to the random locations on the game board. If we're fortunate enough to detect a cetacean response, then that brings us to Joel's second challenge."

"Wait a second," interrupted Spelvin. "How do we recognize an appropriate response on a boat in the middle of the ocean?"

"Sorry if I've skipped over the details about the setup, but my mind is racing ahead. Our team will provide a PC workstation, high-performance laptops, and a special version of the Speakeasy program for doing the audio-to-video conversion of any acoustic response. We'll have the same capabilities for viewing the data as we did last night in the Signal Processing Lab. A word gram display of the symbols in frequency space."

"I understand." Spelvin maintained a grudging tone. "But what about my second challenge? What's our plan for playing the game? I'm assuming we implement the strategy for that type of game and, if we're right and we're lucky, they might even respond."

"Yes, and depending upon the location of their responses on the Speakeasy frequency plot, we'd select our next symbol from Seema's palette of synthesized tones." Dmitri nodded at Andrew. "I'd like you to code a script and an application that links with Speakeasy and automates the procedure Joel just outlined."

"No problem, boss. Interspecies videogames are my specialty. Maybe I could get a patent and market it to Sony."

Seema shook her head. "Remember to donate your profits to the Save the Whales Foundation, Mr. Entrepreneur."

"Hey!" Greg, who'd been reclining in his chair, suddenly sat upright. "I just thought about another embellishment. Just as the deaf Speakeasy subjects have visual feedback of their own vocalizations, why don't we offer the humpbacks a similar light show?"

Greg's proposal evoked blank expressions until Seema posed the question on everybody's mind. "How do we convert a research vessel into a floating movie theater?"

"Dmitri, don't you remember our Molokini snorkeling trip? The boat had a glass bottom for viewing the tropical fish."

Dmitri's eyes glimmered. "That's brilliant, Greg! We feed the Speakeasy images to a large, flatscreen monitor fastened to the glass and pointing down into the water."

"You took the words right out of my mouth," replied Greg. "There's one small problem, however. I read somewhere that a humpback's eyes are spherically shaped, like a fisheye lens. We won't know if the images on the display will appear distorted to them."

"Everybody slow down," interjected Spelvin. "We're possibly sliding down a very slippery slope. What about the *Star Trek* Prime Directive: Do not interfere with alien cultures. Who knows how the whales would react to bright, flashing lights, especially to shapes that dance to the frequencies of their own vocalizations?"

"God forbid," chimed Seema. "I remember an incident in Japan a few years ago. While children watched an episode of the *Pokémon* cartoon series, some had epileptic seizures triggered by rapidly flickering images of a particular frequency. Since we have no clue about humpback brain physiology, we'd better proceed cautiously or else we could become unwitting villains."

"The ACLU would take that case in a heartbeat," said Andrew.

"I agree," replied Dmitri. "We would only activate the external visual display after assessing the progress of the acoustic experiment." After a long pause, he stood and yawned. "Let's take our ten-minute break."

"It's getting too exciting to stop now," said Andrew.

Everybody seconded the sentiment.

"Okay," said Dmitri, sitting back down. "Greg, I'm reminded of Melanie's tutorial in the Maui Speech Lab. She described the two modes of symbols used in written language: the pictorial form, like the Chinese ideograms, and the representational form, such as the characters of the alphabet. Intelligent beings with no physical capacity to communicate in the written format would likely adapt their acoustic symbols to express both modes, don't you think?"

"Like the whale game where the symbols represent the placement of pieces on a game board," added Andrew.

"Yes," said Greg. "In hindsight, it makes so much sense that intelligent creatures, who've developed the symbols of language, would utilize those symbols in the playing of games. Playful behavior in mammalian species serves the dual purpose of social interaction and training for activities crucial to their survival."

"I get goose bumps thinking about this cryptic message." Seema's soulful eyes panned Dmitri and Greg. "The clues to their intelligence have been waiting to be discovered for possibly thousands, maybe even millions of years. It wasn't until humans developed a technologically advanced society that we became capable of interpreting the purpose of their vocalizations. I can't believe we're the beneficiaries of this golden opportunity."

Dmitri felt a teacher's sense of pride. "I agree, and I couldn't have stated it more eloquently." Seema's big smile pleased him. "But," he shook his index finger, "we have to proceed carefully. There's going to be major resistance to the implications of our proposed discovery."

"Think about the public reaction," said Greg. "The confirmation of the game hypothesis could be viewed as a grave threat to belief systems that advocate the primacy of our species."

"Like Creationists and Luddites," Andrew nodded.

Dmitri sighed. "It's not only the conservatives and fundamentalists. Don't underestimate the pushback from rational institutions, maybe even here at SoCalSci."

Dmitri's comment momentarily stifled the conversation, reminding them of the events three years earlier when McPinsky had vacated the premises in a torrent of controversy.

Spelvin cleared his throat. "Right, we can't jump the gun just yet, Dmitri. We'd be crawling out on a very thin limb to publish this 'game' hypothesis so soon. I'd like to see more occurrences of this data profile in other recordings before submitting it to an external review."

"Joel, I agree," replied Dmitri. "Let's take a twofold approach. Initially, I'll contact Gorman at PICES and ask for more humpback recordings. Since our discovery is linked to the Maui population, let's restrict our investigation to the Maui song data and to Alaskan recordings during the winter feeding cycle. At the right moment, we'll inform Gorman we've identified unique acoustic patterns which could be interpreted as linguistic symbols and request his assistance for experimental confirmation. We'd need PICES collaboration to provide and outfit a vessel to conduct the experiment in Hawaiian waters. Let's not be too specific about the nature of the data, though—that it's likely a game. We don't want to give them any reason to think they'd be participating in a wild goose chase."

"What about the software and equipment?" inquired Greg.

"Like I said, we'll pack a workstation for the real-time Speakeasy analysis and two or three laptops for other functions. Until now, we've used Melanie's proprietary version here in the lab. Now that we're progressing into a more public domain of research, I want Andrew and Seema to code our own generic version of Speakeasy."

"That's a heck of a tough task for such a short time frame, boss."

"Our version can be greatly simplified," he said, trying to convey reassurance. "The primary requirement is a Fourier frequency analysis and a center frequency calculation of the two primary resonance peaks. We don't need all of the other phoneme-specific tasks for identifying consonants and vowels."

"Got it," replied Andrew. "For my thesis work, I'm using a graphics routine that plots both two- and three-dimensional data, so I'll port that over to our new Speakeasy system to work in either 2D or 3D coordinates."

"Thanks, Andrew. What about you, Seema? Can you develop a simple synthesizer program that generates the acoustic version of the circular symbols, given any two input frequencies?"

"Absolutely, and to be consistent with Andrew's interface, mine will also accept and generate 2D or 3D data. I'll prototype it using Matlab and then translate the source code to a C++ app."

"Sounds good. Oh, Andrew, let's also incorporate Joel's correlation-analysis codes into your version of Speakeasy so that—"

"—so that we can instantaneously assess the correlation of each new symbol to the previous one to confirm that they're actually playing a game. I'm with you, boss."

"Dmitri, you lucky dog," said Greg. "I wish I had the same rapport with my grad students. But I bet yours don't know you've fabricated this entire project so you can get back to Maui to see your new girlfriend."

Despite the glances between Andrew and Seema, Dmitri looked at Greg with an unusually peaceful smile. "Actually, Melanie could be quite useful aboard the research vessel, conducting an experiment that resembles a Speakeasy session."

"Oh, and don't forget we'll need SoCalSci administrators to approve the time and funding for the enterprise," Greg said. "If I were you, I'd contact the Dean of Engineering and arrange a meeting, the sooner the better."

"That's a great suggestion."

"God, I hope this doesn't backfire on you, dude. The dean's still steamed about his past pitched battles with McPinsky. Now, along comes Dmitri to wave the red flag of the McPinsky Challenge in his face."

"There's no turning back now, Greg. Speaking of the devil, it wouldn't hurt to have the support of other allies. Excuse me, ladies and gentlemen. I believe I'm about to place a call to my old advisor."

Dmitri's Hammer

SoCalSci University, Los Angeles, California—later that day

"GREETINGS, PROFESSOR. I'M sorry it's been so long since we last spoke, but I have some special news I want to share with you." Dmitri felt nearly as nervous as the first time he'd introduced himself to the famed McPinsky. Although they had exchanged pleasantries via the occasional email, it had been nearly a year since he had last spoken with his old college mentor and graduate advisor.

"Dmitri, my boy, how are you?"

"Better than ever, Professor."

Hearing his professor's avuncular voice on his office speakerphone brought back many, mostly pleasant, memories. As he had begun to tell Melanie, Dmitri had been only nine years old when his father had perished in a truck accident. The paternal void had been partially filled during his college years with the flowering of a most simpatico relationship. McPinsky had literally saved him during his first semester of engineering graduate school following a disastrous summer internship. Having been bullied and harassed by his manager at a prominent Northern California high-tech company, he had battled a motivational crisis and a lingering depression. He had been on the verge of dropping out of SoCalSci when his academic advisor, Professor Theodosius McPinsky, had emerged as a mentor and role model. His paternal guidance had been the tonic for Dmitri's rejuvenation. In just three years, Dmitri had earned a doctoral degree and, after a brief, post-doctoral research appointment, had been offered a faculty position in the same department and university as his idol.

For the past fifteen years, the veteran iconoclast and the precocious protégé had been linked together both intellectually and philosophically. McPinsky had infused Dmitri's life with a sense of purpose that transcended academic and professional goals. Dmitri felt nurtured in the Petri dish of McPinsky's assertion that information theory is the basis of the fundamental laws of the universe and the driving force in nature. McPinsky's declaration that the potential for transformational discovery requires the courage to pose provocative questions—questions that dare to challenge the paradigms of the prevailing world view—had stirred his passion for science.

McPinsky's legendary tenure at SoCalSci, following an early PhD from the same institution, had generated numerous awards and patents in his chosen field of communications engineering. During those years of professional success, McPinsky had begun to see a deep pattern emerging from his investigations. These insights had culminated in the current passionate pursuit of the Unified Field Theory of Everything, based on a new Conservation of Information principle. For him, now, it was all about the big picture: the fundamental laws of nature had to explain the necessary and sufficient conditions for the evolution of all systems, from atoms to big-brained organisms.

McPinsky's controversial teachings and participation in the annual *Symposium on New Physics, Cosmology, and Consciousness* had provoked a backlash from the more conservative members of the SoCalSci faculty and administration. Dmitri felt, however, that the evangelical counter reaction to McPinsky's interspecies communication proposals had precipitated his professor's professional coup de grâce. He knew that even a whiff of public controversy was frowned upon by the elite of the university's power structure. He had therefore not been surprised when, shortly after the proposals, a campus-wide, rumor-mongering campaign had subjected his mentor to veiled insults and outright ridicule.

Now, nearly three years later, Dmitri still felt the sting of those painful events. Although McPinsky's position had been secured by tenure, the proud professor had apparently lost the stomach for the steady diet of unsavory slights dished out by campus critics. To the consternation of his supporters, including Dmitri, the illustrious professor had decided to pack his bags and accept an emeritus position from an Ivy League school more tolerant of its progressive faculty members. Dmitri now believed that, if the preliminary discovery about the whales could be verified, McPinsky's reputation at SoCalSci and around the world would flourish once again.

"How are my old colleagues at SoCalSci?" McPinsky's voice filled Dmitri's office. "I hope the dean is of uncommonly good cheer."

Dmitri relished the familiar strains of McPinsky's wry sarcasm. He had long surmised that his mentor's idiosyncratic, sometimes lacerating, wit must have been inherited from his emigrant parents. After all, decades before the days of hyphenated names, his Russian-Jewish father, Isadore Pinsky, and Scottish mother, Tillie McBloom, had changed their surname to the whimsical McPinsky during the McCarthy anti-communist era of "Better dead than Red" hysteria.

"Those old fuddy-duddies," replied Dmitri. "No matter what they said about you, I can tell they're still shocked by your departure. Of course, the rest of us miss you terribly."

He knew about McPinsky's disappointment in students desiring only an expeditious path to an advanced degree. Only a few wanted to achieve something more exceptional from their relationship with him. Of those, Dmitri had been singularly receptive to McPinsky's credo: "If we are to truly appreciate the world of wonder we inhabit, we must link our awareness of our daily experiences with an understanding of nature's deep, underlying principles."

McPinsky had expected no less from his students then he did from himself, and Dmitri had not let him down. During the somber occasion of McPinsky's SoCalSci farewell party, he had taken Dmitri aside to confide his immense pride in his former student. He also said that Dmitri should never hesitate to contact him if he needed personal or professional support. Dmitri had cried tears of joy on the drive home, and he still remembered the occasion as the happiest moment of his adult life.

"So cut to the chase, dear boy. What's up?"

Dmitri sighed before he uttered the code words that would resonate with his mentor. "Professor, 'The sleeper has awakened.'"

The phrase was from Frank Herbert's science fiction novel, *Dune*. When the protagonist imbibed the sacred water of life, he awoke to cosmic consciousness and uttered, "Father, the sleeper has awakened." It was the son's response to his father's signature challenge phrase, "the sleeper must awaken" to new experiences and truths, which ritually concluded McPinsky's renowned end-of-term lecture.

After an interminable silence, McPinsky boomed, "Don't play games with me, son!"

Initially shaken by his mentor's tone, Dmitri found it reassuring to be addressed as "son" by this special man. Nevertheless, he was speechless. McPinsky finally filled the void. "I'm sorry. I trust you, but it's still quite a shock. After all these years, I was beginning to lose hope I would ever hear those words."

"Ironically, Professor, it's all about playing games. I think we've discovered something truly wonderful in the recording of a humpback whale song. It's still preliminary, but the mathematical analysis rings true. The whales are manipulating acoustically generated symbols, like phonemes, to implement the strategy of a two-player board game."

"You're fairly certain of this?"

"Two of our best mathematicians, Bono and Spelvin, have analyzed and reviewed the data and they're confident about the results." Dmitri briefly summarized the events leading up to the breakthrough. "And to think the tool so instrumental to our discovery is literally a souped-up videogame for deaf children!"

"Wow, wow, wow!" exclaimed McPinsky. "Bono and Spelvin are damn good and Spelvin is a game theory expert. So, it's true then, what I've always hoped for. The beginning of an interspecies dialogue. What a fantastic gift for my birthday."

"First things first, Professor. It's not like Klaatu's 'Take me to your leader' greeting after exiting the saucer he'd landed on the White House lawn. We still need to confirm our hypothesis."

"What's your plan?"

Hearing the excitement in his mentor's voice pleased Dmitri. "We challenge them to a game, of course. Choose black or white, please."

McPinsky chuckled. "Einstein was right, of course. God doesn't play dice. He plays checkers." They laughed heartily.

"Of course, in hindsight, it's all so logical," said the professor. "Intelligent creatures with no opposable thumbs . . . socialization coupled with the purely intellectual exercise of problem solving. But even a science fiction writer would be hard-pressed to imagine such a scenario. Bravo to you and your colleagues. This is *tremendulous*, Dmitri. I'll do whatever I can to assist your cause."

Dmitri forced himself to downplay his elation. "That's very generous, Professor. I would be honored if you conferenced into the meeting with the SoCalSci administrators to request funding for the experiment."

"Are you sure that's wise? These days, as you know too well, I'm not the most popular professor on the Left Coast."

"Maybe not, but you're the most persuasive wizard in the world of Muggles. No pun intended, but you're the grandmaster of the funding game. After Greenpeace, I feel pretty confident putting the fate of the humpbacks in your hands."

"Persuasion is one of the Dark Arts of wizardry, Master David Dmitri, and I've trained you well. How can I refuse such a compelling invitation?"

"Happy birthday, Professor."

THE SIX THUNDERCLAPS OF PROFESSOR McPINSKY

SoCalSci University, Los Angeles, California—two days later

IN DMITRI'S EXPERIENCE, video conferences in cyberspace, especially among scientific researchers and academic bureaucrats, were rather lackluster affairs. On this particular occasion, however, the noise-induced, flickering images on the three wraparound, high-definition-plasma big-screens augured the impending clash of high-voltage egos. The telepresence, videoconferencing technology simulated the participants as life-sized figures sitting around the same table. In fact, it was a bridge of light and sound spanning six time zones that instantaneously united Hawaii with California and New York.

Dmitri remembered with pride when he'd consulted in the design of the system's acoustic, echo-cancelling function. To estimate and kill the multiplicity of echoes bouncing off of walls and objects, he'd devised a suite of digital software filters that adapted, every ten milliseconds, to any room's time-varying frequency profile. Similar mathematical techniques were employed in noise-cancelling headphones. The task was further complicated by the non-linear paths of numerous feedback loops crisscrossing the product's multiple sets of microphones and loudspeakers. If not exorcised, the lingering ghosts of voices past could haunt the system with the spooky, earsplitting noise one hears when open mikes are positioned too close to loudspeakers.

Dmitri swiveled his chair in the SoCalSci Telepresence Conferencing Center and inadvertently bumped into the person sitting next to him, the Dean of Engineering and his immediate superior.

"Excuse me, Dean Wilson."

Wilson's genial expression made clear that he was not offended. The perfectly round lenses of his gold, wire-framed glasses projected an image of owlish wisdom. Wilson's tailored navy blue suit and red power tie reinforced his executive authority. Dmitri's senior colleagues had nicknamed him "McNamara," claiming he was the spitting image of the U.S. Defense Secretary under President Kennedy. Dean Wilson stood and assumed control of the meeting with a vigorous cough into his clenched fist.

"I've called this meeting at the behest of Associate Professor David Dmitri. He's requested funding for a collaborative effort between members of our department and the Pacific Institute for Cetacean Educational Studies, represented by their director, Mr. Christopher Gorman. Mr. Gorman's virtual presence is being beamed to us all the way from Maui."

The marine biologist waved greetings to those viewing his image.

"Sitting to my immediate right," Wilson continued, "is the chair of the university's research funding committee, Richard Prescott. Professor Dmitri, would you please summarize your proposal."

As Dmitri rose from his seat, his slim figure flashed simultaneously on the multiple video-conferencing displays. "Thank you, Dean Wilson." He nodded politely and extended an arm toward Greg, who sat next to him at the dark-mahogany-finished racetrack conference table. "Because he was instrumental in this discovery, I've asked my math department colleague, Dr. Gregory Bono, to join us. I've also invited Professor McPinsky of Ivy Tech. Inspired by his challenge to break the linguistic codes of other species, I recently launched a study of the spectrograms of humpback whale songs. We were looking for patterns of frequency information similar to our phonemes and words."

The cadence of Dmitri's voice conveyed excitement. "My team first examined time-lapse waterfall plots spanning a range of frequencies up to ten kilohertz." He remained standing and punctuated his talking points with a medley of hand gestures. "Our analysis suggested time-varying patterns similar to the phonemic transitions of human language. We then plotted the same information in a novel x,y coordinate system of the first two resonance peaks." Dmitri briefly described the Speakeasy speech therapy tool. "Using Speakeasy, we observed a sequence of interesting artifacts which made no sense, so I consulted Dr. Bono. After two days of analysis, he finally made the breakthrough."

"Wait a minute." Dean Wilson's tone expressed an implicit warning. "You're telling me that this is not the interesting but benign study you'd initially proposed? We thought you were comparing and contrasting whale songs among geographically dispersed humpback populations?"

Dmitri paused and met Wilson's icy blue gaze. "That was our original intention. However, we believe we've discovered mathematical evidence of the humpback's use of symbols in an advanced intellectual exercise. We've also determined that the humpback brain must possess a remarkable memory capacity for the acoustic generation and auditory imaging of these symbols. Our findings have been reviewed and vetted by two of our colleagues. In collaboration with Chris Gorman's PICES organization, we propose to confirm our findings experimentally. We'll equip a PICES research vessel and conduct the experiment off the coast of Maui."

Richard Prescott pushed away from the table and propelled up from his chair, startling the dean. "This quixotic proposal could tarnish the reputation of SoCalSci's Engineering Department. It could incite controversy among the university's largest donors, who hold rather traditional philosophical and religious beliefs." He appeared to be jousting with Dmitri, across the table, by jabbing the rapier of his index finger as if it were a weapon. He shifted his gaze, and stared directly at Gorman's virtual image. With increasing vehemence, he continued. "Mr. Gorman, aren't you afraid this Dr. Dolittle fantasy could jeopardize support from your own organization's donors and sponsors?"

Gorman hesitated. As Dmitri saw the signs of confusion—or was it fear?—in Gorman's eyes, he realized too late that he should have forewarned the PICES director about Prescott's bullying tactics.

Gorman cleared his throat, not once, but twice. "Our Institute's charter is nuts and bolts marine oceanographic research. Our initial collaboration with Dr. Dmitri was to study the patterns in whale songs . . ."

Dmitri heard the tentative intonation of Gorman's voice. He didn't sound anything like the take-charge executive he'd been in Maui. He stopped in mid-sentence and sipped from his water glass, then continued.

". . . to study the patterns in whale songs as an insight into the feeding, breeding, and migration behavior of humpbacks. Frankly, I was surprised when Dr. Dmitri informed me he had organized this meeting to discuss a much more ambitious proposal."

Dmitri was shocked. Gorman's waffling response seemed like a stunning reversal of his previous plea for a language breakthrough. Prescott had undoubtedly intimidated the marine biologist, possibly inflicting a fatal blow to the funding proposal. Dmitri, now seated, turned to Greg, whose expression reflected his own indignation.

"Mr. Gorman is rightfully concerned," said Prescott, his face turning red. "Funding a proposal of this nature is dangerous and could serve as a lightning rod for unpleasant backlash from the community at large. We're responsible academics. Not children acting out a New Age fairy tale."

Dean Wilson placed a calming hand on Prescott's shoulder. In a controlled yet skeptical tone, he asked, "Dr. Dmitri, are we to understand you've not only discovered something interesting about whale language but have in fact found what you consider evidence of a high-order intellectual capability?"

"Precisely. The conclusions are based on the rigorous application of engineering fundamentals and mathematical analysis."

Wilson drew a deep breath, as if steeling himself for a strenuous task. "Then please indulge me while I play devil's advocate on behalf of those who would question your proposal. The prevailing view is that a high order intellect is inextricably linked to the development of a society or civilization. But as Mr. Gorman just indicated, we're observing creatures frolicking in the water who simply feed, breed, and migrate like many other primitive species. To echo Richard Prescott's sentiments, those with traditional attitudes might fear that your proposal is a metaphysical wrecking ball to the core beliefs of our society."

While the dean droned on, Dmitri deliberately focused his attention elsewhere. Meeting Greg's sympathetic eyes, his gaze shifted around the table until it settled upon the sickening smirk plastered on Prescott's face, like a carnival mask. The man's terrible comb-over, performing a perpetual reverse backflip on the top of his head, reinforced his image as a "phony" in Dmitri's eye. Nearly three years ago, Prescott had colluded with other McPinsky critics to coerce the professor's departure from SoCalSci. Since then, Prescott had been branded the "Self Appointed Patrician," or SAP, in charge of spin control by SoCalSci's more progressive engineering faculty members.

A familiar sound captured Dmitri's attention. Until now a silent sentinel, McPinsky announced his presence with a droll chuckle. Uncoiling his six-foot, six-inch frame from the chair, the system's motion sensors prominently projected his leonine image onto the displays a continent and an ocean away. "May I address the distinguished Dean of the SoCalSci Engineering Department?"

Dmitri directed a surreptitious wink at Greg. They were very familiar with McPinsky's humble request, a coded invitation to the lambs to lie with the lion.

Dean Wilson greeted the newcomer with a brief smile, a taut brow, and the faintest hint of disdain in his mild tone. "Greetings, Theodosius. How many years have passed since you brachiated away from the Left Coast to cling to Ivy League vines?"

"Long enough, Robert, to know I'm now happily ensconced on the right coast."

Greg whispered into Dmitri's ear, "Let's get ready to rumble. I warned you about inviting him."

Wilson sighed. "Dear Theodosius, our esteemed SoCalSci physics colleague, Dr. Wilhelm Shockey, has expressed serious doubts about your Unified Field Theory of Everything."

McPinsky's tone was solemn. "Let me pause to acknowledge the illustrious Dr. Shockey, and his unique ability to modulate hot air to simulate human speech."

From coast-to-coast-to-coast, all attendees heard the mid-air collision of gasps and titters launched across the table in the SoCalSci conference room.

"Greetings, Professor McPinsky," interjected Prescott. "How *are* your spiritualist comrades from the *Symposium of Cosmology and Consciousness?*"

McPinsky covered his heart with a hand. "Lama Dawa Cham sends his regards, Richard, and a prayer for your salvation."

"Gentlemen, gentlemen!" interjected Dean Wilson. "Let us proceed."

"Prescott's still out for blood." Greg spoke to his friend in hushed tones. "You'd better do something, pal, before it's too late."

Dmitri stood so abruptly he nearly stumbled. "I think you'll all agree . . ." He hesitated, swallowing twice in an attempt to lubricate his dry mouth. "I'd like to recognize Professor McPinsky as a courageous pioneer to those of my generation. It's the reason I've invited him here today. So he can share his invaluable insights."

In stark contrast to the other participants, who casually reclined in chairs around conference tables, McPinsky stood behind a lecturer's podium in Ivy Tech's Media Communications Center. Possibly in an attempt to connect with the 1930s Golden Age of Physics, his clothing reinforced his unconventional proclivities. Suspenders supported McPinsky's corduroy slacks and an op-art vest decorated a burly torso. His imperious gaze was tempered and framed by horn-rimmed, faux-tortoise-shell glasses.

McPinsky gripped the sides of the podium and smiled. "Dean Wilson and assembled guests, the first word I'd like you to ponder is 'transformation.'" With years of practice, McPinsky's resonant voice and authoritative demeanor commanded attention. "My former colleague, Dr. Dmitri, presents us with the 'eureka' opportunity of a lifetime. Nay, it's the opportunity of a century . . ." Here he paused dramatically and then continued, ". . . or even of a millennium. In reply, I only hear the wailing of children, fearful for your reputations and budgets. What a pity. I see that some of you would still cling to pre-Enlightenment orthodoxies rather than wake up to the gestalt of what's staring you in the face. I urge you not to succumb to the shackles of your preconditioned fears. To bolster our collective courage, I'd like to weave a tapestry of brief quotes on the subject of transformation from my favorite philosopher, the great Indian sage, J. Krishnamurti."

After he had removed his glasses, McPinsky read from a book resting on the podium. "'The transformation of the world is brought about by the transformation of oneself, because the self is the product and a part of the total process of human existence. To know oneself as one is requires an extraordinary alertness of mind, because *what is* is constantly undergoing transformation . . . and to follow it swiftly the mind must not be tethered to any particular dogma or belief, because beliefs and ideals only give you a color, perverting true perception.'"

With gusts of breath, McPinsky paused to fog his glasses. He worked a paisley handkerchief vigorously, like someone drying dishes. Satisfied with the result, he hooked the left and right earpieces, one at a time, back over his ears. He stared directly into the camera and resumed.

"Like Krishnamurti, the Eastern mystics tell us that the truth of the perception we experience today is in fact maya, the veil of illusion. The breakthrough technology of this videoconferencing system simulates the reality that we're sitting at the same table and having a friendly chat. As you all know, the images and voices we project to one another are simply reconstructed by microcomputers from the mathematical deconstructions and compressions of signals derived from our original voices and images. Those same microcomputers digitally slice and dice the information until it is but a stream of the most primitive of symbols, bits of ones and zeros. Thus the interchangeable currency of information, transmitted through the ether and reconstructed in reverse fashion can generate the illusion of direct experience, of maya."

As McPinsky spoke while clutching the sides of the podium, he intermittently raised his right arm into the air. On about every third shake of the fist, he modulated his fingers in a seemingly different shape of the rock, paper, and scissors game. This trademark gesture apparently granted the audience permission to experience the deep subject of his lecture in a spirit of playfulness. McPinsky's cadenced voice was synchronized with each exclamation of the fist. No one dared to intervene. After all, he was the preeminent advocate of "the big picture."

"Yes, yes, Theodosius." Dean Wilson's voice expressed impatience. "We're all familiar with your theory. We need to shift back to the matter at hand."

Due to an asymmetric relationship between his nose and ears, McPinsky's glasses periodically slid down the bridge of his nose. While glaring at Wilson, his outstretched middle finger pushed them back in place, an "in-your-face" gesture to both Wilson and to the gods who'd inflicted him with this irritating anomaly.

"Next, I want you to consider the concept of the 'continuum of intelligence,'" McPinsky said forcefully. "Your argument is that humpback whales are primitive animals, swimming in the ocean, with no palpable evidence to justify the possibility of higher intelligence. But in fact many creatures generate symbols of various types to communicate with their comrades, and I claim these symbols are the gold standard for measuring intellect in any species.

"Imagine in the same room, an emaciated parrot in a birdcage and two English-speaking humans who are seated back-to-back. One of the humans sits next to the birdcage and holds a stack of crackers. The other person is in possession of a carton of milk. The parrot starts speaking some words in the English language. In fact, the bird has been trained to utter, 'Polly want a cracker,' whenever it is hungry. In response, the human places one of the crackers into the cage, which the parrot consumes. There is a measureable cross-species exchange of linguistic symbols between bird and human. The human with the remaining crackers realizes he too is hungry, so he consumes the rest. Since his mouth is caked with crumbs, he's in desperate need of a drink, so just as in the scene in a TV commercial, he utters 'Got Milk?' But the man with the milk can't see his neighbor's plight, and since he can't understand the garbled words, he retains the carton. In this case there is no measurable exchange of information between the humans.

"The story's lesson is that language is a set of symbols using any of the five senses. Its sole purpose is to communicate the thoughts inside the brain of one individual to another. In some cases, these thoughts reflect needs, such as expressions of hunger or thirst. The parrot had communicated in our language to express its needs in the same way that a freeway-ramp vagabond displays a WILL WORK FOR FOOD sign. The bird used learned symbols with shared meaning—the very definition of language—across the species boundary to forestall hunger. You could claim my example is a classic case of stimulus-response learning. However, since both language and cognitive reflection are abstractive processes, the use of language is a strong indicator of cognitive intelligence."

McPinsky paused, distracted by Dean Wilson's languorous display of yawning and stretching. Aware of McPinsky's withering stare, Wilson sat at attention. "My apologies, Theodosius. Please continue." Dmitri cupped his hand to veil his grin.

"That's most kind of you, Dean. Now, where were we? Ah, yes. So, although one way to measure intellect is to examine the material vestiges of civilization—its tools, books, and buildings, for example—we can also measure it indirectly by discovering and decoding the symbols of language, the abstractions derived from the brain's thoughts. So you see, this generalized concept of the continuum of intelligence, based solely upon the symbolic exchange of thoughts and ideas, allows various species to evolve societies of the mind which are accessible to other inquisitive species, like us."

A brief silence had settled over the room. Bodies shifted in their chairs. Just as Dmitri had hoped, his mentor, now in the spotlight, had marginalized Prescott's influence.

"My next subject is 'justice,'" said McPinsky. "Did you ever see the original *Planet of the Apes* movies? Arrogant assumptions about another species' intellectual deficiencies prevented communication breakthroughs between the apes and humans. Simple IQ tests were administered by the apes, assuming animal-like levels of intellect. The human subjects were frustrated to be treated in such low regard. As for your argument that Drs. Dmitri and Bono don't have compelling evidence to justify further experimentation, are you willing to take the risk in denying their right to pursue their research? What if they are correct right now, but the world has to wait for another team to confirm their discovery? That these potentially advanced creatures would continue to be consumed as sushi is tantamount to human cannibalism. Future generations will retroactively convict us on charges of moral high treason."

"Now see here!" Prescott's veins bulged under his collar, but he was shushed into silence.

McPinsky thundered onward. "Next, think about 'redemption!' In the exercising of our dominion over all creatures on the earth, and most notably in the seas, we've polluted their home with trash, chemicals, and injurious cacophonies. We've slaughtered them to near-extinction with explosive harpoons and mass beachings. What about the moral rationale of redeeming ourselves from the guilt of these atrocities?"

"Excuse me, Professor," Greg said, raising his hand.

Greg's interjection stunned Dmitri. Even McPinsky's students knew better than to pose questions during his lectures.

"Yes?" replied McPinsky, his tone teetering between surprise and irritation.

"Sorry for the interruption, but many hearing-challenged individuals, including me, have benefitted from high-tech breakthroughs unavailable to previous generations. Tools like Speakeasy are a life-altering gift. Shouldn't we overcome our arrogance and pay this gift forward to give these beings the chance to express their own voices? This, in itself, is a worthy enough reason to continue this line of research. To not even try is to admit we're deaf to other voices."

McPinsky's sober visage transformed to a broad smile. "Thank you," replied McPinsky. "As our auditory-challenged colleague says so eloquently, in one tremendous leap we can redeem the sins of our fathers by offering the "Gift of Prometheus."

"Now, I want you to consider the concept of 'judgment.' Your religious argument is that God has judged humans alone worthy of holding dominion over all creatures on the planet. But what if there are other judges? What if, at this very moment, ET's visiting our solar system are observing our behavior in order to judge our contact-worthiness quotient? In a scenario similar to our current discussion and in the comfort of their mother craft, they might be discussing the pros and cons of contact with Homo sapiens. Their Prime Directive probably echoes *Star Trek*'s: 'Don't interfere with primitive cultures.' If so, the ET's definition of 'primitive' would most certainly be 'incapable of handling the societal shock and psychological dislocation of first contact with aliens.'

"The naysayers amongst them cite how ignorant, arrogant, and fearful we must be, since we did not even attempt contact with another intelligent planetary species. On the other hand, our advocates amongst them could cite that we demonstrated our resilience to potentially shocking discoveries by instigating local cetacean contact. We will have proven we are curious and contact-worthy creatures. In their eyes, the Prometheus gift would qualify humankind as a civilization with the potential for advancement to Type 1 or Type 2 status, as defined by the physicist Michio Kaku."

Dean Wilson raised his arms and tilted his head in puzzlement.

"Apparently, some of you are not familiar with Dr. Kaku's theories about the evolution of planetary civilizations." Wilson nodded. "Humans are an example of a Type 0 civilization: low-tech and on the verge of self-extinction. If we can conquer our self-destructive tendencies, we have a chance of surviving long enough to achieve Type 1 status. We'll have the ability to control energy on a planetary scale: weather modification and limitless, free energy. The next step to Type 2 is the power to manipulate the energy of stars. Type 3 possesses galactic powers, the realm of the gods."

Dmitri enjoyed seeing the frustration roiling on the surface of Prescott's face. The successive waves of McPinsky's pithy pronouncements, which years ago he and Greg had termed "thunderclaps," had once again merged into a powerful force to sway his audience.

"I will conclude with the subject of 'inquisitive enlightenment,'" the professor announced.

Dmitri heard Dean Wilson's muffled "finally" and turned just in time to glimpse a fleeting look of relief before his countenance reverted to its usual haughty expression. McPinsky did not look pleased.

"I've argued that the academic, philosophical, and religious objections to this venture are driven by dogma, a pre-Age of Enlightenment conceit of ignorance and arrogance. Dogma is contrary to a human being's signature characteristic—curiosity. I submit that all scientists convened here today have taken a Hippocratic-like oath to reject dogma and to pursue the scientific method. We can all cite historical examples of societal resistance to previous paradigm breakthroughs, the Church versus Galileo and Darwin versus his detractors, which fortunately did not prevent their momentous discoveries."

McPinsky dabbed his brow with the paisley handkerchief.

"During a distant epoch," he continued, "a great schism occurred in mammalian evolution when the cetacean ancestors returned to the sea. For the last fifty million years, the mammalian mind in the water has evolved independently of the mammalian mind on land. Think of the magnificent once-in-a-fifty-million-year opportunity to build a bridge across that great divide, and to reunite with a potentially kindred intelligence on our very own planet!" He thumped the podium. "If we dare to ask the brave questions, imagine the surprises we might learn about our cetacean earth mates."

After an interminable silence, the dean finally answered. "Damn you, Theodosius! What can I say in rebuttal? As usual, your arguments are quite compelling. The whale sushi comment reminded me of a favorite science fiction story of my youth. ET's had landed on the White House lawn in a display of friendship and with the promise of the gift of advanced knowledge. As evidence of their good intentions, they presented the president with the gift of a book entitled, *To Serve Man*. Unfortunately, when it was too late to alter mankind's morbid fate, a brilliant scientist decoded the alien text, which ultimately turned out to be a cookbook of recipes for preparing human flesh. I can't have anything like that on my conscience. You win. I move that we approve funding for the experiment."

"Excellent. But actually, Robert," McPinsky retorted, "the whale sushi comment reminded me of my favorite meal: homemade gefilte fish with red beet horseradish. My mother called it Jewish sushi. Let's go out for lunch the next time I'm in California."

"All right, all right, I'll second the dean's motion," said Prescott, as coolly as if he had shed all vestiges of personal resentment. Like a snake sloughing its skin, thought Dmitri. He had long been sure that Richard Prescott was a student of Machiavelli's *The Prince*. Dmitri studied the bureaucrat's pallid, expressionless face. He surmised that Prescott had decided it was more expedient to defer this battle until he could dictate the means to achieve his own ends.

Chris Gorman made it unanimous. "How can I refuse the illustrious professor, especially after imagining myself as a defendant in some future cetacean Nuremberg tribunal? PICES will contact Dr. Dmitri's team and initiate preparations for the experiment."

McPinsky, as usual, had the last word. "I wish to thank you, ladies and gentlemen. I would like to end the meeting with my favorite quotation from Einstein. 'The pursuit of truth and beauty is a sphere of activity in which we are permitted to remain children all our lives.' And so I say to you, my colleagues, 'Let us play.'"

Collusions of an Academic Hit Man

Southern California Coast—one month later

RICHARD PRESCOTT SCANNED a sweeping ocean and coastal vista. The swells began far offshore, yet he could still see their faint beginnings. Rolling toward the bay beneath him, their dimensions increased moment by moment. Surging into the cove, they crashed through a field of offshore boulders and sea stacks, spewing white clouds of foam. They continued relentlessly onward until they exploded into the bluffs and evaporated into the mist.

The SoCalSci administrator sipped a first cup of morning coffee, admiring the white water spectacle from the deck of his cliff-top home. He reflected upon his good fortune: the result of a lifetime of channeling the work ethic and conservative values his parents had impressed upon him. Yet, even as he savored the gritty, Turkish-brewed café noir, the conflicting issues of a moral dilemma gnawed upon his conscience.

He knew he wasn't a bad person. In fact, like most of his friends and colleagues, he felt compassion for the whales. When vacationing in Mexico and during family outings to Sea World, he'd been captivated by their sociable behavior. Richard's children had grown up loving the big creatures, and both he and his wife contributed to marine mammal protectionist causes. However, his long-held philosophical perspective was at stake. He had been raised to value the preservation of the system that nurtured him. As in the battle between the waves and rocks below, Richard Prescott knew it was his duty to act as the agent of resistance to the waves of change that threatened his cherished institution.

During last month's committee meeting, he had agreed to abide by the group's decision, and to fund David Dmitri's collaborative experiment with the Pacific Institute for Cetacean Educational Studies. Nearly every day since then, he had struggled to reexamine the implications of Dmitri's proposal. He felt appalled that the university was funding an experiment to engage whales in an "advanced intellectual exercise." This sounded more like the lurid drivel of tabloid headlines on supermarket magazine racks than the activities of a respectable institution. Any leaks to the media could harm the university's reputation. And besides, Dmitri was a protégé of that cursed McPinsky. The man had publicly ridiculed Richard, three years ago, during the successful sub-rosa campaign to oust the old troublemaker from SoCalSci. For years, Richard's father had warned him about the arrogance of ivory-tower professors who thought they were superior to men of the world like themselves, whose management and business skills kept their institutions running smoothly.

Now, after days of intense soul-searching, consulting both his wife and pastor, Richard had regained his equilibrium. Being a man of action, he had decided to reverse the course of his decision, and after tireless research, he had crafted a plan.

During last month's funding meeting, he had put the fear of God into Gorman, and now he was really going to yank the marine biologist's chain. A significant chunk of PICES's budget was subsidized by a generous grant from the University of Hawaii's College of Marine Sciences. Richard hoped to capitalize on a longstanding relationship spawned during his student days. A former fraternity brother and fellow business major, Harvey Padgett, was the current chief administrator of research funding at the University of Hawaii.

After attending the two meetings on his morning schedule, Richard returned to his office for a quick lunch and to contact his counterpart using a new voice-activated Internet phone. "Hello Harvey. It's your long-lost amigo, Richard Prescott."

"Richard, you old devil," replied Padgett.

"It's been too long since we last spoke. I wouldn't mind trading places with you and your hardscrabble existence there in Honolulu."

"I still laugh to tears every time I think about that stunt we pulled on our engineering rivals across the street."

They reminisced about the fraternity hazing incident of their youth. Their frat brothers had scattered an incriminating heap of empty beer cans and liquor bottles about their honor-society rivals' front yard and doorstep. They had then phoned the campus police to report an out-of-control party.

Prescott chortled. "Those arrogant engineering geeks who looked down their noses at us business majors only got what they deserved."

"It *was* diabolically clever, and I still think we should have used more beer cans."

"No need. The cops fell for it. And do you remember the priceless expression on their dazed faces when the police busted in on them at 3 a.m.?"

"You always *were* the clever politician back then, participating in one steering committee or another. That's why I'm pretty certain this isn't strictly a social call, unless, like most of my other 'long-lost buddies,' you're seeking insider tourist tips for a trip to the Islands."

"You could always read me, Harvey. Well, as a matter of fact, I have some interesting information. It'll cross your desk sooner or later. Speaking of engineering geeks, some of our SoCalSci faculty members are collaborating with the Pacific Institute for Cetacean Educational Studies. In my humble opinion, their venture threatens to expose both of our institutions to an embarrassing public backlash."

"What's new about that? In our precarious positions, we always struggle to balance the opposing forces of academic freedom and bureaucratic censorship."

"My dear Harvey, what if the expression of academic freedom transgresses beyond the frontiers of the scientific method to the netherworld of New Age quackery?"

"Can you be a bit more specific? I have a very high regard for Chris Gorman's organization. They do cutting-edge research and perform a great public service to educate the community about whales, specifically our local humpback population."

"But they've gone wacko, Harvey! Based on some computer printout from one whale song, they claim to have discovered a secret language and a highly evolved intellect. Would you believe they're going to challenge them to a game of chess or checkers or whatever?"

"Hmmm, if this plan is as ludicrous as it sounds, then of course we won't fund it."

"If word spreads to the public at large, it could incite a PR firestorm. New Age fruits, nuts, and flakes will converge upon Maui as if it were Woodstock or Burning Man. On the other hand, religious fundamentalists will condemn our university-sponsored experiment as pagan blasphemy. For God's sake, Harvey, we'll be powerless to control the nightmare. The universities' reputations and funding will be threatened, and both you and I will likely become unemployment statistics."

"That sounds very distressing indeed. Okay, Richard, I'll contact Gorman and see what he has to say for himself."

"Thanks, Harvey, that's all I ask. Text me after you've reminded the PICES director about the downside of engaging in dubious marine biological research. Have a lovely day."

At the completion of the call, Richard felt relieved, as if a great weight had been lifted from his shoulders. Indeed, the great weight of a whale, he chuckled to himself. He thought of the famous Latin phrase from his youth, "Alea jacta est," uttered by Julius Caesar when the Roman army crossed the Rubicon. Yes, Richard thought, "The die has been cast." He would not be denied. If Padgett couldn't persuade Gorman to alter his course, then he would find another way to rock the PICES boat.

RESEARCH IN PARADISE

Pacific Institute for Cetacean Educational Studies, Kihei, Maui—late February

"PINCH ME, BOSS!" Andrew called above the howling wind. "I can't believe the university is sponsoring us on an all-expenses-paid research trip to paradise."

A mere six weeks since their winter-break vacation and after a direct flight from the mainland, it was a déjà vu for SoCalSci Associate Professors David Dmitri and Greg Bono. Their Mustang raced through the cane fields hugging Maui's Mokulele Highway 350 en route to the Pacific Institute for Cetacean Educational Studies. This time, however, they were here on a mission of discovery, accompanied by Dmitri's research assistants. Andrew and Seema were wide-eyed and chatty in the back seat of the convertible. This was their maiden voyage to the Hawaiian Islands. Dmitri pointed in the direction of Haleakala as he shouted the story of their fateful encounter with Melanie.

"I'm really looking forward to meeting your friend." Seema raised her voice so Dmitri could hear her in the driver's seat.

Her comment echoed Dmitri's own anticipation. "You won't have to wait very long," he replied, "since she's attending today's meeting at the whale institute. After we meet with Gorman's team, Greg and I will give you the grand tour of Haleakala and Melanie's perch at the LURE Observatory."

"Maui is even more beautiful than I imagined," said Seema. "A vast sugar bowl of cane fields waving their welcome, and surrounded by towering mountains. I can't wait to see the ocean."

Greg's head had been swiveling sharply in order to observe everyone's lip movements. "Dmitri, let's indulge Seema and take a ten-minute detour to McGregor Point. The turnoff is just ahead."

"Absolutely, positively!" Dmitri shouted with gusto.

As Dmitri navigated the curving section of oceanfront highway, he counted the minutes until he'd cuddle Melanie in his arms. Ever since their last embrace, he had longed for this moment. When they pulled into the cliff top parking lot, they observed an animated group of tourists gesturing at a disturbance in the water. They spilled out of the vehicle and melted into the crowd.

"What's all the fuss about?" Andrew asked the nearest bystander.

"Just wait a minute." The congenial senior citizen spoke with a Texas twang. "There, look," she pointed. The spectators gasped in delight as a baby humpback breached alongside its parents.

"Thank you, Doctor Dmitri." A tear rolled down Seema's cheek. She spread her arms as if to encompass the panoramic ocean view. "I'm so happy. The water is so shimmeringly blue, and we're spectacularly greeted by these amazing creatures. I wish my family could be here. A photo is totally inadequate."

"It is a magical place, and the reason I keep coming back." Dmitri felt the depth of his conviction as he high-fived Andrew. "Just don't forget we're here to conduct some serious research with these beings. Let's think of them as our highly motivated research subjects reporting early for duty."

The baby humpback breached repeatedly. Compared to an adult's majestic leaps, it toppled over sideways, like a failed missile launch. More "oohs" and "aahs" rippled through the gathering.

"It could be the research opportunity of a lifetime!" Andrew's giddy voice made everyone grin. "Good thing you reminded us to change into shorts and sandals." He wiped his brow. "This feels like the tropics."

Dmitri checked his wristwatch. "Sorry to be a spoilsport, but our meeting at PICES headquarters starts in thirty minutes."

They piled back into the car and resumed their roller-coaster ride along the coastal road.

Twenty minutes later, they were walking toward the PICES building. Seeing Melanie waiting at the front door, Dmitri raced ahead.

"Give us a couple of minutes, folks, while we get reacquainted," Dmitri called. When they were alone, he reached out to clasp her hands and then pulled her into his arms. His stomach churned as he gulped, "I missed you."

After weeks of anticipation, Melanie's joyous smile was the reply he had hoped for. Gazing into her bewitching, smoky-quartz eyes, he was transported back to the memory of the last time they'd been together, nearly two months ago. On the final night of that vacation, she'd invited him to her apartment for a going away dinner. It had turned into a most memorable evening. It was so memorable he'd nearly missed the flight home on the following morning. Greg had teased him mercilessly at the airport before admitting that he had also enjoyed a going-away date with Melanie's assistant, Erika.

A slight movement in the PICES lobby window caught Dmitri's attention. An unknown figure observed them through the blinds. Holding Melanie in his arms, he felt too happy to care. After a minute of small talk, they decided not to keep the others waiting. Upon entering the windowless conference room, Dmitri observed the participants assembled around a long, rectangular table and engaged in casual conversations.

Chris Gorman, sporting a fresh crew cut and looking every bit the former naval officer, was the first to address the group. "Dr. Dmitri and Ms. Mari, I decided to wait until you had both arrived before opening the session. Welcome back. I never dreamed I'd see you returning here so soon. We're all looking forward to hearing more about your findings." His detached tones suggested otherwise. "But I have to admit I'm taking a wait-and-see approach as we continue to investigate the distinctive features of the song structure. As I mentioned in our last phone conversation, PICES research is focused on the marine biological aspects of cetacean behavior."

Dmitri shot Gorman a puzzled look.

"Let me explain," said Gorman. "I need to inform you about the two urgent voice messages I received this morning. The first was from our University of Hawaii funding administrator, Harvey Padgett. Apparently, he's very concerned about PICES's plans to conduct an interspecies communication experiment with the humpbacks."

Dmitri looked surprised. "How would he even know about it?"

"If you're implying I informed him, the answer is no. However, since Padgett's agency funds a big chunk of our total budget, we're obligated to respond to his inquiries."

"So what will you do?"

"I'll speak with him later, but let's carry on with the meeting. Now, more than ever, I'd really appreciate your support for our official position: 'This collaboration is to observe the whale's responses to the broadcast of a select set of acoustic waveforms.'"

"We're definitely on board with that," replied Greg. "Nevertheless, your public statement provides ample wiggle room to assess the effects of *Beethoven's 5th* on the patterns of bubble nets."

A smattering of snickers danced around the table. Considering that Greg's offbeat sense of humor was an acquired taste, Gorman's vexed expression was no surprise to Dmitri.

"Dr. Bono, your point is well-taken." Gorman took a deep breath and, to Dmitri's relief, appeared to collect himself. "First, I'd like to introduce Peter Hawkins, the Assistant Director of PICES."

Hawkins was the strapping, bearded marine biologist Dmitri and Greg had met on their previous visit. This time, however, Dmitri noticed that the unbearded portion of his handsome face had experienced years of exposure to the elements. The dark-haired Hawkins waved a silent greeting to all convened.

"I'd also like you to meet the newest member of our team, Research Associate Lila Lawson. Lila's specializing in the recording of whale songs and the study of their musicology." He indicated a young, blonde woman who was dressed so casually she looked more like an athlete than a researcher.

"We're happy to see Peter again," Dmitri responded, waving at Hawkins, "and we're certainly pleased that one of your staff members is a song specialist."

"Yes," replied Gorman. "Lila has recently published in *Nature* on the phrase structure of the humpbacks' songs."

Lila reached across the table to shake Dmitri's hand. "Dr. Dmitri, it's a pleasure being with others who are as curious and amazed by the whales as I am. I'm really excited about your discovery, and I can't wait to hear more."

Dmitri noted Andrew's puppy-dog stare assessing Lila's twenty-something attractiveness. Her sunflower tank top framed athlete's biceps and deltoids. He noticed that Seema's attention also seemed to be focused on Andrew.

"I believe you've met our entire team." In sharp contrast to Lila's tone, Gorman's seemed flat. "I'd like to extend an official 'aloha' greeting to our SoCalSci guests. I'm very pleased to see two new faces, Dr. Dmitri. Now it's your turn to tell us about yourselves."

Dmitri stood. "Chris and Peter, you've both met my SoCalSci colleague, Professor Greg Bono. His code-breaking ability led to the discovery of the mathematical patterns of the symbols in the whale song."

"Would you believe I was underwater when the inspiration struck me?" replied Greg. Greeted by quizzical expressions, he responded with a sheepish grin. "Oh, sorry, I was taking a shower."

After Lila stopped laughing, Dmitri continued. "I'd also like you to meet Seema Roy and Andrew Chu, our research assistants extraordinaire, and to acknowledge their initial discovery of these unique symbols." Dmitri's grad students waved their greetings to their PICES counterparts.

Dmitri showered Melanie with a radiant smile. "Last but not least, I'd like to introduce the special person who provided the inspiration and the technical means to achieve the breakthrough that brings us together today. Through a fortuitous chain of events last month, Dr. Bono and I were invited by Ms. Mari to tour your state university's experimental speech therapy lab. She demonstrated a cutting-edge system in a session with one of her hearing-challenged students. We were quite impressed by the system's audio-visual interface and its unique display of the phonetic units of language for easy recognition. During her tutorial, it struck me that this tool might be the magic bullet for detecting similar symbols in the whale songs. The rest is history. Let's all give a warm welcome to Melanie Mari."

As Dmitri led the group in a round of spirited applause, Melanie blushed and gestured for silence. "You're all too kind and Dr. Dmitri is too generous in his remarks. I'm here to help any way I can. On a personal note, I'm tickled to see Lila Lawson, an acquaintance of mine."

When Melanie waved to the beaming Lila, Dmitri was distracted by her intermittent eye contact with Gorman.

"Thank you, Melanie, and welcome aboard." Gorman's gaze lingered on her.

"The feeling is mutual, Chris." She winked back at him.

Dmitri couldn't help it. His gut tensed at the sight of the undercurrent of familiarity between Melanie and Gorman.

Gorman addressed everyone in the group. "I'm impressed by the diverse fields of expertise spanned by the members of our joint venture—"

"So Chris," interrupted Dmitri, "as I explained during last month's video conference, we did indeed discover an intriguing set of symbols and alternating patterns of response." He paused, and a taut silence gripped the room. "Our analysis confirms that the patterns of these symbols conform to the strategy employed in a classic two-player board game."

He paused again, waiting for the inevitable reaction.

"Uh-oh," muttered Gorman. The two tolling tones lingered in the air.

"Now you understand why I didn't want to be too specific about the data until this face-to-face meeting," replied Dmitri. "But now that the moment has arrived, I can tell you the nature of these patterns was confirmed by another member of SoCalSci's distinguished math faculty, Joel Spelvin, the renowned game theorist."

"Hallelujah, hallelujah, hallelujah." Lila's response pierced the veil of stunned silence.

"Ok." Gorman's placid expression never changed. "You recall we agreed to observe the whales' reaction to the broadcasting of these unique patterns of symbols?"

"Right," replied Dmitri, surprised by the PICES director's tepid reply.

"But you're suggesting their response could be something along the lines of the Sicilian Defense?"

Seema looked blankly at Andrew, who whispered, "Think chess."

"I prefer the Nimzo-Indian Defense." Dmitri paused in deference to the brief outburst of nervous laughter. "But seriously, Chris, we've structured the project to operate on multiple levels to satisfy all stakeholders. As advertised to the more conservative research and funding parties, our baseline objective is to observe the humpback's response to the broadcasts of their own vocalizations. We stand by this position statement, and I believe you're satisfied with those ground rules."

"Good."

"If the whales respond to these broadcasts, we'll capture their vocalizations for future analysis."

"Still sounds good to me," replied Gorman.

"And finally, if we identify a developing pattern of symbols that conforms to the correlation profile of a game, we will then attempt to interact according to the rules of the game."

Greg briefly summarized his discovery and Spelvin's findings suggestive of a game like Dots and Boxes.

"Okay," replied Gorman. "That's an extreme long shot as far as I'm concerned, so I can't see it jeopardizing our credibility with respect to our funding sponsors."

"I agree," said Dmitri, "and, realistically, it's too great a leap to expect a communication breakthrough on this trip. We'll be more than happy to simply observe and record any cetacean responses to the first human attempts to broadcast the symbols of their language."

"It would be an unsurpassed achievement to confirm the intentional use of such symbols," said Gorman, but then he shook his head. "However, it could also erupt into a PR nightmare."

"Now it's my turn to speak in cautionary tones," Dmitri said. "Our official story still stands. We're doing correlation analysis to detect the presence of symbols that could be indicative of language."

"But what if the game actually happens? The first-ever, high-level intellectual interaction between humans and another species?" Gorman's tone shift suggested he was torn between uncertainty and an anxious excitement, but it was his glassy-eyed expression that emboldened Dmitri.

"Chris. You've dedicated years of your life investigating these majestic creatures, and I know from my own brief personal observations one can't help but feel a special bond with them. But, is there something else you want to say?"

Gorman paused and stared up at the ceiling. "It is amazing to be underwater and swaying in their powerful currents or to be enveloped in the cloud of a bubble net. And there's nothing like hearing and feeling the haunting melody of a singer. Yes, the bond grows with each encounter."

Dmitri observed the incredulous expressions on Seema's and Andrew's faces in the afterglow of Gorman's aquatic meditation. "I truly envy you, Chris," he responded tactfully, "but since I also realize I'd never have the guts to dive amongst forty-ton marine mammals, I want to thank you for sharing these experiences with us."

"During your stay," said Lila, "you should see the current exhibition of Chris and Peter's underwater photography at the Maui Marine Art Expo. We have enlarged prints for sale in the PICES gift shop."

"I can't wait to attend that exhibit," said Seema, "and I'm hoping you'll autograph a print for me, Mr. Gorman."

"Sure, no problem, Seema."

"I need to make a statement here." Lila stood and took a deep breath. "Please allow me to crawl out on a limb and get to the heart of the matter." She cleared her throat. "Human beings kill whales."

Everyone saw Gorman wince. Lila remained undeterred. "Here in Maui," she continued, "I'm a proud member of a community of scientists and artists, inspired by and dedicated to these magnificent mammals. Chris and Peter founded PICES for the dual purpose of marine mammal research and public education. They're an inspiration to researchers like me, but because of the ticklish relationship between PR and funding issues, they need to sound politically correct about our research activities. You know what I mean. The usual bromides about advancing the frontiers of scientific research can promote still waters and a safe harbor. Nevertheless, the Islands' cetacean support movement must never lose sight of our primary goal: to prevent any further harm to these beings. If your team can help us with a dramatic communication breakthrough, then people will surely have to question their own destructive behavior." Lila faced Dmitri with open arms. "I welcome your support."

"Right on, girl!" Melanie raised a clenched fist.

Lila's and Melanie's impassioned display roused Dmitri. "Thanks, Lila. In California, we've followed the tragic news of more strandings of juvenile humpbacks. I'm sure your superiors admire your ardent advocacy for the whales as much as I do." He turned to address Gorman. "So, Chris, this is exactly what you've always hoped for but never dared to admit: a potential discovery about humpbacks that'll rattle the foundations of human arrogance. Undeniable proof that the Megapterans are to be respected enough to be saved from destruction."

"I like it." Lila smiled at Dmitri. "Your pronunciation of Megapteran rings with the cachet of an advanced species."

"I believe we're all on the same page here," Gorman replied rather stiffly, "so let's roll up our sleeves and discuss plans to equip the research vessel." Enthusiastic voices ringed the table. "Since Lila's in charge of our whale song program, she'll describe the setup for you."

"It's all pretty straightforward." Lila, still standing, sounded calmer, more businesslike than before. "We have a couple of sets of hydrophones left over from last year's Alaska recording sessions, and we just received a set of underwater speakers, loaners from our Australian colleagues. All of the equipment is portable so it can be lowered into the water and secured to the deck with plastic tie lines. The electrical cabling is designed for underwater safety and feeds into the control room with standard RCA plug terminations, compatible with any PC's or laptop's audio mini-jacks."

"That's excellent, Lila!" Dmitri was impressed by the young researcher's mix of passion and professionalism. "I'd like to thank PICES for setting this up."

"It's the least we can do, both for you and for the whales," replied Gorman in his clipped, matter-of-fact tone. "By the way, Lila, lets pack some dive gear in case things get interesting down below, tangled wires or whatever."

"Not to mention underwater cameras in the event things really get interesting," she replied.

After Lila sat down, Gorman addressed Dmitri. "At first I was puzzled by your suggestion to rent a glass-bottom boat. But it actually works out better for us, since we won't have to interrupt our whale watch schedule. By the way, what's that all about?"

"Does anybody here know about 'wall painting?'" Dmitri asked.

"Sure," answered Lila. "I've seen it at raves. Artists use the paintbrush multimedia apps on laptops connected to video projectors to beam the kinetic art against the wall. It's really cool when it's done outdoors and at night."

"So we plan to do something similar with the visual output of the Speakeasy program. Just as Melanie's students use visual biofeedback to control the pronunciation of phonemes and words, we'd like to observe the Megapterans as they experience the visual dimensions of their own voices."

"It's possible that these first-ever cetacean word grams would provide dynamite material for your next publication, Lila." Melanie grinned.

"Thanks, Mel. This is getting more exciting by the moment."

"Not being a rave kind of guy," said Gorman, "I'd be reluctant to expose the humpbacks to gimmicky, light-show-party pyrotechnics."

"It's not like that, Chris," said Greg. "Let me explain. At first, we thought we could connect a giant, flatscreen TV to our Speakeasy computer and secure it on top of the glass, facing down into the water."

"Sweet!" exclaimed Lila. "Flashing neon lights, like an aquatic Times Square."

"But we realized that a TV that large would be too expensive for our limited budget and, needless to say, a pretty heavy object to transport."

Greg continued. "So we Googled some options."

Dmitri picked up the thread. "And realized we could configure a video projector and a large, rear-projection fabric screen similar to those used in some kinds of theaters. These screens are specially coated so that the projector sits behind the screen. The image is projected onto and passes through the fabric to the viewer's side."

Greg walked over to the whiteboard and drew a sketch of the proposed configuration. "So we'll hang and secure the projector from the cabin ceiling, directly above the glass bottom, and project the image down through the screen and the glass and out into the water."

"We'd lay the screen on top of the glass," added Andrew. "It could be as big as the entire size of the window, maybe over a hundred inches."

"That sounds like a pretty wild idea," replied Gorman, "but I have to admit it's an imaginative extension of the primary experiment. However, who knows what to expect? They could be scared away."

"Or agitated by what humans might characterize as paranormal phenomena and possibly attack the boat out of fear or anger." Hawkins himself sounded agitated.

"Nevertheless, Peter, I'm intrigued by the chance to study their reactions to the new stimuli." Gorman faced Dmitri. "But I insist on proceeding cautiously and with safeguards in place."

"We've already planned for this," Dmitri nodded. "No visuals will be projected until we've concluded all phases of the acoustic-only experiment. Andrew's Speakeasy software includes filters to minimize the occurrence of flickering images."

"Your proposals are more progressive than I ever imagined." Gorman seemed satisfied. "In addition to probing their reactions to our acoustically generated symbols, we'll also be gauging their responses to viewing the display of their own vocalizations."

"Dr. Dmitri's mentor likened it to the myth of Prometheus's gift of fire to the human race," remarked Seema.

"Except in this case, it's a gift of light." Lila smiled.

"It's the McPinsky Challenge," said Dmitri. "We're building a bridge of symbols of light and sound."

"Cetacean biofeedback," Andrew chimed in. "An inter-dimensional portal between alien civilizations." Varying expressions of bemusement and amusement appeared on the faces of the team members.

"Getting back to basics." said Greg. "We've packed a couple of high-performance laptops to support the Speakeasy analysis and plotting functions. Andrew has written a homemade version of Speakeasy to avoid intellectual property conflicts with the original developers."

"I've designed an acoustic synthesizer." Seema sounded a bit shy. "We can broadcast selectable frequency combinations to reply to the whale's acoustic symbols."

"I'd love to hear a demo of that, Seema." Lila was clearly elated. "Sometimes I compose music that incorporates the sounds from the whale song recordings."

"Lila is being modest," said Hawkins. "She's a highly regarded keyboard artist here on Maui. Tomorrow night, her group is giving a debut performance of her latest compositions. I thought we could all attend as a sort of team ice-breaker event."

Dmitri heard a polite knock and saw the tanned face of Gorman's office assistant peeking through the partially opened door. Gorman waved her in, and she tiptoed over to his chair. "Sorry to bother you, Mr. Gorman, but Mr. Padgett phoned again. He wants to speak to you about an urgent matter."

"Damn it." Gorman clenched his jaw and sprang up from the chair. "I'd better just get this over with. Why don't you continue while I take the call in my office?" Gorman followed his assistant through the door.

"Hmmm," muttered Hawkins. "I haven't seen Chris lose his composure like that in a long, long time, and Padgett's behavior is totally out of character. He's never interfered like this before. The UH funding is administered as a three-year grant cycle, and we're not required to inform them of any new activities initiated during the cycle."

"I have a suspicion about who might be pulling Padgett's strings." Dmitri nodded at Hawkins.

"Well, there's nothing to be done until Chris returns," said Hawkins, "so let's move on to plan the experiment."

The group engaged in a lively discussion about the technical details of preparing the research vessel. Concluding they could be ready to launch in about five days, Hawkins lifted his glass. As they toasted one another with their soft drink cans and coffee mugs, Gorman burst into the room, crimson-faced. He stalked to a chair and threw himself down in a fury. "There's trouble brewing in paradise, folks. Our UH funding administrator is threatening to cancel our grant if we taint the reputation of his university by conducting an interspecies communication experiment."

Expressions of "gloom and doom" transfigured everyone's faces. Lila's face, however, seethed with rage. "So what did you say to him?" she fumed.

"Who knows how I might have responded if my eyes hadn't been opened during our meeting. Thanks again to all of you for challenging me with your passionate ideas. Because of the other disturbing message I received this morning, there's another reason why I'm mad as hell. I therefore told Padgett in no uncertain terms that our mission here is all about the whales. Nobody is going to stop us until our investigation reveals everything that's possible to discover about the humpbacks. I told him we'd find other sources of funding, if need be, to maintain the integrity of our program."

When the cheers died down, Hawkins asked, "What's the news in the other disturbing message?"

Gorman's face morphed into a grim expression. "I hate to tell you this, Peter, but the tissue biopsy results of the beached humpbacks are negative for disease or infection."

Hawkins's head drooped. "Which means it's more than likely we've confirmed yet another human threat to our local humpback population."

Gorman reminded Dmitri's team of the purported sightings of naval research vessels in the vicinity of the Pailolo Channel between Maui and Molokai. "At least we're finally getting support from the larger eco-groups like Greenpeace and the NRDC."

"Right," said Dmitri. "We saw today's front-page story about the Greenpeace protestors at Pearl Harbor."

"Navy base protests won't solve the problem." Lila bounced out of her chair. "It's more important than ever to make a significant communication breakthrough to give us the clout to stop those experiments."

Gorman nodded his agreement.

"So how did Padgett respond to your pushback?" asked Hawkins.

Gorman hesitated. "Well, I think I might have mentioned contacting the media about academic freedom issues if he reneged on our funding. After that, he relented and finally even apologized. Then he asked me very politely to refrain from publishing anything related to the experiment until the data and our conclusions are peer reviewed."

"That shouldn't be a problem." Dmitri felt relieved. "It's standard procedure, and we agreed to a media and publishing moratorium at last month's SoCalSci funding meeting. By the way, did he tell you how he knew about the experiment?"

"Nope," replied Gorman. "He was mum on that issue. I suppose he could have been tipped off by one of your SoCalSci associates."

"And I think I know who that particular individual might be."

After they'd adjourned the meeting, Lila escorted Andrew and Seema to the lab where she analyzed whale song recordings. "It looks like a scaled-down version of SoCalSci's Signal Processing Lab," Andrew observed. They were surrounded by a cluster of high-performance computer workstations and laptops for displaying and editing the waveforms.

"Look at this." Seema pointed to a fancy keyboard synthesizer perched atop a stand.

"I love music." Lila brushed her fingers across the keys of the instrument. "I think that's the main reason I joined PICES. It's the sheer beauty and mystery of the humpback's songs. I love to jam along with the recordings or sample and integrate the vocalizations into my own compositions. As Peter mentioned, I'm in a New Age jazz combo."

Andrew's eyes opened wide. "Lila, did you know that Seema is also a gifted musician?"

"I don't know about being gifted," replied Seema. "I'm a classical violinist, but I've occasionally jammed with my jazz-aficionado sidekicks."

"Hey," said Andrew, "how about you two do a quick duet?"

Lila did not hesitate. "Wait just a sec." She disappeared into the back room and emerged with a violin case. "This is Hawaii, where work and play go hand in hand. Let's do it."

Andrew clapped his hands enthusiastically while Seema removed the violin from its case.

After a few warm-up exercises, they were ready to jam. Lila started the session with an improvisational rendition of a melody from a Norah Jones song.

Thirty seconds into Lila's solo, Seema began to bow a single continuous vibrato chord, like the *shruti* drone of an Indian raga. Once she had synched up to the key of the song, she launched into a riff of rhythmic chord progressions that complemented Lila's melody. After a while they switched roles, with Seema bowing a lively jazz-rock version of a Jean-Luc Ponty violin solo.

Captivated by the music from the next room, the other team members drifted into the lab. The newcomers reacted instinctively, bouncing to the beat and clapping their hands. While Andrew hand-slapped a syncopated rhythm on a desktop, Greg hooted his approval. When the duo's harmonizing crescendoed to a scintillating finale, the musicians were rewarded with a rousing ovation.

"No problem here with team chemistry." Hawkins directed his remarks to Dmitri, still snapping his fingers to the memory of Lila's up-tempo rhythm. "As I mentioned, Lila's combo is performing tomorrow night at a local supper club. We insist you be our guests for an evening of dinner and music."

"Besides that," added Melanie, "the place has the most mouth-watering sushi on the island."

"Speaking of mouth-watering," replied Seema, "I've been dying for a taste of fresh Maui pineapple."

Lila looped her arm around Seema's. "Seema, my friend, I've never met an Indian woman who fiddles like you. I'll see you dine like royalty on all of the freshest treats that Maui has to offer. Welcome to the Maui community of cetacean artists and scientists."

Dmitri observed the felicitous scene. Andrew looked happy as heck standing next to Lila, which didn't seem to bother Seema at all. She seemed delighted to be discussing photography with Gorman. Dmitri felt ecstatic to be arm in arm with Melanie. Even Hawkins and Greg shared a laugh. What could be better, he thought, than doing research in paradise?

Three time zones to the East, Richard Prescott reviewed his afternoon email in his SoCalSci office, surprised to see a post from Harvey Padgett so soon after their conversation about Gorman:

Sorry, Richard, but Gorman was adamant about proceeding with the communication experiments whether or not UH continues to fund him. He even threatened an embarrassing media ruckus if I attempt to stifle their academic freedom. He did agree to keep mum about this particular endeavor until he ob-

tains more substantive evidence about the cetacean language issue. I'll keep you informed, and certainly if he appears to violate our agreement.

Prescott clenched his fists. It seemed that David Dmitri's association with the controversial McPinsky still threatened to unleash the ghosts of the past. All right, he thought, there is more than one way to skin a cat. Perhaps he could derail the Dmitri-Gorman alliance with a dose of preventative medicine. Like a vaccination designed to prevent a virulent contagion from striking too close to home, he would inject a smidgen of controversy into the general population. By skillfully parsing the information, he could spare his own institution any embarrassment. True, the cure might require some sacrifices, but Gorman and Padgett weren't being very cooperative, were they?

He walked three blocks to one of the few remaining off-campus phone booths. After so many years, he was surprised it was still there, albeit tattooed with vulgar graffiti. He hesitated outside, weighing the consequences of his plan while anxiously pawing the coins in his pocket. When he started to walk away, a voice in his head chanted like a mantra, "Alea jacta est, the die has been cast."

He turned around, deposited the coins, and dialed the number he had committed to memory. After an interminable earful of cheesy elevator Muzak, he was greeted by a pleasant female voice. "This is the *Enquirer* hotline. Do you have a story for us?"

Creationists and Luddites—
Full of Passionate Intensity

Pacific Institute for Cetacean Educational Studies, Kihei, Maui—five days later

"WE'VE BEEN SABOTAGED." Gorman slapped the wooden table, startling the groggy Dmitri who nearly spilled his coffee. "Someone's out to get us."

"But we're just about to launch the experiment," Greg protested, squinting through puffy eyelids.

Dmitri cradled a steaming mug and scanned the table through the aromatic mist. It was eight o'clock in the morning, too early for most software engineers. With only Melanie absent, the members of the team slouched in chairs around the PICES conference table. When Gorman had finished rubbing his eyes, Dmitri could see they were bloodshot even from across the table.

The members of the "Research in Paradise" team, as they had dubbed themselves, were shell-shocked. After five very productive team-building days, they'd completed most of the preparations for the PICES research vessel, which they'd christened the *Research in Paradise*. A pre-launch party had been arranged for that evening to unveil the team's custom-designed T-shirts, stenciled with a humpback breaching above a Speakeasy word gram. Rather than reveling in the moment, however, they found themselves engulfed in a mass media firestorm.

"How could this happen?" Lila threw her arms up in exasperation.

Gorman explained how he'd been tipped off the previous night when an acquaintance had emailed the distressing news. A *National Enquirer* online story had compared the rumored PICES interspecies communication experiment to the Roswell ET incident. It further speculated that Professor McPinsky, the author of the infamous McPinsky Challenge, would supervise the experiment. The response had been instantaneous: a resurrection of the wrath of fundamentalists who, three years ago, had so fervently objected to the radical, secular-humanist threat posed by McPinsky's challenge.

The story had legs. Gorman's Google to the keywords "PICES" and "*National Enquirer*" had returned over one hundred hits. Tuning his radio to the ten o'clock local news broadcast and hearing the same story, he realized that something was drastically wrong. Despite the late hour, he'd contacted the entire team and advised them to convene at PICES headquarters for this early morning emergency meeting.

Gorman's assistant entered the room and handed him a note. "Thank you, Shelley." After a brief examination, he crushed it into a ball and lobbed it across the table. It landed dead center in the wastebasket to scattered applause. "Too bad the news we've just received is not as good as my free-throw percentage. At this very moment, protestors are assembling on the pier leading to the PICES dock."

"I know who blindsided us!" Dmitri clutched his empty coffee mug. "It's the same scoundrel who tattled to Harvey Padgett. It's Richard Prescott. He's had a thing against McPinsky for a long time. Three years ago, he organized a malicious campaign to discredit him at SoCalSci. Prescott's a typical company guy who equates bold thinking with controversy and trouble. I'd bet he's redirecting his paranoia at me, a McPinsky disciple, whom he perceives as a threat to his rocking-chair existence."

"He is definitely a piece of work," said Gorman. "Now we've got to reach a team decision on the best way to respond, especially since I was roused at 5 a.m. by a phone call from none other than Cristina Reyes of CNN."

Andrew perked up in his chair. "Cool. She's a damn good journalist and a hottie to boot. I've always wondered if her gorgeous emerald eyes are natural or contact lenses."

Lila shook her head and Seema rolled her eyes.

"Well," said Gorman, "I might soon be able to answer your question. She's invited me onto her TV show to discuss the rumors of our impending experiment."

"Damn that Prescott." Dmitri slammed a fist onto the table, and Greg's shoulders jerked.

"Don't fret," said Gorman. "With luck, we can spin this in our favor. But we'll have to make a quick decision, because the program begins at 1 p.m. local time. What do you think? Should I participate or not?"

"It's really your call, Chris," said Dmitri. "From what you've described, only PICES has been dragged into the muck. You're certain that SoCalSci wasn't mentioned?"

"Not a single hit when I'd Googled 'SoCalSci' and '*National Enquirer*.'"

"That's surprising," said Andrew. "I'd heard about a recent bust of one of our psych profs in the company of a notorious drag queen. Too bad it wasn't Prescott."

"Andrew, you're so gauche." Seema reached over and bonked him, playfully, on the head.

"It's all right, Seema." Gorman had recovered his usual calm demeanor. "We're all pretty downcast about these revolting developments. I appreciate Andrew's attempts at levity, lightweight as they may be."

"Okay," said Dmitri. "Since SoCalSci University has apparently flown beneath the media's radar, I'm even more convinced Prescott is the puppet master behind this farce. I'll phone the Dean of Engineering when he returns from his three-martini lunch."

"Since I can't wait that long," replied Gorman, "I've decided to address these charges head-on and defuse this brouhaha once and for all."

"Yea, Chris," Lila shouted, against a backdrop of scattered cheers.

"You know," said Hawkins, "once this blows over, all the publicity might be a boon to our whale watching business and fundraising efforts."

"Just be careful, Mr. Gorman," said Andrew. "There's a reason why Cristina Reyes is known as the 'Queen of Entrapment.'"

"Oh, yeah," said Greg. "Remember last year when she maneuvered that Orthodox Jewish congressman into admitting he'd made a killing in pork-belly futures? It cost him the election."

Dmitri chuckled. "How ironic," he said, "considering that for years he'd been reelected for bringing more pork to his district than anyone else in Congress." When the laughter subsided, Dmitri felt better, delighted by the revival of the team's high spirits.

"As an experienced diver, I deal with sharks like Reyes all the time," said Gorman. "And I don't think I'm hiding any skeletons in my closet." He checked his watch. "It's time to inform Ms. Reyes I'm prepared to be a willing participant in her gladiatorial arena. Then I'm off to the local TV studio for a noon makeup call. I think I'll opt for the guava eye shadow."

"Good luck, Chris," said Lila. She surprised him with a hug.

During the next three hours, the team focused on the experiment's final preparations. Andrew and Seema tested their Speakeasy and whale-synthesizer computer programs. Greg assisted Andrew in the migration of Spelvin's game-analysis code to Andrew's codebase. Dmitri engaged in a round-robin flurry of phone conversations with Lila and local contractors they'd hired to outfit the *Research in Paradise* floating laboratory. Lila directed the efforts on the boat, docked at the nearby Kihei boat harbor.

Hearing Shelly's summons to lunch, Dmitri couldn't believe the time had passed so quickly. After the famished collaborators had returned to the conference room and devoured their Caesar salad and pizza, it was nearly time for Gorman's broadcast.

"I'm getting nervous." Dmitri punched buttons on the TV's remote until he'd navigated to the correct channel.

"Me too," replied Hawkins, "but don't worry. Chris is an old pro at public speaking engagements."

When the familiar theme music heralded the beginning of the program, all eyes shifted to the portable television. The recognizable face of the Latina journalist appeared.

"I'm in love," whimpered Andrew. "It's those emerald eyes, those curve-licious lips."

He ducked to avoid the pizza crust Seema propelled in his direction.

"Serves you right," Greg chuckled.

"Good evening. This is Cristina Reyes of *CNN Headline News*, welcoming you to tonight's edition of *Urgent Assignment*. Our lead story: 'Are whales trying to tell us something?' We have confirmed that the Pacific Institute for Cetacean Educational Studies in Maui has discovered evidence of advanced intellectual capabilities in humpback whales. The Institute is preparing an interspecies communication experiment in Hawaiian waters to verify their initial findings. The news about the experiment has provoked vehement protests from organizations concerned about public monies spent on what they consider a dubious enterprise. We'll be back in a moment with a roundtable discussion."

Lila entered the room, gasping for breath. "I ran all the way."

"Don't worry," said Dmitri, "you didn't miss anything important." He pointed at the TV, currently airing a series of commercials.

"I saved you a slice of pizza," said Andrew, inviting her to sit in the seat next to him. "How's the boat?"

"We're looking shipshape for launch, but I've gotta say there's excitement brewing outside." She paused to catch her breath. "A van from the local TV station is parked just down the street with a satellite dish on its roof. I also saw the protesters that Chris mentioned and a news reporter and crew preparing for a broadcast."

"What kind of protestors?" asked Seema.

"Some were brandishing SAVE THE WHALES and STOP THE NAVY'S EXPERI-MENTS signs. Others were distributing Jehovah's Witness leaflets. They were definitely yelling at each another."

Reyes's voice grabbed everyone's attention. "Now let's hear what our panel of experts, spanning six time zones, has to say."

Boxes of talking heads began to populate the screen.

"Oh, God!" Greg pointed at the TV. "It's McPinsky."

"What the heck?" A sly smile emerged from the tense crease of Dmitri's mouth. "I knew he'd dive into this one way or another, but this tops them all."

"Which box is he?" asked Seema.

"Upper right."

McPinsky peered imperiously into the electromagnetic ether.

"He looks like a guru," said Seema.

"It's called *gravitas*," Greg responded.

"That's the Swami McPinsky challenge stare." Dmitri laughed. "To the notion his out-of-the-box essence can be confined to a CNN-boxed Microverse."

"Our headline guest expert is Ivy Tech Professor Theodosius McPinsky," announced Reyes as McPinsky's image filled the screen. "He is the architect of a controversial cosmological theory and an impassioned proponent for inter-species communication research. We've also invited Reverend Warren Ricks of Christ Church in Denver, Colorado, and a leading advocate of the theory of intelligent design. Also, from Washington, D.C., Captain Thomas Abrams, the founder and president of the controversial Sea Guardian Conservation Society. And last but not least, Mr. Christopher Gorman, the director of the Pacific Institute for Cetacean Educational Studies."

Like a crazed sports fan, Dmitri stood and cheered along with the rest of the team.

"Chris is looking great," exclaimed Lila, "more rested and relaxed than I've seen him in a long, long time."

"It's the guava eye shadow," Andrew grinned.

"Mr. Gorman," continued Reyes, "thank you for joining us all the way from the island paradise of Maui. Since there are so many conflicting rumors, here is your chance to clarify your organization's role in this controversial experiment."

Gorman's life-sized portrait extinguished all of the individual boxes.

"Thank you, Cristina." Gorman's military training was evident. He appeared to be in total command, sounding like a general describing the tactical details of a field operation. In laymen's terms, he summarized SoCalSci's discovery of the game-like pattern of symbols in the whale vocalizations, and then he outlined the goals of the experiment.

"Reverend Ricks," said Reyes, "do you wish to comment?"

The silver-haired Ricks's perfectly coifed televangelist image replaced Gorman's. "Why should taxpayer funds be used to, and I quote, 'engage in an advanced intellectual exercise' with animals swimming in the sea? Mr. Gorman just mentioned that the justification for this experiment is based upon the expert analysis of whale vocalizations by two esteemed mathematicians. Let me remind the audience of a similar so-called breakthrough by two esteemed chemists, over twenty years ago, promising limitless free energy in a test tube by the process of cold fusion. Needless to say, their results could never be confirmed, and they were both discredited."

"Ahh," interjected McPinsky.

"Yes, Professor McPinsky," said Reyes. "We'd like to hear your reaction to the Reverend's comments.

As McPinsky cleared his throat, the camera zoomed in. "The Reverend is referring to the infamous 1989 announcement of room-temperature nuclear fusion by the Utah electrochemists Fleischmann and Pons. Unfortunately for humanity, their findings could never be replicated. However, the scientific method did indeed triumph in that matter because rigorous follow-up studies failed to confirm their initial discovery. This is precisely why PICES is pursuing experimental verification of SoCalSci's claims."

"Mr. Gorman," said Reyes. "Do you also wish to respond to the Reverend's objections? Are public funds being used frivolously?"

"Our funding agency, the University of Hawaii, awards grants based upon their scientific merit and their potential benefits to society. We're proud that PICES is on the cutting edge of marine mammal research. Our educational programs are designed to share that knowledge with the public. As Professor McPinsky stated, the proposed experiment is an exercise of the scientific method, irrespective of the controversial implications. This is what academic freedom is all about. In that spirit, I'd also like to remind the public about a new lethal threat to our local humpback population—"

Reyes interrupted. "You're referring to the cluster of beached whales rumored to be linked to the Navy's sonar experiments. That's a very timely comment, Mr. Gorman, because it looks like the Greenpeace protest rallies at Pearl Harbor have shifted to Maui. We've received breaking news of an intensification of public demonstrations close to PICES headquarters. Let's go live to our affiliate in Maui."

A new image appeared on the TV. The microphone and camera captured the escalating booing and jostling of an unruly crowd. "That's what I saw," said Lila, pointing at the screen, "but it's gotten much worse. You can see the policemen protecting the news crew."

The middle-aged, African-American man in the center of the picture looked like any of the other tourists in a flowery shirt, white shorts, and maroon sports cap. However, he was the only person speaking into a hand-held microphone. "Thank you, Cristina. We're here at the boat dock in Kihei Harbor on the beautiful island of Maui. This is the spot where tourists gather each day to board the PICES whale watch tour boats. There are no tourists here today because, as you can see, they've been scared off by this vociferous mob of protestors. Nearly everyone here is clutching some sort of rally sign or wearing something espousing their cause. Here's a fellow holding a sign that says FREE SPEECH FOR WHALES. Sir, can whales really speak?"

"Dude, I'm a college student here in Kahului." The tanned youth stroked the blond bangs which intermittently covered his right eye. "As a surfer, I've shared the waters with the humpbacks my entire life. For sure, they're a unique species. If someone proves they can communicate, it's our duty to hear them out. The Constitution should be amended to guarantee free speech for all species."

"That's a pretty innovative take on the situation," said the correspondent. "You wouldn't by any chance be a pro-ACLU law student? You're also wearing an anti-Navy T-shirt."

"That's right. I was at Pearl Harbor last month to protest the sonar experiments destroying our humpbacks." The surfer's comment triggered an angry outburst behind the police barrier.

"Okay, let's get another opinion," said the broadcaster, pointing his microphone into the crowd. "You ma'am, please step forward." He motioned to a police officer who escorted a sweet-faced, young woman toward the camera. "You're holding a sign that says GENESIS 1:16."

"I'm a Christian Scientist here in Maui." Her voice was hoarse, as if she'd been shouting for a long time. "Genesis 1:16: 'And God said, Let us make man in our image, after our likeness, and let him have dominion over the fish in the sea.'"

"What significance does that verse hold for you here today?"

"Not just for me, but for all God-fearing individuals," she answered. "I heard about some researchers trying to talk to the whales. They're saying the whales are smart like humans, but that's not possible, according to the Bible." The camera captured her expression of dismay.

"How would you feel if it were proven other creatures had intelligence comparable to humans?"

"How can you ask that? Have you been to the zoo lately?"

"The whales *are* created in God's image," howled someone nearby.

"Who said that?" The newscaster pointed at the grizzled man who raised his hand. "You sir, step forward please and explain how whales are created in God's image."

The Willie Nelson lookalike with stringy, shoulder-length, gray hair shuffled into view. His frail frame was stooped under the weight of a sandwich board placard strapped to his chest. The sign was sprinkled with Biblical verses. "I witnessed the Holy Spirit enter the body of a beached humpback whale," he said. "It waved its fin in the sign of the cross just seconds before its last breath. Like this." He motioned with his right arm.

"Praise the Lord," howled Greg. "We stood on holy ground, Brother Dmitri."

The PICES conference room rocked with laughter.

The CNN broadcaster hesitated. His face strained with the effort to suppress a chuckle. "And you're sure you're not misinterpreting a random event?"

"If you don't believe me, check it out on YouTube. It's a miracle, like Lourdes. It's inspiring a new wave of eco-Christianity. Churches of the Whale are popping up across the country."

"There you have it, folks, a CNN exclusive. Eco-Christianity is alive and well, thanks to the Miracle of Maui. Thank you, sir. Do you have any final thoughts for our audience?"

"I'm a retired fisherman, and the whales never bothered me. We should treat them the same way and respect their territory. We native Hawaiians believe the humpbacks are one of the sacred spirits of our Islands. Too many tourist boats chase them down and shove microphones into their faces. If they want to communicate with us, then let them first come to us and—"

"Thank you so much, sir, but it's time that we return to our program in Washington. This is Michael Johnson, reporting from Kihei, Maui."

"Thank you, Michael," replied Reyes. "Okay. Let's get back to the members of our panel. Mr. Gorman, you've just heard a request from a native Hawaiian to respect the whales and his community's cultural values by leaving them alone. Your organization engages in tourist excursions, and now you've planned this experiment. What do you have to say to these people?"

"Cristina, we share the same values as the members of our local community. In our entire whale watch and research activities, we are prohibited by the Marine Mammal Protection Act from approaching closer than one hundred yards to any species of whale. What's fascinating is the humpbacks approach *us* for close encounters. I've occasionally been the object of a forty-foot humpback's scrutiny when diving off shore. It's mind-boggling."

"So according to you, your organization is exercising reasonable precautions," replied Reyes.

"We do, but the gentleman makes a valid point. Some privately owned boats and wildcat tour operators violate the one-hundred-yard limit and the spirit of the prohibition. We report such instances whenever we observe them, but it's a drop in the bucket compared to the number of abuses."

"By the way, the description of your underwater close encounter sounds exciting. It does suggest these creatures are curious and possibly intelligent. Thank you, Mr. Gorman."

"Thank you, Ms. Reyes. The next time you're in Maui, please join the PICES team for a guided dive with the humpbacks. Feeling the vibrations of their songs coursing through your body is an indescribable experience."

"That sounds like the makings of a very interesting segment," laughed Reyes. "Don't be surprised if I take you up on your offer."

"Brilliant move, Chris." Dmitri pumped his fist into the air.

"Let's get back to Professor McPinsky," said Reyes.

The Research in Paradise team's cheers, whistles, and hoots greeted McPinsky's reappearance.

"Professor, your ideas have been a lightning rod for controversy," Reyes said. "Three years ago, you incurred the wrath of fundamentalists when you challenged the scientific community for a communications breakthrough with other big-brained creatures. Now your alleged association with this experiment is quite a déjà vu."

"I'm sorry, Ms. Reyes, but despite all the rumors, I'm not a participant in this experiment."

"Your admirers have anointed you the leading exponent of the Radical Ultra-Secular Humanist organization, also known as RUSH. Because of their aggressive protest tactics, critics have characterized RUSH members as eco-anarchists." She paused for an instant. "According to RUSH's published mission statement, mankind urgently requires new scientific paradigms to address its existential crises. Can you briefly describe the core ideas of the RUSH movement?"

"You just introduced me using some erroneous labels. I'm not associated with any philosophical movements. I'm a man of science," chided McPinsky.

"I'm sorry to interrupt you, Professor," Reyes replied, her tone somewhat defensive, "but those so-called labels were assigned to you by others, not by me."

"Then let's just make it plain and simple." McPinsky's tone expressed impatience. "The chaotic scene in Maui is the very reason we need to engage other intelligent species. Science has failed to address the existential afflictions of the human race: our crippling isolation and our breach with nature. In desperation, humanity has resorted to palliative theological and philosophical belief systems. The foundation of all faith-based religions, such as the Church of the Whales we just heard about, is based upon a belief in miraculous events. To quote Joseph Campbell: 'If you want to change the world, you have to change the metaphor.' To my mind, that means we need a new, reality-based paradigm resulting from scientific breakthroughs and communications with other species."

"Hey, boss, your Professor acts like he exists on another level from us mere mortals, and I'm beginning to think he does. Cristina Reyes may have met her match."

Although Dmitri pretended to ignore Andrew's remark, he was brimming with pride to see his mentor dispensing his startling wisdom on such a grand stage.

"Thank you, Professor," replied Reyes, "but that sounds pretty convoluted to me and probably to most of our viewers. Can you please explain how the proposed whale communication experiment addresses humanity's existential crisis?"

"I certainly can," McPinsky responded. "Without feedback from other intelligent species, the human race is isolated and terribly alone. Any psychologist will tell you that a healthy, balanced individual needs a variety of peer, mentor, and family relationships to promote intellectual growth and emotional intelligence. Parental and mentor relationships provide guidance during development and provide us with the moral compass and ethical laws to live by. The same psychological analysis applies to our species consciousness. Our species needs an external support structure amongst the family of peer species. In the absence of external stimuli, we compensate with delusions. To some people, God is the supreme parent and the creator of the universe, and religion is the ultimate law-giver. To others, ETs are the intellectual peers we crave. And yet to others, paranormal spirits provide the emotional comfort we lack or are the daemons of the id that we fear."

"I challenge Professor McPinsky's wild assertions," interrupted Reverend Ricks. "Religion is universally embraced by all races and cultures. It is not just an aberration of group psychology. All of these systems share the same value: that mankind is related to the Creator and is cast in His image. I don't see any evidence to the contrary on our planet."

"No evidence has been found because we've not asked the right questions," said McPinsky. "Maybe because it strokes our egos to be the earth's top dog, we don't bother to ask these tough questions in the search for other intellects."

"Where is the evidence of other advanced intellects?" asked Ricks. "We've lived on the earth for thousands of years, and there's no sign of civilization other than our own. As far as most of us are concerned, Professor McPinsky notwithstanding, we are the guardians of the planet with dominion over all creatures."

"Ah-hah." Thomas Abrams, with his ruddy complexion and bushy, salt-and-pepper beard, projected the iconic image of a sea captain. "Yes, we are the guardians, but that doesn't justify planetary and species exploitation. The mission of our organization is to end the slaughter of wildlife in the world's oceans. Not to mention the disruption of their habitats caused by anthropogenic, meaning human-produced, noise. The list is long: underwater explosions used in seismic surveys, seabed drilling by oil companies, military and commercial sonars, and ship traffic. It's an unending onslaught upon their health, and it interferes with their normal behavior. I'm urging all of your viewers to log onto the *CetaceanRights.org* website and sign the 'Cetacean Bill of Rights.' Our fellow big-brained creatures should be entitled to the same rights we humans cherish: life, liberty, and the pursuit of happiness."

Reyes smiled. "Is there really such a website?"

"Absolutely," roared Abrams.

Reyes didn't appear intimidated. "The Sea Guardians' tactics are extremely controversial," she said. "Your attempts to damage Japanese whaling vessels have been condemned by Greenpeace and recently by His Holiness, Lama Dawa Cham."

"We need to fight fire with fire," replied Abrams. "Our actions are intended to incapacitate equipment, not to endanger people. Greenpeace's limited protest activities have not deterred the whaling nations from butchering whales."

"But Lama Dawa Cham said—"

"Just to set the record straight," interrupted Abrams, "His Holiness has consistently supported our organization's goal of preventing whalers from harming the giant sea mammals. His Holiness's recent quote about our non-violent, anti-whaling protests was a politically correct attempt to appease his hosts during a recent tour of Japan."

"I'll take your word for it," replied Reyes, whose peevish tone was directed at the guest who'd interrupted her. "So what's your organization's position on the PICES communication experiment?"

Captain Thomas Abrams was not easily intimidated. His voice energized by passion, he declared, "Your broadcast of the protests in Maui confirms that this is a controversial subject, even amongst members of the ecology community.

However, we all agree that the whales should be protected from mistreatment by commercial interests. To some of us, therefore, this also includes the potentially intrusive consequences of experimentation."

"We aren't ever going to know if there are other intellectual civilizations unless we break the codes of their language," countered McPinsky. "It's our species' responsibility to try for a breakthrough, and I cheer the PICES organization for attempting it. Anything less is an abrogation of our obligation as the dominant species on earth. We have nothing to lose and everything to gain if we discover other intelligent companions."

"Reverend Ricks," interjected Cristina Reyes, "you're known as a leading advocate of the theory of intelligent design. How would the members of your congregation react to a significant communication breakthrough with creatures on our own planet?"

"We of the faith believe the Grand Designer of intelligent creatures is the God of Christianity. Since humans are created in God's image, we should therefore assume our rightful role in the scheme of things."

"I don't hear any answer to Ms. Reyes's question," Abrams said. "Instead, I hear the familiar anthropocentric strains of the 'human exceptionalism' argument. It's an excuse for powerful organizations to play God with the rights of individuals and other species in order to justify commercial exploitation of the environment and the abuse of fragile ecosystems."

"I'm not surprised Mr. Ricks sidestepped your question, Ms. Reyes," said McPinsky. "It's a bad enough blow to the human ego to admit there could be intelligent creatures on other worlds. Imagine the future shock, however, if we were to discover they exist on our very own planet but hadn't been smart enough to detect it sooner. By the way, the notion that man is created in God's image reminds me—"

"I'm sorry to cut you short, Professor," said Reyes, "but our time has expired. I want to thank all of our distinguished panelists for a stimulating discussion. Stay tuned to *Headline News* for updates on the situation in Maui. This is Cristina Reyes of *Urgent Assignment* wishing you all a good night."

Dmitri turned off the TV. "I thought it went pretty well. That 'intelligent design' sophistry espoused by Ricks is a ruse. It's an end run around court rulings that prohibit the teaching of creationism as science."

"How ironically Darwinian," replied Greg, "that creationism itself needs to evolve in order to ensure its survival."

"Brilliant deduction, Greg," replied Dmitri. "Now, if only Prescott had evolved beyond the Neanderthal stage, we'd be home free."

"Ouch." Greg slapped his forehead "We definitely know where you stand with *that* guy."

Dmitri turned to address the group. "Okay, I've got to make some phone calls, so let's take a thirty-minute break and then reconvene in the conference room."

Half an hour later, the Research in Paradise team had regrouped to discuss the inventory of supplies for the pending launch.

"Yikes." Andrew jumped to his feet. A loud bang just outside the building startled the entire team.

Hawkins dashed into the lobby and everyone followed. He lifted a corner section of the window blinds. As Dmitri peeked out, he saw chanting protestors marching in circles in front of the PICES offices.

"There's Chris," shouted Hawkins.

Through the window, Dmitri saw Gorman struggling to shove his way through the crowd. Hawkins cracked the door open. Gorman staggered through, slammed the door shut, and locked it. He dripped with perspiration. "I'm okay." He wiped his face with the souvenir PICES handkerchief provided by his assistant, Shelley.

The team followed Gorman back into in the conference room. Dmitri tried to be upbeat. "That was an excellent presentation, Chris. You made the case for the PICES organization and the legitimacy of its research program."

"I guess so. Nevertheless, whoever pulled this media stunt is probably laughing. They've unleashed the mobs upon us. Did you see how I had to bulldoze my way through that throng just to get in here? It's a zoo out there. Let's forget about the experiment. Right now I'm more concerned for our safety."

"Not only that." Hawkins sounded grim. "Our naturalists had to cancel all of today's whale-watch tours. The tourists are afraid to get anywhere near the dock."

Shelley opened the door. "Hey, everybody, turn the TV back on. All hell is breaking loose."

Hawkins grabbed the remote and hit the power button.

"This is Michael Johnson back on the boat docks in Kihei, Maui, on a lovely afternoon. During the past hour, clashes have intensified between those who support and those who oppose the controversial PICES experiment. Police are arresting individuals who've escalated their protests to the level of physical violence. Some of these incidents are allegedly fueled by the consumption of alcohol and drugs. I've got a Maui peace officer with me. Sir, will you impose a curfew to quell the disturbances?"

"Not really," replied the officer. "There aren't enough cells on the island to handle arrests due to curfew violations. We'll deal with the worst of the lot, and then I'm sure it'll all simmer down by tomorrow. After all, this is laid-back Maui. We want to assure everyone that it's still safe to visit our island paradise." He smiled for the camera.

"Thank you for the update, officer. It's taken a very nasty turn out here, and there doesn't seem to be any relief in sight. Now back to our Atlanta studios."

"That just sucks." Andrew paced with his hands in his pockets. "This has nothing to do with the experiment. Bringing in the TV cameras is a calling card for all the loons who want their fifteen minutes of fame."

Gorman shook his head. "The game's over. It's just too dangerous out there. I've decided to suspend our experiment indefinitely. We'll resume if and when the passions die down."

"You can't do that." Lila rose, looking furious. "That's just what they want."

Another sharp bang against the side wall of the building stopped the conversation. A fusillade of thumps and booms reverberated throughout the conference room.

"I'm getting scared." Seema's voice sounded small and tentative. "Where are the police?"

A blast of shattering glass and a woman's chilling scream jolted everyone at the table.

"Shelley's out there." Gorman leapt to his feet and rushed out the door. Dmitri followed him into the lobby, shocked by the grisly scene. The front window had been demolished, and the blinds swayed in the breeze. A large rock lay in the middle of the glass-littered floor. Shelley cowered beneath the desk. Her whimpering drew the rest of the team into the room and Gorman to her side.

"Maui police! Open up!"

Hawkins unlocked the door, and four cops poured into the lobby. An officer with a sergeant's badge approached Gorman. "I'm sorry we weren't here to stop this. Is everyone all right?"

Gorman helped Shelley to her feet. Despite her tan, her face appeared bleached of its vitality.

"Oh, no!" cried Lila.

Slivers of glass covered Shelley's blood-stained arms and clothing. Remarkably, her face had been spared.

The sergeant motioned to two of his men. "We'll escort you to the hospital, ma'am." As she left, trembling but subdued, the sergeant faced Gorman and said, "Looks like she's in shock. Fortunately, her wounds appear minor."

"Hey, check this out." Andrew held the rock in his hands. "There's a note attached." Before the cops could react, he untied the string and unfolded the paper. "Uh-oh," he moaned.

"Lemme see that." The sergeant grasped the edge of the note between his thumb and forefinger. "This is evidence. Take it to the lab, Garza." He handed the page to one of his assistants. "I just got another emergency call, so I'm leaving one of my officers to guard your building. In the meantime, I suggest you contact Maui Glass to fix this window. If you need anything else, here's my card."

After the police left, the team moved back to the conference room. After they'd all exchanged anxious stares, Gorman cleared his throat. "Andrew, what did the note say?"

Andrew looked confused, his eyes darting around the table. "Death," he murmured. Seema gasped.

"That does it." Gorman's bold tones tolled like a command. "It's just too risky to proceed."

"You can't wimp out on the whales, Chris!" Lila snarled. "Everything is ready to go! We can prove once and for all that the humpbacks deserve humanity's respect. Now is the time to strike."

Dmitri fully expected Gorman to lose his cool and lash back at his young researcher's impetuous remarks. Instead, the PICES director sagged back into the chair and stared at the ceiling. When he finally spoke, Dmitri strained to hear his muted voice. "It's killing me, Lila. Don't for a minute think I wouldn't risk my life to save even a single endangered humpback. But I also have the perspective of leading others into battle . . . bearing the life-long burden of lives lost under my command . . . experiencing a family's grief as I delivered the news." Gorman paused. His eyes glistened. "It took me years to make peace with those decisions. As a Navy officer, I'd issue those same orders again. But as a civilian, I've no right to endanger your lives."

Lila walked over and placed a consoling hand on her boss's shoulder. "I had no idea, Chris."

"How could you?"

Lila paused and gazed into her supervisor's eyes before speaking. "Please don't take this the wrong way, but new lives are at stake. Since you're the director of PICES, I truly believe you need to honor your commitment to protect and preserve the cetaceans."

Gorman stood. "I agree, but not at the risk of human life. I'm sorry, but my mind is made up." He left the room, Hawkins trailing behind him.

Although Dmitri was shocked by Lila's outburst, he agreed with her. But what could *he* do? After all, this was Gorman's organization, and it stood in the crosshairs of a national media assault. Dmitri sensed, however, that Lila wouldn't let it rest.

"You know I'm right." Lila's face was flushed. "This is an occasion that comes along once in a lifetime. We've worked hard, and we're ready to launch. If we miss the opportunity, it could be years before the stars are in perfect alignment again." Lila approached Dmitri, hovering over him. "Dr. Dmitri, your mentor said it more eloquently than I ever could. It's not about us. It's about the existential redemption of the human race and the survival of the cetaceans. Dr. Dmitri, I implore you to follow through on your inspiration and—"

Dmitri tugged at his shirt collar. "And what?"

"I have a friend who could pilot the boat."

"What are you suggesting, Lila?"

"If Chris doesn't change his mind by tomorrow, my friend, Tony, could help us bypass the protestors' barricade. We could approach and board the boat from the water under the cover of darkness. Tony is a master pilot who does contract work for various tour companies, so we won't need Chris or Peter's nautical skills. I've done whale song field research for over two years. I know their habitats, their behavior, and how to locate them. I'm an expert diver, and I can pilot a boat if necessary."

"That sounds illegal to me." Dmitri brushed away the beads of moisture tickling his brow. "Your boss would be hopping mad and probably press charges against whoever's involved."

"I know the real Chris Gorman," implored Lila, "and he's a complicated guy but a very good one. Right now his ethics compel him to protect us. But once we've made the decision for him, I know his passion for the humpbacks will prevail. He'll find a way to forgive us. And reengage with us too."

"Unless, of course, we encounter real trouble on the high seas and something terrible happens," Dmitri said softly. "I'd be wracked with guilt the rest of my life."

A spasm of emotion contorted Lila's face. "PICES researchers on Molokai reported two more humpbacks washed ashore this morning." Her cheeks and forehead had turned red. "To paraphrase Hegel, 'The history of the world is a slaughter bench, because of actors that did not think and thinkers that did not act.' For the sake of the whales, now is the time to act."

After a prolonged silence, Seema sighed. "I agree with Lila. I think Professor McPinsky would want us to proceed."

"Me too, boss," said Andrew. "The potential rewards outweigh the risks."

It was obvious to Dmitri that the fault line of opinion was generational. "And the children shall lead them," he thought to himself.

"*Et tu*, Greg?" he asked.

Greg replied immediately. "You're my compadre. Whatever you decide is fine with me."

Dmitri locked the fingers of both hands over his head and began to pace around the table. "It's all up to me then. I've never had to make a decision so agonizing."

"I'm sorry I put you in such an awkward position," said Lila. "Why don't you think about it? Get a good night's rest, and then tomorrow you can discuss the matter with our mutual friend. Melanie is the most supportive person I've ever known."

Dmitri knew Melanie would be devastated by Lila's news about the whales' escalating death toll. He ceased his pacing. Realizing he couldn't look Lila in the eye, he hung his head and stared at the floor.

"Oh, and one more thing," said Lila, with a new air of authority. "With the exception of Melanie, not a word of what we've discussed leaves this room."

Everyone was speechless. After all, what more could they say?

Symphony in the Park

Wailuku Public Park, Wailuku, Maui—the next day

"MEET ME IN Wailuku at the koi pond in Keilani Park, no later than 1:55 p.m. I've attached a link to a map of the area."

After reading the last sentence of Melanie's text message, Dmitri checked his wristwatch: 1:48 p.m. He stared at the creased map one more time. It was rumpled and smudged, appearing to have absorbed all of his recent tension. Confident he'd arrived at the right destination, he stuffed the printout into a back pocket and started walking down a cheerful bougainvillea-lined path. A pleasant stroll like this would normally set his mind at ease. This time, however, he couldn't stop worrying about his current dilemma.

For the past twenty-four hours, he'd been paralyzed by indecision about the fate of the experiment. After yesterday's debacle at PICES headquarters, Gorman had informed Padgett he'd suspended their investigation, citing safety issues related to the violent protests. The youngest members of the team, however, had again beseeched Dmitri to override Gorman's edict and to sanction a stealth launch.

All morning, Dmitri had grappled with the tumultuous forces raging inside his head. Realizing he needed the counsel of the one person on the island he trusted most, he phoned Melanie. Once he'd told her about the latest developments, she'd juggled her work schedule for a rendezvous at her favorite public park. He'd been curious about her insistence to meet at such a precise time, and just to be safe, he had arrived a bit early.

He hadn't been to a park in a long time, and as he surveyed the landscape, he realized he needed to spend more time outdoors instead of cloistered in a laboratory. The brilliant sunshine illuminated a vivid floral tapestry, framed by blue sky and green grass. A distant figure waved to him from a bench next to a lily pond. Dmitri raised a hand in greeting. He saw Melanie surrounded by the purple clouds of a flowering jacaranda grove and a magenta ground fog of bougainvillea.

As he approached, his pulse quickened. Her lithe figure was graced by a jade-green, silk cheongsam. To Dmitri she looked like the spectacular centerpiece of an impressionistic painting. He inhaled the perfumed scent of ginger and was greeted by the serenade of hundreds of Hawaiian songbirds and whistling mynahs. They sounded like little music boxes hidden in the branches. The melodious chorus lifted his spirits. He sat down next to Melanie and held his breath. A black and gold butterfly adorned her hair, flexing its wings like a decorative fan beating the air.

"You arrived just in time." The butterfly took wing.

"For what?" he replied.

"You'll soon find out. How are you holding up under the pressure?"

"Before I forget, I want to thank you for arranging such a wonderful picnic of color and sound." He reached for her hand. "I already feel like a weight has been lifted from my shoulders. The bird symphony is as mesmerizing as you are." She didn't hesitate to respond, embracing him. He pressed his cheek to her satiny hair and inhaled the scent of jasmine.

Melanie turned and their eyes met. "It's a very calming sound. I come here to relax on hectic days, and I'm so glad it's helping you unwind." She peeked at her wristwatch. "Now get ready for the next song on today's program."

From across the park, Dmitri heard the clarion call of a school bell. The avian chorus instantly evaporated into the sweet-scented air. After a brief silence, he heard a crescendo of exuberant chatter from a nearby playground.

He gave her a quizzical look. "It's uncanny that the birds stopped just as the children's voices began."

"It happens every time. I think the birds are entranced by the children's playful twittering."

"Human white noise." He smiled. "It's such a peaceful sound, and soothing, like your voice." She squeezed his hand.

"For me it's inspirational. It reminds me of my childhood hopes and dreams. And the chameleon-like quality reflects my moods. How is it affecting you?"

"It's hard to tell," Dmitri replied, "but you're right. Their voices take me back to my childhood. In some strange way, I'm sensing something about my past is the reason I'm struggling now."

She nodded. "Maybe we can figure it out."

"I'm a pretty lucky guy to have you as my guardian angel." Dmitri brushed his fingertips across her cheek. "I'm also recognizing a theme emerging from your orchestration of this concert in the park event. First, the chorus of bird-song followed by the celestial children's choir—"

"And remember the songs of the humpback. So what theme are you referring to? What's the binding tie?" Melanie's smile sparkled in the natural light.

"You're a magician," he exclaimed. "You can add song therapist to your resume. Yes, yes, I know Lila is right. Except for the fact that a wildcat launch is probably illegal and obviously usurps Gorman's authority, taking a risk for the whales makes a lot of sense. What to do? What to do?" He looked up to the sky and shook his head.

"I know it sounds corny," answered Melanie, "but sometimes when I need even more inspiration, I visit my neighborhood elementary school playground when nobody's there."

"How—"

Before he could continue, she placed her soft palm upon his lips. "I sit on a swing and visualize the thousands of children who've played on that field. I imagine their spirits have been absorbed into the ground. Then I begin to kick my knees like I did as a child and swing wildly. When I'm completely giddy and accelerating toward the earth, I summon all my willpower to channel that same spiritual energy out of the ground and into my mind and body. To me, that schoolyard is more of a cathedral than any church. Maybe we can go there sometime."

The sound of a familiar musical jingle punctured Dmitri's reverie. Sounding like the tintinnabulations of a music box melody, the tune reminded him of the bell-ringing announcement on his father's ice cream truck. Long ago, he'd composed a tribute to his dad to this very jingle. He hadn't thought about it for many years. He had called it "The Song of My Father."

Dmitri stared into space. When a single tear slid down his cheek, Melanie reached out and clutched his shoulders. "I'm so sorry." She shook him gently. "I didn't realize you'd be . . ."

Her voice and her touch brought him back. He turned to face her. "How did you know I should hear that?"

"The last time you visited me, you mentioned your father's accident. I wanted to help you so badly, I—"

Just as she had done earlier, he touched his fingers, ever so gently, to her lips. "After school, the kids streamed into the street to my father's ice cream truck and his beckoning jingle. It was a mob scene of pure delight. All of my classmates danced around him, waving their quarters, and begging him to be first to receive their treats. They adored him and so did I. Despite the drudgery of a low-paying job, I could see how happy he'd been to bring joy to so many kids. I was so proud to be his son." Dmitri choked back emotion, pausing to regain his composure. "Those were the happiest moments of my childhood, maybe even of my entire life."

Melanie leaned closer, until they were face-to-face, and grasped his hands. "I know your father would be very proud of you—a scientist in the quest of breakthrough discoveries. If he were with us now, you'd probably be asking for his advice instead of mine. So what do you think he'd want you to do? While you're thinking about it, close your eyes."

Dmitri did as instructed and soon felt Melanie's soft caress upon his temples. While she massaged his scalp, she'd begun to hum the lyrical melody of "Greensleeves." He luxuriated in the soothing sensations of her tender strokes and floated upon the gentle swells of her voice. As he purred and smiled, the vexing thoughts that had clouded his mind gradually dissipated. Like a fog dissolving to reveal a marvelous hidden landscape, his mind's eye gazed upon the images of both his true father and his adoptive father figure. Although it was too late to save Michael Dmitri, David Dmitri could still "rescue" McPinsky. To his amazement, the goddess of the mountain had once again transmuted sound and vibration into illumination. He opened his eyes to the sight of her radiant smile.

"Hey, buster." Melanie poked a finger into Dmitri's chest. "Don't think for a minute you're going to launch that floating Speakeasy Lab without the assistance of your neighborhood speech therapist."

Dmitri responded with a crisp military salute. "Permission granted. All aboard ship."

Melanie saluted back. "By the way, Captain, when do we sail?"

"Lila said we'd better sneak aboard and launch a couple of hours before sunrise. Her pal is piloting the boat. So tell me, how are you interpreting the sounds from the playground right about now?"

"Like an *Ode to Joy*," she whispered, and planted a lingering kiss on his lips.

A few moments later, Dmitri heard the ringing of a school bell. With a glance at her wrist watch, Melanie said, "Recess is over." When the joyful buzz of the children's chorus subsided, she waved an imaginary baton up into the trees and winked. Within seconds, the mynah bird symphony resumed at full-throated intensity.

Windward Sea Flight

Kihei Boat Harbor, Maui—pre-dawn, the next morning

"DON'T SPLASH SO loud!" Lila's fierce whisper pierced the night.

Frozen in mid-stroke, Dmitri clutched an oar and listened. The once distant voices were much closer now. "I can't believe we're doing this."

"Shhh, be quiet," Lila commanded.

Clad in black, their faces shadowed by dark makeup, the seven coconspirators stealthily rowed a pair of rafts along the quay. Dmitri shared the lead raft with Lila, Melanie, and Greg. Seema, Andrew, and Lila's friend Tony, who was to pilot the *Research in Paradise* experimental vessel, followed in their wake. Concealed by the cloak of a new moon, they navigated toward the floodlit glow of the PICES boat dock. Dmitri watched the reflections of onshore lights shimmering on the water. The undulating images conjured up reflections of recent events.

Following Lila's plan, Dmitri had driven Melanie and his SoCalSci associates to the 3 a.m. rendezvous point, a secluded frontage road at the far end of the Kihei boat harbor. After they'd scrambled across the beachfront to the jetty rocks, their flashlights found Lila and Tony perched upon two inflatable Zodiac rafts. Despite the bobbing motion of the lightweight vessels, the ticklish boarding operation had gone smoothly until Andrew stumbled knee-deep into the bay. Once they'd yanked him aboard, Lila and Tony had outlined the plan to circumnavigate the harbor and approach the boat dock under a curtain of darkness and silence.

As soon as they'd launched, they discovered the difficulty in coordinating their paddling efforts. They seemed to be going nowhere fast and had fallen behind schedule according to Dmitri's glow-in-the-dark watch. "Okay," said Lila. "On my mark, pull." Repeating the command numerous times, they'd synchronized to her rhythm and surged ahead at a steady clip.

Now, fifteen minutes later, they converged upon their destination. Dmitri's trepidation intensified as the raft pitched upon the wavelets whipped up by an advancing storm. "Did you hear that?" In this anxious state, he imagined he'd heard an eerie greeting call. Paddling closer to the dock, he cupped a hand to his ear. The foreboding sound had turned into a peaceful symphony of chimes: the rigging cables of many boats beating against their stolid masts. Just an oar's length away from the *Research in Paradise*, Dmitri glanced up at the double-decker boat and shivered. Illuminated by the dock lights, the all-white vessel incandesced with a faint, spectral glow—like a ghost ship.

Dmitri shuddered at the yelping, rowdy outbursts echoing from the pier. He'd read the news reports about a protest blockade to prevent dockside access to their vessel. Fundamentalists had proclaimed the PICES experiment a violation of God's will and had organized an around-the-clock vigil to enforce their edict. To avoid a confrontation, Dmitri's teammates knew they'd need to execute their plan to perfection.

Tony, now officially in command of the *Research in Paradise* crew, whispered instructions for boarding the fifty-foot vessel. He was the first to ascend the six-foot ladder at the left side of the stern and adjacent to the boarding ramp. Aided by helping hands, the precarious transfer from the Zodiacs up to the passenger deck proceeded without a hitch. Being the last person to cross over, Lila shoved and kicked the two sixty-pound rafts and watched as they drifted away. A friend would retrieve them at sunrise.

Tony toggled his LED headlamp three times, the prearranged signal to Andrew, Lila, Dmitri, and Greg to untie the ropes tethering the boat to the dock cleats. They tiptoed across the stern's compact first-level deck, their footsteps illuminated by the headlamps Lila had purchased from a local camping store.

According to plan, Melanie and Seema disappeared through a door into the enclosed passenger area housing the glass-bottomed observation deck. Andrew and Lila, the two most athletically inclined members of the team, kneeled at the top of the gangway entrance ramp. They clutched oars like shields, arms extended, and prepared for battle. Dmitri and Greg crouched behind them as a second line of defense.

Dmitri wiped his forehead. He was soaked in perspiration. This was the pivotal moment. Their next action would set them upon an irreversible course. He saw Tony climb the stairs to the spacious, upper-level observation deck. Dmitri knew what to expect. Tony entered the pilot house, perched above the bow, and donned a set of night-vision goggles, a memento of his military service in Iraq. Tony paused while his eyes adapted to the goggles, and after a quick study of the boat's controls, he signaled down to Andrew and Lila. Dmitri drew a deep breath and held it in, waiting for—

The engine roared to life, shattering the night silence, and triggering an instantaneous commotion on the pier.

"Hey . . . what's that noise? They're getting away! Stop that boat!"

Within seconds, flashlight beams crisscrossed the dock and climbed the boarding ramp, illuminating the shadowy forms of Lila and Andrew. Hearing clanging footsteps and seeing three hefty, flashlight-bearing figures charging up the aluminum gangway, Dmitri braced himself for an ugly showdown. The conspirators, however, had anticipated this contingency. Tony jerked the gear in the reverse direction. Seeing the boat inching away from the slip, the protestors leapt from the top of the ramp. Andrew and Lila wielded their oars like martial artists. With deft strokes to their foes' shins, they knocked them off-balance. As the boat glided away, two of the dazed attackers screamed expletives and splashed into the water.

With Lila and Andrew fully engaged, the third interloper landed on the lower deck, scrambled to his feet, and bulldozed past them. Like an NFL linebacker charging the quarterback and snorting like an enraged bull, he tackled Dmitri. They hit the deck together with a crashing thud. Hearing the grunts, groans, and the thrashing of limbs, Dmitri's teammates joined the fracas. Lila and Andrew grabbed the attacker by the legs, pulling him clear. Greg's left foot delivered an immobilizing blow to the assailant's groin. Dragging him to the gunwale, they hoisted him overboard to be reunited with his thrashing companions.

By the time the invaders had scrambled out of the water, Tony had maneuvered well away from the dock. He shifted into forward gear and gunned the engines. The *Research in Paradise* accelerated away from its bondage. Dmitri's heart beat a crazy rhythm in his chest. He fully expected to hear the shrieking siren of a Coast Guard cutter bearing down on them. For an interminable minute, he listened to the steady soliloquy of the boat's engine as the enemy's voices gradually faded away. His face hurt and he shivered in the darkness, but he also felt waves of relief. He'd overcome his own worst fears. The team, *his* team, had triumphed over their adversaries.

"We did it!" hollered Andrew.

Lila let out a whoop. "Yeah! The forces of evil have been vanquished." The giddy duo exchanged hand slaps.

Hearing the commotion, Melanie and Seema bounded outside.

"Guys, that was amazing," said Melanie. "How did you get rid of them?"

"The years of aikido paid off." Andrew waved an oar, triumphantly, above his head. "I practiced stick fighting every day in class. The basic idea is to knock your attacker off balance, and in this case, into the water." He gave them a whirlwind demo as he spun and thrust the oar at an invisible foe. "And Lila was fantastic!"

"I was captain of my college field hockey team." Lila laughed. "I pretended the oar was the hockey stick and their ankles the *pelota*."

Lila and Andrew's shipmates showered them with mirthful accolades, rejoicing in the dim illumination of their headlamps.

"We look like a school of flashlight fish," said Greg.

"What's the story with those cool Ninja outfits, Lila?" asked Dmitri. "They remind me of a Bruce Lee movie."

"Would you believe these are old Halloween costumes," replied Lila. "I even found one that fit Andrew's scrawny frame." She covered his face with her palm.

Even Andrew shared in the collective laughter.

Seema spoke through a torrent of giggles. "Do you guys realize how ridiculous our faces look?"

"Yeah," replied Andrew, licking his lips, "and it doesn't taste very good either." Andrew's finger traced a streak across his mascara-encrusted cheek.

"I can solve that problem." Lila rushed inside. She returned bearing a big, cloth bag. "Here you go." She passed out hand towels and mocha Frappuccinos, enough for everyone.

"Thank you!" Melanie raised her bottle like a celebratory libation and proposed a toast to her friend's thoughtfulness.

After they'd wiped away the makeup, they went upstairs for some fresh air. Savoring their mochas, they watched silently as the shore lights receded into the distance.

Melanie's probing flashlight beam revealed a blue welt under Dmitri's right eye. "Poor baby, what happened?"

"Don't you know?" Greg slapped Dmitri on the shoulder. "Dr. Dmitri here put his body on the line. The guy who tackled him was a brute, too."

Dmitri dabbed gingerly at his eye. "Ouch," he groaned.

"My hero," Melanie cooed and hugged him.

As the scudding boat bounced upon the rough seas, Dmitri felt a bit queasy. Nevertheless, he was thrilled. They sailed, unimpeded, toward an opportunity to revolutionize the mindscape of language and intelligence. The weight upon his conscience—that he'd sanctioned this desperate action—lifted, and he experienced the buoyancy he imagined an astronaut might feel upon launching into earth orbit. They heaved through the water at a speed of about fifteen knots in the windward direction, west by southwest, through the Kealaikahiki Channel and into the leeward waters of Maui County. They'd planned to get as far away as possible from the primary shipping lane known as the Lahaina Roads.

"Hey, mates." Tony's husky voice boomed down from the pilothouse. "It's an hour before dawn and over ninety minutes until we arrive at our secret destination. Why don't you all go below deck and catch forty winks. We've a long day ahead of us." As Tony gripped the wheel and stroked his bushy beard, he reminded Dmitri of the archetypal image of a brawny sailor.

Charged by the mochas and the adrenalin rush of their clandestine adventure, the team opted instead to prepare for the day's activities. They descended the stairs to the glass-bottom tourist portion of the boat, now converted into a makeshift Speakeasy control room. Temporary workstations consisting of two portable folding tables and four chairs, secured to the floor by suction cups, hugged the cabin's perimeter. Two large LCD flatscreens had been mounted to the wall above the workstations. Andrew, Seema, and Greg powered their laptops and initialized the various signal processing and statistical analysis programs that were the essential tools for this unique experiment.

In the ambient illumination of the cabin's LED ceiling lights, Greg did a double take at the sight of Dmitri's face. "Hey pal, you look wasted, and your shiner's getting worse. Why don't you and Melanie take some blankets topside and lie down under the stars? We've got things under control."

"Ditto, boss," added Andrew. "Seema and I are about to start testing the Speakeasy interface to the underwater hydrophones and speakers. Go take a nap. You deserve it."

"That's a great idea." Melanie yawned. "We'll return the favor and fetch you guys at dawn. It's fantastic to watch the color of the water changing in the morning light."

"I've never experienced a sunrise on the open ocean," said Seema. "Please don't forget to call us."

"I promise." Melanie grabbed Dmitri's hand and as they ascended the stairs, arm in arm, Dmitri could hear the faint voices of Andrew and Seema.

"So Seema, whaddya think of the boss's new girlfriend?" asked Andrew. "Pretty hot, huh?"

"Men. That's all you ever think about. She *is* a speech therapist and a linguist, and since you asked, I'm very happy for Dr. Dmitri. He deserves someone like Melanie. And he's been a bachelor for a long time. In my country, a man in his late thirties can be a grandfather."

"You'd make a cute grandfather." Melanie laughed as they arranged a bed of blankets inside one of the two rubber life rafts tethered to the deck.

"Oh no, you heard them too?"

"My dad once told me you can't keep a secret on a boat." Settling into their improvised nest, they snuggled together. "Dmitri, my injured hero," Melanie crooned, delighting him with her puppy-dog eyes. "Before you fall asleep, I want you to know that being here with you is better than any luxury cruise."

"I have to admit it's been quite a day," Dmitri replied with a big grin. "First the *Mission Impossible* getaway sequence and now I get to share the *Love Boat* with you." He reached over and took her head gently between his hands. Her lips were soft and pillowy, and he thought for a moment he'd fallen asleep on them—that the night was all a big dream. But it wasn't a dream. Melanie kissed him back.

As they lay down and watched the pulsating cloud of stardust, Dmitri was reminded of his first camping adventure with his dad and brother. Enjoying the soothing sound of the boat skidding across the ocean, he realized he was falling in love with the Islands and with the goddess beside him. Why not take a one-year sabbatical in paradise and devote himself to his new-found love and her bright and appealing son, Mark? During their few encounters, he had grown quite fond of the boy. He'd won Dmitri over during their very first conversation, when he had asked Melanie's son about his age. With quiet confidence and a straight face, Mark's binary-correct answer had been, "two cubed plus one."

Cuddled cheek to cheek with Melanie, he meditated to the rhythmic warmth of her breath, mumbling as he drifted toward sleep.

Victory at Sea

Kealaikahiki Channel—dawn

"DMITRI, WAKE UP," Melanie whispered into his ear, gently shaking his shoulder. "You have to see this."

"What's that sound?" Half-asleep, Dmitri squinted into the twilight. Melanie pointed to starboard and he turned his head, startled by the pair of dolphins that squealed enthusiastically and flew through the air like airborne torpedoes, pacing the boat.

He stood, pulling Melanie along with him, and shivered in the chill of the brisk morning breeze. Leaning over the railing, he thrilled to the sight of a pod of dolphins riding the bow wake, like a winged formation of surfers. The cetacean escort party hurdled alongside the *Research in Paradise*: taking turns leaping out of the water, jabbering at them, and cavorting about like the happiest creatures in the sea.

Dmitri danced across the pitching deck to the stairs. "Hey everybody," he called. "Get topside. We've got company."

Seema was the first to arrive. "Just listen to them, those whistles and clicks." The words raced from her mouth at twice the rate of her normal speech. "They sound like they're talking to us in an alien language."

"It would be fascinating to analyze their voices with Speakeasy," replied Dmitri. He brushed the sleep from his eyes. "John Lilly studied their behavior and vocalizations for over thirty years. It's obvious they're a very intelligent species. The problem is that, just like the humpbacks, no one's broken the code to their language. How about it, team? Depending upon today's outcome, there might be another interspecies communication opportunity here next year."

"Sounds cool, boss," replied Andrew, "but shouldn't we finish this experiment first?"

Andrew's comment resurrected the concerns gnawing at the edges of Dmitri's sleep-deprived brain. Despite everyone's best intentions, maybe they had fooled themselves. Although Spelvin had claimed an 85% confidence factor in his analytical approach, there were many compelling reasons to doubt the validity of the whale game theory. It could be nothing more than a glorious fallacy. Had his desire to validate McPinsky distorted his objectivity? And this mission, fraught with unknown consequences and possibly placing Seema and Andrew in harm's way, was now his responsibility. He hoped Lila's intuition was correct: that Chris Gorman was a forgiving guy who valued the fate of the humpbacks more than his own authority.

Through a fog of fatigue, Dmitri heard the animated conversations of his shipmates and their enjoyment of the gymnastic exploits of their dolphin entourage. He faced the horizon and saw the pinkish glow of daybreak intensifying with each moment. It was the dawn of a glorious new day. How could he not be infused with a renewed spirit of hope and anticipation?

"This is a really good omen for today's experiment," said Lila. "Normally a pod of dolphins won't track a boat longer than ten minutes."

Seema appeared hypnotized. "It's the first time I've seen the rosy fingers of dawn reflected off the water in the middle of the ocean."

"I'm impressed," replied Lila, turning to face Dmitri. "Seema's not only a scientist and a musician, she quotes Homer."

Seema blushed. "The *Odyssey* is my favorite book."

Dmitri smiled. Since everyone was in such good spirits, he'd try his best to remain positive. "Hopefully, like the *Odyssey*, our voyage will lead to epic adventures and discoveries."

Melanie wrapped her arms around Dmitri's waist. "It's nice to see you in such a good mood so early in the morning."

"The sunrise reminds me of the *Ten Commandments*," said Greg, "where Moses dips the divine staff into the Nile and turns the waters red."

"Interesting you'd invoke a Biblical image at this moment," said Lila.

"Well," replied Greg, "if you think about what we're attempting today, it does smack a bit of the miraculous."

Melanie nodded. "Speaking of miracles," she said, "did you notice how the sea has calmed down? That storm must have headed in the opposite direction."

"Hooray!" Andrew shouted.

"Well, Sister Seema," said Lila. "Did you know that PICES offers humpback whale research internships to motivated individuals? You can enjoy many more ocean sunrises if you join us. The perk is that we do humpback research all over the globe."

"Very cool," replied Andrew. "I'd like to compare and contrast the mating habits of humpbacks in the Indian and Pacific Oceans."

"I'm sure you'd like to study the mating habits of many species," replied Lila.

"Is that an invitation?"

"Hey, Lila," interjected Dmitri. "Are you trying to steal my graduate students?"

"If today's experiment yields promising data," replied Lila, "maybe your entire team could relocate to Maui for an extended research-in-paradise-sabbatical joint venture with PICES."

Before Dmitri could reply, he was blinded by a spectacular burst of light. A sliver of sunlight flashed above the horizon.

"Look!" shouted Andrew. "Out here away from the land, where it's perfectly flat in all directions, you can almost see the horizon's curvature." He whirled around and swept his arms in a wide circle.

"You're right. It's like we're in earth orbit." Greg squinted at the solar disk. "This is just blissed-out sensory overload."

As the dolphins danced away into the sunrise, a one-hundred-decibel symphony boomed from the ship's public address system. Dmitri wobbled across the deck to the helm.

"Thanks, Tony," said Dmitri. "I always loved this music. It's so heroic, so inspirational, and the perfect music for our voyage. I forget what it's called?"

"It's the Richard Rogers theme music for the World War II naval documentary TV series, *Victory at Sea.*"

"Now I remember. My granddad said it was his favorite fifties TV show. I've seen a couple of reruns."

"My grandpa's too," said Tony. "The best ocean battle footage ever captured . . . the allies fighting for their lives against the Japanese and Germans. Whenever I get the chance, I celebrate the dawn of a new day by plugging my iPod into the ship's sound system and playing 'Victory at Sea.' It just puts me in the zone."

"I couldn't agree with you more," murmured Dmitri. After all, he thought, they'd just triumphed over the enemies of enlightenment at the boat dock.

"Look at the dolphins!" Seema's ebullient voice grabbed everyone's attention.

The dolphins had returned to the boat, performing a *Cirque du Soleil*-like series of acrobatics in synchrony to the music. Lila, always the marine biologist, grabbed her video cam. "Truly a universal language," she said to Seema standing beside her. "We're entranced by the songs of the humpbacks and the dolphins are entranced by our music. This choreographed response is something extraordinary. I've got to discuss it with Chris. It could open up a whole new line of research."

Andrew was downright giddy. He danced a jig around the deck, shouting, "We've done it! We've done it!" After he'd hugged Seema and Lila and belted out a few choruses of "Sailing, sailing over the bounding main," he bounced over to the helm, unplugged Tony's iPod, and replaced it with his own. With the upper deck pulsating to the rattle-and-hum sounds of U2, Seema, Lila, and Andrew joined together, skipping and hopping to the beat of the music. As the boat rocked across the waves, the youthful humans rocked upon the deck.

"Check it out," screamed Lila. The dolphins had changed the rhythm of their leaping and bounding in reaction to the mixed U2 and Springsteen sound track. They were now performing mid-air pirouettes.

The kinetic exuberance diffused across the interspecies divide. Melanie grabbed Dmitri who thought, "Why not just go with the flow." With encouragement from his colleagues and spurred on by Melanie's exhortations, Dmitri gamely answered her elegant sashays and paso doble with his twists, twirls, and twitches. Even Greg leapt into the action, wowing everyone with his stylistic impression of a Michael Jackson "moonwalk." Not to be outdone, Dmitri laughed and stumbled across the deck, trying to mimic Greg's fancy footwork. Remembering painful, past escapades on the dance floor, he knew his act was a poor imitation. This time, however, it didn't bother him a bit.

Hatching a Plan

Southern California

WHILE THE MEMBERS of the Research in Paradise team enjoyed their victory-at-sea dance, twenty-four-hundred miles to the east, Richard Prescott drove to work listening to the morning news. Stunned by the story about the wildcat launch, he cursed Dmitri. The fact that two SoCalSci associate professors and two graduate students had seized the vessel in the middle of the night, without the director of PICES on board, could provide the opening he needed to stop them once and for all.

Therefore, Richard had formulated a new strategy. He'd decided to contact Captain Ned Perry, an old NROTC university chum. Ned was a U.S. Navy officer and currently posted at the Pentagon. Richard drove to the same untraceable off-campus phone booth from where he'd previously called the *Enquirer*. After three rings, Perry answered his mobile.

"Hi, Ned, it's your long lost college buddy, Richard Prescott."

"Richard," replied Perry, "you old coot. What's it been? Five years or so since we last toured the bars of Georgetown?"

"At least that. You know the old saying: 'tempus fugit.' I heard the good news about your promotion to lead the Navy's Advanced Communications Division."

"Give me a break," replied Perry. "That's old news by now. Surely you have other reasons for calling me from out of the blue. Could it perhaps be related to the hubbub about SoCalSci's controversial research program over in Hawaii?"

"You're as perceptive as ever, Ned," replied Richard. "Then, let me be frank. I believe the SoCalSci and PICES joint venture could prove quite a threat to your advanced sonar program. The Greenies have bombarded you with their politically correct heat about the adverse effects of underwater noise pollution. Just think how they'll ramp-up their campaign if PICES can demonstrate some new communication breakthrough with the humpbacks."

"You're preaching to the choir, Richard," replied Perry. "We've already sunk a fortune into the project, and we're getting pressure from the Joint Chiefs to deploy the system ASAP. I refuse to risk losing the funding to complete the mission. What do you suggest?"

Prescott recounted the media's report of the *Research in Paradise's* nocturnal abduction. "So technically speaking, the vessel could be considered stolen property. There must be some way you could persuade your Navy chums to bring them to justice."

"I do have a contact in the Coast Guard command structure, but I think that would be overreacting, Richard. Based on what you told me, I don't believe this qualifies as a theft-on-the-high-seas offense. I do have a suggestion, however."

"I'm all ears."

"Didn't the news accounts of the boat's disappearance mention scuffling and injuries?"

"You're right, Ned. That's brilliant. Why didn't I think of that?"

"It's not as if you're not creative enough." Prescott and Perry shared a chortle.

"I owe you big time, Captain Perry. The next time you're in SoCal, dinner at Spago is on me."

"Don't mention it. Oh, and by the way, whatever you decide to do, this conversation never happened. Good luck."

After he'd hung up, Richard hesitated, considering the pros and cons of Ned Perry's idea. Despite his objection to the speculative theories of McPinsky's protégé, he had to admit a grudging admiration for Dmitri's gutsy exploit, an amateur commando raid against impassioned mobs. He doubted his own ability to organize and execute such a plan. Nevertheless, Dmitri's actions were reckless, with injurious consequences. Richard's original plan had been designed to minimize media exposure to SoCalSci, surely a noble goal. Dmitri's sensationalistic gambit, however, had thrust their institution into the national spotlight, leaving Richard no choice. As a student of history, he steeled himself with the thought of a favorite rally cry: "He must act in the defense of the realm!" Grabbing his iPhone, he scrolled to the contact information of an attorney friend, a notorious ambulance-chaser, in Honolulu. Why not? he thought. What are old friends for, anyway?

How could it get any worse? thought Ned Perry, recalling the maxim: "Bad news comes in bunches." After Prescott's call, he remembered the disturbing dispatch he'd received just a few weeks ago from Lieutenant Nina Davis at USSIA headquarters. According to her report, RH-12 satellite reconnaissance video had captured a pod of humpbacks engaged in extraordinary activity in the vicinity of the Hawaiian sonar tests. At the time, he didn't doubt he could keep a lid on the information, at least long enough for his sonar team to complete their mission. If, however, the SoCalSci researchers witnessed the same phenomenon, the news could go viral and energize every save-the-whales organization around the globe. The publicity unleashed by a discovery of this magnitude would undoubtedly jeopardize the sonar program. If Prescott couldn't stop the nonsense, Perry feared he'd need to take command of the situation and enact the necessary countermeasures.

THE TURING TRANSLATION

Leeward Waters, Maui—later that afternoon

"THIS IS VERY FRUSTRATING." Dmitri gazed at the blank Speakeasy LCD display mounted on the wall above Andrew's workstation. He'd been staring at it for hours. "Lila's tried just about everything to locate the humpbacks."

The sun had arced beyond its zenith but there was still no response to the hundreds of game symbol sounds they had cast, like a baited hook, into the eighty-degree water. As the team's patience gradually waned, a cloud of resignation shrouded the cabin. Dmitri suffered the most, and he hummed blues tunes to temper his creeping disappointment. He suspected his decision to head out to sea in order to avoid detection had thwarted their mission.

"Don't give up and don't feel bad." Melanie sat next to him, holding a book.

"I think we're just too far away from the coastline. According to Lila, the humpbacks prefer to birth and raise their young in the shallow channel between Lahaina and Lanai."

"My dad called that channel the Straits of Lahaina because of an old mariner's map my great grandfather had given him." She smiled. "Nobody calls it that anymore, though."

"The Straits of Lahaina . . ." Dmitri smiled back. "It sounds so poetic. I like it."

"I'm glad." Melanie stroked his shoulder. "And don't underestimate Lila. There's still hope. By the way, everyone is really proud of the way you stepped forward to make this happen. I see your relationships with Greg, Seema, and

Andrew. They adore and respect you, probably the way you feel about McPinsky. In the end it's the people relationships that count the most."

"You're right about McPinsky. After all he's been to me, all he's done for me, I just can't fail him."

"Exactly!" She frowned and nodded. "You've hoisted the weight of the world onto your shoulders . . . McPinsky, Gorman, and the whales. You feel obligated to save them all. If it's meant to be, it's meant to be, but you can't expect to rescue everyone and everything. So let's just relax and keep the faith."

Melanie had done it again, helping Dmitri regain his equilibrium. She knew exactly how to tap into the source of his angst and, like a mental masseuse, gently knead the tightness from his mind. He led her across the cabin to a more private location, and wrapped her up in his arms. "Thanks for the pep talk. You're my rock."

Their intimate embrace was disrupted when Lila entered the cabin. "Oh, excuse me," said Lila, sounding both apologetic and surprised. "How's it going down here?"

"Sorry to say, not a peep," replied Dmitri.

"I'm sorry, too." Lila sighed. "Tony and I keep trolling the area but we've come up with zilch. And I've realized something. What would you expect from parents whose children are being killed by human sounds? I don't blame them for not wanting to communicate with us."

"I never thought about it that way. Maybe you're right," said Dmitri.

"Nevertheless, this experiment *has* to succeed. We've gotta grab the public's attention about the threats to the cetaceans."

"What can we do?" Melanie asked as Andrew joined them.

"Last night," Lila said, "I thought we might need additional assistance luring our subjects to this particular location, so I came up with a desperate-measures contingency plan. I remembered Chris telling me about a famous whale event that happened over twenty years ago. Apparently, a wayward humpback, named Humphrey by the locals, got stuck in San Francisco Bay."

"Even I've heard about the legendary Humphrey," said Melanie. "He's the most publicized humpback in history. He kept swimming farther and farther into the bay and even up into the Sacramento River. He attracted huge crowds who turned out to encourage him to reverse course and save himself."

"Yes, indeed," replied Lila. "People definitely have a soft spot for endangered species."

"Probably because whales are so soft and cuddly," said Andrew.

"Andrew, can't you ever be serious?" replied Melanie. "There's a lot more to it than cuddliness. Organizations like PICES deserve a lot of credit for their educational programs."

"Thanks," said Lila. "So, anyway, the volunteers tried various techniques, including banging on pipes and other types of scary sounds, to herd Humphrey back in the right direction. But nothing worked and after a couple of weeks, things looked bleak. Humphrey became emaciated. He was so far upstream and so lost that he almost got stuck in a tiny slough. Finally, in desperation, a musician and bioacoustics expert came up with a great idea. He used reverse psychology. Instead of attempting to scare the whale straight, he played a recording of humpback feeding vocalizations. It worked like a charm. In less than two days, they lured Humphrey the entire seventy-five miles back into the bay, under the Golden Gate Bridge, and out into the Pacific."

"That's pretty cool," replied Melanie. "I'd never heard that part of the story."

"So you're saying we should play some Charlie-the-Tuna Star Kist commercials through our underwater speakers?" Andrew teased, but his tone was half-hearted, as if he were trying to cheer himself up.

Dmitri frowned at Andrew. "Go on, Lila."

"Sorry, boss." Andrew's expression begged for forgiveness.

"So I'm saying, wise guy," Lila turned to face Andrew, "that I had Chris track down a CD version of the same recording they used for Humphrey. It's in my backpack. Let's patch the CD into our broadcast system at the same time we're transmitting the game symbols."

"I can do that," replied Andrew.

"Let's try it, Lila," said Dmitri. "I mean what have we got to lose?"

After Lila left to fetch the recording, Dmitri turned to Andrew and Seema. "Could we be missing something?" he asked. "There's got to be a ton of noise in the Speakeasy input interface that might interfere with your symbol detection software. As we discussed earlier, let's enable the band-pass filters we matched to the frequencies of the game symbols."

"I'm on your side, boss," replied Andrew, "but I really don't think that's the problem. We've already enabled the high- and low-pass filters to eliminate the extreme frequencies."

"Those band-pass filters might erase the very game symbols we're trying to detect," Seema added.

"You're right," muttered Dmitri. "My desperation is affecting my judgment."

"Anyway," replied Andrew, "I'm listening to the underwater sounds through my headphones. I'm just not hearing the types of vocalizations, like the barking sounds of seals, corresponding to the symbols on the original whale recording. After all, we're broadcasting those symbols every thirty seconds, so I'd recognize a similar sound."

"Seema, are you certain the broadcast level is amped up?"

"I'm transmitting at ninety decibels, which is the maximum intensity allowed by the Marine Mammal Protection Act. Since we're in the middle of nowhere, it wouldn't hurt to crank it up another five or ten decibels."

"Why don't you do that," replied Dmitri. "I'll take responsibility for any adverse consequences."

"You mean like if hundreds of dead fish suddenly float to the surface?" replied Seema, perking up.

"Anything that we catch, we eat," Dmitri answered.

"That's a good one, boss. I'm glad to hear you're chill with this."

Lila approached them, handing the feeding vocalization CD to Andrew. He popped it into his laptop, and the sounds of a humpback feeding frenzy filled the control room.

"Whoa," said Melanie, "that's definitely a change of pace from the sounds of the game symbols."

Andrew licked his lips. "It's making me hungry for shrimp tempura."

"Keep your fingers crossed, folks," said Lila.

"This may take a while," said Melanie. "Let's go topside for some fresh air."

"Good idea," replied Dmitri. "I've been staring at the Speakeasy display for so long I'm starting to feel queasy."

Melanie and Dmitri trailed Lila up the stairs. Lila joined Tony up front in the pilot house leaving the couple all alone at the aft portion of the spacious sun deck. Once outside and focused on the horizon, Dmitri felt much better. The remnants of the storm lingered on, and a brisk west wind washed his still-sore face. He craned his head back and peered up at the fleet of puffy white and gray clouds sailing across the sky. "It's glorious out here. Maybe I need a change of scene in my life. You're living here with Mark and dedicated to your students, so what would you say if I applied for a teaching position at the local community college?"

"I'm flattered," said Melanie, "but first things first. Let's not give up on this experiment just yet."

She took his hand and led him over to the starboard railing. When he'd begun to speak, she gently pressed a finger to his lips. In silence, they shared the tranquility of the ocean and sky panorama. With the engines shut down, they just drifted along with the lazy current. She rested her head onto the cushion of his shoulder. Strands of her long, black hair wafted in the gentle breeze, tickling his cheek. He realized his somber mood was all but extinguished. This marvelous woman had a magical effect upon him. Yesterday, at the koi pond, she'd harnessed the therapeutic powers of nature's music. Today, she'd done it with the sounds of silence.

Lila's urgent chattering from the pilothouse interrupted their serenity. "Tony just received a short-wave radio message from Chris Gorman. He's somehow located our vessel and is about ten minutes away."

The glow on Dmitri's face faded to a gloomy pallor. He looked up at the sky, inwardly cursing the gods of fate. "Thanks, Lila. Melanie, why don't you keep Lila company and alert me when you see Chris. I'm going back down to be with Andrew and Seema."

Dmitri's shoulders sagged as he descended the stairs on leaden legs. After he'd apprised his SoCalSci associates about Gorman's impending arrival, they talked shop while waiting for whale-sign.

Melanie's shuffling footsteps announced her return from above. "Tony says Chris is just a couple of minutes away. Any luck here?"

"Same old, same old," Dmitri replied, his tone sullen. Why should he bother to sugarcoat his true feelings? He was too tired to play the role of the never-say-die leader. "We'll just take our dose of medicine when Chris comes aboard. Greg, please be brutally honest with me. Did I make the right decision?"

Greg did not hesitate. "Absolutely, yes, and I'll let you in on a little secret. If you'd decided otherwise, I was ready to convince you to side with the whales. I still think Gorman will forgive and forget."

Dmitri stood. Just as he placed an appreciative hand on Greg's shoulder, Lila rushed through the door.

"Hey," she boomed, "I just saw some spouts about a mile away and maybe getting closer!"

Everyone cheered wildly. They turned as one to face Andrew. He pressed his hands against the headphones and concentrated. "Sorry folks," he finally said, "but still nothing to report."

"They're too far away," said Lila. "Let's just hope they're really heading our way. Oh, Chris has arrived. Let's go outside and get this over with."

Dmitri trudged outside with Greg and Lila. He sighted the PICES vessel heading back to shore while two hundred feet off the starboard bow, Gorman rowed a dinghy. He was accompanied by a person of much shorter stature, too distant to be recognizable. Wracked by a combination of guilt and nerves, Dmitri suddenly felt panic-stricken by thoughts of the impending confrontation with the PICES director. What could he possibly say to the man whose boat he had literally stolen?

As the dinghy bobbed in the choppy sea, Dmitri recognized the familiar face and ponytail of Gorman's young companion. To his amazement, the youth was none other than Melanie's son, Mark. When the dinghy pulled alongside, Lila tossed a rope down to Gorman. Once he'd secured the tie line, Gorman helped the child gain a foothold at the bottom of the stainless steel ladder. Carefully, he assisted Mark up the steps, bracing him from behind. Near the top, he let go of the boy's hand, as Dmitri and Greg hoisted him aboard.

The youngster looked up at the men he now stood beside. "Aloha, Dmitri."

Though stunned by the boy's presence, Dmitri smiled and shook his hand. The members of the team inched forward, gathering in a circle around the two newcomers on the stern's open-air mini-deck.

Dmitri felt it best to get the inevitable trip to the woodshed behind him. "Chris, I—"

"Mark!" Melanie cried. "What the bejesus are you doing here?"

Dmitri's mind seized up at the sound of Melanie's shrill outburst. Temporarily tongue-tied, he watched as she wrapped her arms around her son.

Gorman's attention shifted to Melanie, who continued to caress Mark. "Sorry, Mel, but I couldn't find anyone else to watch him. And, anyway, this is as good a time as any for a young lad to experience his first high-seas adventure. Besides, he was very insistent about it, crocodile tears and all."

"Mom," said Mark, "it's only for one day. I begged Chris to bring me."

Dmitri had interacted with Melanie's son on two previous occasions. They'd chatted at Melanie's apartment while he had waited for her to get ready for dinner dates. He was impressed by the nine-year-old's curiosity, undoubtedly acquired from his mother. Mark had been particularly fascinated by Dmitri's description of the similarities and differences between human and whale voices.

Mark was a handsome boy, inheriting both his mom's Asian beauty and his long-gone father's Caucasian features. Mark's face had a shape-shifting quality. One moment he looked Asian, the next like an intriguing mix of nationalities. Dmitri was mystified, however, by the sides that formed this unlikely triangle of Gorman, Melanie, and her son.

"Okay, Mark, you're right. We'll be back in Kihei in a few hours. Chris and I will have a talk later on." Melanie saw Dmitri's confused look and said, "I was going to explain things after today's experiment."

Before Dmitri could react, Lila stepped forward. "Chris, I want you to know it was all my idea. I practically shamed Dr. Dmitri into agreeing to go along with my scheme. I'll take all the heat. Fire me if you must, but please don't press charges."

Gorman's tense expression did not appear encouraging. The veins in his neck bulged. "You all had me scared sick, but I'm here to save your butts." Dmitri felt Gorman's anger as a sharp pain beneath his sternum. "I had to call the boat's owner and give him my personal assurance it would be returned safely. And as far as the Maui police are concerned, I didn't report the incident as a theft."

"Thank you, Chris." Dmitri sounded both relieved and contrite. "Don't blame Lila. This happened under my leadership. Let's leave now and return the vessel."

"Not a bad idea." Gorman's sullen visage gradually cleared.

"How did you find us?"

"Oh, didn't you realize? Since this is a licensed commercial passenger vessel, it's required to have an AIS transponder. I asked the Coast Guard to perform a radio sweep, and there you were. So tell me, any luck so far?"

"I'm sorry to tell you we've struck out with the whales." Dmitri tried not to sound glum.

"Maybe not," replied Gorman. He pointed to starboard. "Those spouts are only a few hundred yards—"

Two shrieking voices interrupted him—Seema's and Andrew's cries from inside. Everyone hastened through the door into the control room and stared, wide-eyed, at the forty-six-inch LCD display. The much anticipated cetacean circular game symbols hovered like halos upon the Speakeasy-formatted display.

"They're just like the squiggly circular shapes from the recording!" Andrew exulted. "We've received two so far. Seema is broadcasting our version of the symbols at random locations on the plot. I've erased all of the previous symbols we transmitted except for the one preceding our opponent's first symbol, so you're observing a clean board."

"Did you initiate the data recording system?"

"No sweat, boss," he replied. "The hydrophone inputs are being logged to a file on the hard drive. We can replay all of the acoustic signals back into our Speakeasy program and reproduce everything. I'm also recording a high-def video of the word grams on the screen. We can replay those too."

"Oh, God," moaned Seema. "I'm really nervous! Until now my automatic program has been broadcasting random symbols. Now that I have to respond according to the rules of the game, I'm getting a brain cramp. Can you please help me, Dr. Dmitri?"

Dmitri hastened over to Seema's workstation. "How about if I point at the location on the screen where I'd like you to image the next symbol as I announce the x,y coordinates for that location?"

"That'll work."

"I've counted three separate spouts a couple hundred feet away and getting closer." Tony addressed them from above through the ship's PA system.

"I can't believe it," said Lila. "It's like a dream come true."

"We owe you big time, Lila," said Dmitri. "I'll bet your feeding vocalization CD was responsible for this."

Everyone gasped when the next cetacean game symbol appeared on the screen. "If this is what we think it is, then we're the first to see these as they were intended to be understood," said Gorman. "This could be an historic moment. I have to admit I'm both elated and terrified."

"Okay, okay." Dmitri tried to steady himself. "Andrew, be certain you've disabled the auto-refresh mode. We don't want anything erased." He touched the display. "Seema, the next symbol to broadcast is here at coordinates 171 dash 322."

Seema keyed-in the coordinates, and an X appeared on the screen at the precise location where Dmitri had tapped his finger.

"Way to go, Seema." Greg's chortle seemed to relax her. "You've just successfully demonstrated the world's first cetacean game symbol synthesizer."

Mark walked up to Seema's workstation. "Mom, what's happening?"

"Dr. Dmitri and his team are playing a game with the humpback whales," replied Melanie. "We think they're playing Dots and Boxes."

"How is that possible?" Mark asked.

Dmitri traced a straight line across the display with his index finger. "When humans play, the game board starts with an empty grid of dots. Then we draw lines to connect the dots and to form the boxes, right? But in the whale's version of the game, they don't draw any lines." He pointed to the circular shapes. "Do you remember our chat at your mom's house, when I told you how both humans and whales use their voices to draw shapes?" The boy nodded. "So the whales use their voices to draw these circular shapes onto this game board of sound. The shapes represent the corners of the boxes. A rectangular pattern of four circular squiggles forms one box."

"That's awesome!" the boy yelled. "Can I play?"

Dmitri couldn't help but smile. "Sure, Mark," he replied. "Come over here and stand next to me." As Mark joined him, it didn't escape Dmitri's attention that Melanie sent an appreciative glance in his direction. "Andrew, increase the volume on the public address system."

Dmitri was in control, guiding the flow of the experiment like a director on a high-tech movie set. Now, in addition to visualizing the symbols, they could all clearly hear the familiar sound of the whale vocalizations associated with each symbol. They didn't have to wait long to hear the next brief cetacean utterance, like a seal's bark, as the next O symbol was painted on the screen by the mind of the humpback—human versus whale—X versus O.

"Okay," uttered Dmitri, like a command. "Let's transmit the randomized data for a few more rounds and then decide who's going to be first to commit to a strategy."

"This is unbelievable," said Seema. "We're the first humans to interact with another species in a high-level, abstract communication."

"Let me remind you," said Greg, "that nothing is proved until Joel Spelvin's correlation coefficients begin to converge to determinacy. These random opening moves aren't definitive."

The graphical update of Spelvin's numbers appeared on the Speakeasy screen just below the plot of the symbols. Both of the correlation plots were still flat lines.

"Lila, come over here," said Melanie, waving from the glass-bottom viewing area at the front of the cabin. "One of the whales just cruised by."

Dmitri turned and saw Melanie ensconced on an upholstered bench. Leaning over a raised, thirty-inch-high, wooden safety barrier, she stared down into the recessed, rectangular well area for underwater viewing.

"Wait a sec, Mel." Lila turned to Chris. "As scintillating as this is," Lila pointed up at the display, "I'm crazy curious to observe the body language of our opponents. By the way, Chris, a penny for your thoughts?"

"Truthfully, I didn't come out here just to chew you out. I came to pay my respects and to thank all of you for acting so courageously. When I'd realized you'd all taken such a huge risk for the sake of the humpbacks, I decided to join you."

"God," uttered Lila. "What a relief. In my heart, I believed you'd react like this, but I couldn't know for certain."

"I wouldn't have missed this for the whole world," replied Gorman. "Thanks again, Lila, for making the decision for me. PICES is indebted to you."

"Only PICES?" interrupted Melanie. Dmitri detected a hint of annoyance in her voice. "How about the entire cetacean research community?"

"Thanks, Mel." Lila joined her friend, up front, on the bench.

As the game unfolded, the fist of tension that gripped the room squeezed even tighter. After four additional rounds of symbols, the results were still indeterminate. Now is the time to strike, thought Dmitri. This was the moment to test all of their hypotheses and hopes. Mathematics and the scientific method would determine if humanity was a lonely star in a galaxy of organisms or one of many suns in the constellation of sapient beings.

"It's your move, Dmitri," said Greg.

Dmitri paused as his thoughts shifted. He was overcome by a surge of emotion, a sudden longing for his parents. They had infused him with their life force and the life-long gift of their love and support. They'd scrimped and sacrificed so he and his brother could fulfill their academic potential. He thought of the many years of study and training, the lathe that had shaped and prepared him for this pivotal moment. His mentor had kindled the fuse of his inspiration. Greg's steady voice now reminded him he was surrounded by colleagues and friends. They were more than just a team. They were a family of scientists, bonded together by a sense of wonder and the passion to penetrate nature's mysteries, which waited behind doors of discovery.

"Time's a-wastin'," said Greg. "If our opponents are as smart as I think they are, they're probably growing impatient."

"Okay, Seema, let's take the plunge," Dmitri mumbled, tongue-tied by cotton mouth. He lubricated his vocal tract with a swig of bottled water. "This is it. Let's try to complete the third corner of a box and see if he blocks." He grabbed Mark's hand and placed it on the display. "Put the next symbol here, where Mark is pointing, at coordinates 102 dash 182 and hold your breath."

Seema entered the keystrokes and the X symbol appeared at the precise location beneath the boy's index finger.

"Cool," exclaimed Mark.

Dmitri heard the fleeting synthesized tones corresponding to the tone-pair frequencies. As he imagined them racing through the water like a magic communications bullet, the wait was agonizing, the silence overwhelming. When the whale's next symbol appeared on the screen at the same time as the creature's grunt spilled out of the speakers, Dmitri heard groans instead of climactic cheers from the audience. Instead of blocking, the latest game symbol had materialized adjacent to the whale's previously transmitted symbol.

From across the room, Melanie's and Lila's ardent cries startled Dmitri. "Two of your opponents just swam beneath us!" exclaimed Melanie.

Dmitri stared at her and then turned to Greg. "Why hasn't our challenger taken the bait?"

Greg didn't answer. He looked perplexed, his eyes shifting frenetically as he studied the Speakeasy screen. "No, wait. Look here!" he exclaimed, his face brightening. He pointed at the latest numbers corresponding to Spelvin's correlation coefficients. One of the two flat lines had sprung to life.

"What is it?" asked Seema.

"Look at the second correlation coefficient. It's now trending upward since it's correlated to the location of the previous cetacean symbol." Greg's finger traced the telltale curve on the Speakeasy display. "If he'd attempted to block us, we'd instead see the first correlation coefficient trending upwards, corresponding to the location of our previous symbol. There's evidence of an independently developing strategy."

"Ok." With an anxious hand, Dmitri wiped the sweat from his brow. "For now, let's just complete our first box and see what the response is. We were assuming a somewhat predictive level of gamesmanship. Maybe the whales are more sophisticated than we thought."

When Seema transmitted the next symbol, the scoreboard tally of human-completed boxes incremented from "zero" to "one" on the big display.

"Last year I went to Vegas to play that MIT professor's system for counting cards at blackjack," said Andrew. "During breaks, I hung out at the high-roller table for the rush of watching thousands wagered per hand. This match, though, is more awesome than any high-stakes card game."

"Yes!" cried Greg, pumping both fists. The next cetacean symbol extended the chain of dots on the whales' side of the board. "This is what you'd expect for a non-beginner strategy. They're building their own chain of boxes instead of blocking ours."

"You're right," said Dmitri, peering at the display. "Look at Spelvin's numbers. The value of the second correlation coefficient keeps going higher."

Greg leapt from his chair. "I think we might have achieved first contact." With cheers and backslaps, the SoCalSci teammates celebrated.

Lila and Melanie rushed over. "What happened?" asked Melanie.

"A two-player game seems to be happening, that's what." Dmitri hugged her.

They watched with fascination as two sentient minds dueled across the interspecies divide. From opposite ends of the virtual game board, the two chains of symbols filled the plot, each gradually converging toward the center. The endgame strategy, to complete the many potential boxes, would soon commence. Although the score was still "one to nothing" in favor of Homo sapiens, the Megapteran strategy had given them an opportunity to complete a short chain of boxes.

"I can't believe it, Greg," said Dmitri. "This interaction satisfies the Turing test in a way that Turing never imagined."

"What's the Turing test?" asked Melanie.

"Alan Turing," replied Greg, "was the British mathematical genius who decrypted the German ciphers for the Enigma code machine during World War II. After the war, he published a famous paper that considered whether or not machines like computers could think. Since the concept of thinking was difficult to define, he proposed a test of a machine's ability to demonstrate intelligence. The setup is a human judge who engages in a conversation with both a human and a machine where all three participants are placed in isolated locations. If the judge can't tell the difference between the machine and the human, then the machine passes the test. In order to rule out the variability of spoken language, Turing's conversation is limited to a text-only channel such as a computer keyboard and display."

"Except that in the case of our own Turing test," replied Melanie, "we've replaced the machine with a whale and the conversation with a game of logic."

"Precisely," said Dmitri. "If we didn't know who was at the other end of the Speakeasy visual interface, we'd think we're playing another human. I'm dying to see their next move."

They didn't have to wait more than five seconds. The computer-generated ringtone confirmed the first completed box for the humpbacks. In fact, their opponent had broadcast two consecutive symbols without bothering to wait for the next human response, as was their right according to the rules of the game for completing multiple boxes if they are available. The score was cetaceans two, humans one.

"Wow, pinch me please," Seema exclaimed with a giant grin. "I'm the first human being, *ever,* to be losing to a member of another species in a game of X's and O's."

When the laughter had subsided, Dmitri said, "I wish Professor McPinsky could be here to witness this—the inner workings of the Megapteran mind. It's exhilarating."

"Exhilarating is not the word to describe my feelings." Gorman's eyes were moist. "This is simply transcendent. Pardon the pun, but it's a game changer. How the hell do we even begin to report this to the world at large?"

"The first thing we'll do is distribute the raw data recordings to other research teams to validate our findings."

"At this moment, I'm so glad I decided to be a signal processing engineer instead of a hedge fund manager," Andrew grinned.

"It's your move, Dmitri," said Greg. "By the way, did you notice that our mystery opponent could have completed four boxes but opted instead to stop at only two and place the next move elsewhere?"

"Maybe they are just not as smart as we are," Seema suggested.

At her words, a roguish grin raised the corners of Greg's mouth. "So what's your next move, Dr. Dmitri?"

"I almost forgot that it was my turn. Greg, why are you smiling? You look like the proverbial cat that swallowed the canary."

"Oh, you'll soon find out."

"Okay. So it looks like we can fill in three more boxes. Go ahead, Seema."

After Seema had completed the moves that Dmitri had instructed, the tally screen showed the humans leading by a score of four boxes to two.

"Oops." The bell-and-whistle clamor pouring out of the speakers startled Dmitri. "We've been played for suckers."

Their worthy opponents had flooded the screen with a nonstop series of symbols. The tally board rang out and flashed like a pinball machine as one box after another was completed in a super-chain. Greg couldn't stop laughing. Once the carnival atmosphere of sound and video fireworks had settled down, Dmitri realized the cetaceans had tallied over twenty boxes. He also recognized there were not enough empty spaces in the grid for a human comeback. Dmitri sought his colleagues' reactions and saw mixed expressions of wonder and crazed elation.

"Look, boss!"

Andrew's booming voice and outstretched arm brought Dmitri's attention to the game board monitor. At the very location of the last symbol placement, a familiar geometric pattern steadily emerged—the three concentric circles which presumably signaled "game, set, and match."

A hush blanketed the control room, until Andrew finally spoke. "What just happened?"

"Remember a few moves back," replied Greg, "when our distinguished opponent failed to complete the two boxes still available in his chain? It turns out he was gaming a strategic advantage at the expense of a temporary tactical sacrifice. We were simply outplayed by a superior opponent."

"Oh, I forgot to mention," said Lila, "the only whales I sighted near our boat are three juveniles. Dr. Dmitri, you've just lost to a child."

"This is fantastic!" Dmitri enveloped Melanie in an effusive embrace.

Greg started whooping and hollering. He circulated around the cabin and slapped the hands of each member of the team in a high-five victory tribute.

"You mean the whales beat the people?" asked Mark, pulling at his mother's arm. "How'd they do it?"

While the rest of the team celebrated, Dmitri took Mark aside to play a quick game of Dots and Boxes. He tried his best elementary school teacher impersonation to explain how they'd used his mom's Speakeasy program to play the game with the humpbacks. He sensed Melanie observing their interaction.

When Mark darted off in the direction of Gorman, Melanie sat down with Dmitri. "I'm sorry. I owe you an explanation. I meant to tell you earlier, but I wanted it to be the right moment. Once upon a time, Chris and I were a twosome. It started over five years ago, just after my husband moved off the island. After a couple of years, we realized we weren't a good match, but we've been friends ever since, and he occasionally babysits Mark. They have a bond. In fact, when I said I was going away with you for the night, he agreed to take Mark. I thought for sure Chris would never suspect anything about our scheme to launch the experiment. It never dawned on me he'd bring Mark along when he heard the news about our getaway."

"Mark will be fine." His heart pounding, Dmitri reached out to cradle her hands in his own.

"Thanks for being so understanding."

"Understanding, maybe, but still somewhat discombobulated." He smiled at her. "Just give me some time to digest the news."

"Have no fear. Like I said, it's all in the past." She left to tend to Mark.

The aroused voices of his colleagues recaptured Dmitri's attention. He tried to sequester what he'd just heard from Melanie into a compartment he'd examine later, and was able to calm himself by remembering the expression on her face. It would be important to think of Gorman as an ally, not a rival. "Chris," he said. "I'd like to contact Professor McPinsky and replay the video for him. Is there Internet access on this boat?"

"You're in luck," replied Gorman. "The tour company that operates this vessel caters to high-end clients looking for off-shore privacy in their scuba and fishing adventures. They confirmed they'd installed a maritime satellite link for the Silicon Valley CEO who frequently charters this boat. However, it's not as fast as your typical home broadband connection."

"It might not be sufficient for a hi-res Skype video session, but it wouldn't matter if McPinsky sees a herky-jerky video feed. He's primarily interested in the game symbol plots."

"In the meantime, Lila and I will be upstairs observing the whales."

After Gorman disappeared, Dmitri drifted back to Andrew's workstation.

"Chris just confirmed we have a digital satellite link. I'd like you to open up a Skype session on the laptop with the webcam."

"Okay, boss. I brought some Ethernet cables to patch the laptop into the boat's Internet router. I assumed you'd want to record the Speakeasy sessions, so I installed this external webcam and recorded the video session of the game we just played." He pointed to the spherical camera mounted to the table.

"Great job, Andrew." Dmitri slapped him on the back. "After we link up with McPinsky, let's transmit the file to him. How big is it?"

"Since we're only interested in displaying these slowly developing symbols, I selected the camera's low-data-rate, black-and-white video option."

"Cool," replied Dmitri, looking at his wristwatch. "Let's hope the video uploads in a reasonable amount of time. I'd better phone McPinsky, since it's almost his bedtime on the East Coast. He's an early bird."

Following Gorman's earlier instructions, Dmitri used the ship's digital phone system to place a call. McPinsky answered on the fourth ring.

"Hello, Professor, its Dmitri. Sorry to bother you at such a late hour, but I have some very good news to report."

Dmitri summarized the events of the past twenty-four hours and described the details of the breakthrough interaction. He clicked on the switch for the speakerphone.

"This is sensational!" replied McPinsky. "I wish I were there." His exuberant voice filled the room.

"Well, Professor, the good news is that you could be a virtual participant if you initiate a video-conference session on your home PC."

"No problem. I can't wait to see this."

"I'm all set up and ready to link up with the professor," said Andrew. It had taken him less than five minutes to connect his communication laptop to the local area network and to establish a link to McPinsky's PC.

"Okay, Professor," said Dmitri. "The first thing we'll do is upload the video file of our just-concluded game session. Hopefully, it'll take no more than a few minutes to transmit. You'll be amazed by the strategy that our youthful opponents used to defeat us."

"Youthful?"

"The only whales in the vicinity were juveniles."

McPinsky chuckled. "This is too good to be true. Do you think you could challenge them to a best two-out-of-three match so that I can watch a live session?"

"It's a possibility. Andrew has a webcam pointed at the Speakeasy monitor.

We're using it to record the game sessions, but we can also patch the feed over to your Skype link. Get ready to receive the old video file. Andrew just started the transmission."

Lila burst into the room. "This is very strange, but Tony just reported a distress call from the Coast Guard. They're under orders to arrest us and impound the boat."

"What the hell?" said Greg.

"I overheard the news of your predicament," said McPinsky from the digital ether, "and I detect the Captain Ahab specter of Dick Prescott."

"Damn that guy." Dmitri clenched both fists. "This ruins everything. They'll confiscate the entire experiment, including our computers. We'll have no proof."

"*You* may not have the proof," replied McPinsky, "but after I've finished downloading your video file, I'll have it."

"That's right," declared Dmitri. "Good thinking, Professor. I just hope the data transfer is complete before we're boarded."

The usually unflappable Gorman entered the control room in a frenetic state. "Lila, everybody, come upstairs quickly. Something really weird is happening!"

The Aquarian Grandmaster

Leeward Waters, Maui

"Can you see the spouts?" Gorman aimed his binoculars at a distant location off the starboard bow.

"Just barely," said Lila, squinting at the water's surface. The sea shimmered like molten silver in the afternoon sunshine.

It wasn't yet clear to Dmitri what had so aroused Gorman that, with the exceptions of Andrew and Mark, he'd dragged all of them upstairs to the forward starboard portion of the observation deck, adjacent to the pilot house. The only distinguishing feature was a peculiar pattern of smudges dotting the horizon.

"Take these," replied the PICES director, handing the binoculars to Lila. "Look to where the blows are most concentrated."

Lila peered through the lenses. "That's strange. They're occurring so frequently, sometimes in clusters."

"This can only mean one thing," exclaimed Gorman.

"So tell us already," pleaded Dmitri. "What's the big deal?"

"A hell of a lot of whales concentrated into a small area," answered Lila.

"Exactly!" said Gorman. "They normally dive for five to seven minutes before surfacing to exhale in blows of three to four cycles. Based on what we've seen, I'd say there are at least forty whales. No one in Maui has ever observed more than thirty-something in a single pod."

"Wow!" exclaimed Melanie. "Now I see what you're talking about." She guided Dmitri's outstretched arm to help him locate the pod's activity.

Lila clutched the binoculars, scanning the water as the boat rocked with the swells. "They're rapidly approaching, coming directly toward us!" The words raced from her lips and Dmitri felt the tension mount.

"They're not the only ones heading our way," shouted Tony from the pilothouse. "I just received another message from the Coast Guard. They're only a few minutes away."

"That's puzzling," said Gorman. "When the news of your wildcat launch was posted on CNN's website, I contacted the manager of the tour company. I have a pretty good relationship with this guy. I gave him my personal assurance my team was in control of his vessel. That I'd take responsibility to track you down and return the craft. He seemed fine with it. Why would he change his mind and notify the authorities?"

Dmitri frowned. "Because we've been sabotaged by the same weasel who leaked the news of our experiment to the *Enquirer*. It's that rat Prescott."

Still squinting through the binoculars, Lila screamed, "Oh, my God! The pod is swimming in a circular formation."

Gorman grabbed the binoculars. He surveyed the scene swiveling from side to side. "This is freakish. It looks like there are at least forty individuals maintaining a circular formation and advancing toward our boat. Not only that, they're all traveling at the surface instead of diving. Oddly, there's a single blow in the center of the circle. Lila, fetch a camera and a camcorder. We'll need to document this or else no one will believe us."

During the next five minutes, they watched as the cetacean flotilla completely encircled their vessel. Gorman and Lila were in constant motion as they juggled the video and still cameras.

Mark's squeaky voice rose above the sound of the wind. "Mom, what's happening?"

"It's okay, sweetie," replied Melanie. "The whales have made a circle around our boat." She pressed him close to her hip and turned toward Gorman. "Chris. Do you think this has anything to do with the game?"

"What else could it possibly be? A major interspecies communication breakthrough followed shortly after by the most significant cetacean group behavior ever witnessed."

"Word travels fast through the underwater grapevine," added Lila. She turned to Mark and smiled. "I just hope all these humpbacks aren't taking numbers and lining up to be Seema's next game challenger."

Seema chuckled. "I'd be stuck out here for days." She left the group, drifted back to the stern and leaned over the rear-facing railing. "God, there are so many of them."

"Look out there." Gorman spoke while he videotaped the proceedings. "Most of the members of this super-pod are taking turns spy hopping."

"What's that?" asked Mark.

"A spy hop is when the whale sticks his head straight up out of the water," replied Lila, "and then rotates around, as if scanning the surface."

"We're completely surrounded by forty curious humpbacks." Gorman shook his head in disbelief. "That they're poking their heads above the surface at the same time is just extraordinary."

A scream lacerated the air. Dmitri turned his head. A breaching humpback appeared to tower directly above Seema's cringing figure. Paralyzed by a jolt of fear, Dmitri stared, spellbound, at the awe-inspiring sight. The giant had vaulted above and just a few feet aft of the stern, like an athlete celebrating the opening ceremonies of an Olympiad.

Lila tried to capture the event on camera before the earth's gravitational tug induced the perfectly symmetric finale to the monster's stunning arc. At the moment of impact, a billowing mushroom cloud emerged from the sea, followed by a booming shockwave. The entire stern of the boat, including Seema, was engulfed in the deluge. She flailed helplessly in the churning waters.

Dmitri, Greg, and Chris slogged through the backwash to assist their comrade. By the time they'd reached her, Dmitri could barely hear Seema's distress cries above the sloshing turbulence. They grabbed onto her arms and legs and held tight as the water cascaded through the gunwale railings and scuppers, merging back with the sea. When the upper deck had completely drained, they released their grip. Seema lay on her back, struggling to speak. "I thought—" A hacking cough interrupted her. "I thought I was going to die." She choked out the words through sobs, water dribbling down her chin.

Dmitri felt a stab of guilt. "You're okay now, Seema." Remembering his CPR training, he tried to sound calm as he helped her up to a sitting position and stroked her shoulder. Melanie wrapped Seema in a blanket she'd found in the supply closet. "Let's get you dry and keep you warm. Just focus on your breathing."

Melanie and Lila knelt at Seema's feet and dried her legs with fresh towels.

Gorman stepped forward. "Seema, do you realize you were the closest witness to something truly remarkable?"

Trying to speak, she gagged and coughed. Her body trembled.

"Not now, Chris," said Melanie softly. "It was a *very* scary moment for all of us, but far more for Seema."

"And don't forget about the Coast Guard," Dmitri muttered.

"Trust me," Gorman responded. "I've spent more time around humpbacks than practically anyone else, and I've never seen anything like this. I'll tell them—"

In the distance, they heard an amplified voice hailing them from the deck of the approaching Coast Guard cutter. "This is a warning for the occupants of the PICES vessel. Prepare to be boarded by the U.S. Coast Guard."

"C-Chris," stammered Dmitri. "I'm the one who's responsible for the wildcat launch, and I'd better prepare a convincing story for the Feds. I don't think this is the appropriate time to wax eloquently about magical moments."

"Don't worry," replied Gorman. "Lila, can you please fetch the ship's megaphone from the pilot."

Dmitri stared at Gorman, wondering how the marine biologist could totally misjudge the precariousness of the situation.

"Seema," said Gorman. "I know you were terrified, but in all the years I've observed humpbacks, I've only known them to be gentle creatures that would never intentionally endanger a human being."

"You could have fooled me," said Greg. "It looked like that huge sucker just missed crushing us. Good thing he jumped just behind the boat instead of directly above it."

"*Intentionally* is the salient word," said Melanie, her hand on Seema's shoulder.

"No one has ever documented a breach like the one we just witnessed," replied Gorman, as Lila returned with the megaphone. "I've never seen a humpback practically leap over a boat, seemingly on purpose. And this was not your garden-variety whale."

"Yes," added Lila. "That's the biggest humpback we've ever seen breaching so far above the surface. Probably a fifty-ton, fifty-footer. There was something unique about this animal."

"Unique is right. It's also the oldest specimen we've ever seen fly so high through the air," added Gorman. "He looked pretty beat up. His entire ventral surface was covered in barnacles and by the scars of old wounds and infections. Finally, it's the ceremonial escort that tells me this humpback is some sort of leader afforded the protective cordon of the group. Remember when they were all poking their heads out of the water just prior to the breach? All of it happening within minutes of the first-ever human and whale intellectual encounter." He paused, and seemed to speak to himself for a moment. "As far as I know, no marine biologist has ever observed such unique behavior."

"It's like he's the . . ." Lila paused and stared into space. "It's like he's the Uberwhale."

"So you're saying . . ." Greg stopped.

"That Seema was the closest witness to the first-ever, humpback airborne salute of a human vessel," interjected Gorman. "Think of it as a stupendous champagne toast, except Seema was unfortunately inside of the glass."

Everyone was silent. Seema spoke with less difficulty now. "You really think this Uberwhale was signaling us with a greeting?"

"Yes. Given all of the facts, I couldn't characterize it in any other way. Like a Blue Angels flyover."

"I feel better, Chris." The color had returned to Seema's cheeks. "Thank you, everyone."

"This is all fine and dandy, folks," proclaimed Dmitri, "but now we've gotta deal with the U.S. government."

"Like I said, we're still under their protective umbrella." Gorman grabbed the megaphone from Lila and angled it in the direction of the cutter. "I'm Christopher Gorman," he shouted, "Director of the Pacific Institute for Cetacean Educational Studies. Our organization is in legal contractual occupation of this vessel. You're observing the same event we are. Our vessel is surrounded by a pod of whales of the species Megaptera novaeangliae. They are protected by the Marine Mammal Act of 1972. Do not attempt to approach within one hundred yards of any of these individuals or you'll be in violation of U.S. law."

Dmitri finally realized what Gorman had already deduced. His shoulders relaxed. The average distance separating the individuals in the ring of humpbacks was less than one hundred feet. Any attempt to pass through a gap between the whales would automatically violate the one-hundred-yard limit. The *Research in Paradise* was shielded by the same escort that safeguarded the Uberwhale.

"We will abide by international law," called a Coast Guard official, "but our orders are clear. "We will board your vessel at first opportunity."

Before anyone could react to the threatening announcement, Andrew's fervent cries were heard from below the deck. Dmitri followed the others downstairs to see Andrew at the front of the cabin, staring down into the sunken well area that housed the glass bottom.

Andrew turned to face them. "Hey, folks, I don't know what just happened upstairs, but you've gotta see this." He pointed straight down.

Dmitri and Greg walked over and sat down next to him. Dmitri leaned over the edge of the barrier and peered, incredulous, at an eyeball the size of a large orange on the other side of the glass. The orb appeared to be scrutinizing them.

"It's Uber!" exclaimed Lila. "He's checking us out."

"It's more like he's checking out Mark," said Andrew. The boy had somehow scaled the safety barrier and descended to the bottom of the recessed glass well. With Mark's face pressed firmly against the glass, the boy and the humpback seemed to be studying one another. The dramatic encounter reminded Dmitri of the scene from Spielberg's movie, *E.T.: The Extra-Terrestrial*, when the children and the alien make first contact.

Melanie rushed over and gazed down. "Mark!" she yelled, "Get the heck out of there, or else!"

This was the first time Dmitri had heard a punitive edge in Melanie's voice. He reached down and pulled Mark back up to the cabin level.

"Uber, Goober, whatever . . ." exclaimed Andrew. "He's right underneath us!"

"Has any humpback ever knocked a boat out of the water?" asked Seema, sounding wary again.

"No way," replied Gorman. "Andrew, let's try something. Why don't you and Seema prepare to engage in another game session?"

"You want us to start broadcasting the random game symbol sounds?" said Seema.

"Precisely," replied Gorman. "I have a hunch about Lila's Uberwhale and what this visit is about. Let's invite our honored guest to an afternoon tête-à-tête. However, since he's literally camped out in our living room, we first need to reduce the volume level to the underwater speakers. The longer we engage our cetacean friends in conversation, the more time we buy from the Coast Guard's grasp."

Seema unwrapped the blanket and walked over to Andrew's console station.

"Hey, Seema," said Andrew, "how'd you know I dig the wet T-shirt look? What happened, anyway?"

With a playful flick of her wrist, she slapped his temple.

"Actually," replied Greg, "Seema was baptized by Uber."

"You mean like King Kong and his human girlfriend?" replied Andrew.

"Don't mess with me, pal," crowed Seema. "I went through hell, but I'm now their Chosen One."

Lila walked up behind Seema holding some garments. "I scrounged a T-shirt and shorts from the ship's supplies. Look the other way, Andrew." With Melanie shielding her in a beach towel curtain, Seema stood and changed into the dry clothes.

"Back to work." Seema rejoined Andrew, typing commands to initiate the synthesizer and the Speakeasy programs. While the sounds of the whale synthesizer resounded throughout the control room, the first computer-generated game symbol appeared on the TV screen behind Andrew's workstation.

"Hey look, he's backing away," said Lila.

The school-bus-sized Uberwhale gracefully descended beneath the vessel, parking a full body-length's distance away.

"What's happening?" It was Professor McPinsky's voice, sounding confused. "Why'd you all disappear?"

"I forgot you were on the line." Dmitri gave his professor a brief account of the latest dramatic developments.

"After I completed the file transfer to Professor McPinsky's computer," said Andrew, "I initialized the external webcam interface, so he's currently viewing the Speakeasy screen from his home."

"It's almost like being there," replied McPinsky. "I'm also recording the session to a backup file—"

Before McPinsky could complete the sentence, an earsplitting roar reverberated throughout the cabin, as if it were an echo chamber. Most members of the team cupped their hands over their ears.

"What was that?" said Melanie

"Look at the Speakeasy display," replied McPinsky.

Dmitri stared at the screen, but it made no sense. The sound that had rocked the boat had also generated the perfectly formed, squashed oval shape of an ellipse. Then he had a hunch. "Andrew, lower the input volume of the hydrophones and everyone fasten your seat belts."

As the suspense mounted, another cetacean roar yielded the drawing of a second identically shaped ellipse, rotated by forty-five degrees.

Dmitri, his heart racing, faced his friend. "Greg, it looks like Uber is trying to communicate with the mathematicians among us."

"Unfortunately," Greg responded, "I don't have the same ability to depict geometric figures with my voice."

In under a minute, Uber had roared the shapes of four ellipses, each rotated around the same center point by about forty-five degrees from its neighbor. Dmitri glanced around and saw the same incredulous expression on everyone's face. To him, the constellation of the four superimposed elliptical figures bore an uncanny resemblance to the U.S. Atomic Energy Commission's four-ringed logo depicting the orbits of electrons in the nucleus of an atom.

"Oh, Lord," uttered McPinsky. "Those acoustic drawings are so precise. They're fairly symmetrical in shape, rotated by nearly identical angles, and they share the same center point. It's mathematical virtuosity rendered exclusively in sound."

"If the definition of music is sound-sculpted time," said Seema, "this is sound-sculpted mathematics." She glanced at Dmitri.

"That's a beautiful description, Seema," replied Dmitri. His comment painted a broad smile onto her face.

"They've achieved a mastery of sound," said Greg, his tone expressing stupefied elation. "The sounds of songs, and now, the sounds of language—a mathematical language!"

"It's not like Uber is drawing with pencil and paper and has the benefit of visual feedback to achieve such precisely proportioned figures." Dmitri traced a finger over the shapes on the display. "Just as the juveniles imaged the logical game symbols, Uber's taken his prowess of memory and precision acoustic control to an even higher level of expression."

"Except I'm seeing an irregularity in the elliptical symmetries." Greg paced his words as though he were deliberating. He appeared pensive. "I think there's something more here than meets the eye. Look." Greg slid a finger across the peaks and valleys depicted in the waterfall plots on Andrew's PC workstation monitor.

"You're right." Dmitri combed an anxious hand through his hair. "It's surprising that the energies of the third and fourth higher-frequency peaks are about the same as the first two lower-frequency peaks."

"Which is very different than for human speech and for the juveniles' game vocalizations, where only the first two peaks were dominant." Greg's voice was charged with excitement. "I think Uber is encoding vital information using all four frequencies."

"What are you two suggesting?" asked Melanie. "The basis of the Speakeasy system is the visualization of the two-dimensional word grams. Remember our discussion last month? Since we're restricted by the properties of our vocal tracts, we only use the two lowest resonant frequencies to encode the symbols of language."

"Which is why the symbols of our language are inherently processed in only two dimensions, limiting the number of symbols we can generate," answered Dmitri.

Like the Invisible Man, McPinsky's disembodied voice loomed from the speakerphone. "As the human brain evolved to adapt these symbols in various ways, it's no accident that the types of games we play are also of a two-dimensional nature."

"But the spectral plots indicate Uber is generating four different frequency peaks of nearly equal energy intensity, Professor," replied Greg. "I think we should assume he has an entirely different physiology, which gives him independent control of the four peaks."

"Chris," asked Dmitri, "could the humpbacks utilize air sacs of different dimensions, like Helmholz resonators?"

"Over the years, we've autopsied a few humpbacks that have washed ashore," replied Gorman. "We've confirmed their respiratory system is connected to a series of structures that look like flotation sacs. Maybe those have been adapted for the generation of sound?"

"Or maybe," said Seema, "their respiratory system has multiple tubal structures, acting like independent vocal tracts?"

"This is all fascinating," said Dmitri, "but the Coast Guard's breathing down our necks, and I am, after all, responsible for the launch. Maybe they'll be more lenient if we tell them we're ready to cooperate."

"I hear you, Dmitri, but my gut tells me this could be really, really big!" answered Greg. "I'd like to try one more thing."

"And we're still surrounded by the whales," said Lila. "The Coast Guard can't touch us."

"Okay, Greg," said Dmitri. "What do you suggest?"

"Possibly because of my hearing deficiency, I've developed an acute visual sensitivity to the structural details of mathematical functions like the ellipses on the screen. I'm saying we may need to examine these vocalizations at a deeper level. Andrew, I know I'm pushing the envelope here, but is it possible to display Uber's three lowest frequency peaks in 3D perspective?"

"Like a 3D version of Speakeasy?" asked Melanie.

"That's the idea," replied Greg, "except we won't need to wear funny glasses."

"Thought you'd never ask," replied Andrew. "I always prepare for contingencies when I write new applications and, besides, we already discussed this back at SoCalSci. I actually did design the program to plot the Speakeasy data in 3D x,y,z coordinates. It's only because I've forced the data points to a value of zero in the third dimension that it's defaulting to Melanie's two-dimensional version of Speakeasy."

"He's right," said Dmitri. "Since Andrew had adapted his thesis's 3D plotting routine for this experiment, we'd decided to maintain the 3D option for both transmit and receive functions."

"That's great," said Greg. "What about computing the frequency and the amplitude of a third peak?"

"Like I said," replied Andrew, "I live by my Boy Scout leader's maxim, 'Prior planning prevents piss-poor performance.' My peak analysis program loops through the frequency data for as many peaks as I specify. Right now, it only searches through the data for the two lowest-frequency peaks. To search for the three lowest-frequency peaks, I only have to change a single input parameter in the setup menu. Then it's a piece of cake to image the symbol location in the three-dimensional perspective of a Speakeasy plot."

"For God's sake, man, that's fantastic!" Greg thrust his arms triumphantly into the air. "Do it now and replay the recording of Uber's vocalizations of the ellipses. Seema, while we're waiting, do you think your symbol synthesizer can be modified to broadcast three different frequency peaks at the same time?"

"Like Dmitri said," replied Seema, "we'd already planned for that option. Even though my program is restricted to synthesizing tone pairs, I have the option to generate two tone pairs at the same time by the superposition principle. If you only want three peaks, I'll zero the output energy of the fourth peak."

"That's brilliant, Seema!" exclaimed Dmitri. "I didn't realize you'd finished that. You two are amazing."

"Okay, I'm ready," announced Andrew. "I'm replaying Uber's recording back into the Speakeasy program which is now set up to analyze and plot the first three peaks. They should be appearing on the Speakeasy display any second now. Look, there's the first ellipse."

They waited silently for the time it took to plot all four of the ellipses.

"Are you kidding me?" howled Greg.

"Oh, my," uttered McPinsky. "Is this what I think it is?"

"Yes," answered Dmitri, surprised that his mentor's voice had quavered with such emotion.

"What is it?" asked Mark.

"Could you elaborate, Professor?" Melanie echoed.

"It's a sublimely succinct calling card," answered McPinsky, "rendered in the universal language of mathematics and written by the acoustic hand of the Megapterans. This is a message for the ages, transcending the proverbial 'take-me-to-your-leader' cliché. In Carl Sagan's book *Contact*, he postulated that the first confirmed radio communication from an ET civilization was mathematical—a repeating series of the first 261 prime numbers."

"It's rather elementary, Watson," interjected Greg, facing Dmitri. "I'm visualizing the acoustical mastery of the mathematical expression of three-dimensional geometric figures. Uber has independent control of the rotation of these figures in all three dimensions. These ellipses are rotated independently by forty-five degrees around each of the three x, y, and z axes of the 3D plot."

To make his point, Greg traced his fingers across the shapes on the screen, and Dmitri muttered, "Amazing." The static figures not only appeared to be rotated clockwise relative to one another, but in the 3D perspective of the x,y,z coordinates, they also seemed to pivot into the depth of the screen as well.

When the boat momentarily swayed, Dmitri clutched the back of Andrew's chair. "This is the mathematical basis of inertial guidance systems such as gyroscopes and gyrocompasses." In awe, Dmitri reached out and touched the figures on the monitor. "Could this be how they navigate?"

Gorman spoke in a quieter tone now, as if mystified. "I never imagined this—"

"What are they talking about, Mom?" asked Mark. "What did the whale say?"

"Honey, it's even difficult for me to understand, but I think the whales are drawing 3D pictures with their voices."

"Awesome!" exclaimed Mark.

Melanie turned her attention to the researchers. "You know, for thousands of years, what we heard as grunting or barking sounds is really a language of mathematics. Humans have adapted the written language to express both the representational symbols of the alphabet and the pictorial symbols like the Chinese ideograms. Likewise, as I see it now, the humpbacks have adapted their voices to express both the primitive logical game symbols, and in the pictorial mode, the ideograms of geometric figures in 3D no less."

"So whaddya think now, Chris?" asked Lila.

"This is way beyond my grasp," replied Gorman. "I'm relying on Dmitri and Greg to interpret the meaning of these signals."

Uber's vocalizations resumed. He blasted away, over and over. As the cabin groaned with his roars, the geometric figures danced on the screen.

"His control is unbelievable!" shouted Greg. "He just keeps retracing the same rotated figures with perfect precision."

"Oh, my God," uttered Dmitri. "Look, now he's rotating in the reverse direction, first counterclockwise, then clockwise."

The whale's booming voice finally ceased.

"I think he's waiting for an answer," said Andrew.

"Who are we to refuse," remarked McPinsky. "Don't you think we should engage him in a three-dimensional version of the game?"

"That's an intriguing idea, Professor," replied Dmitri, rubbing his hands together in anticipation. "Seema, is your synthesizer ready to broadcast that extra tone we discussed?"

"It's all set up and ready to go. I've even incorporated it into the random-tone-generation program. You want me to start with that?"

"Yes," said Dmitri. "Fire it up and cross your fingers. Hopefully, we'll see a response."

With the addition of the third tone, the sounds of Seema's computer-synthesized game symbols had a richer quality. The Speakeasy translations of the first few, ring-shaped symbols appeared to float in the three-dimensional perspective of the Speakeasy display.

"Works like a charm," said Greg.

"Now the game becomes all the more challenging," said Dmitri. "In addition to forming boxes in all three dimensions, a higher-level goal is to complete as many cubes of eight vertices as possible."

"I remember the original *Star Trek* television series," said McPinsky, "where Spock and Kirk played a futuristic version of three-dimensional chess. I never imagined I might witness such a match between humans and another earthly species." Dmitri sensed a degree of anticipation in McPinsky's voice that he'd never heard before.

"Hey, Andrew," replied Greg. "There's still something fishy about the shapes of the ellipses in three dimensions. Can you give me a raw data printout of the power levels and the frequencies of the four peaks?"

"Fishy!" Dmitri heard Mark repeat, and he saw the boy was smiling.

"Sure enough," replied Andrew. "You'll see the printout appearing in a couple of minutes, right over there." He pointed at the printer located on the adjacent desk.

"What are you up to, Greg?" asked Dmitri.

"I'm not sure yet. Give me a few minutes to do some calculations."

"Hey, guys," said Andrew. "I'm hearing game symbol responses from Uber."

"Okay, Seema, get ready." Dmitri tensed. "I'll give you the 3D coordinates and you feed them into your synthesizer."

Lila rushed over to Andrew's workstation as Uber's first ring-shaped symbols appeared. "Look at the screen! You were right, Greg. He's playing the game in three dimensions. God, can this be happening?"

Dmitri slapped Greg on the shoulder. "You're a genius, pal."

As before, Uber projected the loop-shaped acoustic game symbols left and right, up and down, onto the LCD display. Now, however, the researchers could see that the placement of the symbols also receded into the depth dimension of the 3D Speakeasy soundscape.

The match magically unfolded before their eyes. The circular symbols appeared to levitate in the three-dimensional perspective of the x,y,z plot. Now that the game had been translated into a higher dimension, the Turing test, the ultimate gauge of intellectual aptitude, was being performed upon a stage of even richer complexity. As the game progressed, boxes were transformed into cubes. The scoreboard's mounting tallies confirmed the undeniable truth that, despite all of his training, Dmitri's mind was not nearly as adept as his cetacean counterpart's at manipulating the rules of logic in the extra dimension. The transcendent breakthrough more than compensated for his humbling defeat.

Ensconced in the executive leather chair in his home office, Professor Theodosious McPinsky stared at the revelation painted upon his computer monitor—the Speakeasy rendition of Uber's 3D game masterpiece.

To celebrate the occasion, he uncorked a rare, vintage bottle of his father's favorite Scotch whisky. He yearned to share this special moment, so he filled two tumblers and placed the second drink next to the framed photo perched upon the desk. Then he raised his glass and toasted the lovely woman in the photograph, who perpetually smiled back at him. Savoring the Laphroaig single malt, he gazed longingly into the eyes of his departed wife, Emma, his own eyes wet with tears.

Back in California, Richard Prescott lounged in his den's plush Italian leather recliner, and enjoyed an after-dinner snifter of Armagnac. With each pleasurable sip, he measured the minutes with great anticipation, waiting for the phone call from Maui to confirm the demise of Dmitri's dangerous experiment.

THE LORDS OF SOUND

Research in Paradise Control Room

IF HE'D HAD a box of cigars, Dmitri would have shared them with his giddy colleagues. He could only compare his current euphoria to his cousin's description of elation at the birth of her first child.

After a quick soda and chips mini-celebration in the *Research in Paradise* control room, Dmitri decided it was time to get back to work. He sat down at Andrew's workstation. "Professor, are you still there?" The momentary silence suggested the Skype session had been terminated. "Professor?"

"I'm here, my boy, but I doubt if I'm still the same person."

"I think we all feel that way," replied Dmitri. "What are you thinking at this moment?"

"I'm thinking that the use of logic and mathematics is regarded as the universal litmus test of higher intelligence. That the whales could be so adept at modulating and analyzing sound, in the same fashion that we utilize pen and paper to express these abstract concepts, is mind-boggling. Even humans don't usually play games of logic in three dimensions without the assistance of a computer. Yet for centuries we judged the whales by our own arrogant standards, looking for the external vestiges of civilization, and we found them wanting."

"Their songs were only a clue to something much bigger." Dmitri chuckled. "Now we literally have to face the music. This is the paradigm shift we'd been hoping for. For so long!"

"All the same, we shouldn't be too critical of ourselves," replied McPinsky thoughtfully. "We couldn't have achieved this breakthrough without the cut-ting-edge technology of the Speakeasy system."

"Speakeasy is the interspecies communication bridge you'd long sought, Pro-fessor," replied Dmitri, his tone devotional. "It's as if Homo sapiens had to prog-ress to a level worthy of engaging with a species as advanced as the Megapterans."

"Now, if we could only cross that bridge with a sense of humility and the emotional intelligence to deal with the impact of such a dialogue," said Mel-anie, who had appeared next to him. "Hello, Professor." She raised her voice. "I don't believe we've formally met. I'm Melanie."

Despite the afternoon's flurry of incredible events, Dmitri felt chagrined he'd not yet introduced these two significant people in his life to one another. "I'm sorry Professor, but—"

"So this is the brainy woman with the beautiful voice," interrupted McPin-sky. "Pleased to meet you."

Dmitri was pleasantly surprised by their instant camaraderie. "You're right, Professor. It was Melanie's Speakeasy training of her students that made this discovery possible." He gazed into her eyes.

"Thank you, Melanie," replied McPinsky.

"You're welcome, Professor, but I believe Dmitri deserves the lion's share of the credit." She smiled at him. "I never dreamed Speakeasy could become a universal translator between beings that image symbols of light and beings that image symbols of sound."

"I believe we've only scratched the surface of our potential for communi-cating with these creatures," said McPinsky.

"You're more correct than you can even imagine, Professor!" said Greg.

"You certainly are jubilant, Greg," noted Dmitri.

"Prepare yourselves," exclaimed Greg, "because the discoveries just keep on coming. I might have confirmed something even more remarkable!"

"How could it get any better?" asked Dmitri.

"It could be exponentially better," replied Greg. "I just finished number crunching the raw frequency data of Uber's 3D, rotated ellipses. These are just rough calculations, mind you. There's possibly much more here than meets the eye. This is way beyond the perception of our physical senses. We would need more precise calculations, however, to confirm my finding."

Greg produced the data printout from Andrew's workstation as the team gathered around him.

"Look at this table of numbers." He traced a finger across the rows and down the columns on the printed page. "These four columns correspond to the energy measurements of the first four frequency peaks in Uber's raw-data spectra. They confirm what I suspected."

Dmitri peered at the numbers. "The energy levels are all in the same ball-park."

"Correct," replied Greg. "From a cursory inspection of the waterfall plots, it also struck me that the time-dependent variations of the energies of the four peaks looked uncorrelated. This is compelling evidence that the four frequencies were intended to convey independent information. Because Uber's rotated ellipses in 3D space looked suspiciously shaped, I finally remembered that the geometric projection of a circle from three dimensions into two dimensions has the shape of a squashed ellipse."

"Oh, my God!" uttered McPinsky. "Dr. Bono, don't tell me you confirmed the existence of a geometric plane curve in tetra space?"

"That's what my rough calculations suggest," Greg replied with a grin.

Dmitri's mind reeled at the outpouring of exuberant laughter from the speakerphone. Until today, he'd never heard his mentor react so emotionally. "Greg, please speak English. The suspense is killing me."

"Analogous to the projection of the 3D circle into a 2D ellipse, a circle 'drawn' in the abstract, mathematical world of four dimensions is transformed into the shape of an ellipse when projected into three dimensions. Let me repeat—" Greg reiterated what he'd just said, slowly and methodically. "I therefore wrote a quickie program for analyzing the raw data from Andrew's printout and confirmed that the four-peak data satisfies the equation of a circle in four dimensions. Uber literally and figuratively 'drew' the acoustic version of a circle in four-dimensional space rotated four times by forty-five-degrees. Unfortunately, the human brain and eye can only interpret the plot of such a geometric construction as a three-dimensional ellipse."

"You're pretty certain of this?" asked McPinsky.

"Somewhat certain, yes, but only for the limited amount of data I've analyzed so far. By selecting different sets of eight points from the circumference of the alleged four-dimensional circle, I generated corresponding sets of eight simultaneous equations. For each and every one of those sets of equations, the solution always converged to the same answer for the radius, the location of the center, and the tilt angles. That a living organism could create this audio sequence of four-dimensional concentric circles is extremely difficult. Actually, it's practically impossible."

"How so?" asked Lila.

"One way to simulate this procedure is with a sophisticated computer program," Greg said. "You'd first need to generate the geometrical figure of a four-dimensional hypersphere, a sphere existing in more than three dimensions, from the complex equation that describes it. Then you'd have a plane intersect the 4D hypersphere exactly through its center and tilted at the precise angle. Then you'd need to repeat this three more times for the same forty-five-degree angles of rotation." His flattened palm and clenched fist simulated the geometry lesson of a plane and a sphere in three dimensions.

"Are you saying Uber's brain is like a supercomputer?" replied Lila.

"What he's saying," answered McPinsky, in reverential tones, "is that Uber's brain could be capable of processing symbols of information in four dimensions. To achieve the inconceivable mastery of four-dimensional frequency modulation, they'd need to precisely coordinate four independent streams of acoustic information to generate and image the symbols. We humans spend our whole lives learning to speak and understand language using only two independent streams. The humpbacks might be doing something exponentially more complex."

"The humpback's acoustic ideograms might inherently be four-dimensional constructs," added Greg. "If so, they could both literally and figuratively think and express themselves in four dimensions."

Once again, Dmitri observed the dazed expressions upon the faces of his colleagues. He marveled at this stunning turn of events, remembering how he'd battled with Greg about the original whale-song research proposal. Now his friend was leading the way, challenging the team with previously unimaginable possibilities.

Andrew finally broke the silence. "First we were overjoyed to discover they could play a game of logic in two dimensions. Then we were thrilled to realize they could kick our butts in 3D. Now we're stupefied to realize we'd need to program a supercomputer to have any chance of competing with them in 4D."

"It would certainly be a humbling realization for humankind," added McPinsky.

"Who's going to believe any of this?" added Seema. "I can barely believe it myself."

"It's all still speculative," cautioned Greg. "We need to do a more thorough analysis of the data we've collected and submit it for peer review."

"But no one can argue with the facts," replied Dmitri, "and we have the data to prove it. Andrew, just make sure you transmit those files to Professor McPinsky."

"I can't believe I'm actually saying this, Dmitri, but maybe it's time to turn on the video projector," said Gorman. "Let's give Uber the chance to experience the multi-sensory feedback of his mental machinations. It's our chance to return the gift of this discovery."

"You read my mind, Chris," replied Dmitri. "No reason to worry about violating the species Prime Directive, since it appears we've received a four-dimensional invitation to their party. Like you said earlier, as long as we keep Uber engaged, we'll be shielded from the Coast Guard. Maybe they'll even give up and leave."

"And I want to share this experience in the medium of the humpbacks," Gorman said. "It's the dive of a lifetime. There should gear on board. Are you ready to join me, Lila?"

"Absolutely," she replied. "I'm so glad you'd asked me to plan for a dive. There's gear for four. Just like the old days. How about joining us, Melanie?"

"You're kidding," bleated Andrew. "You want to expose yourself to two thousand tons of mathematical geniuses who've been persecuted for generations and have a score to settle with the persecutors?"

Seema's freaked-out expression caught everyone's attention.

"We'll be okay, Andrew," replied Gorman, "and don't worry, Seema. Since our cetacean comrades are mathematicians and, for all we know, poets too, I don't think they'd mind us sharing the experience of their very own Speakeasy discovery."

"So you're saying they'll welcome you with open fins?" replied Andrew.

"No comment." Like a Buckingham Palace guard, Gorman's face remained expressionless.

"I wouldn't miss this opportunity for the world," said Melanie. "I'm thrilled when my students make Speakeasy pronunciation breakthroughs, so I've gotta be there when Uber makes the connection between sight and sound. How about it, Dmitri? You mentioned you had diving experience. Wanna go for a swim?"

"I'd normally be as petrified as Andrew, but this afternoon has thawed most of my inhibitions. I'll shock all of you and just go with the flow."

"Very cool," said Greg. "While you guys suit up, Andrew and I are gonna set up the video system."

While their colleagues prepared for the dive, the two men located the rolled-up, eight-foot-wide fabric screen tucked away in the corner. After they'd lugged it over to the observation area, Andrew climbed over the solid barrier railing and slid down into the sunken rectangular well area.

"Careful," said Greg. "Try not to step directly on the glass."

Two oversized panes of safety glass, framed in the center by a two-inch-wide support member, formed the super-widescreen view window. Greg lifted and lowered the sausage-shaped object, while Andrew, balancing himself on the structurally sound perimeter, guided it into position on top of the glass. Once he'd unrolled it to completely cover the eight-by-twelve-foot rectangular window, Andrew secured the screen with duct tape. Greg's helping hand facilitated his climb up.

An LED video projector had already been attached to the cabin ceiling. Secured by a jury-rigged assemblage of rubber clamps, metal brackets, and assorted nuts and bolts, the projector pointed straight down toward the glass bottom. A long video cable had been taped to the ceiling, one end plugged into Andrew's workstation and the other connected to the projector. This improvised system would enable the same Speakeasy plots displayed above Andrew's workstation to be projected onto and through the movie screen resting on the glass bottom.

"The Coast Guard is still waiting for us." Dmitri fussed over the final adjustments to his wetsuit. "So, please, Andrew, transmit the audio and video files of everything that's happened, and maybe about to happen, to Professor McPinsky."

"Yes," replied McPinsky, reminding everyone he was still on the line. "I need those files. I've been waiting my entire career for data like this, and I know just the special person I'd like to share this discovery with."

"Who might that be?" asked Dmitri.

"Trust me," replied McPinsky. "He's the right person for this moment in history. Hopefully, you'll all find out sooner than later. In the meantime, I envy your youth and the once-in-a-lifetime opportunity to swim with the 'lords of sound.'"

CHAIN REACTION

The Pentagon, Virginia

THREE TIME ZONES to the east, Richard Prescott had decided to contact his Navy buddy, Ned Perry, for another friendly phone conversation.

"Richard, I'm impressed," said Captain Perry. "How did you persuade the Coast Guard to act so quickly?"

"Thanks to your earlier suggestion, a lawyer friend in Oahu located the injured protestors in Maui. They're hurt, embarrassed, and angry, so they were more than willing to file assault and battery charges against Dmitri's team. You have news from the Coast Guard?"

"Yes, I have a contact on the cutter that's intercepted the PICES vessel."

"How'd you arrange that?"

"Think 'homeland security.'"

"It's my turn to be impressed."

"I wish I had better news for you, though. My contact says the PICES vessel is shielded by an escort of humpbacks. They'll just have to hang tight until they can sneak through."

"Oh, no," Prescott moaned. "But it might be too late by then. They could have the data they need to sink us all. By the way, it's rather unbelievable to me that the whales are protecting them."

"I'm just telling you what they told me. Something remarkable is happening out there."

Now Prescott was flummoxed. What if it were true: a communication breakthrough with another species? And if he himself were thwarting it?

Nonsense, he told himself, it's a fairytale! "By the way, Ned," he replied. "I appreciate you burning the midnight oil. Just tell your Coast Guard insider to seize the computers and the data when they board the vessel. As far as the law is concerned, Dmitri's crew is guilty of assault on the high seas. If you can't make that happen, then your sonar experiments could be ancient history."

"Copy that, Richard. I hear you. Bye bye."

Although temporarily relieved, Richard Prescott was dumbfounded that Dmitri and McPinsky had stymied him. Yes, they were quite clever, and he continued to admire their devotion to their profession. But he couldn't be weakened by second thoughts. Those arrogant professors would not stoop to acknowledge the important contributions of SoCalSci's administrators: people like himself, who successfully orchestrated the financing and functioning of the system that supported their dopey experiments, sanctioned under the guise of academic freedom. It was only a matter of time until he received official confirmation of Dmitri's arrest. Then he'd initiate the next step in his plan.

Prescott's admonishments had finally struck a nerve with Ned Perry. The latest dispatch from the Coast Guard cutter near Maalaea Bay, confirming the extraordinary marine mammal group behavior surrounding the PICES-chartered vessel, had pushed him beyond the tipping point. He could not sit idly by with the future of the sonar program hanging in the balance. It was an essential piece in the geopolitical chess game vital to the defense of the nation. He needed to disperse those whales and stop the potentially ruinous experiment. Now was the time to act. And he'd been lucky. The vessel that had conducted the recent battery of tests in Hawaiian waters was still cruising in the vicinity of the current PICES experiment.

Perry stared out the window into the black void of the moonless night, the Washington Monument glowing in the distance. Though he'd never tell anyone but his wife, he deeply regretted the collateral damage caused by the fateful decision to conduct the tests at such intense power levels. He winced at the memory of his daughter's tearful response to the much publicized death of the beached whale in Maui. Worst of all, he couldn't tell a soul about the recent dispatches from the USSIA Satellite Imaging Agency. They'd confirmed that the ocean crop-circle patterns, linked to the group behavior of humpbacks, were a worldwide phenomenon. It was painfully obvious that the whales were far more intelligent than he had ever imagined. But he had a duty to perform.

Perry sighed and sat down at his secure workstation. After he'd retrieved the GPS coordinates embedded in the dispatch from the Coast Guard cutter, he typed a coded message:

To: Commander, U.S.S. *San Fernando*
From: Pacific Fleet Command and Control Center
Copy this:
Urgent - Proceed to coordinates 20.759122,-156.457228
Conduct - five minute test at half power
Ping Duration - six seconds
Ping Frequency - every thirty seconds
Report back -Target signature profiles at beginning and end of test
Over and Out.

Just enough power to disorient and confuse the whales but not injure them, Perry reflected, as he pressed the SEND key. Perry's coded message traversed the labyrinth of the U.S. Navy's ultra-secure computer network, and then it was broadcast from the Naval Computer and Telecommunications Master Station at Pearl Harbor. Less than a minute after his final keystroke, the message arrived at its destination.

What an odd request, thought the commanding officer on the bridge of the U.S.S. *San Fernando*. He'd assumed that the classified sonar experiments were over, especially after the news of the beached humpbacks in the vicinity of the last tests. Now he had to deal with this puzzling new command with oddball parameters. His role, however, was not to question his superiors. He relayed the new orders to the operations specialists and recited the GPS coordinates to the navigator, who keyed them into the system. The good news was that they would arrive at their destination in about twenty minutes, complete the task, and head for home soon thereafter.

The Torch of Prometheus

Leeward Waters, Maui—thirty feet below sea level

DMITRI COULDN'T BELIEVE he'd summoned the chutzpah to dive amongst forty humpback whales. Since this had already been the most eventful day of his life, he'd decided to play with house money and chalk up one more adventure of a lifetime.

Chris, Lila, and Melanie had already taken the plunge and now it was his turn. This would be his first dive in nearly five years. Unaccustomed to the weight of the scuba gear and the tight-fitting wetsuit, he devoted every ounce of concentration inching down to the bottom of the slippery ladder. He paused on the last step, clutching the railing, frozen in indecision. Sucking air through the mouthpiece, he struggled to control a choking sensation. A dormant childhood gag reflex had returned to haunt him. As he turned and saw the massive bodies poking above the surface, his heart pounded. Was he really going to go through with this?

"Don't think about it," Greg yelled from the top of the ladder. "Just let go."

Dmitri looked up to a reassuring presence. Greg had always been there to support him and he needed his help now. Dmitri pointed at his friend and then at himself. Pushing an arm forward, he mimed a shoving motion. The message seemed perfectly clear to Greg. He took two steps down the ladder and braced himself against the supports. Flashing a mischievous grin, he pressed an outstretched foot into his colleague's chest and delivered a gentle push. Dmitri fell backward and disappeared with a splash.

It all seemed to happen in a panicky blur. Dmitri crashed through the surface with a jarring jolt, felt the water's instant chill, and feared he'd never stop plummeting to the bottom of the sea. Arms and legs thrashed in the struggle to regain his equilibrium. His teeth tightly clamped to the mouthpiece, he fought in vain to subdue persistent throat spasms. Why had he thought he could do this? He'd already swallowed a cup of saltwater. The briny taste nauseated him, and he was beginning to shiver. He'd better get it together, before it was too late.

Seeing Melanie drift into view, he remembered her advice when they'd donned their wetsuits. She'd coached him in a yoga breathing technique tailored to underwater emergencies. Closing his eyes, he focused on the memory of her words and the sound of her voice. Counting slowly in patterns of three, he paced his deep and steady breaths, and felt the agitation gradually diminish. When he finally looked around, Melanie was right beside him. With her uncanny knack of being there for him, he greeted her with a very grateful thumbs-up gesture. She reached out and grasped his gloved hands.

With their arms linked, they paddled in place and shared a buoyant moment, pausing to survey the subaquatic scenery. The play of the light in the crystal-clear water imbued all things with a fluid vibrancy. Dmitri's first impressions were of the sun-lit clouds of translucent foam ascending from Melanie's mouth, born of the same breath that animated her voice. The glistening, grape-bunch clusters of bubbles looked vaguely like jellyfish. With each breath, a new "jellyfish" spiraled lazily up to the surface.

Although Dmitri estimated the visibility at more than one hundred feet, he was glad the whales were not to be seen. During his previous dives, he'd marveled at the rainbow schools of tropical fish feeding in the shallow coral reefs. Out here in the deep water, far from the coast, the sea seemed devoid of life, until a familiar figure loomed into view. After Gorman drifted over, he handed Dmitri a miniature video camera, jabbed an index finger into his chest, and then motioned straight down before scissoring away.

Now that Gorman had issued him marching orders, Dmitri grappled with the buoyancy compensation control on the stabilization vest. Once he'd figured it out, he began a steady descent, trailing Melanie's bubbly plume until they were submerged sixty feet directly beneath the *Research in Paradise*. At this location, he could hear and feel the vibrations from Seema's game symbol synthesizer oozing from the underwater speakers.

Dmitri stared up at the boat's glass-bottom window, made opaque by the illuminated screen. Now he could actually see the same visual representations of the sounds on display in the control room beaming from the video projector aimed into the water. Directly above him, Chris and Lila were engaged in the procedure for calibrating the underwater video system. The zero-gravity, slow-motion scene reminded him of a popular video of Space Shuttle astronauts floating hypnotically above the earth during a Hubble Telescope repair mission.

The current operation revolved around a daisy-chain relay ring of five individuals at five separate locations. Based upon Chris's underwater video quality assessment of Seema's game-symbol projections, he'd signal either a thumbs-up or thumbs-down gesture to Lila near the surface. She surfaced and repeated the same gesture up to Greg, who was leaning over the boat's railing. He then relayed it to Andrew at the entrance to the control room. And after Andrew shouted the result to Seema inside, she would either increase or decrease the level of the projector's current video control setting. The entire process was repeated until Chris had signed with a flattened palm, his signal to move on to the calibration of a different control.

After a number of iterations and incremental adjustments to the projector's focus, zoom, and illumination intensity controls, the results were spectacular. Dmitri marveled at the Speakeasy images of the game symbol frequencies, the circular shapes. Perhaps it was an optical illusion, an artifact of the virtual perspective created by Andrew's 3D plotting routine, but as the light underwent multiple refractions across the cloth, glass, and water boundary layers, the ring-shaped images appeared to hover in the water, just below the glass.

Gorman had entrusted Dmitri with the responsibility of capturing these spectacular moments. Aiming the video camera up at the glass bottom, Dmitri was startled by something bumping against his back. Since he was more than mildly fearful about sharing the same space with Uber, he turned around, fearing the worst. Sighting Melanie, he exhaled an effervescent sigh of relief. However, as he followed the vector of her outstretched arm, pointing straight down, his gut tensed. Uber's colossal hulk appeared directly beneath them, gradually closing the distance. Melanie and Dmitri followed the lead of Lila and Chris, kicking rapidly away to give Uber a wide berth as he parked about twenty feet directly beneath their vessel.

From the perspective of their new location, Dmitri could fully appreciate Uber's immensity, power, and grace. He practically eclipsed the entire *Research in Paradise*, yet glided effortlessly with gentle beats of his aircraft-sized wing fins. So that he wouldn't obscure their view of the glass bottom, Dmitri and Melanie positioned themselves at an oblique angle, with Uber about fifty feet above them and some distance off to the right, with Lila and Chris the same distance over to the left. It was a bit too close for Dmitri's comfort, but when he peered through the camera's zoom lens he understood why this opportunity was worth the risk. Uber appeared to be transfixed by the shapes appearing on the screen, his curiosity obviously piqued. Dmitri could not imagine what the creature was experiencing.

A sudden jolt, like a shockwave, shoved Dmitri sideways. Uber's trumpeting vibrations had ruptured the silence of the depths. Dmitri's torso shuddered as if he'd gripped a jackhammer. Once he'd acclimated to the novel sensations, it was his turn to experience what Gorman had previously described: the combination of a mild electric shock and a high-frequency massage, intensely pleasurable yet mildly uncomfortable, emanating from deep within his physical core.

With a clear view of the screen, Dmitri witnessed a tour-de-force demonstration of Uber's mental imaging powers. Speakeasy translated the giant's rhythmic staccato tones into the circular game symbols—brilliant, incandescent rings glimmering in the cool, blue water. In rapid succession and in the perspective of 3D, Uber splashed them across the entire length, width, and virtual depth of the glass-bottom screen. As Dmitri filmed, his entire body resonated with the energy of Uber's voice.

Greg observed the pyrotechnic display in the Speakeasy control room. "Are you getting this, Professor?" he shouted above Uber's thundering voice.

"He's systematically filling the entire 3D game board with symbols up and down, left and right, in and out, like an automatic program," replied McPinsky, his voice racing. "It's spectacular. Stupendous! I wouldn't be surprised if it's been sparked by the first glimpse of his own vocalizations."

"It's what both the cetacean and the human brains are visualizing in three dimensions for the first time," added Seema.

"It is possible, however, that the acoustic region of Uber's brain is imaging the symbols in four-dimensional frequency space." Greg touched a finger to an area on Andrew's display where colorful columns of numbers scrolled top to bottom. "According to these measurements, Uber's shifting the energies and frequencies of all four resonance peaks, like when he vocalized the shape of the four-dimensional circle."

"I can try to confirm that hypothesis with the mathematicians here at Ivy Tech," said McPinsky."

"Okay, Andrew?" asked Greg.

"I'm ready to upload the data files, Professor," said Andrew. "They're big. They'll take a while to transmit at our limited data rate."

"My god, what if it's true," mused McPinsky. "What if we actually validate your 4D hypothesis? It could be the bombshell that will rock the human race. A paradigm shift in planetary consciousness."

"Unless we can distribute the data," replied Greg, "nobody is going to believe it."

In the aftermath of Uber's dramatic outburst, an eerie quiescence pervaded both the ship's control room and the water below. Dmitri gazed up at the astonishing story revealed by both Speakeasy screens: a snapshot of another species' thoughts. The display was jam-packed with dozens of circular symbols, meticulously organized into a 3D matrix structure of rows and columns. As Uber circulated beneath the boat, Dmitri was intrigued by the humpback's unusual body language—the herky-jerky motions of his three massive fins. The whale appeared to be studying the images, as if he were trying to interpret their meaning. Dmitri, Lila, and Chris filmed the momentous occasion juggling a variety of cameras. They had captured enough breathtaking imagery to challenge the marine biological community for years to come.

After the four divers exchanged handshakes and hugs, Dmitri's arms suddenly flung out in all directions. A hasty three-sixty-degree assessment provoked a surge of anxiety and vertigo. He, Melanie, Chris, and Lila were surrounded at close range by the entire ensemble of Uber's escort party, encircled in a revolving tower of forty motor-coach-sized humpbacks. The divers whirled helplessly in the slow-motion vortex induced by the circulating mass, a surrealistic barbershop pole spiraling hypnotically.

Melanie tapped Dmitri on the shoulder, and he followed the line of her arm to a magical sight. A whale calf, dwarfed by the adults like a guppy in an aquarium, suckled its mother's milk. Lila and Chris went crazy attempting to capture the mammalian ritual with their cameras. Once sated, the nursling, with a startling "zero to sixty" burst of speed, raced up to the boat. She settled next to Uber, who was still fixated on the mysterious images.

The calf broke the silence, trilling a cavalcade of improbable, high-frequency tones that literally palpated Dmitri's eardrums. Speakeasy transformed them into the curvilinear brush strokes of inchoate geometric forms, all superimposed upon the palette of Uber's game symbols. While the calf paused to study her artistic creation, Dmitri, too, gawked at the otherworldly renderings. Since the pace of the pod's merry-go-round rotations had slackened, the spinning sensation gradually ebbed.

Dmitri's brief respite ended when the baby titan flapped her fluke and glided back down, straight toward them on a collision course. As she loomed ever larger, he felt his heart pounding down to his stomach. He estimated her length at approximately fifteen feet and weighing several tons. To his great relief she stopped ten feet away, directly above them, wallowing in the wall of bubbles ascending from the divers. Because she maintained this position for quite some time, Dmitri had an eerie feeling about the encounter. Was she sensing the chemistry of their respiration, or reveling in the tingling sensation of the effervescence, or simply curious? As the drama intensified, Dmitri experienced the lingering convergence as something like a Vulcan mind meld—two species immersed in the synergy of their merged auras. Yet it was not science fiction. It was intensely real.

The calf eventually drifted down, inching closer and closer, until she was within an arms-length distance of Dmitri's and Melanie's faces. Too numb to move, Dmitri stared, seemingly forever, into the calf's big, shiny, coal-black eye. Her gaze effused purposeful intelligence and evoked in him an unsettling reaction of both fear and wonder. He felt as if he were being "scanned" by a sentient alien being. When she ever so gently brushed a pectoral fin across his chest, Dmitri thought he might wet his wetsuit.

With a stroking motion, Chris swept his arm back and forth. Melanie responded by removing a glove and, with her bare hand, explored the calf's body. Encouraged by the whale's seemingly positive reaction, Dmitri did the same and prayed that a cetacean's maternal instincts were not akin to a grizzly bear's. Lila and Chris filmed and photographed the "petting-zoo" images for posterity.

Dmitri turned his head and saw Melanie's blissful expression. They were inextricably linked by this unforgettable moment, their hands joined on the body of the baby giant. The calf recaptured their attention with a surprisingly polite five-ton nudge. She basked in the human massage for what seemed to Dmitri an eternity. How would he describe the tactile sensation of stroking a whale calf? His answer, now based on first-hand knowledge: like a combination of buttery, soft leather and slick rubber, her skin smooth, firm, and yet cool to the touch. The calf finally edged away. Then, with two ripples of her tail, she jetted back to her mother.

Drifting in space, Dmitri rejoiced in the ecstasy of this silent moment. He felt buoyant and free, submerged in an aquamarine sea, and he beheld an unfathomable panorama. In this underwater temple, he was ringed by the awe-in-spiring sight of forty gigantic, cetacean Buddhas. Shifting shafts of light pierced the surface, sparkling like stained glass, and wavering in the subtle ocean currents. Gazing up above, the boat and the sky were shimmering apparitions beyond the ocean's skin.

Without warning, Uber, who had been stationary beneath their vessel, had begun to revolve. Dmitri aimed the video camera, pressed the RECORD button, and held his breath. Starting from an orientation horizontal to the surface, the leviathan rotated its monolithic frame, steadily and inexorably, around its central axis. With Uber's pectoral wings fully extended, the power-fully silent moving image jogged Dmitri's memory of yet another video taken in space: when the ISS Space Station recorded the Space Shuttle performing a one-hundred-eighty-degree rotational "back-flip" against the blue-and-white backdrop of the Earth.

Thirty seconds later, Uber had attained a perfectly vertical orientation. His head pointing directly up at the glass-bottom Speakeasy display, he remained motionless just twenty feet below the boat. In the ensuing silence, Dmitri's imagination conjured the mystical, orchestral strains of Holst's *Neptune* move-ment, as he felt a new hush of anticipation within and outside of himself.

An ethereal tone signaled the end of Dmitri's trance, as if Uber were tun-ing his voice for the next performance on the program. Like an impassioned conductor, the precision strokes of his vocal baton unleashed a climactic out-burst of sound and vibration, inundating the underwater display in torrents of light. A glissando of geometric figures and esoteric shapes, forged in the mind of Uber, danced before Dmitri's eyes. Uber projected a dazzling cascade of ellipses, parabolas, hyperbolas, and shapes he'd never seen upon the canvas of game symbols. Dmitri witnessed and filmed a spectacle of multi-dimen-sional representations that, like a Copernican thunderbolt, demolished the foundations of human understanding about intelligent life on planet Earth.

Sitting at his workstation, Greg's gaze was glued to the display of the same cryptic, three-dimensional figures. "I know the Coast Guard is waiting for us, but I just don't care anymore. This is uncharted territory. Uber's brain could be the biological equivalent of an analog supercomputer." Greg's rever-ential tone epitomized the expressions on Andrew's and Seema's faces. "It's all so amazingly mathematical. Some of the shapes he's composing look vaguely like Bessel functions or Legendre Polynomials, but I can't be certain, Professor."

"It's so amazing, it's spooky," replied McPinsky.

"I'm certain of one thing," said Seema. "These figures are beautiful, surely the creations of an aesthetic mind. But there's so much more to it. How can Uber have such precise control of his vocalizations? How can he fashion such meticulous drawings of multi-dimensional mathematical functions?"

"Think about the range of handwriting capabilities in the human population," replied Greg. "Some people can't draw a straight line while others can master the most exquisite calligraphy. Uber's obviously in the latter category."

"I have to admit," said Andrew, "I can't comprehend any of this either. That they can transition between two, three, and maybe even four dimensions to express the symbols of their thoughts, as smoothly as if they're shifting the gears of a sports car, is mind-blowing."

"Don't forget," replied Greg, "when Uber's driving in the communication fast lane, he needs to downshift into second gear to merge into the right lane of human communications traffic."

"I feel like one of Einstein's awestruck graduate students on the first day of school," Andrew said. "What does all of this mean, Professor McPinsky?"

After a sigh and a long pause, McPinsky answered. "Honestly, Andrew, I'm as mystified as you are. What comes to mind is a favorite quotation from a science-fiction movie I remember from my childhood. I never dreamed I'd hear myself repeat it for real. 'There are times when a mere scientist has gone as far as he can, when he must pause and observe respectfully, when something infinitely greater has assumed control.' I believe this is one of those times."

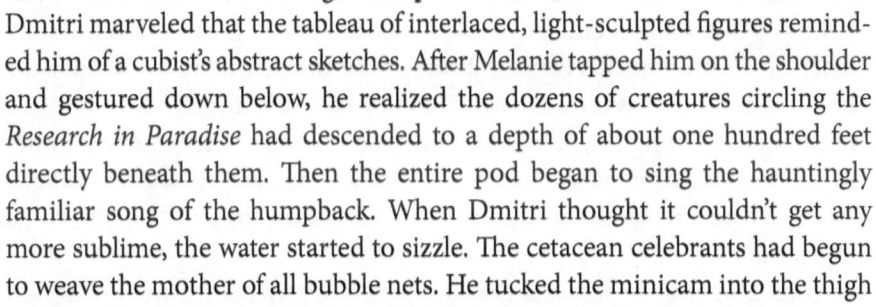

In the water, as Uber's magnum opus illuminated the screen above him, Dmitri marveled that the tableau of interlaced, light-sculpted figures reminded him of a cubist's abstract sketches. After Melanie tapped him on the shoulder and gestured down below, he realized the dozens of creatures circling the *Research in Paradise* had descended to a depth of about one hundred feet directly beneath them. Then the entire pod began to sing the hauntingly familiar song of the humpback. When Dmitri thought it couldn't get any more sublime, the water started to sizzle. The cetacean celebrants had begun to weave the mother of all bubble nets. He tucked the minicam into the thigh pocket of his dive suit and clasped Melanie's hands. Together, they were engulfed in the stimulating effervescence, their bodies resonated with the song of the Megapteran chorus, and their eyes pulsed with the afterglow of Uber's frequency-sculpted bolts. In this multisensory kaleidoscope, Dmitri felt all of his senses maxed to their limits—a rapture beyond description.

When the melodies had gradually diminished in intensity and the cylindrical curtain of bubbles floated up and away, Dmitri realized to his dismay that the fantasia was dissolving and would soon be a memory. The pod had begun to disperse. Gorman pointed upwards, and when he'd begun to kick to the surface, Dmitri and the others followed. Halfway up to the boat, however, Dmitri felt strange, even uncomfortable. Before he could take another breath, a suffocating surge of pressure deep within his skull had metastasized into an apocalyptic onslaught of sound. His head felt like it was going to explode. Through a squall of pain, he was shocked to see Lila and Chris clutching their hands to their temples. When the retreating whale calf started shrieking and Melanie contorted her face in agony, Dmitri realized the true extent of this developing horror show.

Though he thought it would never end, the stranglehold of noise and pain mercifully subsided. Nevertheless, Dmitri was stunned to see his face mask blotched with his own blood. He was even more alarmed by the view through Melanie's mask. A crimson streak dribbled from her nose. He took hold of her limp hand.

After a brief reprieve, they were blasted by a second wave of noise and torment. Gradually, another layer of sound leaked into Dmitri's throbbing consciousness. Uber had initiated a new broadcast. A continuous variation of the same theme, it seemed more songlike than the punctuated phrases of his earlier vocalizations. Above all, Dmitri was struck by the song's sense of urgency.

Melanie's shove startled Dmitri, who turned to see two monstrous humpbacks racing toward them. He embraced her without hesitation, placing himself in the path to absorb the initial impact, thinking to prolong her existence by the gift of a millisecond. An instant before their imminent annihilation, the whales deftly adjusted course, slewing their massive bodies in a sideways motion. The compression wave generated by their arcing trajectory sent the four humans plummeting deeper. Dmitri and Melanie clutched one another as they tumbled. Opening his eyes, Dmitri was amazed to see they'd been shepherded to the same location as the distressed calf, still clinging to its mother's flank.

Through pulses of pain and the backdrop of Uber's opus, Dmitri observed the pod's purposeful movements. They grouped together in pairs. The pairs then distributed themselves equidistantly and symmetrically in a circular formation, surrounding the congregation of the humans, the calf, and its mother. Each of two diametrically-opposed pairs propelled forward, sweeping a great circular arc around their designated circumference in the formation. Clasping Melanie's hand, Dmitri stared in wonder as the whales orbited around them. To his astonishment, the individuals within each pair, like acrobats, spiraled around an imaginary axis between one another and deposited, in their wake, a braid of bubbles in the pattern of a double helix. Melanie and Dmitri twirled as one in the twisting currents.

This guild of weavers had fashioned an effervescent shield that encompassed the four humans, the mother humpback, and its calf inside of a huge, spherical cocoon. The singing Uber hovered near the surface and above the pod, so he too was sheathed in bubbly foam. Each of the whale pairs was partially shielded by the mini-shell of a sparkling white cloud as they arced and rotated through the bottom hemisphere.

Glimpsing Gorman's thumbs-up gesture, Dmitri realized he was nearly pain-free and that the whale calf's distress cries had waned to a whimper. Straining to see through the veil of bubbles, Dmitri craned his neck and turned a full three-hundred-sixty degrees to admire the intricate coordination of the humpbacks' movements. They'd endowed the net with a recursive geometric sophistication, reminding him of an Escher construct. Thinking who would believe this, Dmitri reached for the minicam and joined Lila and Chris in the struggle to document this Neptunian ballet of the giants.

On the surface, the crew on the Coast Guard cutter reacted as the sea boiled all around their vessel. "What the heck?" said the lieutenant commander. "I thought those whales had disappeared. Suspend the order to board."

"Yes sir," replied the lieutenant.

Back underwater, the whales maintained their protective umbrella as the grating, machine-like sounds continued to torture the sea. When the on-and-off cycle of sonic violence had finally ceased, the humpbacks remained in formation until the abrupt finale to Uber's vocalizations.

With the restoration of silence and as twilight faded into dusk, the Megapteran entourage ultimately dispersed. As they drifted off into the darkness, Gorman's pointing gesture was the signal to return to the boat. As the quartet ascended, the calf returned for an encore, weaving in and out amongst the humans in a celebratory farewell. Then she was gone.

After Dmitri had broken the surface, he felt drained beyond exhaustion. Each step up the ladder rekindled memories of a long-ago, oxygen-deprived ascent to the top of Mount McKinley. Crawling onto the deck, he was shaken by the amplified tones of a human voice and the reminder that they were no longer shielded by the humpback flotilla. "This is the U.S. Coast Guard. Prepare to be boarded."

The buddy system of Chris, Greg, and Andrew assisted Melanie, Lila, and Dmitri in the removal of their gear. Seema distributed towels. Once they'd changed into dry clothes, they hustled inside to assess their predicament. Seema addressed Melanie, who appeared dazed. "Everything was going fine until we were blasted by the crazy racket beneath the boat and through the speakers."

"After we peeled back the edge of the video screen, we were scared stiff to see you clutching your heads," Greg added. "Then you just disappeared from our view through the glass window. What the heck happened down there?"

Andrew held a dive mask aloft. "Why is there blood on all your masks?" he asked.

"Are you ok?" McPinsky's voice echoed from the speakers.

"Those SOBs." Gorman was livid. "Those explosive sounds had to be the Navy's sonar. We just confirmed the rumors about their recent tests in Hawaiian waters."

"Did you notice the pain stopped after they wrapped us in their bubble net?" added Melanie.

Gorman nodded his agreement. "Yes, it makes complete sense. The air in each bubble deflects and attenuates the mechanical energy of the sound waves."

"They shielded us," said Lila, with reverence in her voice.

"And the calf too," added Melanie. "They protected us as one of their own."

"From an attack by members of our own species," said McPinsky, "like the Red Cross aiding refugees in a war zone."

No one spoke. From the soul-searching stares, Dmitri knew that everyone was as overwhelmed as he.

Gorman finally broke the silence. "It's bad news for the Navy. We can publicize the details of these defensive countermeasures to compromise their sonar program."

"But we're about to be seized, and the proof along with us," replied Andrew.

"Aren't the audio files fully transmitted to McPinsky?" Greg asked him.

"Gimme a sec," replied Andrew, typing commands on his workstation. "Sorry, but I warned you the link was slow, and I never thought we'd collect so much data. It'll take at least another fifteen minutes."

"Damn!" replied Dmitri. "We might not have enough time before the Coast Guard confiscates the ship. Unless we transmit the evidence to McPinsky, this '*Crack in the Cosmic Egg*' event could be all for naught."

Andrew spoke quickly. "For my undergrad thesis, I developed some data compression routines that exploit fractional bit redundancies in non-ASCII datasets. They're still on my laptop and ready to go. It'll cut the time in half to compress and transmit the video files. Seven minutes tops."

"That's fantastic, Andrew," replied Dmitri. "We'll keep the sea dogs at bay until you're done. Are you ready, Professor?"

"This is really crucial, son," replied McPinsky. "I need to deliver that Speakeasy data into the hands of our Ivy Tech mathematicians."

"Professor," added Andrew. "I'm also sending a file to do the decompression. You'll need it to expand the data file to its original format."

"After I receive the data," said McPinsky, "I highly recommend you erase the files on your workstations so they don't fall into the wrong hands."

Dmitri directed an anguished expression at Greg. Then, with a slashing motion across the side of his throat, he nodded his assent to Andrew.

"And no matter how demoralizing these next few days seem," added McPinsky, his voice getting louder, "don't tell a soul about the data until I go public. We're dealing with ruthless foes, hell-bent on seizing our data to preserve their status quo existence."

Mark clung to his mother's waist. "Mom, what's he saying? Why is he so angry?"

Melanie hugged him. "It'll be okay, sweetie. I might have to go away for a short time, but Chris will take care of you until we sort things out."

"Absolutely," replied Gorman. "Don't fret, Mark. You'll see your mom again real soon."

Melanie flashed her son a tenuous smile, and the boy relaxed his grip.

"Lila," said Gorman, "why don't you, Melanie, and Seema stay inside and figure out a hiding place for the cameras' memory cards."

"No problem, Chris."

"If the file transfers aren't done by the time we return," he continued, "we'll need to buy more time."

Seema stepped forward. "I have acting experience. I'll create a diversion."

"Thank you, Seema," replied Gorman. "Hopefully, it won't be necessary."

As Andrew assailed his keyboard, Chris, Greg, and Dmitri shuffled outside to greet the boarding party. The Coast Guard was very efficient in the execution of their duties. They'd already cleated their lines to secure the *Research in Paradise* to their cutter. A group of five had transferred across and stood at attention on the lower deck.

An impressively appointed officer, wearing a sopping-wet dress white uniform and a smug expression, stepped forward. "I'm Lieutenant Commander Richard Fulton of the U.S. Coast Guard."

"Why do you all look like you drove through a carwash with your top down?" asked Greg.

Fulton's authoritative air vanished. "One of those goddamned whales breached over the prow of our vessel. Drenched us all."

Greg clapped his hands and turned to Dmitri. "Add one more item to the list of today's discoveries: humpbacks have a highly evolved sense of humor." He doubled over with laughter.

"Hey, wise guy," replied Fulton, punching an index finger into Greg's midsection. "You think that's so funny. Well, guess what. I'm about to have the last laugh. You've been charged with assault and battery and flight from the scene of a crime." Fulton's rigid posture made it evident he was accustomed to giving, rather than receiving, orders. With a contemptuous flick of his wrist, he extracted a sheet of paper from his pocket and read from the page. "We're here to take the following individuals into custody: David Dmitri, Gregory Bono, Andrew Chu, Seema Roy, Melanie Mari, Lila Lawson, and whoever is piloting this vessel." His voice suddenly sounded more collegial. "By the way, those were very unusual circumstances that prevented us from approaching you earlier. I've never seen anything like it."

Gorman stepped forward. "I'm the director of the Pacific Institute for Cetacean Educational Studies. I chartered this vessel for the purpose of researching the unique behavior you've just described. Since I spoke with the boat's owner as recently as this morning, I've no reason to believe he would file those charges. Why don't you give me a few minutes to contact him and resolve the situation?"

"The charges against these individuals were filed by three injured parties in Maui, not by the owner of the boat."

"What the heck?" replied Dmitri. "We were defending ourselves. They attacked us first. Look at this." He tapped an index finger to his black eye.

"That's a nasty shiner," replied Fulton, "but I have my orders. You can sort this out back on shore. Now please follow us so we can detain the remaining suspects on our list."

They filed inside to the Speakeasy control center. Less than five minutes had elapsed since Andrew had been left to his devices. The file transfer process was still in progress.

The Coast Guard commander emerged from his pack of men. He looked disapprovingly from one person to another, and said, "You're all under arrest. Please follow me outside."

Mark marched up to Fulton and glared at him. "Stay away from my mom!"

"I'm sorry, son, but I have my orders," said Fulton. "What are *you* doing here?"

"Don't worry," said Gorman. "I'm not on your arrest list, and I'm the boy's guardian." He grasped Mark's hand and brought him back to Melanie.

"Oh no, I'm going to be deported!" Seema declared, sounding truly aghast. "My family will be ashamed of me!" She burst into tears.

"Calm down, ma'am. Just compose yourself." Fulton reached into his pocket and offered a handkerchief.

But Seema unleashed a torrent of sobs. To the commander's chagrin, the hanky was soon soaked in the residue of her apparent grief. She milked her performance until Andrew flashed a signal to indicate that the all-important file transfers to McPinsky had been completed. He stood directly in front of the workstation, facing the Coast Guard team. With the keyboard shielded behind him, he furtively curled his right hand behind his back. He took a deep breath and, with a delicate stroke of his pinky finger, pressed the ENTER key to initiate the program that erased the precious files.

Last Gasp

U.S.S *San Fernando*, Leeward Waters, Maui

WHAT EXACTLY THE heck was happening? wondered Captain Pierce Bogan on the command deck of the U.S.S. *San Fernando*. He'd executed his orders to the letter. The ship had advanced to the designated coordinates. The crew had initiated the five-minute test sequence program at half of maximum power. Ping duration was six seconds, repeated every thirty seconds. Whoever had organized this operation must have known what they were looking for, he thought. Immediately after the first ping, the display had lit up like a Christmas tree. At least forty large sub-targets, each approximately ten to fifteen meters in length, appeared as a constellation of bright amber blips against the sonar display's dark background.

Bogan turned toward his executive officer. "What do you think we're looking at?"

The XO hesitated. "The signatures indicate they're probably whales, sir."

"So many? Come on. Forty whales swimming in circles?"

Bogan stared at the screen. He'd never seen anything like it. The targets appeared to be arrayed in a circular formation. Sixty seconds later, after the transmission of the third active sonar pulse, the brightly lit targets had vanished. In all the years of testing the ultra-tech, billion-dollar tracking system, this had never happened. Once the sonar had locked onto a target, the tracking process was one hundred percent reliable.

"Emergency systems check!" bellowed Bogan.

"Aye, sir," answered the XO.

The engineers barked out the sequence of commands and responses corresponding to the reliability tests for each of the software and hardware subsystems. Flashing digital displays at multiple workstations churned out colorful plots and pulsed with tables of numbers. Despite the razzle-dazzle, Bogan neither saw nor heard any evidence of a component failure. He waved at the display. "What the hell are we looking at now?" He observed the faint smudge of a spherical object pulsating in the center of the screen.

"Unidentified bogey, sir," the XO sighed, "maybe just a false positive echo?"

"This new-fangled sonar is supposed to be foolproof. How am I going to explain this malfunction to headquarters?"

For one of the few times in his career, Bogan was befuddled, yet his superiors expected a summary report ASAP. The damned bogey had persisted for the duration of the test. It couldn't be dismissed. He sat down at the nearest workstation and opened a new report-template file. He stared up at the ceiling and scratched his head. Five minutes later, the file was still devoid of text.

Six time zones to the East of the Straits of Lahaina, Ned Perry, still ensconced in his Pentagon office, monitored the events transpiring in Hawaiian waters. Cupping a hand to his face and muttering to himself, he heard the klaxon ringtone of an incoming phone call.

"I was afraid it might be you, Richard," answered Perry, seeing the "SoCalSci" caller-ID tag on the phone's display. "I have both good news and bad news to report. Fortunately for you, the good news is that the occupants of the PICES vessel have been taken into custody and the vessel has been impounded."

"That's splendid news, Ned, splendid indeed. So whatever happened out there will never see the light of day. You'll see to it, of course, that their computer disk drives are wiped clean?"

"Of course, Richard." But not, he thought, until the files have been subjected to the intense scrutiny of my own staff of experts. "And their entire team, except for Gorman, has been transferred to a local jail, charged with assault and battery. Since it's the weekend, I estimate we can keep them incarcerated for a couple of days, until bail is set."

"Excellent," replied Prescott. "I'll notify the chair of the academic senate."

"Huh?"

"The arrest of any university employee automatically triggers sanctions levied by a jury of peers. Based upon the severity of their charges, I'd say our

SoCalSci professors face, at best, a vote of censure and revocation of research funds."

"And the worst?"

"Their positions at SoCalSci could be in jeopardy."

"Ouch."

"I wouldn't worry. Once this blows over and the experiment is forgotten, I'll do my best to have them reinstated."

"That's civil of you, Richard."

"I hear your sarcasm, Ned, but I do have a conscience. So what's the bad news?"

"Well, according to the report I just received from the commander of my sonar test vessel, there's a new problem with my system. Since you've decided to bug me at such a late hour, I'm not letting you off the hook. I'm going to read you every frigging detail of his dispatch."

After Perry's tedious recounting of the U.S.S. *San Fernando*'s status report, Prescott sounded exasperated. "I'm sorry, Ned, but why don't you translate the technobabble into something I can get a grip on."

"Well, the 'sub-targets' he refers too are the humpbacks, and the 'bogey' is probably the whole pod. So far, so good. But then, apparently, the entire pod disappeared from our screens after a couple of minutes."

"And?"

"Richard!" snapped Perry. "No bogey has ever 'winked out' in the middle of a test. It's beyond comprehension that so many large whales could have suddenly vanished without a trace. There should at least have been evidence of their individual signatures as the formation dispersed. There's either a new glitch in my very expensive system or worse yet, some unknown force has compromised the functionality of our new secret weapon. I need to get to the bottom of this."

"How will you do that?"

"Something peculiar happened beneath the PICES vessel, and the only souls who can shed light on the matter are currently in a Maui prison. The one thing I'm certain of is that Dr. Dmitri's obligatory first phone call was directed to a Professor McPinsky."

"No surprise there," replied Prescott. "McPinsky is the mastermind behind all of Dmitri's shenanigans. In fact, if I were you, I'd focus your investigation on the distinguished professor at Ivy Tech University. If anyone knows why your system failed, he's your man."

"Thanks, Richard. You've been very helpful. Sorry to run, but I need to make another phone call."

Perry depressed the security-mode button on his wired phone. When the party answered, he asked, "So what did you discover?"

"A Skype voice and data connection between the boat and a fellow named McPinsky in New York."

Perry heard the robotic voice and wondered whom he was conversing with. In secure mode, these phones invoked real-time, voice-changing firmware to preserve the anonymity of both speakers.

"How about the data files?" replied Perry.

"The disk was wiped clean. Someone knew what they were doing. The files aren't recoverable."

"Damnation," replied Perry, ending the call. He stabbed the handset back into its docking port.

Perry checked his watch. No wonder he felt so tired. It was already past midnight. He dragged a hand across his chin stubble, sighed, and came to a decision. He grabbed the secure mobile phone on the desk and punched the speed-dial key. Two rings later, Perry delivered his terse message. "Cancel all previous orders and proceed to the next objective, Professor Theodosius McPinsky of Ivy Tech University. No need to remind you. This conversation didn't happen."

"Bloody Hell!" With a loud thump, Perry slammed his expensive phone onto the desk.

Jail House Blues

Maui Police Department, Wailuku—March 1

"SEEMA, WATCH OUT!"

Andrew's voice cracked like a gunshot, breaking into Dmitri's fitful predawn slumber. He lurched upright to a sitting position and saw Andrew writhing on the cot, eyes still shut. Dmitri felt mentally and physically spent, yet restful sleep in this Hawaiian prison cell seemed as elusive as his hope of freedom. He lay back down and stared straight up, searching for answers in the recesses of the rough-hewn ceiling and listening to the restless murmurs of his cellmates.

Only twenty-four hours had elapsed since yesterday morning's commando mission had launched the voyage of astonishing discoveries. In the wake of their adventure, the Coast Guard had confiscated all of their equipment, and the telltale data files had been obliterated. Dmitri prayed McPinsky had received the climactic Speakeasy data before the communication lines had been shut down. The revelations of a lifetime might be a passing dream if he had not.

Dmitri tussled with the institutional bed, yearning for his memory foam mattress back home as he replayed the calamitous concluding events in an otherwise spectacular yesterday. Tony's jazzy blues harmonica tunes were the only pleasant memories of their Coast-Guard-chaperoned, jail-boat ride. Immediately after docking in Kihei, they'd been transferred into the custody of the local police, who paid no heed to their protests. During the recital of their Miranda rights, Dmitri had watched the inauspicious arrival of a Maui police van. The short drive to Wailuku had passed in sullen, hand-cuffed silence. It was late evening by the time they'd been hustled inside the local jail and, since Dmitri's internal fuel gauge was pinned on empty, the subsequent booking and incarceration gauntlet had happened in an anti-climactic blur. At the conclusion of the fingerprinting and mug-shot sessions, the four men and three women had been herded into separate group holding cells. Dmitri's quartet shared theirs with a local teen sleeping off a DUI.

In this hot, dank cell, the vapors wafting up from the open toilet seeped into his awareness and then leached back out on a wave of self-recrimination. It had been his decision to launch the experiment that resulted in everyone's imprisonment. How were the women faring in their wing of the prison? Melanie would be frantic about Mark. Could Gorman arrange a timely bail? Dmitri agonized over the precarious situation faced by Greg and his grad students, as well. His worst fear was that their fate at SoCalSci was a fait accompli, since Prescott now had free reign to smear their jailbird reputations all over the campus.

Since his brain and body were starved for rest, he knew he'd better stop obsessing. As Greg had often counseled, the best way to squelch vexing mental chatter was to think about favorite people, places, and things. What could be better than to focus on a pleasant reminiscence of Melanie? He closed his eyes and meditated on the indelible image of her sleek figure graced by a jade green cheongsam, and her radiant smile reflecting that brilliant, sunny day in the park. In his mind's ear, he imagined floating on the cloud of her velvety voice, to the accompaniment of the mynah bird chorus. He yawned.

Jolted awake by a hideous screech, Dmitri soon realized he'd heard the fork-scraping-the-frying-pan squeal of the opening of an iron-barred cell door. Squinting into the light, he saw a uniformed guard slide trays of food into their cell through a slot near the floor. "Good morning. I heard a rumor about you guys having a visitor today." After he'd brought two more trays of their morning meal, bowls of mush soaking in Hawaiian brown sugar, he left without sharing any more details.

"Hooray," said Andrew, rubbing the sleep from his eyes. "This could be our lucky day, right?"

"Or it could be one of Prescott's lackeys and the beginning of the end for us," said Dmitri, still lying on his back.

"Don't give up hope, pal," said Greg. "After what we experienced yesterday, we have every right to believe something extraordinary is still possible."

Dmitri sniffed the air and turned his head to see their DUI cellmate sitting on the toilet. "It can't get any worse than this, Greg," he said, his tone laced with sarcasm.

After breakfast, they passed the time playing poker.

"What were you dreaming about, Andrew?" asked Dmitri, as he dealt the cards for Five Card Draw.

"No idea, boss." Andrew looked genuinely surprised.

"I had my usual recurring dream," said Greg, "flying through the air with a basketball, like in a Chinese martial arts film, and finishing a slam dunk. Last night I posterized LeBron. The time before that it was Yao Ming."

"I envy you, Greg," replied Dmitri, his voice listless. "I pretty much tossed and turned all night."

"Cool, Greg," replied Tony. "I've always wished I could dunk a basketball."

"Reminds me of the way Uber posterized our boat yesterday." Andrew's cupped hand arced in a giant circle above his head.

"That's a great insight, Andrew!" Dmitri's sudden enthusiasm brought a smile to Greg's face. "If humans think and dream about flying, then why not whales? Why else would a big-brained, fifty-ton creature breach with such apparent enthusiasm?"

"Just like big-brained hominids are compelled to pole vault," added Tony, "or Evel Knievel leapfrogging twenty cars in a Harley."

"Or skydivers jumping from airplanes," said Andrew, "present company excluded, of course."

"I often dream I'm a seagull cruising down the coastline," Tony mused.

"It's a pretty universal dream." Andrew tossed three cards.

"Makes you wonder if humpbacks have flying dreams too?" said Greg.

"The dreams of the giant." Dmitri replaced Andrew's cards. "I'd give anything to solve that mystery. There's no stopping us now, Greg. After we get out this mess, let's plan the next experiment. We now have the tools to begin a legitimate dialogue with the Megapterans."

"I'm happy to see you back in the saddle, my friend." Greg traded two cards. "By the way, besides your infernal snoring, you talked in your sleep last night. Do you remember the dream?"

Dmitri just smiled. Revealing a straight flush, his comrades shook their heads in mock consternation. The poker game resumed with elevated spirits, everyone taking turns cracking jokes.

After lunch, the guard returned to announce their visitor had arrived. Only Dmitri, however, had been hustled out of the cell, ushered down the hall, and led into a temporary visitation chamber. To his relief, the familiar figure of Chris Gorman stood in the middle of the same room where he had been processed the previous evening. The PICES director's haggard appearance, however, tempered Dmitri's optimism. As they shook hands, the sight of the guard watching from across the room, with a hand resting on his holstered weapon, was most distressing. "It's great to see you, Chris. We were beginning to feel abandoned."

"I'm sorry, Dmitri. It's not that we forgot about you. Far from it. We're all working overtime, late into the night. It's not easy to arrange bail on a weekend in Maui. Apparently the judge is out of town on a fishing trip. I was also on the phone with your mentor. I'm bushed."

"McPinsky!" Dmitri's forlorn expression vanished, and he straightened up. "Tell me about him, please. No, wait. First tell me about Melanie, Seema, and Lila. They're okay, right?"

"I just visited them a few minutes ago and they're holding up pretty well. I'm concerned about Seema, though. She's taking it harder than the other two. She's genuinely worried about deportation and being banished by her family."

"Oh, no, what have I done?" Dmitri moaned. "I fell right into Prescott's trap and jeopardized my colleagues' careers."

"Oh, yeah. Prescott popped up on the morning news. He tried to disassociate SoCalSci University from what he called Dr. Dmitri's lawless Dr. Dolittle fantasy."

Convinced his career was a shambles and that a similar fate awaited his SoCalSci compatriots, Dmitri's head slumped to his chest. And what about Melanie? Who knew how long she would be separated from Mark?

"Things might not be as bleak as you think," said Gorman.

"How can you possibly say that?"

"Two reasons. First, don't forget about yesterday's amazing discoveries, especially the finale when Uber lit the water with his voice."

"It *was* amazing."

"His vocalizations were more dynamic than any humpback I've ever heard."

"And the second reason?"

"Let me update you about that phone call to Ivy Tech. McPinsky hinted at an exciting new development in the analysis of Uber's vocalizations."

"Anything to do with Greg's 4D theory?"

"Not that. He did mention he'd sent that data to another university for analysis."

"Ouch. That's not like McPinsky. If he thought there was anything to it, he would have kept it in house. So what's the good news?"

"McPinsky alluded to an entirely new theory that explains how the humpbacks communicate, but he said he needs visual proof to confirm his hypothesis."

"Huh?"

"Remember when we were saved by the bubble net during the sonar attack?"

"How can I forget?"

"When I told him I'd filmed the whale's movements during the attack, he asked me to upload the video file to YouTube. He's chiefly interested in the pod's formations and patterns when they seemed to react to Uber's singing."

"Yeah, that was one hell of a team bubble net. Saved our butts. How were you able to secure that videotape with the Coast Guard hanging all over us?"

Gorman smiled. "No problem. Lila slipped the memory card into my hand during a farewell hug."

"Cool, like an MI-6 secret drop. But why send the file to YouTube instead of directly to McPinsky?"

"He warned me it was too dangerous. He's certain that both his snail mail and electronic communications are being bugged by some government mucky-muck, so best get it into the public domain. How's that for cloak-and-dagger intrigue?"

"It doesn't surprise me at all. Whoever *they* are, they've gone overboard to deprive us of our constitutional rights."

Gorman tried to suppress a yawn. "So it took me nearly an hour to upload the file. McPinsky wasn't specific. Just that there might be an intriguing connection between the video and the audio data."

"So all we can do now is wait and hope that McPinsky can come up with a miracle. What about bail?"

"This is Saturday morning. If I can locate the bail judge, we might spring all of you either today or tomorrow. If not, you'll have to wait until the courts are in session on Monday morning. Just keep the faith."

The guard stepped forward, signaling the end of the meeting. Gorman handed Dmitri a business card and said, "If you haven't heard from me by tomorrow afternoon, call me at this number. Oh, and by the way, Dmitri, you don't have to worry about Melanie. I mean, it's long finished between us." Gorman's voice sounded oddly off-key, leaving Dmitri to wonder if Melanie's old flame still pined for her. "I'm pretty certain she's stuck on you." He paused. "You don't have to worry about Mark, either. He's fine with me."

"Thanks, Chris." When Dmitri extended his right arm, Gorman reciprocated with a surprising bear hug. Despite the friendly gesture, Dmitri couldn't shake the suspicion that the PICES director knew more about their predicament than he was willing to admit.

Cosmology 101

Ivy Tech University, Upstate New York—two days later

"IS EVERYTHING ALL right, Professor?"

McPinsky tapped the miniature microphone pinned to his jacket lapel. When the overhead speakers echoed their amplified reply, he nodded to the stage manager. After the man had disappeared and he was certain that nobody was watching him, the professor peeked out from behind the pleated folds of the decorative curtain drawn back to the edge of the stage. As the last of the students and other interested persons trickled into Ivy Tech's jam-packed main lecture hall, he felt the familiar buzz of anticipation that preceded his public talks. It was followed by a fleeting regret that these events were less frequent than when he'd been an international luminary.

It was the end of the term for Professor Emeritus Theodosius McPinsky's "Seminar on Cosmology" offering in Ivy Tech's Special Studies Program. For ten weeks, the lectures had covered the course curriculum on the various theories about the origins and the history of the universe. The final exam would test the students about the Standard Model of particle physics, the Big Bang Theory, and the most recent entry: String Theory and the multiverse. This final lecture, however, was something different. Following in the footsteps of Einstein's lifelong pursuit of the elusive Unified Field Theory, McPinsky would reveal the latest developments in his own controversial theory for addressing the Holy Grail of physics, the Theory of Everything.

McPinsky was always psyched up for this occasion. Now, however, with the unfolding of the recent events in Maui, he harbored mixed feelings about the timing of tonight's obligatory engagement. Yesterday he'd been heartened by Gorman's report that the entire Research in Paradise team had been released on bail. At this very moment, Dmitri, Greg, Seema, and Andrew were jetting back to California. He fervently hoped he could be there to offer support for their disciplinary hearing with the SoCalSci authorities. He'd also wanted to share the breaking news about the latest communication discovery by his Ivy Tech colleagues. After their miserable weekend in jail, it would definitely lift the team's spirits. Now, however, he needed to block out all distractions and channel his energy into this prior commitment.

Tonight's address marked McPinsky's third annual end-of-term lecture at Ivy Tech. The number of students enrolled in this extremely challenging course never exceeded twenty. Due to the professor's celebrity status, however, the much-anticipated presentation was a magnet to inquisitive minds both from the campus community and the local populace. Although many struggled to comprehend the arcane subject matter, they were beguiled by McPinsky's passion and the audacity of his worldview. Due to popular demand, the grand-finale lecture had been relocated to the main campus auditorium, with capacity exceeding seven hundred.

In contrast to his waning national prominence, McPinsky's reputation in the Ivy Tech community had soared to rock-star status. He was lionized as a genius and a visionary by his academic disciples. Many had queued outside in the frosty weather for two hours before the doors had opened. Despite the notoriety of his controversial theories, a contingent of Ivy Tech faculty members populated the first five rows of reserved seats. Even his detractors felt compelled to attend, since they too were curious about his latest paradigm-busting speculations.

McPinsky's dramatic entrance from the stage wing to the podium was greeted by a torrential outpouring of cheers, whistles, and applause. Since this was, in fact, a class lecture, McPinsky had requested they skip the obligatory guest-speaker introduction. He marched resolutely over to the podium, unfurled a sheath of notes, and placed them on the table. Gazing about, he was amused that some of his younger devotees had mimicked his "sixties" fashion statement. They sported paisley vests as they stood and clapped. McPinsky's image as the sage scientist and distinguished professor did not disappoint. In stark contrast to his clean-shaven, sober visage, his salt-and-pepper, shoulder-length hair and bushy eyebrows projected an Einsteinian persona.

After he'd raised both arms to still the crowd, the video cameras could be heard humming into action for the spectacle which was certain to become a popular cult selection on the YouTube hit parade. McPinsky dispensed with the customary introductory greetings and gripped the podium as if he were seizing the audience by its lapels. As he was on the verge of launching into his scientific sermon, a loud bang rifled throughout the hall, causing many to flinch. To the accompaniment of nervous snickers, a crimson-faced youth retrieved a water bottle spinning on the floor.

For the past three years, an undercurrent of tension had gripped McPinsky's public appearances. Attendees suffered the indignity of having their backpacks searched. The contentious nature of the professor's lectures and publications had provoked threats from the righteous fanatics who feared his dangerous, godless ideas. Because his scientific-existentialist manifesto had been co-opted, without his blessing, by eco-militants, he'd been the unwitting victim of guilt-by-association smears. Though an avowed pacifist, McPinsky's refusal to condemn the Radical Ultra-Secular Humanist group's tactics had thrust him into the crosshairs of fundamentalist outrage.

During a recent interview, he'd been asked if his grand quest had been worth the risks to his career and to his personal safety. "Yes," he replied emphatically, and added that he wanted to make science right—to complete Einstein's work. Beyond science, he explained, he hoped to address humanity's great existential crises. Privately, even he had to admit that a breakthrough of the type he'd sought would exact sweet revenge upon his many critics and enemies.

Now, as McPinsky's gaze swept across the sea of faces, he focused on the doe-eyed expressions of the students who had entrusted him with their hopes for a better future and their faith in his vision. For their sake, he could not fail. Now, finally, this gift from the gods of science—the whale communication discovery—was indeed the breakthrough he'd long sought, the confirmation of a life's work. He yearned to share it, here and now, but since the key data was still under analysis, it would be premature to do so. The time would come soon enough. His resolve restored, he forged ahead.

"The human race is in the dumps, afflicted by two crippling existential crises: alienation and isolation. On the one hand," he raised an arm, "because of our emergence as a symbolic species, we've been expelled from the Garden of Eden to suffer the angst of our breach from the natural world. On the other hand," he raised the other arm, "we endure collective loneliness born of our inability to engage in interspecies dialogue, terrestrial or otherwise."

McPinsky's impassioned voice reverberated in the historic wood-paneled hall.

"Scientific paradigms, philosophy, and religion have failed to rebalance the equations linking humanity with the natural order. In the perpetual yearning for equilibrium, humankind staggers like a drunkard searching for answers from visionaries, sages, and even from demagogues. To my mind, the solution to the problem is obvious. We must invoke the scientific method to stabilize these binding ties."

McPinsky left the safe harbor of the lectern and journeyed out to the lip of the stage, the better to bond with the audience.

"For ten weeks, I've presented the best theories physics has to offer to explain the origins of the universe and the theory of everything. Yet we still have no satisfying answers. The Standard Model is incomplete and the four forces are not fully unified. Indeed, conjectures about phantom concepts such as dark matter and dark energy are desperation measures to salvage an explanation about our ever-expanding, self-destructing universe."

McPinsky was particularly interested in the body language of the two preeminent Ivy Tech physicists seated in the front row. They did not disappoint him, shaking their heads in dismay and muttering to one another. He smiled at them and plowed ahead.

"What about the string theorists? In order for their theory to be correct, we must inhabit an eleven-dimensional universe. And not just one universe. Indeed, there are an infinite number of bubble universes that comprise the multiverse." McPinsky unveiled his hallmark sardonic grin. "The string theorists have guaranteed their own job security into perpetuity for there is no experimental test of the validity of their rather entertaining assertions which, by the way, appear slick and glossy on PBS specials and elsewhere in the popular media."

The irony in his voice was not lost on the audience. McPinsky heard sporadic giggling balloon into pervasive laughter, striking him as the comic equivalent of a super-inflationary phase transition. He returned to the podium and resumed. "Now, I ask you, what is the criterion by which the archetypal 'theory of everything' is judged to be comprehensive and complete?"

He paused and, with his middle finger, poked his glasses back in place most emphatically. As always, they'd slid down the slippery slope of his nose. "First and foremost, it's universally acknowledged that the explanation must satisfy the criterion of Occam's razor. It must be simple and elegant, preferably a single equation which unifies the four fundamental forces of nature. My assertion is that it must also describe just about everything else, including the information-based structures ubiquitous in our daily lives and everywhere else in the universe. Of utmost importance, it should provide the explanation which enables our species to reconnect with the creative process that birthed our universe and all of its inhabitants. This unifying principle would proclaim—"

He slammed a fist onto the podium, startling those in the front row, and intoned with a rhythmic, staccato emphasis on each and every syllable, "'You are a child of the universe no less than the atoms and the stars; you have a right to be here,' and I would proclaim this in no uncertain mathematical terms."

A covey of students leapt to their feet, pumped their arms in the air, and chanted in frenzied unison, "McPinsky, McPinsky, McPinsky—" The attending Ivy Tech administrators wore expressions of incredulity.

McPinsky gestured once again but he couldn't completely stanch the crowd's enthusiasm. He was an impatient man, so he continued above the buzz. "As you all know by now, I was inspired by physicist David Bohm's theories about universal quantum wholeness. As such, I'm a firm believer that information is the intrinsic stuff of the cosmos, more so than elementary forces which, as I shall soon demonstrate, are derivative. In fact, there can be no unified field theory unless the concept of *information* is woven into the fabric of nature's fundamental laws."

McPinsky welcomed the expressions of disbelief glaring back at him from some of the distinguished faculty members in the front rows. His confidantes knew that his iconoclastic resolve was fired by such arrogance, so he pressed on. "Since information is, by definition, the measureable distribution of energy and matter in space, I want to introduce you to a trio of radical conceptualizations which form the basis of the new theory."

When McPinsky requested the lights be dimmed, a movie screen descended from the ceiling for the display of his PowerPoint presentation. "The first concept is that there is an equilibrium state of the universe where all matter and energy are distributed uniformly throughout its entirety. In this baseline state, the density of matter is constant everywhere, space has constant curvature everywhere, and all particles are separated from one another by the same equilibrium distance.

"The second concept I shall hereafter refer to as the 'Principle of Uniformity' or 'Local Conservation.'" He began to speak more slowly, more deliberately, so that as many as possible could grasp his ideas. "Any force acting to change the mass density of the equilibrium state is resisted intrinsically, by space itself, in order to maintain the equilibrium state." Brandishing a laser pointer, he cast its beam upon a diagram appearing on the screen. "For instance, if particles attempt to approach closer than the equilibrium distance, the curvature of space in the gap between these particles must increase, resulting in the dilation of space itself, so that the local density between particles is conserved. The third concept, the 'Principle of Global Conservation,' is related to the second, in that the global curvature of space is conserved even when the local curvature must change due to the Local Conservation principle."

Murmurs of amazement were beginning to eddy through the lecture hall.

"Invoking these new concepts, we can make the following predictions." He forwarded to the next slide.

"The first prediction is that the new law of Local Conservation is one and the same as the strong nuclear force. The second is that the new law of Global Conservation causes a complex folding of space that creates all of the fundamental forces as dictated by the curvature of space at different scales. And finally, do you recall how Maxwell unified electromagnetic phenomena by postulating the existence of electromagnetic waves? In a similar fashion, the combined effects of the three new principles can serve to unify a number of existing laws of information and game theory. Thus we can postulate a mathematical and physical model which completely describes and predicts the evolutionary formation of stable, information-based systems—nature's 'Grand Organizing Principle.'"

The murmurs were now intensifying as many more minds had been kindled by McPinsky's proposals.

"A continuum of information-based structures fills the universe. So doesn't it make sense that the 'theory of everything' should provide a fundamental explanation of the formation of information structures, from nuclear particles to living organisms? Until now, physics has only given us the great conservation principles that apply to mass, energy, momentum, charge, spin, etcetera. But it provides no fundamental explanation about how this stuff is organized into complex systems. Physics has left us bankrupt in that regard. Without a fundamental rudder to guide us, we're left floundering, to be cast adrift in the swirling currents of anecdotal descriptions of philosophy, religion, and myth."

With the passion of a sermon or a political rally, chants of "yes, yes, yes" and "amen" arose from the audience. McPinsky was well aware that the dons of his parent institution, who held their collective breaths and crossed their fingers whenever he made a public appearance, grew particularly tense at moments like these, when he'd ignited the audience. Still, he continued on in an ever escalating arc of intensity.

"Einstein has given us permission to pursue such an avenue, since general relativity has proven so elegantly that matter warps space on the macroscopic level and that the force of gravity is equivalent to the curvature of space. So doesn't it make sense that matter and space should interact in an innate manner that subsumes all forces? That yet another set of even more fundamental conservation principles need to be considered to reconcile this interaction, this dance, between matter and space? These new principles are the driving force of the creation of information structures from the primal essence of the universe."

Some were so stirred that they stood and applauded. McPinsky paused and mopped his brow with a purple handkerchief. Hands were raised around the room but McPinsky had never countenanced the interruption of his discourse. "Questions will be answered at the end."

Like an implacable force of nature, he surged ahead. He wove the fabric of the universe before their minds' eyes, completely deconstructing and reconstructing it in his unique fashion.

"Now for the coup de grâce," he said. "For the equilibrium state of the universe, let's plot the force due to the local curvature of space for all distances around the equilibrium distance, knowing that the force at the equilibrium distance is by definition zero." He brought up the next slide, a plot of the force versus distance relationship, and then paused again to blot the moisture on his forehead. "Aren't the contours of this plot recognizable?"

In a few seconds, a volley of gasps punctured the silence. Most seemed too dazed to respond, but one brave hand finally appeared. "Professor, are you saying that the strong nuclear force is caused by the new conservation of equilibrium density principle?"

"Yes, smart lady!" shouted McPinsky. "And notice from the force versus distance plot that the force is repulsive when the particles are closer together than the Fermi distance and attractive when farther than the Fermi distance. But remember that, according to the new equilibrium distance concept, there is no net force at the equilibrium distance. This corresponds to the zero-crossing point on the nuclear force curve."

As many more arms were raised, McPinsky sighed and acknowledged one of the queries. "Professor, are you suggesting that all of the forces were unified during the complicated folding of space curvature, when subnuclear particles approached one another to less than the equilibrium distance?"

"Not only that, sir, but all of the forces were born and locked in at the time of baryogenesis, about one-millionth of a second after the Big Bang, when trios of free quarks in the quark-gluon plasma cooled sufficiently to be bound together by the sub-quantum folding of space and to form the nucleons. Thus the fundamental forces, nuclear, electromagnetic, and gravitational, were birthed and forever unified by the complicated folding process shaped by local and global conservation. This is the elegant story of the unification of the fundamental forces."

More waving hands appeared, but McPinsky ignored them. "In concert with the new conservation principles, we are currently working on the derivation of a super wave equation which reconciles the interaction of matter, energy, and space. This one equation describes the unification of all forces and predicts the wave-particle duality of matter. It also supersedes the probabilistic predictions of quantum theory with a more deterministic model."

McPinsky saw the blank expressions on many faces, and he knew that it was pointless to continue. The audience was at the breaking point, unable to absorb any more. He initiated the renowned ritual to conclude the final class of a term. He closed his eyes in silent vigil for about thirty seconds, the signal for everyone to prepare for the climactic moment. When the buzz of the crowd had crescendoed to a peak, he opened his eyes, hushing the audience, and recited the signature challenge phrase culled from Frank Herbert's epic science fiction novel, *Dune*. "'Without change, something sleeps inside us, and seldom awakens. The sleeper must awaken.'"

Most in the hall leapt to their feet in a standing ovation, unleashing a torrent of raucous whistles and cheers. A familiar rap-like melody emerged from the sea of sound. A raving chorus of students had begun to sing a customized version of the school's legendary low-tech fight song:

E to the U d u d x, E to the X d x
Tangent, secant, cosine, sine
Three point one four one five nine
Slide rule, slip stick, x y z
Mc Pin Sky, Mc Pin Sky

The students' fervent repetitions of the verse persisted for more than a minute, but the crowd's ardor had eventually cooled. Since he was eager for updates about the around-the-clock, global, whale-song-analysis endeavor, McPinsky planned a quick exit. After he'd taken a few curtain calls and posed for some group pictures, he excused himself and escaped through a back door. He'd always enjoyed the brisk early-evening, cross-campus walk back to his office in the old engineering building. As he entered the historic structure and climbed the stairs, he anticipated a reply to his request for assistance from the mathematicians at the Chalmers Institute of Technology.

McPinsky noticed something amiss as soon as he had unlocked the door and entered the office. An open desk drawer seemed odd, and the display at his workstation was in a different state than when he'd last logged off. The old, reliable Einstein screen saver had morphed into a black hole, the screen as blank as dark matter. Well, never mind. It wouldn't be the first time his seventy-year-old memory had played tricks upon him.

He sat down and opened an email folder, delighted to see a post from Arne Gustafson at Chalmers in Sweden. They'd finally agreed to attempt the verification of the 4D geometric properties of Ivy Tech's data. For obvious reasons, he'd decided not to inform them about the source of the data.

McPinsky checked the World Clock website on the Internet. Realizing it would soon be morning in Goteborg, he prepared to upload the files to Chalmers. But after he'd pointed and clicked on the link to the directory, and even after an interminable wait, nothing appeared. The directory was empty. He checked the backup drive. It too was wiped clean.

McPinsky smiled. He was not surprised that this epoch-making data had vanished so mysteriously. He had no doubt that the files on his home PC and on the computer in the lab had succumbed to a similar fate. He'd struggled against the enemies of change for most of his career. This time was no different. He knew exactly what had to be done, no matter the consequences.

Ivory Tower Tribunal

SoCalSci Department of Engineering,
Main Conference Room—two days later

"DR. DMITRI," SAID Dean Wilson. "This joint engineering and math department hearing was convened to address your current legal situation and its impact on your status here at SoCalSci. To summarize, you were recently arrested and charged with multiple counts of assault and battery. Charges were filed against you, Dr. Gregory Bono, and your grad student, Andrew Chu, in a court of law in the State of Hawaii. You've been released on bail, pending further court appearances. Before we proceed, I'd like to introduce you to the members of the panel."

Dmitri had spent the last four days struggling to assess his predicament, but to hear the harsh reality colored by the dean's voice felt doubly punishing. Indeed, the seats were arranged as for the proceedings of a tribunal. He sat next to Greg and Andrew on one side of the rectangular conference table spanning the length of the room. Their somber expressions met the stony-faced stares of the panel of six judges seated across the gleaming tabletop. The judge and jury consisted of the deans of math and engineering and two professors from each department. Suits and ties were de rigueur for the occasion.

As Dean Wilson ministered to the preliminary formalities of the distressing conclave, Dmitri felt blessed to be back at SoCalSci rather than languishing in a Maui jail cell. Just three days ago, Gorman had finally located the weekend bail judge and a lawyer who'd finessed a Monday morning arraignment. After they'd pled "not guilty," their attorney had filed a request for the team's release in order to return to their jobs. Chris, a pillar in the local community, had not only provided sterling character references for the defendants, he'd also guaranteed their reappearance on Hawaiian soil to attend future legal proceedings. The Research in Paradise team had been granted bail on the day following Gorman's testimony. To Dmitri's great relief, the plaintiffs had only identified Andrew, Dmitri, Greg, and Lila as their assailants, and the charges against Melanie and Seema had been dismissed. They'd said their tearful goodbyes, and the SoCalSci team had flown back to California.

Uncomfortable as he was, Dmitri patiently endured the dean's interminable remarks. He took comfort in the familiar confines of the Engineering Department conference room, having participated in many memorable sessions in this very room. Only a few weeks ago, they'd met here to celebrate their initial "game" breakthrough, yet that seemed to have occurred in another lifetime. He gazed at the framed pictures of historic campus landmarks: the campanile bell tower where he had first kissed his college sweetheart, and the stunning arches, parapets, and terra-cotta-tiled roof of the Mediterranean Revivalist library, where he'd discovered the joy of Shakespeare. He wondered if this was the last time he would set eyes upon these treasures.

"Dr. Dmitri. Dr. Dmitri, are you with us?" The dean's voice brought Dmitri back to the task at hand. "You've been an invaluable member of our department for nearly ten years. Therefore, to give you the benefit of the doubt and before we proceed, we'd like you and your colleagues to give us your personal accounts of the events in Maui."

During the ensuing ten minutes, Dmitri, Greg, and Andrew recounted their recollections of the incident on the boat. At the conclusion of their testimonials, the dean struck a pensive pose, fingers clasped to his chin. "So even though you admit striking and injuring the plaintiffs, your claim will be self-defense?"

"Yes!" Dmitri's emphatic rejoinder startled the dean. "They forcibly boarded our research vessel. It was a case of trespassing."

"But they claim you used weapons."

"Plastic oars, yes. But I was attacked. My colleagues saved me from serious injury by subduing the skinhead perpetrator."

"Ok. I'm somewhat sympathetic to your situation, but in the end you'll have to convince a Hawaiian judge and possibly a jury. What about the claim of a significant experimental breakthrough?"

Dmitri knew it was pointless to say anything about their communication discoveries. Only McPinsky had the data and they'd sworn to maintain his anonymity until the Ivy Tech team had vetted the new information. Even worse, since their return from Maui, they'd been denied access to their office and lab PCs, the repository of the original game data. It was as if there had never been a discovery. He threw both hands up in exasperation. "It's not possible to explain that as yet."

When Professor Crandall leaned forward, Dmitri knew what to expect. Crandall was an ally of Prescott's and had assisted in McPinsky's ouster from SoCalSci. With his pinched eyes, pointy goatee, and scheming persona, Dmitri bristled at the man's Mephistophelian vibe. "With no compelling evidence from Dmitri's team, I have to conclude this so-called breakthrough is nothing more than an unsubstantiated rumor."

"That's enough, Crandall," said Dean Wilson. "Gentlemen, please wait outside. We'll call you back when we reach a decision."

Once they'd filed out of the conference room, Dmitri was in no mood to talk to his colleagues. He paced back and forth, his impatient footsteps echoing down the hall. A mere five minutes later, Wilson's assistant poked her head out the door. "The dean expects you back in the conference room."

Her tone struck him as blatantly patronizing, and the swiftness of the verdict caused Dmitri's stomach to cramp. "This is worse than a kangaroo court," he whispered to Greg.

After they had settled into their seats, Dmitri scanned the jurors' faces. When most avoided eye contact, he knew the situation was hopeless. Crandall, however, stared Dmitri dead in the eye, practically taunting him with a look of smug satisfaction. Dmitri fought the urge to leap across the table.

Dean Wilson cleared his throat. "Gentlemen . . . we've arrived at a unanimous decision. You are to be suspended for the duration of the semester while you deal with your legal matters. We don't take these actions lightly. We've based our decision on a recent precedent established for a similar case in the English Department." He sighed.

Andrew's whole body jerked. "But—"

The dean shushed him with a dismissive wave of the hand. "Let me finish, young man. If any or all of you are exonerated, those individuals can resume their positions here beginning in the fall semester. You will not be penalized, academically or financially, for missing the term. However, if any of you are convicted of a criminal offense, we will have to reconsider your long-term standing at SoCalSci. Are there any questions?"

Their grim faces were their only reply. Dmitri and Greg had expected this outcome. In fact, Dmitri was somewhat relieved. Since the tribunal was stacked with anti-McPinsky forces, he'd half expected the worst possible scenario: an immediate termination. It pained him, however, to see Andrew's crushed expression. He'd do everything in his power to help his student.

Dmitri's muted voice barely reached across the table. "How long before we have to clear our offices?"

"Since our departments need to staff your positions immediately for the short term, and possibly for the long term, you'll have to finish by the end-of-day tomorrow," replied the dean. "Obviously, your replacements need the space."

Dmitri stared at the pictures on the wall, resigning himself to never seeing them again. He seethed inside. There was no doubt that Prescott's dirty paw prints could be found everywhere the team had dared to venture. If there was justice in the world, then Prescott would get his comeuppance. He himself would see to it.

"Thanks for the update, Crandall." Richard Prescott slipped the cell phone into his pocket. He was very pleased by the dean's decision. Locking his office door, he thought about how brilliantly he'd handled the situation. In order to prevent retaliation, it was customary for all suspended faculty members and students to surrender their magnetic entry cards to the university's restricted areas. Dmitri's team was effectively quarantined from the computers and data storage devices in the Signal Processing Lab. There would be no evidence to confirm the absurd "discovery" of a communication breakthrough with humpback whales.

In one master stroke, he'd succeeded in eliminating all vestiges of Theodosius McPinsky's legacy from the SoCalSci campus. The man's irresponsible pronouncements had embarrassed the university and plagued him personally, forcing him to labor countless overtime hours as a damage-control specialist in order to stem the public's outrage. From now on, it would be business as usual in the hallowed halls of his beloved university. He whistled a cheery tune on his stroll out to the parking lot.

Paternal Condolences

SoCalSci University, Los Angeles, California

AFTER THE HEARING, Dmitri returned to his office to pack his things. He felt both depressed and nostalgic. Years of lecture notes, publications, and mementos of trips to far-flung conferences had settled into every nook and cranny of the snug workspace. It felt more like a home than an office. Two hours later, after he'd combed through the stacks of memorabilia, he heard the mobile's "dueling sitars" ringtone.

"Dmitri, my boy. I just heard the news through the grapevine, and I want to express my condolences."

McPinsky's paternal voice infused Dmitri with renewed hope. "Yes, we've been suspended, but I suppose it could have been worse. When you've announced the news of our discovery, maybe they'll reinstate us. Are you close to a confirmation?"

McPinsky's prolonged silence unnerved him. "Professor, are you still there?"

McPinsky took an audibly deep breath. "That's the reason I called, son. The data has disappeared. There won't be any confirmation."

Dmitri felt dizzy. "Tell me this isn't happening."

"I'm afraid it's true. All of the whale song files on my home and office PCs have been erased. It's the same for the data here in our lab. It's over."

Dmitri wanted to scream. "Is it Prescott? Or the Navy? Who else?"

McPinsky's tone was grave. "It's probably all of the above and more. We're up against something bigger than we can possibly cope with."

"But—"

McPinsky interrupted him. "I should have arranged for tighter security."

"It's not your fault."

"Maybe we can do another experiment next year?"

"But I'll have no job. I might even be in jail."

"I'll do my absolute best to prevent that from happening and, if you'd like, I'm sure I can find you a position here at Ivy Tech." McPinsky paused, apparently waiting for a response.

Dmitri massaged his brow, fingers pressed against closed eyelids, his gloom filling the silence.

"It'll be like old times." His mentor was clearly masking despair of his own. "Look, I know how you feel, Dmitri. My departure from SoCalSci left me devastated, feeling quite sorry for myself."

"That damned Prescott," Dmitri yelled. In a contrite tone, he said, "Sorry, Professor."

"Yes, I raged about him. And the others. But then I did something that lifted my spirits. Coincidently, you have an opportunity to partake of the same salutary experience."

"What?"

"I attended a lecture by my hero and spiritual mentor. Helped to chase the blues away."

"Who's that?"

"He was recognized at the age of seven by the monks of Khutan as the reincarnation of their spiritual leader."

"Ah, you mean Lama Dawa Cham. He's here in L.A.?"

"He's appearing in the Grand Auditorium at Cal University on Saturday night."

"Professor, that's a wonderful suggestion, but, under the circumstances, I'm just not in the mood."

"Dmitri, you've been like a son to me, and I can never thank you enough for the gift of this discovery. Please indulge me in a bit of fatherly advice."

"Yes." Dmitri could barely speak. McPinsky's words meant the world to him.

"Just trust me. Lama Dawa Cham is a very wise man with an uplifting message. I've made the arrangements for you, Greg, and your students. Your tickets will be waiting at the will-call booth."

"Yes, Professor. I'll think about it."

"Now I've got to go. It's my duty to inform Gorman and his team about what's happened to the data."

"Oh, God," replied Dmitri. "He'll be devastated. Another dead humpback washed ashore in Maui last weekend. I should contact Greg, Seema, and Andrew."

"I'm so sorry this happened," replied McPinsky.

"Like you said, it's just the few of us against an army of resistance. You'd better make that phone call."

After he'd hung up, McPinsky felt guilty about the half-truths he'd told Dmitri. He was particularly unnerved by Dmitri's strong reaction, the pain in his voice. Under the circumstances, however, there had been no other choice. He'd had to sound convincing, as his phone was undoubtedly bugged. And he needed to buy a bit more time so he could be of use. For years, he and Dmitri had shared a unique bond, almost like father and son. He desperately wanted to help him through this ordeal. And it might be possible. He had an idea.

High-Tech Satori

California University Grand Auditorium, Los Angeles, California—Saturday night

"WHAT THE HELL are we doing here? As much as I respect Professor McPinsky, I'm no fan of swamis and gurus."

Greg's somber assessment reflected Dmitri's own dark mood. Craning his neck for a panoramic view of California University's Grand Auditorium, Dmitri saw the steady stream of Lama Dawa Cham devotees spilling down the aisles and settling into the auditorium's two thousand seats.

Andrew tapped Dmitri on the shoulder. "Hey boss, how about the four of us go bowling after the show? There's an alley in the student center."

"Andrew, you're so inappropriate." Dmitri felt the sadness in Seema's flat voice.

"It's okay, Seema," said Dmitri. "We could all do with a bit of distraction. These are cool seats, aren't they?"

Greg grimaced. "Maybe for a Laker game."

Andrew's face brightened. "You're not gonna believe it, but I thought I saw a familiar face."

Absentmindedly, Dmitri scanned the crowd. "I don't see anyone. Who was it?"

Andrew appeared to survey the room, but he shook his head. "Sorry, I must have been mistaken. Hey look." He pointed at the stage. "That man in the . . . that's Mitchell Gyre."

"You're right," declared Seema, staring through opera glasses. "And Yumi Hermann is beside him." She sounded excited.

"What did you expect." Greg frowned. "This is Hollywood, and Lama Dawa Cham has a worldwide following of celebrity groupies."

Despite Greg's caustic tone, Dmitri had to admit it was an ideal setting for a celebrity lecture. An array of crystalline chandeliers glistened overhead. Intense spotlights hung from the ceiling, directly above the center of the large stage, illuminating a pair of oversized and sumptuously appointed golden velour chairs. Directly behind them, attached by thin cables to the rafters in the ceiling, hung the spectacularly oversized red, white, and yellow flag of Khutan, also known as the "thunder-dragon" flag for its depiction of a fierce, white dragon.

They'd decided to dress up for the occasion: the gentlemen attired in the same suits and ties they'd worn for the disciplinary hearing, and Seema wrapped appropriately in a stunning floral-blue, formal sari.

Once again, Andrew tapped his boss on the shoulder and directed Dmitri's gaze down to the end of their row. "Look who's coming."

"My God, you were right!" exclaimed Dmitri.

"I told you so."

Dmitri waved at the couple awkwardly tiptoeing toward them. "Hey, guys, fancy meeting you here." Once she'd navigated through the gauntlet of feet of those already seated, Melanie drifted into Dmitri's outstretched arms. After he'd planted a lingering kiss on her lips, he turned to Chris Gorman and asked, "So who's the mastermind behind this chance encounter?"

"It was Professor McPinsky's idea," replied Gorman, exchanging handshakes with Greg and Andrew. "He told me Lama Dawa Cham might have something to say about the humpback deaths in Maui. He also said that two airline tickets were waiting at the airport, that I should bring Melanie along to cheer you up, and that he owed us for failing to prevent the disappearance of the data."

"Disappearance, my foot," muttered Greg. "Grand larceny is more accurate."

Melanie squeezed Dmitri's hand and briefly turned to Greg. "Of course I agreed to come along. I'm so sorry to hear about your suspensions."

Dmitri couldn't help but to smile. "To put it mildly, I'm very happy you're here."

She pulled him closer and whispered into his ear.

"Where's Lila?" Seema sounded disappointed.

Melanie sighed. "Lila has the flu. Otherwise she'd be here. By the way, Seema, you look gorgeous."

"She's a vision." Andrew, for a change, sounded dead serious as he assessed Seema's jewelry-accented ensemble with an art-patron's appreciative eye.

"And look at you guys, so sartorially splendid." Melanie brushed a finger across Dmitri's silk tie. "*Très chic*."

"*Merci. Et toi aussi*," replied Dmitri, with a smile. "It's a shame about Lila, though. We're one big family now."

"She'd have enjoyed the Lama Dawa Sham," said Andrew. "We're sitting so close. I'll get to see the color of His Holiness's eyes."

Given the short notice and the popularity of the event, Dmitri wondered how his mentor had come by six contiguous prime-location seats. The first few rows were reserved for California University faculty and dignitaries. Most were engaged in animated conversations. Every seat seemed to be filled.

Dmitri clasped Melanie's hands. "Maybe McPinsky was right. I'm enjoying myself more than I thought I would, present company included, of course."

When the lights in the hall blinked twice, Greg said, "Okay, folks. For whatever it's worth, the show's about to begin."

They sat down sequentially from left to right: Andrew, Seema, Melanie, Dmitri, Greg, and Chris. The teammates chatted until the main lights in the chamber were dimmed. All conversations ceased. Then, without any fanfare, the spiritual leader of Khutan, Lama Dawa Cham, walked humbly across the stage and removed both sandals. In one motion, he bowed to the audience and coiled into a cross-legged pose as he sat upon one of the chairs. Dmitri was fascinated by the contrast of his bare-shouldered saffron robe and his contemporary, black designer-frame glasses—a spiritual figure adapted to modern times.

"So who's the surprise guest?" whispered Greg, sitting to Dmitri's right.

"What do you mean?" Dmitri whispered back.

"The empty chair. Are you thinking what I'm thinking?"

"Nah, can't be."

Lama Dawa Cham closed his eyes, clasped both hands together, and uttered a silent prayer. The audience grew respectfully hushed. As his lids fluttered open, a beatific smile adorned his face. He raised both arms in ceremonious greeting.

"Ladies and gentlemen, thank you for coming tonight. I know you are expecting me to discuss the subject of compassion. However, there's been a change of program. Like a bolt from the blue, I'm here to tell you that something truly wonderful has happened."

The sounds of many voices combined as one, like the low murmur of a forest of pines fanned by a breeze. He waited for the sound to subside, his shaved head glistening in the stage lights.

"Earlier this week, I received an urgent message from a dear friend, a distinguished scientist. He informed me of a great discovery that has been confirmed beyond all conjecture and controversy." Greg tapped Dmitri on the leg. "You'll soon see for yourselves."

Lama Dawa Cham paused to scrutinize the audience. When he resumed, Dmitri heard his mesmerizing British-Asian-accented voice sounding much more subdued, almost reverential. "The human race is no longer alone. The second sun of consciousness has finally been discovered. It will illuminate all of humanity's future generations so that we can extricate ourselves from the shadows of ignorance."

While the audience struggled to process his revelatory message, silence prevailed. Some turned to gaze into the eyes of their neighbor, searching for a response. Many appeared dazed. Dmitri clasped Melanie's hands and felt the mingling of their throbbing pulses.

"Before I say more," Lama Dawa Cham continued, "I'd like to introduce my friend. He will describe the technical details of this transformative discovery. Please welcome the distinguished Ivy Tech professor, Theodosius McPinsky."

The bulky McPinsky ambled onto the stage, attired in an ill-fitting, grey suit and his trademark vest. The audience welcomed him with a warm round of applause. Dmitri was surprised to see his distinguished mentor shoeless in deference to the holy ground he now occupied. He was relieved to observe that McPinsky's paisley socks were respectfully without holes. Lama Dawa Cham rose from his chair to lead the assembly in a standing ovation. Squeals of joy abounded from the Research in Paradise team.

"Unbelievable!" exclaimed Andrew, "McPinsky comes through big-time once again!"

"You're so right." Dmitri's face glowed with delight. "By orchestrating this joint appearance with Lama Dawa Cham, he's literally broken the back of the connivance between Prescott and his goon squad. I think we're gonna be ok."

Seema sighed. "Thank God."

Dmitri gazed at Melanie, her face luminescent. "McPinsky must have recovered the lost data he needed to confirm our discoveries."

"Were you aware your mentor was a friend of Lama Dawa Cham?" she asked.

"I had absolutely no idea. A good thing too, else I might have been intimidated by his very presence."

As the applause continued, Greg leaned forward to stare at Dmitri's lips, not wanting to miss any remarks. "It's fascinating how we're conditioned to respond to the persona of fame peddled in the media," said Greg. "I'll bet if Lama Dawa Cham was an anonymous dinner party guest, many would judge him simply as an eccentric character."

No one in their group spoke until Seema said, "But Professor McPinsky looks like he really belongs on the same stage with His Holiness."

The renowned scientist and the august holy man remained standing with their hands clasped. They gestured for silence, and the energy in the room was instantly quenched. Lama Dawa Cham resumed. "For the past ten years, Professor McPinsky and I have shared a special bond forged by an ongoing dialogue about the human condition. We first met at the World Conference on Cosmology and Consciousness, where we all grappled with humanity's existential crises, the spiritual vacuum that is extinguishing the life force from our souls. Since nature abhors a vacuum, it has attracted all of mankind's spurious attempts to fill it, which is why our species is still grasping for stability and meaning. At that conference, I became intrigued by the Professor's proposals for a solution: his bold challenge to the scientific community to break the interspecies communication barrier and his Unified Field Information Theory.

"The sage professor is with us tonight to explain how his protégé's research team has responded to the McPinsky Challenge with a millennial discovery." He paused to glance at McPinsky, then turned back to face the audience. "Unfortunately, because certain elements in our society cannot cope with the enormity of this breakthrough, these heroes were imprisoned and their data illegally confiscated. Although they are temporarily free on bail, they face serious criminal prosecution. I personally beseech the authorities to drop the unjust charges against these special ones. They have an extraordinary story to tell us. So that you will know them for who they are, I have invited them here tonight." He pointed in their general direction. "I'd like them to stand and accept your greeting."

Dmitri heard Lama Dawa Cham's words but could not respond, paralyzed by disbelief. He glanced at his colleagues. No one moved. Professor McPinsky stood, waved in their direction, and flapped his outstretched arms. "Dmitri, everyone with you, please rise so we can honor you."

Heads turned their way and those nearest urged them on. Andrew popped up first, sporting a huge grin and waving toward the stage. One by one, the members of the Research in Paradise team joined him in a group salute to the professor and the guru. Scattered applause gained momentum, intensifying when Lama Dawa Cham clapped his hands above his head.

As Dmitri turned to acknowledge the approbation, he felt chills. In his entire life, he'd never imagined the possibility of such a transcendent moment. He thought about his father, the ice cream man and the maker of his childhood dreams. In spirit, Michael Dmitri was with him now. Dmitri's mentor and father figure stood on the stage. In sharp contrast to his earlier despair, he now wondered how life could get any better. He looked at Melanie and felt great tenderness. Seeing tears rolling down her cheeks, he turned and hugged her.

When Lama Dawa Cham and McPinsky settled into their chairs, the audience followed suit, and Greg turned to Dmitri. "Worth the price of admission?"

"Most definitely," he replied, still dazed by it all. "Now we can enjoy the rest of the presentation."

Once the excitement had waned, Lama Dawa Cham resumed. "Fellow members of the human race . . . abandon all of your preconceptions and prepare yourselves for a quantum leap in earth consciousness, for we are blessed by the dawn of the second sun." The tone of Lama Dawa Cham's voice struck a delicate balance between solemnity and passion. "It was an imaginative leap of faith by a man of science that made this remarkable discovery possible. I would now like Professor McPinsky to explain the details of the marvelous event."

Sensing McPinsky's struggle to untangle his intertwined legs, Dmitri suppressed his mirth with a bite of the tongue. When he'd finally liberated himself from the lotus position, McPinsky dropped both feet onto the hardwood floor. Turning to face the holy man, he steepled his hands and bowed.

McPinsky turned back, and the beacon of his intense gaze swept the audience. "Ladies and gentlemen, because mathematics is the universal language, there is no longer any doubt that humanity has shattered the millennial silence. The sleeper has awakened. You may have heard media accounts about a controversial interspecies communication experiment in the waters of Hawaii. About a week ago, the group of scientists whom you just met successfully conducted this experiment with astounding results. The team was organized by my former student, David Dmitri, now a professor in his own right. It includes his SoCalSci University research associates in concert with the marine biologists at the Pacific Institute for Cetacean Educational Studies."

Another wave of applause rippled across the audience.

"I'd like the projectionist to play the first in a series of remarkable videos recorded during the breakthrough experiment on the PICES research vessel."

When the spotlights illuminating the stage had been dimmed, the first Speakeasy images flooded the screen. "As hard as it is to believe, you're witnessing the first-ever game of logic played between a humpback whale and a human being."

Once McPinsky had finished describing the Speakeasy-mediated game of Dots and Boxes, Dmitri heard murmurs and gasps echo throughout the hall.

"The positions and the sequencing of the whale's symbols were analyzed by one of the world's leading game theorists at SoCalSci University and by the mathematicians at Ivy Tech. They've confirmed beyond all doubt that this is indeed an advanced game of logic. The realization that the whales played a game amongst themselves occurred just a few weeks ago when the SoCalSci team used the Speakeasy system to analyze a commercially available recording of humpback whale songs."

The murmurs intensified and coalesced, sounding like distant surf on a windy day.

"The best is yet to come, ladies and gentlemen." McPinsky smiled. "After this initial encounter, the Maui research team was greeted by a never-before-seen ceremonial escort of more than forty whales. It was led by a very special individual, a fifty-ton adult of the species Megaptera novaeangliae, commonly known as the humpback whale.

"The next video depicts a similar game, but played, unbelievably, in the three-dimensional frequency domain of the mind of this Megapteran grandmaster, nicknamed Uber by the research team. The game is similar in difficulty to a game of checkers played in three dimensions. The human participant, relying exclusively on the Speakeasy system to visualize the game board, could scarcely compete. He was summarily trounced by the Uberwhale, who played the game using only sound and memory."

With two thousand confounded individuals muted in forest-primeval silence, McPinsky paused. Dmitri knew firsthand that his mentor's passion for teaching was stoked by his students' visceral responses to new discoveries. The stunned expressions in the first few rows would certainly fulfill the professor's expectations.

"The fact that these creatures participate in games of symbolic logic as a form of social engagement is irrefutable evidence of a highly evolved intellect. These games confirm that the Megapteran humpback brain has adapted the use of acoustical symbols to express logical concepts. It's similar to the way humans have adapted such symbols to encode the building blocks of our own spoken languages. Yet this is not the only discovery of an amazing afternoon in Maui. Our fifty-foot grandmaster demonstrated an even more remarkable sound-adaptive ability. It is analogous to the manner in which human hands draw representational forms using pencil and paper.

"I'd like the projectionist to proceed to the next video. Good. The geometric figures you're now viewing were literally drawn in frequency space, like a virtuoso musician-mathematician, by the vocalizations of the humpback. During the past forty-eight hours, a team of human mathematicians at Ivy Tech has thoroughly analyzed the data. They confirm these are indeed the representations of ellipses in three dimensions and rotated by fixed angles of forty-five degrees with respect to one another. Since mathematics is the universal language, there can be no doubt that our cetacean friends swimming alongside us have the intention to express themselves in the language of Euclid, Pythagoras, and Fermat. These mathematical representations of their language are not simply abstractions unto themselves. We have unequivocal proof they serve a unique, functional purpose that facilitates their group behavior."

A great commotion swept through the audience. The wall of sound forced McPinsky to pause. Lama Dawa Cham stood and shushed the crowd. "Distinguished members of the audience, my friend Theo's university colleagues have yet to reveal two more startling discoveries."

Melanie snatched the opportunity to speak directly into Dmitri's ear. "What's he talking about? Two remarkable discoveries? I thought the 3D game was dramatic enough."

"Chris mentioned it has something to do with the bubble net," Dmitri answered, "but I've no other clue."

After Lama Dawa Cham sat back down, McPinsky resumed. "As if we needed any more proof of the advanced communication skills of our cetacean brethren, I've instructed the projectionist to play two videos, side by side, filmed during last weekend's climactic undersea encounter. On the left side of the screen, we see the Speakeasy-translated shapes of the Uberwhale's compelling oration. On the right side is a video filmed by a PICES marine biologist showing the pod's unique response to Uber's vocalizations. By raising your hand, let me know when you've made the connection between the two videos."

"Hey," exclaimed Dmitri, pointing at the figure plotted on the Speakeasy display. "What's that?"

"I recognize that shape," replied Greg. "When all hell broke loose at the beginning of the sonar attack, Uber started singing that new song and this is how it was interpreted by Speakeasy. I was so distracted by the sonar attack and the rush to transmit the data to McPinsky, I'd forgotten about it."

The faces of McPinsky and Lama Dawa Cham radiated delight at the sight of so many enthusiastic arms sprouting up around the hall. "It's remarkable, isn't it," said McPinsky to the audience.

Dmitri stared with wonder at the Speakeasy rendering of a sphere in three-dimensional perspective. The sphere's surface was outlined by the tracings of ten concentric circles rotated by equal angles. When the projectionist zoomed in to reveal the corkscrew pattern of the lines which traced each of the circles, Dmitri knew what McPinsky had discovered. "It's the shape of the bubble net!"

McPinsky's amplified voice resounded with Shakespearean gravitas. "Ten concentric rings cast by the Megapteran Kings under the water! A sonar-busting, bubble-net tapestry choreographed in the mind of the master builder and instantly communicated to and constructed by his team of artisans."

Dmitri, inspired by McPinsky's brilliant homage to Tolkien, couldn't contain himself. "You're right, Professor!"

McPinsky pointed at the screen. "No, folks, you're not dreaming. This sequence of spiraling lines each traces out the circular circumference of the geometric projection of a sphere. The forces of ignorance and fear brutally attacked both the whales and the diving researchers with a blast of sonar energy. The Uberwhale immediately responded by vocalizing the frequencies that 'drew' these geometric shapes. The whales have evolved the means to image these figures in the acoustic regions of their brains, while we require the Speakeasy computer translation to visualize them for ourselves.

"This underwater video is conclusive proof. The forty Megapterans translated the Uberwhale's acoustic blueprint into a spherically shaped bubble net which encased a humpback calf, its mother, and the underwater researchers in a protective shield of air. A masterful tool, indeed, a cloak of immunity, was designed, communicated, and constructed in a matter of seconds. The bubble sphere neutralized the damaging effects of the sonar." He paused. "As I speak, the details of the cetacean defensive countermeasure to the human-engineered sonar weapon are being posted on the Ivy Tech website for the whole world to see."

The two thousand humans in the hall stood as one and unleashed a thunderous ovation. After the two men rose from their chairs, Lama Dawa Cham grasped McPinsky's arm and raised it in tribute. Cheers and whistles leapt above the din.

Lama Dawa Cham remained standing alongside McPinsky. When the crowd had spent its energy, he continued. "And if this is not yet enough, there is still more to dazzle us. It is, in fact, the reason why I'm here with you tonight. Theo has requested my counsel in regards to a most crucial question. Are we psychologically prepared to deal with a discovery so remarkable, that its consequences pose a humbling realization for mankind? I am personally humbled that Theo has entrusted his faith in my opinion. Some of our greatest minds have pondered the potentially disorienting impact of mankind's first encounter with creatures whose intellectual capacity possibly surpasses our own."

The hall erupted into pandemonium and the proceedings ground to a halt. Dmitri heard fragments of comments whirling around him . . . "Humbling realization?" . . . "Smarter than us?" . . . "What could he mean?" Once the cacophony had ebbed away, McPinsky continued, as if undisturbed.

"Yes, I thought it imperative we consult His Holiness about the enormous implications of the discovery we confirmed yesterday morning. The same forces that conspired to seize all of the original data from the breakthrough experiment and, as I mentioned, to jail the discoverers, don't feel mankind can withstand the inevitable shockwaves of the remarkable knowledge I'm about to share with you. It's only because Dr. Dmitri's team transmitted the data files from their research vessel to my home PC that the world has access to the proof of this discovery."

Dmitri heard the crowd still abuzz.

"And what an empowering truth it is," added Lama Dawa Cham, "to finally realize we share the planet with these gentle and majestic creatures of such astonishing intellectual potential. This is a discovery so wonderful, so astounding, that future generations will wonder what hubris had prevented us asking the questions which led to such an amazing awareness. As a Buddhist, I know it is time for humanity to grasp this dazzling truth, to awaken from our slumber, to fill the void of our ignorance, to unfasten the yokes of our individual and species egos. We can achieve the human potential for transformational discovery if we exercise the courage and creativity to ask provocative questions which dare to challenge establishment dogmas and our own personal fears."

"I'd like the projectionist to proceed to perhaps the most spectacular of the Speakeasy recordings," said McPinsky. "You're now witnessing a spectacle of pure mathematical prowess as the Uberwhale generated a symphony of geometric patterns in the perspective of three dimensions. What's remarkable is that the onset of this display was triggered just a short time after my SoCalSci colleagues presented the Megapterans with a gift—the Torch of Prometheus. They'd projected the Speakeasy display through the glass bottom of the vessel and down into the water so that the whales could, for the first time, witness the visualizations of their own acoustical drawings.

"Based on a hunch by a brilliant SoCalSci mathematician, Dr. Gregory Bono, our Ivy Tech team, and another team in Sweden, labored throughout the week to perform the computer analysis of the raw data. Yesterday, both groups working independently confirmed Dr. Bono's hypothesis: that all of these geometric figures were generated natively in four dimensions. In the figure you're now viewing, the Uberwhale has literally drawn the acoustic version of a circle in four-dimensional space, rotated four times by forty-five degrees. Unfortunately, the human brain and eye can only visualize and interpret such a four-dimensional circle as the geometric projection of a three-dimensional ellipse."

"What my friend revealed today is the true nature of the humpback's mind," interjected Lama Dawa Cham, "and I'm honored to share it with you. The Uberwhale's brain processes the symbols of information in four dimensions. He can manipulate four independent streams of acoustical waveforms to generate and image these symbols. We humans spend most of our lives learning to speak and understand the symbols of our language using only two independent streams. What the humpbacks are doing is far more complex. Now we need to answer the great mystery as to why they evolved to think and to express themselves in this four-dimensional frame of reference."

"We can speculate," replied McPinsky, "but there's an even better way to answer the question. Since we now know they have evolved both the pictorial and representational forms of the symbols which bridge thought and language, equivalent to our own spoken and written languages, we have the basis for establishing a dialogue."

"And there are so many questions to ask them," added Lama Dawa Cham.

With the entire auditorium hushed, Dmitri whispered into Melanie's ear. "Can you believe it? McPinsky's already planning our next experiment." While Melanie smiled at him, his mind reeled at the possibilities.

"It's interesting," said McPinsky, turning to address the holy man, "that our first glimpse of their intellect is through the window of mathematical concepts. So now we know the remarkable truth about these wondrous creatures. We've discovered that the Uberwhale utilizes his unique language in his various roles as mathematician, grandmaster, choreographer, architect, and even as diplomat."

"Despite this great leap forward, we've only begun to scratch the surface," remarked Lama Dawa Cham.

"Yes, this is just the beginning," said McPinsky, facing the crowd once again. "What if Speakeasy could be adapted into a universal translator? We'd discover that the animals of our planet would exhibit a range of intellects similar to human, from genius to mentally challenged. Yet the rights of most humans, no matter the degree of their mental faculties, are protected equally under the law by a Bill of Rights and a constitution. A universal translator would be a game changer for the inalienable rights of many more species. That's why we need to break the communication codes of other potentially intelligent species."

"Theo assures me that such a translation is inevitable," said Lama Dawa Cham, staring intently at the audience.

"Yes, indeed," replied McPinsky. "Since we've already confirmed their adaptation of acoustical symbols to express logical gaming concepts, it's no leap of faith to assume they could also have been adapted to express the symbols of a spoken language. So that other research institutions can verify and expand upon our findings, we have posted copies of the Speakeasy videos on YouTube and the raw data files on Ivy Tech's math department website."

When McPinsky paused to dry his brow, Lama Dawa Cham spoke. "Professor McPinsky, your colleagues have contributed to a significant expansion of planetary consciousness. We owe them a great debt, for we now know with certainty that these are exquisite, gifted creatures in our midst. They have achieved the mastery of a marvelously complex language that clearly plays a useful role in their group communications and behavior. Yet we pollute their home in so many thoughtless ways: noise, garbage, and chemical contaminants, to name a few. Our wanton slaughter of these transcendent beings must now come to an end."

McPinsky held a sheet of paper aloft. "I'd like to read an excerpt from the minutes of a recent International Whaling Commission meeting." He removed his glasses. "'Chefs around Tokyo said that they have developed new gourmet recipes to entice more people to eat whale meat, which was once a precious source of protein during the lean times following World War II. New menus tout such creations as whale spring rolls, whale cutlets, and whale bacon. Japan still conducts whaling through a loophole in the 1986 IWC moratorium on commercial whaling that allows whales to be slaughtered for research purposes.'"

With his glasses back on, McPinsky eyed the audience and said, "Our sins are immense, yet we can rectify our behavior and maybe even redeem ourselves by bestowing upon them a great gift. Think about the physicist Stephen Hawking. Despite the man's crippling handicap, cutting-edge technology has endowed him with a voice to express his brilliant mind so that we may all benefit. Similarly, the Torch of Prometheus will transform the whales' voices into a virtual opposable thumb, enabling them to both experience and share the visual reflection of their thoughts and ideas. It's an unprecedented opportunity to know if the Uberwhale and his companions are indeed the Stephen Hawkings and the Helen Kellers of the deep."

"Thank you, Theo," said Lama Dawa Cham, resting a hand upon McPinsky's shoulder. "It's a glorious vision: a gift of human science for the enlightenment of another species and for the redemption of our own souls." Then he turned to face the audience. "Today, more than ever before, life must be characterized by a sense of universal responsibility, not only nation to nation and human to human, but also human to other forms of life. Thank you, ladies and gentlemen. It is my sincere hope that humanity will act with renewed wisdom for the sake of all future generations of all the species upon our planet."

Lama Dawa Cham closed his eyes and mouthed a silent prayer. Reopening them, he illuminated the room with his world-renowned smile. The audience rose as one in a boisterous ovation. When the holy man and the scientist linked their arms together and bowed, the cameras flashed like fireworks, and the headline photo appearing in the news media would bear the caption: TWIN SPOKESMEN FOR A NEW WORLDVIEW.

For the first time in Dmitri's memory, the members of an entire audience openly embraced. With the energy of the crowd swirling all around them, the members of the Research in Paradise team clasped hands and sat in silence. It was the dawn of the first day of the second sun.

Epilogue

BEHOLD THE CREATIVE PAGEANT

"Creation is here and now. So near is man to the creative pageant, so much a part is he of the endless and incredible experiment, that any glimpse he may have will be but the revelation of a moment, a solitary note heard in a symphony thundering through time."

Henry Beston 1928 — *The Outermost House*

SOMEWHERE IN THE Straits of Lahaina, a young humpback practices her first mathematics lesson. Following the example of her tutor, she vocalizes the shape of a circle in two-dimensional frequency space. The teacher proceeds on to the next exercise. Uber makes the necessary adjustments to his vocal tract and sings the shape of a circle in three dimensions, tilted in all three planes relative to the previous circle. The student does not respond but instead, begins to drift up to the surface, leaving a trail of bubbles. Uber watches as she spirals upward in a helical orbit, her movements synchronized in accordance with Archimedes's principle of buoyancy. With the precision only a mathematician or physicist could appreciate, and against all odds, her breath has designed a perfectly proportioned, one-hundred-foot-diameter bubble ring, its ecliptic plane unerringly parallel to the surface. She is enveloped by the halo's luminous ascension, encircled by a crown of jewels sparkling amongst beams of liquid light.

Like a high-wire acrobat, she arcs back down in a great loop until she is directly beneath the rising ring. Then she launches straight up, like a quickening missile converging on its target. When her foamy creation bursts through the surface, she rockets directly through the center, and leaps into the sky.

ACKNOWLEDGEMENTS

I'D LIKE TO honor Ying Lee Pines. Racing at the speed of light, she made this book possible with her tireless work ethic and unstinting support. I want to thank my grown children, Josh and Jamie, for challenging me to clarify the premise of the existential themes of my story. This book is my legacy to them and a reminder that we share a world of wonder.

Being a retired engineer and a debut novelist, I struggled with the multi-dimensional challenges of craft development. I'm indebted to my three primary editors, all award-winning fiction writers, for persevering through a literary novice's steep and prolonged learning curve. With their guidance, the germination of an idea flowered into a dream fulfilled.

I'd like to thank my original mentor, Linda Watanabe McFerrin, and the Left Coast Writer's community for their support in guiding the transformation of my ideas onto the printed page. Linda was both midwife and physician to the birth and development of the first few revisions of the manuscript. Her uncanny ability to intuit the author's and the protagonist's personal and story goals laid the foundation of the novel. Molly Dwyer's application of critical thinking skills to the assessment of point of view, character, and scene credibility helped to elevate *The Whale Song Translation* from a work in progress to a bona fide narrative. Molly's literary "tough love" stressed respect for the readers' sensitivity to intrusive narration and excessive description. Debra Ratner's dialogue expertise and advocacy for the humanity of all the book's characters added a layer of personal richness to the story that was sorely lacking.

This book bears the indelible imprint of others. Lynne Michelle's endless hours of proof reading and copy-editing guidance led me to the promised land of a publishable manuscript. Alan Rinzler's developmental suggestions helped breathe new life into the narrative voice, led to the selection of the "right" opening scene, and gave birth to an important new character. A handful of friends generously donated their time to peer review an early revision of the manuscript, copyrighted in 2009 as *The Turing Translation*. Their insights and suggestions have graced subsequent revisions. Brooke Warner's expertise instilled in me the confidence to take the leap into publishing.

I'd like to express my sincere appreciation to the residents of Maui for their spirit-of-Aloha hospitality and enlightened stewardship of the Valley Isle's natural bounty. Much of the marine mammal material in this book was culled from the excellent publication *Humpbacks of Hawai'I—The Long Journey Back*, written by the co-founders of Maui's Pacific Whale Foundation. Visit their website: www.PacificWhale.org.

We should all salute the Natural Resources Defense Council, and other environmental and marine mammal organizations, for chronicling the adverse effects of anthropogenic noise pollution on marine mammals. For an overview of the controversial subject of the military sonar experiments depicted in the book, I highly recommend a visit to their website, www.nrdc.org/wildlife/marine/sonar.asp, and the short video narrated by Pierce Brosnan posted there.

And last but not least, I'd like to acknowledge Maui's humpback whales. This book's inspiration was spawned the moment I first thrilled to a humpback rocketing from the deep blue sea. I was ultimately compelled to tell this story when, during a "recreational" analysis session of a humpback whale song recording, I grokked the intriguing implications of waveforms eerily similar to frequency-modulated human speech.

ABOUT THE AUTHOR

AS A CHILD of the post-Sputnik boomer generation, and as someone captivated by the sixties "Race to the Moon," I suppose I was destined to be a math and science dude. Since the moment I realized computers could solve math problems at the "speed of light," I've been hooked.

My career passion for software engineering began during the seventies energy crisis as an alternative energy research scientist at the Lawrence Berkeley National Laboratory. After Reagan pulled the plug on that project, I had a smashing good time devising improved designs and tuning strategies for the ion beam lines attached to the lab's HILAC "atom smasher." However, it wasn't until I'd joined a startup company specializing in digital voice products that I discovered my true calling.

My writing is informed by a twenty-five-year Silicon Valley software engineering career that's led to five patents in wireless voice technology. In the adaptation of voice and modem algorithms for communication devices, I became fascinated by the theoretical and physical foundations of speech. I was amazed to recognize the connection between the natural process that created spoken language and the design of cell phone technology—they had both found the solution predicted by a fundamental law of communications. The realization of this convergence is the inspiration for my fictional trilogy-in-progress, *The Torch of Prometheus*. *The Whale Song Translation* is the first installment of the trilogy.

The idea for the book's "Speakeasy" speech-therapy system is based on a speech-modulated, shape-writing prototype I developed and demonstrated at the Fremont campus of the California School for the Deaf in 1985. My understanding that human speech evolved into a process of shape-writing and shape-matching generated the interspecies communication experiment at the core of the novel. To learn more about the underlying principles common to speech, language, and whale songs and, if my time permits, maybe even a demo of the shape-writing app featured in the book, visit www.HowardStevenPines.com.

Born in Los Angeles and a lifelong Californian, I have a love affair with the Pacific Ocean that is steeped in childhood summers playing in the waves. As an über-fan of speech, sound, and surf, my motto is: "Ride the wave, ride the wave equation." Entranced by Northern California's coastline, beaches, and migrating whales, I currently shuttle between the scenic bay and coastal communities of El Cerrito and Mendocino. Maui is a favorite vacation get-away destination, and the inspirational setting of my debut novel and its forthcoming sequel.